Acclaim for J. A. Redmerski's Novels
SONG OF THE FIREFLIES

"Flawlessly and compellingly written, this is a story that made me live every page, every emotion, every unconventional facet of this truly epic romance." —NatashaisaBookJunkie.com

"A stunning and heart-wrenching novel...Redmerski captures the intensity of love so beautifully in each book she writes...[This book is] fantastic, fast-paced...It will keep you on your toes until the last page!" —GutterGirlsBookReviews.com

"I adored *The Edge of Never* and *The Edge of Always*...[This book is] equally amazing...I love Redmerski's style! It's so easy to read, flawless, and addictive. She has amazing talent."

—ReviewingRomance.com

THE EDGE OF ALWAYS

"This was so good!...This book certainly throws its characters quite a few curveballs. Stuff that had my adrenaline racing and my heart skipping beats." —Maryse's Book Blog

"Another fabulous journey with Camryn and Andrew...This series will take you on a ride down roads you never thought to travel, and when you return you'll be nothing like you were before you started." —MyBookAddiction.com

"I was blown away by this book in so many ways...The perfect closure to one of the most emotional and deep love stories I've ever read...*The Edge of Always* is a must-read. All you'll want to do is read it and read it again." —BookishTemptations.com

THE MOMENT OF LETTING GO

ALSO BY J. A. REDMERSKI

The Edge of Never

The Edge of Always

Song of the Fireflies

THE MOMENT OF LETTING GO

J. A. REDMERSKI

FOREVER

NEW YORK BOSTON

Forever

Hachette Book Group

1290 Avenue of the Americas

New York, NY 10104

hachettebookgroup.com

twitter.com/foreverromance

Printed in the United States of America

RRD

First Edition: August 2015

10 9 8 7 6 5 4 3 2 1

Forever is an imprint of Grand Central Publishing.

The Forever name and logo are trademarks of Hachette Book Group, Inc.

The publisher is not responsible for websites (or their content) that are not owned by the publisher.

The Hachette Speakers Bureau provides a wide range of authors for speaking events. To find out more, go to www.hachettespeakersbureau.com or call (866) 376-6591.

Library of Congress Cataloging-in-Publication Data

Redmerski, J. A.

  The moment of letting go / J. A. Redmerski.—First edition.

    pages ; cm

  ISBN 978-1-4555-3153-0 (paperback)—ISBN 978-1-4789-0336-9 (audio download)—ISBN 978-1-4555-3154-7 (ebook)   1. Man-woman relationships—Fiction.   I. Title.

  PS3618.E4344M66 2015

  813'.6—dc23

2015018093

THE MOMENT OF LETTING GO

ONE

Sienna

*T*ripping over my suitcase, I land on my knees, which take the brunt of the fall as I skid across the carpet. Biting back the burning pain, I stumble out of my bedroom to answer the front door.

"Sienna!" Paige calls out from the other side.

"One sec!" I say and slide the chain lock away from the door.

"You're not even *up*?" Paige's mouth falls open.

She pushes past me and comes inside.

"I've been calling and texting you for the past hour."

As I run both hands over the top of my head and through my hair, a long, deep sigh escapes my lips.

"I overslept."

"Thank you, Captain Obvious," she says and brushes her hands toward me in a hurrying fashion. "Let's go; we have half an hour to make it to the airport."

In my camisole and panties, I rush past her back toward my room, still trying to fully wake up. I yank the outfit I set out last night from the back of my desk chair and throw everything on in seconds. I'll have to forget about a shower because there's no time. There's not even time to brush my teeth, so I swig back a mouthful of mint—gargle, swish, and spit—and then graze my deodorant sloppily underneath both arms so fast that I think I missed the left pit altogether. No makeup. Dark auburn hair pulled into a messy something-or-another at the back of my head. I look like death.

Finally, when I'm as ready as time will allow, I shoulder my purse and yank on the pull-out handle of the suitcase I tripped over, rolling it behind me as I rush toward the door. Stepping into my red Chucks without stopping long enough to push my heels into them properly, I slam my apartment door behind us on the way out, wincing as I hear the photograph of my parents hanging by the window hit the floor with a *thump* and a *crash*.

I'm hardly ever late for anything. Ever. My fear of flying has everything to do with why I didn't hear the alarm this morning. I want to go to Hawaii—more than anything—but I know the next several hours of my life as I'm moving through the sky in a glorified sardine can forty thousand feet above an abyss of ocean will cause enough stress to take years off my life—if the plane doesn't crash and kill me first.

Everything about this trip so far is going wrong.

We make it to the airport just in time, surprised I didn't have anything suspicious in my purse that I forgot to take out before going through security, and we're on the plane minutes before takeoff.

"You sure you're gonna be all right?" Paige asks, sitting next to me in the window seat.

"No, I'm definitely not sure," I say, trying to settle myself, "but nothing I can do about it."

"Want me to knock you out?"

I smirk over at her.

"No, I think I'll pass, but thanks for the generous offer."

She grins and shakes her head, peering down into her phone. I know she's itching to tell me how ridiculous it is to be so afraid to fly, but she's doing well to hold her tongue. For now. I give her an hour and she'll cave to the urge and tell me anyway. Because that's what best friends do—they give each other shit.

Paige is slender and tanned like a Hawaiian Tropic model, wearing a pair of short shorts and a pink ball cap that fits snugly over her small, blond head. My boss, Miss Cassandra Harrington, glamour girl extraordinaire with a passion for money and all the things it can buy, agreed to hire Paige on as my assistant, even against her initial concerns about Paige being my best friend. We love the new arrangement—me because she helps keep my head on straight in this hectic profession, and Paige because *she* started out as Cassandra's assistant and that's enough to break anyone ten times over. I should know because I also started out there.

So I don't have an anxiety attack and embarrass myself on this flight, I slip my earbuds in and lay the back of my head against the headrest, hoping to soothe my rattled nerves somewhat with the constant sound of rain pattering and swishing in my ears. It's not nearly as effective as a Valium might be, the sound of rain, but it helps a little and I'll take what I can get. I keep several variations of rain sound effects on my iPod for times like these.

As the plane takes off, I grip the arms of my seat so tight it feels like my fingernails could pierce the hard plastic. *Breathe, Sienna. Just breathe.* Paige is sitting next to me with a big smile that I assume is supposed to be her way of saying, *See, there's nothing to it—look at me. I'm *not* afraid.* She means well, she really does, but like a lot of people, she just doesn't *understand* the fear.

I close my eyes and listen to the rain, picturing myself sitting on land, watching the droplets fall all around me and sink into the earth. And I think about my twenty-two years of life as if it's my last chance to be intimate with my happiest memories.

Six hours later I'm on Oahu in one of the most beautiful places in the world. And I'm still alive. I'm equally excited and disappointed to be here—excited because, well, it's Oahu, disappointed because I'm not here to inhale the beauty of the island or spend days photographing it as I'd always dreamed, but instead to work my butt off arranging someone else's wedding. But I can't complain. The trip is fully paid for and not a lot of people can say they've even *been* to Hawaii, much less went on someone else's dime—I'm a lucky girl.

"I'm so excited!" Paige says over the buzzing of conversations in the airport. "Our first time in Hawaii. It's going to be awesome."

Paige reaches out a ring-decorated hand for my duffel bag. "When we get to the hotel I'll get you checked in and make sure your room is up to par." She's trying so hard to play the assistant—carrying one of my bags for me, pretending she's not my best friend, speaking to me in a sort of proper way that just comes off as weird to me.

I laugh. "*Up to par?* I'm not Cassandra," I remind her. "No need for a white-glove inspection or phrases that aren't typically part of your vocabulary."

Paige grins, shoulders my duffel bag, and then slides the handles out from one of my two rolling suitcases, in addition to her own.

"*What*, no servant waiting on hand to dispose of your chewed gum?" she jokes.

I laugh with disbelief. "Tell me Cassandra didn't do that—though I wouldn't put it past her."

Paige shrugs. "Nah. I read that somewhere and immediately

thought of *Miz* Harrington." Her pale blue eyes flutter as she raises her head high and mimics Cassandra's dramatic personality.

We make our way outside into the perfect summer Hawaiian breeze to find a cab. While I'm standing on the sidewalk, my cell phone buzzes around inside my purse, and I fish it out just in time before the voice mail picks up.

"I got a call from Mrs. Dennings. She couldn't get ahold of you. I guess your phone was off," Cassandra says into my ear as Paige waves at a cab making its way toward us. "They'll be there later tonight, but she said you can go ahead and start without her. The bride's sister—her name is Veronica—is already there."

The cab stops and the driver gets out to help Paige store our bags in the trunk.

I slide into the backseat.

"How late did Mrs. Dennings say they'd be?" I close the cab door and adjust myself on the squeaky leather seat. "I can't do much until she gets here with the rest of the supplies."

"She didn't say," Cassandra answers. "But do what you can with what you have."

A smile warms my face as sudden thoughts of non-work-related ideas begin to materialize in my mind.

"Well, maybe I'll get to relax and have a look around before they get here with everything," I suggest, hopeful.

"Perhaps," she says simply, as if she were telling me in her most cultured and sympathetic way, *No dear. I'm sorry, but that's not possible, though you may continue dreaming about it if it makes you feel better.*

I knew that before I came here; there's no such thing as relaxing when you work as an event coordinator for the most high-profile event planning business in California. One hundred percent of Cassandra's clients are wealthy, half of them are famous, and the rest are people who know someone famous. There's a lot of money in it, but it's very demanding and often so stressful that most who get into the business quit within the first month—at least, those who work for Cassandra Harrington do, anyway.

I still can't believe I lucked into this job with all its perks. Like all-expense-paid trips to Hawaii, a career in a creative field where I'm paid generously and have job security that allows me nowhere to go but up. They don't come along often and one would be crazy not to take it. I grew up with financially struggling parents. I made up my mind long before I was out of high school to not go through life as they have had to. Like they still do. And now, with Dad's failing health—prostate cancer, though they caught it early and he's in remission—I'm more determined than ever to have a good-paying job so I can help my parents; they've done so much for me.

Paige slides onto the backseat with me and shuts the door behind her, cutting off the sudden stream of voices from outside. Knowing I'm on the phone with Cassandra, she gives me that look, suppressing her playful comments about our boss, and leaves me to our conversation.

"Two days setting up," Cassandra says into my ear, "a one-day wedding, and then it's back to San Diego." She pauses. "After that, you're off to Jamaica."

Blinking back the stun, I turn my head to lock eyes with Paige on the seat next to me. "Jamaica?" I say into the phone.

Paige's face lights up.

"Thought you'd like that," Cassandra says with a proud air. "A client I've known for a long time in San Francisco is getting married in Montego Bay. And he's loaded, honey." I picture her brushing her thumb and fingers together rapidly to demonstrate money. "It'll be your biggest commission yet."

My face stretches into a smile as I gaze past Paige toward the window as palm trees and colorful landscaping fly by—it's not the money I'm thinking about, but photographing Jamaica. Paige sits there quietly but anxiously, waiting for the details.

"Getting used to this kind of money is hard, I know," Cassandra teases, followed by a dramatic sigh. "But I'm afraid you'll just have to stick it out."

"Oh, the hell you put me through, Cassandra," I tease her back.

"Think you can handle it?" Cassandra asks suspiciously.

I laugh. "Of course I can! Didn't you say on our last event that I'm the best coordinator you've ever hired?"

"Well, I was referring to the flight," she says, and my smile fades with the realization. "It's a little over nine hours to Jamaica."

My heart picks up a nervous pace just thinking about it. Nine hours on an airplane. Thousands of feet above the ocean. Humans weren't born with wings for a reason.

"I can handle it," I half lie, and make a mental note to schedule an appointment with my doctor soon to get some Valium because I think somehow the rain sound effects on my iPod just aren't going to cut it this time.

"Jamaica?" Paige asks eagerly when I hang up with Cassandra. "Please tell me I get to go on *that* job."

"Well, *yeah?*" I look at her as if she'd just asked a ridiculous question. "You're my assistant. You get to go wherever I need you to go."

"Awesome." Her smile seems a permanent fixture on her face, along with that thoughtful, dreamy look *I* usually have when I first learn I'm going somewhere I've never been. Only difference between me and Paige is that she has yet to learn that these trips never turn out the way we dream about them. She was Cassandra's assistant for only a month before becoming mine and didn't travel farther than Chicago. Not that Paige couldn't afford to travel anywhere she wanted on her own—she has plenty of family money—but she's not above being appreciative of all-expense paid trips, either.

We arrive at the hotel. I turn to Paige, who's trying to steady my heavy duffel bag, suppressing an uncomfortable look.

"What the hell did you pack in this thing?"

I laugh.

"I think I packed everything I own—Cassandra must be rubbing off on me."

"God, I hope not." Paige chuckles and readjusts the duffel bag strap on the opposite shoulder, her wispy blond hair poking out from underneath the ball cap.

"Well, you know me," I say with a shrug, "prepared and organized as always."

"Yeah, yeah, I know." I don't see it, but I sense Paige's eyes rolling dramatically.

When we finally make it up to my suite, I gasp as I open the door. Immaculate. Lavish. And with a beautiful balcony view to die for.

Paige places my bags next to the wall.

I kick off my Chucks and plop down on a wicker chair with a soft teal cushion near the sliding glass balcony door.

"Nice, isn't it?" Paige says, looking about the room.

"Nice is an understatement." I run the palm of my hand across the smooth surface of the table next to me and I think of my parents momentarily, about the only time we ever went on a vacation when

I was younger. We stayed in a cheap roadside motel one night on the way to visit friends of my parents somewhere in Texas. It wasn't much of a vacation really, but I was glad to see my parents spending time together, doing something other than working sixty-hour weeks and too tired to talk to one another when they saw each other in passing.

Paige plops down on the end of my perfectly made bed, her tanned legs dangling off the edge, her feet dressed in an expensive pair of Louboutin gladiator-style sandals.

"How much time do you think we have?" she asks, bouncing gently on the bed to test the feel of the mattress.

I don't even want to think about work because I just got here, but it was inevitable.

"I've gotta take a shower," I say, raising my back from the comfort of the chair, "and put on my makeup and fix my hair—we'll head down to the pavilion in about an hour."

Paige nods and gets up from the bed.

"Well, I'll leave you to it. I'm gonna get a bite to eat. I'm over in 510. Call me when you're ready—unless there's anything you need before I go...*boss*?" She winks.

I shake my head and smile, leaning my back against the chair. "No, I'm good, but thanks. See yah soon."

The door closes with a *click* behind her.

Finally I'm alone. In Hawaii. I'm in *Hawaii*! I can hardly believe it. I glance over at my hard-side suitcase sitting upright on the carpeted floor and I contemplate pulling out my camera gear packed safely inside of it—I bring it pretty much wherever I go. Then I glance at the clock on the nightstand beside the bed and a long, deep sigh escapes my lungs.

Accepting that it's not a good time—unfortunately, it rarely ever is—I erase the camera gear from my mind and get up from the chair, sliding the glass door open and stepping out onto the balcony. The warm eighty-degree breeze greets me as I make my way out, pushing through wandering strands of dark auburn hair pinned sloppily to my head. I shut my eyes for a moment and breathe in deeply, taking the wind into my lungs and savoring the moment of peace while I can. Because once I step out that suite door to head down to the wedding site near the beach, peace and tranquility will be nothing but a memory.

TWO

Sienna

I meet Paige in the hallway an hour later and we're on our way to the elevator. She's changed into another pair of shorts and a cute lacy top. Her blond hair has been brushed and lies softly over both shoulders.

"I've already met a guy," she admits.

I look over at her.

"You're kidding." This doesn't really surprise me much; Paige has always been a social girl; not to mention she's beautiful, with a magnetic personality to boot—she dreams of becoming a model someday, and personally I think it's just a matter of time.

Her slim mouth spreads into a grin.

"Hey, it's not like I went looking," she says as she moves a few long strands of hair away from her face, tucking them behind her ear. "I went to check things out and ended up in the bar downstairs."

"The *bar*? *Paige!*" I shake my head disappointedly.

The elevator dings and stops on the fourth floor, the doors parting. A thirtysomething couple steps in.

"I wasn't *drinking*," she whispers, rolling her eyes. "I was just looking around and getting a feel for the resort." The woman looks in our direction. "Anyway, he works at the bar and told me to stop in and have a drink sometime when I get a chance." She grins and lowers her voice even more. "He's not the kind I usually go for, but he's hot enough I'm willing to make a few adjustments on my requirements list."

The elevator stops on the third floor and the couple gets out, leaving us to our privacy.

Paige has quite a requirements list—I'm surprised she's not still a virgin. I'm not as picky, but I admit my list isn't all that short. Difference is that mine is more reasonable.

"Just remember we're here to work," I say. "And unfortunately, I doubt we'll have time for hot breakfast, much less hot bartenders."

"I know, I know," she says. "But there's nothing wrong with flirting while we work, y'know. Am I right or am I right?" Her lips spread into a broader grin and she looks across at me under hooded eyes the way she always does when she's trying to shift my attitude.

She wins.

"Yeah, you're right." I give in and then shake my finger at her. "But don't make me regret getting you hired on under me, Paige."

She turns to me, a bright smile plastered on her sun-kissed face. "I'd never put you in a bad position, and you know it," she says, collapsing her hands about my upper arms and pretending to look all serious.

I smile, pursing my lips on one side, and then slip my arm around her.

When we arrive at the glass wedding pavilion on the wave-washed edge of the beach, a tall, dark-haired girl with long bare legs swishes her hips underneath a pastel flowered dress, sashaying like a model down the center aisle toward us. Her hair is like a wave of dark silk flowing unrestricted against her bare back.

"You must be Sienna Murphy," she says in a confident, dramatic voice, reaching out a dainty ring-decorated hand to me. "I'm Veronica Dennings, sister of the bride-to-be."

I get the feeling she expects me to be impressed. I'm not, so I fake it. I'm good at faking these kinds of things—a skill I'm proud to have mastered in this job.

I know the look of disgust on Paige's face without having to actually see it.

Veronica barely touches my hand with her fingers, as if she's afraid to mess up her newly manicured nails.

"It's nice to meet you, Veronica," I say brightly, strategically placing my fingers about her hand without touching her nails. "This is Paige Mathers, my assistant." Veronica's dark blue eyes barely skirt her. "You must be *so* excited for your sister."

"Of course," she says. "As I'm sure Valerie will be excited for me when *my* wedding day comes." Her hand goes up and lightly brushes against her dark hair, pushing it away from her shoulder with such a self-important grace that it actually makes me feel momentarily inadequate—until I realize how ridiculous that is.

I smile slimly in response and glance around the area suspiciously, noticing right away that she has already been draping the guest chairs with extravagant fabric—made of a design that is entirely different from what was agreed on two weeks ago. Paige notices the look on my face, and I straighten it out quickly before Veronica sees it, too. But I'm too late and she notices anyway.

Veronica waves her hand about the room in a sophisticated fashion. "I know my sister's taste better than our mother," she says about the fabric. "That hideous floral pattern Mother chose without consulting me just *had* to go; don't you agree?" An arrogant smile glows on her face.

That "hideous" floral pattern is what your sister, the bride *picked out.*

I nod slowly. "I respect your concerns," I say with a kind expression, "but I think it's best we keep what the bride chose. I'd be happy to talk with her about your ideas, if you'd like."

Veronica looks quietly stung, but she raises her chin as if to look important and then shrugs it off as if she doesn't care either way.

"Whatever. Do what you like. But it's hideous."

Then she motions for Paige as if she were merely an errand girl and puts her to work right away, insisting she find a Starbucks before she loses her damn mind.

Paige eyes me secretly from the side and mouths, *You've got to be kidding me.*

"What will you have?" Veronica asks me.

I put out my hand, palm forward. "No, I'm good, but thanks." Really, I just don't want to contribute to the balancing act I'm sure Paige will have to do carrying the drinks back. And sure enough, she's got a list with the needs of Veronica's two assistants who just walked up—petite, bubbly, one more stuck-up than the other, pretty, and wearing Daddy's bank account from their colored roots to their glittery pedicures.

What's happening here? Did Paige and I just become *Veronica's* assistants, too?

I swallow down my disappointment; my kind, professional smile is still intact as always, though already it's becoming more difficult to pull off. I like my job. I enjoy creating an event to remember for my clients, but every now and then I get one like this where I don't really get to put my creativity to work.

Once Paige is out of earshot, I say in a respectful, even manner,

"You know, Paige has a great eye for this stuff. She can really help out with the setup."

Veronica tosses her head back majestically and laughs in a gentle manner so as not to overly alter her smooth complexion. I'm not sure what to make of that, her laughing, but it leaves a sour taste in my mouth.

I look over when I feel her hand touch my shoulder.

"I'm sure she's helpful," she says with a twinkle in her deep blue eyes. "But today she's the perfect coffee girl. Come. I'll show you what I intend to do with the archway."

Wow. Talk about a sour taste...

————

Long after Paige gets back with the coffee, she and I are listening to Veronica's harping demands and superior personality. But it looks like I'm the only one of us who can let it all roll right off my back. For the most part.

"And I thought *Cassandra* was bad," Paige mumbles under her breath. She ties another long ribbon around the back of a chair.

I tie a ribbon around the chair next to hers, afterward wedging a finger behind the satiny material to straighten out the fabric pinched beneath it.

"It comes with the job sometimes," I tell her quietly. "You just have to learn to ignore it."

"I don't know how you *do* it," she says, standing up, her lips pinched in frustration.

Sometimes I don't either, but somehow I manage.

Veronica walks up carrying a clipboard pressed against her breasts.

"I guess this is all we can do until my parents get here later," she says. "They're due around six, so until then I suppose we can all take a break."

"Thanks, but I have a lot to do," I say. "Phone calls to make and—"

"Suit yourself," Veronica says, twirling a wrist, "but if those phone calls have anything to do with the wedding, I've got all that under control."

I just look at her, surprised, not liking the sound of that at all.

Veronica smiles importantly—her assistants stand next to her, staring down into their phones.

With that famous fake smile of mine, my teeth grind harshly behind my closed lips. "You already called the caterer and—"

"Not yet, but it's next on my to-do list," she interrupts me again. "Take a break, girl. You look like you need one."

I'm sure that last comment wasn't meant in the kindest of terms, but like everything else I dislike about her, I let it slide. Paige isn't as forgiving, and glares at Veronica with flames in her eyes. I step in front of Paige quickly to distract Veronica before she notices.

"I appreciate the help," I say, "but don't worry yourself with the phone calls; I'll take care of them. We'll finish up here and then I'll take you up on that break." I smile, hoping Veronica takes the bait. I want to get her as far away from the arrangements—and the vendors—as possible.

Veronica, probably not used to being struck down once, much less twice, in just a few hours, manipulates the inside of her mouth with her teeth and just looks at me, wordless and quietly disapproving. Then she says something about how she needs to go lie in the sun, and walks away with her assistants, sashaying her hourglass hips down the center aisle as if *she* were the one getting married tomorrow.

"I swear, Sienna," Paige says, "I feel like I need to shower every time she's within five feet of me so I don't get infected with cuntilitis."

As Paige's best friend, I would have to agree with that, but as her boss, I decide to keep my mouth shut this time rather than fueling the fire.

"Do me a favor," I tell Paige, "and call the vendors to make sure everything's on schedule. I'm going to finish up here and check on a few more things just in case Veronica got any other ideas."

"I'm a step ahead of you," Paige says. "Was thinking the same thing."

———

Later I do find time for a short break and I end up on the beach with my camera. Hawaii is too beautiful not to photograph, and so I sacrificed lunch to take advantage of it while I could. As I inch closer to where Veronica is sitting on her towel with long, tanned legs stretched out like landing strips in front of her, I make it a point to keep my distance. I just want to get a few shots of the surfers riding the waves. A few guys—and girls who are probably girlfriends—are among the group. All of them are tall and tanned and look like they walked right off the pages of a Hawaiian magazine.

Squeals pierce the air as Veronica's assistants are sprayed by water from a small, boisterous wave. Veronica throws her head back daintily and laughs like a wannabe 1950s movie star—I suddenly feel embarrassed even though I'm not sitting beside her.

I peer back into my lens as two more guys from the group head out together into the wave-capped water, surfboards in hand.

Snap, snap, snap.

Suddenly the tall guy with a nice body in the red and black wetsuit looks in my direction briefly. Through my lens I see his eyes looking right at me, and I suck in a sharp breath, dropping my camera from my face with a pang of embarrassment settling in my stomach. I hope he doesn't think I was photographing him, even though I was.

Maybe he wasn't looking *at* me—I mean, I *am* across the beach. Though I'm sure, with them being surfers and all, they get tourists out here all the time taking photos of them.

I watch the group for a short while as they ride the waves. It's said that the North Shore is the best place to surf in Hawaii, but I guess I expected giant waves and bodies disappearing underneath a frightening, towering tunnel of water only to shoot out the other side to the gasps of onlookers. This isn't as nail-biting, but it's still impressive. I doubt I could stay up on a surfboard for more than a few seconds—these guys make it look easy.

The guy wearing the red and black wetsuit emerges from the water and walks onto the beach with his surfboard tucked underneath his arm. He looks over in my direction as he walks forward, pushing a hand over the top of his wet golden-brown hair. My heart leaps a little. I think...yeah, he was definitely looking at me.

My awkwardness comes back full force, accompanied by a hot blush in my cheeks.

Veronica pushes herself to her feet, dusting sand from her fingers, and walks toward the group, her little bubble butt swishing beneath her black bikini bottom as she moves through the sand.

A little baffled by her sudden brazen decision, I watch as Veronica approaches the guy in the black and red wetsuit. He looks right at her. He smiles and nods. Veronica twirls the end of her long, dark hair around the tip of one finger, cocking her head coyly to one side.

Words are exchanged.

Then a few more.

The guy's smile fades.

Did his brows just furrow?

Uh-oh.

Veronica's arms navigate upward and fall into a locked position, crossed loosely over her chest.

The guy shakes his head at her with a look of...Is that *disgust?*

He bends over and picks his surfboard up, turning his back to her, and then heads back out toward the water.

Veronica spins angrily on her heels and marches back over to her towel and beach bag with the most offended expression I've ever seen on a face before. She snatches her towel from the sand, thrusts her feet into her flip-flops, kicking up sand around her toes, and goes to leave, headed straight in my direction.

"Unbelievable!" she says as she steps up. "The locals around here are rude, that's for sure." She shoves her towel angrily into her canvas beach bag.

"What happened?" I ask.

"He was an asshole—*that's* what happened."

Even more baffled now, I just stare at Veronica for a curious moment, part of me wondering whether she's actually going to cry, the rest of me just wanting to know what he could've possibly said to someone like her to spark the urge. Her assistants move in right behind her, just now catching up, but they aren't the ones I notice when I look up—the guy in the red and black wetsuit is looking in my direction again, and suddenly I feel embarrassed standing here with Veronica.

I look away quickly, just as he does.

"I guess they don't like tourists around here," she says. "Better watch your back." Then she saunters off back toward the hotel, leaving me on the beach. The guy never looks over at me again, and while it's probably for the best because I'm here to work, I can't help but be bummed by it just the same.

————

I spend the next thirty minutes in my suite alone, expecting to get a call from Veronica any minute telling me that her parents have finally made it. Paige texts me to let me know that she finally got ahold of all the vendors and that everything is on schedule. Sitting outside on the balcony with my legs drawn up on the chair, I take in the view, letting my mind wander thinking about all the other things I could be seeing right now, the beautiful things I could be photographing. Before I came here, I spent a week poring over photos of Hawaii on the Internet, dreaming about seeing each and every majestic place with my lens: the towering waterfalls, the sprawling green mountains, the glowing golden fire of Kilauea, and the whales and the fire dancers. But all I can see when I come back to reality are the glass walls of the chapel closing in on me, the decorative Mason jars hanging precariously from the trees, the lavender ribbons choke-tied around the chairs, and Veronica's sour expression accompanied by fake smiles and heavy doses of vanity and pity.

My phone buzzes against the glass-top table, snapping me out of my thoughts.

Looking down into the screen, I'm expecting it to be Veronica, but I'm surprised to see that it's my mother.

"Hi, Mom," I answer cheerily.

"Hi, baby," she says sweetly into my ear—I'm twenty-two and she still talks to me like I'm ten and probably always will. "I take it you made the flight all right. How long have you been there?"

"Just a few hours." I pull my head away from the phone and run my finger over the speaker icon. "I was going to call you, but I got tied up with the client." I set the phone down on the table.

"So what's Hawaii like?" my mother asks eagerly, the speaker cracking faintly with her voice.

I feel bad that she isn't here with me; I'd've loved to have been able to bring her along. She hasn't seen much outside of San Diego in her forty-three years of life.

"It's beautiful," I say. "Well, what I've seen of it anyway."

"I'm sure you'll get some free time to explore," she says. "You took your camera, didn't you?"

"Yeah, you know I always do."

"I'm so proud of you, Sienna."

I pick the phone back up and hold it near my face, balanced within my fingertips.

"So is your father," she goes on. "You landed a great job with perks most people who've been working for twenty years never see. We're just really proud of you."

I smile. Nothing makes me happier than to know that my parents, who had such a hard life before they had me and an even harder one after I was born, are proud of what I've done so far and continue to do.

"Thanks, Mom." I pause, looking out at the endless blue ocean. "I wish you were here. Y'know, I've thought a lot about it and I know you've got work and all, but I really want to take you and Dad on vacation in the fall. I thought maybe we could go on that Alaskan cruise you've always talked about and—"

"Oh, honey," she cuts in, "you know I can't take the time off work, and neither can your dad. We've got two mortgages, not to mention the hospital bills and the car payment—we just can't afford the time off."

A heavy sigh deflates my chest. "I told you I'd help you pay off the mortgages. I lived in that house most of my life; the least I can do is help pay for it now that I can. I'll even help pay Dad's hospital bills—"

"Absolutely *not*." I can picture her auburn head shaking in refusal. "We wanted so much more for you than what we were able to give you growing up, Sienna, and I'll be damned if we start taking from you the things you've worked so hard to earn for yourself." I swear I can sense Mom slashing her hand in the air. "Honey, I really appreciate you wanting to help us out, but we're doing just fine, and as much as I'd love to go on that cruise, I just can't give Mr. Towers any reason to lay me off."

I know there's no arguing with her about any of this. We've had this discussion many times since I started drawing a good income. I just wish they were more open to my help than they are.

I sigh again and run my free hand through the top of my hair.

Another call beeps through.

"Mom, I have to go. It's the client."

"OK," she says, already her cheery, smiling self again so quickly. "But call me when you get a chance and let me know how everything's going. I just know you're going to have a wonderful time."

"Thanks, Mom. I'll call you soon."

I rush through the day in a nerve-racking haze, barely stopping long enough to take a bathroom break.

Working long after the sun is swallowed up by the Pacific, we finally call it quits minutes after eleven o'clock, and I take immediate advantage of it. Instead of hanging around long after everyone else has turned in for the night so I can triple-check everything, I call it a day and go straight up to my suite.

I take a long hot shower, and I'm asleep moments after my head hits the pillow. Before I fall asleep, I find myself thinking about that guy in the red and black wetsuit. He was gorgeous from where I was standing—but I'm not here for that! Maybe Paige is rubbing off on me.

I wipe the guy from my mind and eventually fall fast asleep. I dream about that dreaded wrench all event coordinators fear will be thrown into the gears and ruin everything. It's always there, looming in the back of my mind.

And then it happens.

THREE

Sienna

*A*fter putting on my makeup, I glance at the clock beside the bed just to make sure that I'm not running late, and am relieved to see that it's not even eight in the morning. I'm not expected downstairs for another thirty minutes. But when my cell phone starts vibrating in my hand and I see that it's my boss, Cassandra, I get a panicked feeling in my gut.

"Hello?"

"Sienna," Cassandra says into the phone with a frantic tenor in her voice, "what on earth is going *on*?"

"I-I don't know. What do you mean?"

My heart is beating a hundred miles a minute all of a sudden.

"Mrs. Dennings called me," Cassandra says, "saying something about the caterer thinking he was supposed to be on Oahu a day later"—my palms are sweating—"and that the band received a *cancellation* notice? Sienna, I don't know what this is all about, but you need to call me back as soon as you find out."

My head feels like it's on fire. I can't imagine how high my blood pressure is right about now, but it would undoubtedly alarm a doctor.

"Yes, ma'am. I'll call you right away. I'm sure it's just a misunderstanding. I'll get it cleared up."

"You better. If I lose this client, you lose your commission… and maybe more than that." The acid in her voice, although laced with regret for having to resort to threats, burns right through me.

I hang up and step into my heeled sandals, my heartbeat pounding in my ears. I swing open my room door and rush down the hallway to the elevator. When the doors open on the ground floor, I pick up the pace and practically glide toward the reception building.

It's a nightmare. And possibly the beginning of the end of my career. Veronica, the Evil Queen of Oahu, went behind my back and made phone calls to all the vendors even after I told her I had it under control, telling them God knows what. She must've done it later in the afternoon, after Paige made the calls for me, because everything was on schedule at that point.

Mrs. Dennings chews me out for a good five minutes, embarrassing me in front of at least fifteen people. I *could* tell Mrs. Dennings that Veronica is the one who did all of this, but now isn't the time to point fingers. What little time there is left, I know I have to use trying to fix what Veronica broke.

Paige is nowhere to be found, having no idea what's going on and still thinking she doesn't have to be down here for another half hour. But I can't even will myself to call her to help me because I know Paige, and she might make things worse by saying something to get us both fired. Paige's fuse is much shorter than mine.

"This is a *disaster*," Mrs. Dennings tells me with an angry pinched mouth. Her arms come uncrossed and she gestures her hands out in front of her angrily. A muscle begins to twitch rapidly at one corner of her mouth. "I hired Harrington Planners because I thought they were the best. And I will not accept anything *less* than the best for my daughter. Did I make a mistake?" Her glare pierces me like a hot poker to the face.

My mouth is incredibly dry. I can't think straight, much less answer her straight. I need to buy some time, although I know that time is both expensive and elusive this close to the wedding tonight, and I've got to think of something quick.

If I can't buy time, I'll have to manipulate it.

"I'm on this right now," I say, putting up a hand as a sign of assurance. "I don't know how any of this happened"—a total lie—"but I'll fix it." I start to walk away, putting my phone to my ear as the caterer's number begins to ring. "Ten minutes!" I call out to Mrs. Dennings as I get farther away. "Don't worry about anything!"

I've never lied so much in my life in such a short time.

Four minutes on the phone with the caterer and after some begging and convincing and an offer to pay a convenience fee, they were able to rework their schedule to squeeze us in for today. I'm assuming Veronica told them the wrong day by accident when she called to verify—I don't even *want* to know.

One disaster down, one to go.

Wiping beads of sweat from my forehead caused mostly by the stress and not the heat, I scan the contacts in my phone—ignoring the stream of text messages from Paige—for the number for the band when Paige walks up briskly.

"I've been looking all over for you," Paige says, a scowl etched in her face.

"What is it now?" I ask, exhausted, afraid of the answer.

Paige stops and motions her hands up and down in front of her, indicating her clothes.

"Does this look 'suitable' to you?" She makes quotation marks with her fingers. "These shoes cost more than Mrs. Dennings's facelift," she snaps. "Yet it's *still* not good enough for her. I think she just has it out for me."

I put up my hand to stop her, not looking her in the eyes, but at the ground instead.

She hushes in an instant.

"I can't *deal* with this right now," I say, throwing my hands in the air, surprising not only her, but myself. "Paige," I say more calmly, "just stay as far away from Mrs. Dennings, Veronica, *and* the wedding as you can, OK?"

Paige blinks, stunned.

"Please," I say before she has a chance to start with the questions—in addition to everything else that's gone wrong, I feel like the worst best friend in the world. "Just go to your suite, or hang out with the bartender—whatever you want to do. I don't care right now. All right?"

Baffled by my reaction, she stands there with deepening creases around her blue eyes.

"But what about—"

I turn my back to her and walk away, leaving her standing in her statuesque form, and with the rest of her words on her tongue.

Where I'm going, I have no idea, but I know it's not to do any of the things I *should* be doing. I have to get away. I need to clear my head. Or jump into the ocean and let a wave sweep me out into oblivion, never to be found again. I should be tougher than this! Working in this kind of hectic environment and feeding off the stress instead of letting it feed on me, I'm usually good at. Maybe two years of running my butt off nonstop and trying to prevent disasters has finally caught up with me.

I drift farther away from the building, my feet going smoothly over concrete until the concrete becomes sand and it's harder to trek through in my favorite blue-mint heeled sandals. Shoes I never would've worn to do a setup, but felt obligated because of Mrs. Dennings's excessive expectations of others.

Steady footing becomes wobbly and uneven as my heels sink into the sand step after step. But I keep on walking, letting the sounds of voices and vehicles and other manmade things fade into the background, replaced by the crashing of the waves against the shore. The light wind brushing through the trees and the nearby bushes are becoming more numerous the farther I drift. The birds. The sand crunching beneath my shoes. I want to shut myself off from the world just long enough to breathe, but the voices and images swirling tumultuously inside my head are too loud and only drown out the peaceful things that nature has to offer.

As unexpected as having the wind knocked out of me, my fuse finally burns to the end and I fall against the sand on my bottom and bury my face in my hands, sweat and all. My eyes begin to burn as I smear mascara into them, but I don't care. I don't care if I look like a raccoon when I go back into that building—sometimes you just have to throw your hands in the air.

"Are you all right?" I hear a voice say.

Raising my eyes from the confines of my hands, I look up to see a tall, gorgeous guy in red swim trunks standing over me—the same guy who was looking at me across the beach in the red and black wetsuit yesterday. The same guy whose brief glance made my stomach flutter.

FOUR

Sienna

*A*lthough I only saw him from afar, he has the kind of face that would be hard to forget: defined cheekbones brushed by a five-o'clock shadow. Deep hazel eyes that seem to contain everything between devotion and mischief, framed by tousled golden-brown hair, short in the back but a little longer on top. It looks like he woke up this morning, shuffled his hand through it a few times, and, *voilà*, perfection.

"Yeah, I'm fine," I say with no distinguishable emotion, wiping underneath my eyes with the edges of my thumbs.

I quickly pull the ends of my skirt farther down near my ankles to make sure I'm not on display.

"I see," he says, crossing his arms loosely over his plain white T-shirt. "You must not be from around here then."

I look up at his tall, tanned form looming over me and brace for the same tourist treatment that Veronica received.

"What's that supposed to mean?" My nose wrinkles around the edges.

The guy smiles, close-lipped, and though it's charming enough that it borderlines infectious, I'm not sure what to make of it.

"Well, people from Hawaii," he says matter-of-factly, "when they cry like that, it usually means something's wrong." He shrugs.

I blink confusedly and just stare up at him for a moment.

I'm not crying.

"Is that so?" I say out loud, my voice faintly laced with sarcasm. "I'm curious to know where you think I could be from then, based on that observation." I'm usually not this impolite, but he caught me at a really bad time.

His lips turn up faintly, matching the charming look in his eyes.

"I dunno," he says. "I was hoping *you'd* tell *me*."

I look away and down at my phone crushed in one hand. A stream of unread text messages from Paige await me. Sighing heavily, I drop the phone on the sand beside my shoes, not wanting to think about any of that right now.

The silence grows between us.

I wonder why he's even still standing there.

Finally I stand up and dust sand off the back of my long flowered silk skirt, and then my hands. My heels sink deeply into the sand again, causing me to lose my balance. I catch myself before I fall, but it doesn't stop him from collapsing his hand around my elbow, just in case. My stomach flip-flops a little when he touches me, but I quickly brush that aside.

"Well, I'll leave you alone then," he says suddenly and takes a step back. "Whatever it is, just let it go. You'll feel better a lot sooner." He smiles. His strange advice seems sincere and not at all arrogant or all-knowing—this alone makes me infinitely curious to know more about him.

He starts to walk away, his white T-shirt clinging to him in the breeze, his bare feet moving easily over the top of the sand as if he's had time to master it, but then something urgent grows inside me and my mouth suddenly has a mind of its own.

"I'm just under a lot of stress," I call out, finally giving him an answer, and stopping him in his tracks.

He turns to face me.

Nervously I glance down at my toes and the blue-mint beads running along the bottom strap of my sandals, buried partially by the sand.

He walks toward me again, but I don't look at him. It feels awkward to look. I don't want to risk giving him the wrong idea.

"That must be some serious stress," he says, stepping back up. "To reduce you to tears."

"Yeah, I guess you could say that." I point at him playfully. "I wasn't crying though."

"Yeah, yeah—well, you *do* realize where you are, right?" he asks.

I look around briefly without moving my head, not exactly sure what he's getting at, but I think it's mostly because he's caught me so off guard.

His smile softens around his eyes.

"Hawaii," he says as if making a very serious point. "People come here on vacation to *de*stress, not to create more of it."

I kind of feel bad for dragging my issues over here from the mainland, like I've brought the plague with me.

Finally I look at him with a steadier gaze. "I know," I say with regret, "but I'm not here on vacation."

"Well, that's your first mistake." He points his index finger upward.

"An *unavoidable* mistake," I say. "It's my job."

"Ah." His head tilts back slightly, his lips parting. It's as if he just realized something. "Well, that explains it, then," he says with what seems like relief.

"Explains what?"

"Why you were hanging around that crazy chick yesterday."

I remember him seeing Veronica talking to me on the beach right after she stormed away from him. But I take immediate offense to his choice of words.

"Well, that's a little rude, don't you think?" I cross my arms, letting my fingers drape over my biceps. "Not to mention whatever it was you said to her yesterday."

He laughs lightly and then looks at me with raised eyebrows, but he doesn't say anything in his defense. I'm not sure what to make of it, but I don't like the arrogant vibes he's putting off, and that's a shame because I was beginning to like his company.

Then something dawns on me.

"It, uh . . . well, whatever you said to her, she probably asked for it, right?" I wince a little, feeling like an idiot.

He shrugs his shoulders, his muscled arms hanging freely down at his sides, the white T-shirt stark against his bronzed skin.

A breeze blows by, pushing the fabric of my loose, flowing skirt embarrassingly between my legs.

"I'm sorry," I say, ignoring my skirt altogether. "I should've known."

I stumble again—stupid shoes.

"I barely know her," I go on, pointing at him briefly, "but what little I do know doesn't help her case any."

He chuckles and then crouches down in front of me.

Surprised by the sudden movement, for a second I can't move anything but my eyes, which follow him. His fingers lightly touch my foot as he unzips the tiny zipper at the back of my sandal, collapsing the other hand around my ankle and then easing my foot out. There's that fluttering in my stomach again; my skin breaks out in chills—I hope he doesn't notice. Baffled by this otherwise intimate gesture, I still can't do much but stare down at the top of his golden-brown head, my lips parted and my eyebrows scrunching up in my forehead. When I don't protest, he takes off the other shoe, and before long I'm standing on the sand in my bare feet. He pushes himself back into a stand two inches taller than me and places my sandals into my hand, hanging them on my fingers by the thin straps.

I stare at him in bewilderment, swallowing nervously.

"Umm, so what exactly *did* happen yesterday?" I ask, feeling the need to change the subject—not because I was offended by what he did . . . No, I certainly wasn't offended.

It was something else.

"Luke Everett," he says, holding out a hand to me.

I glance down at his hand and back up at his gorgeous sculpted face and deep hazel eyes, undecided what's confusing me more: the way he's smiling at me or the way he keeps avoiding my questions.

"My name is Luke," he repeats, urging me to shake his hand the charming smile never faltering. "We should get that much out of the way, I think."

Reluctantly I place my hand into his, and in an instant I feel a sense of security.

"Sienna Murphy."

"It's a pleasure to meet you, Sienna," he says while still holding my hand.

Finally he lets go.

"To answer your question," he says, "she came over to talk to me, and when she asked me to show her how to surf, I told her—as I would any other customer—that I was already booked for the day and that she'd have to set up an appointment." He laughs lightly, shaking his head. "She didn't like that much."

I make a face just thinking about it.

"I saw you talking to her yesterday," he goes on. "That worried me a little. Thankfully you're nothing like her—that would've been a disappointment."

Luke sits down on the sand, drawing his knees up and resting his forearms atop them.

"You teach surfing?" I ask.

He nods. "Yeah. I'm not a pro, but I know my way around the waves enough to offer lessons." He points in the direction of the hotel. "I work part-time for the surf school."

I smile on the inside, assuming that the girls in his group yesterday were likely just customers. I drop my sandals and sit down next to him, crossing my legs underneath my skirt.

"Then I guess you're not just some stuck-up surfer with territory issues?"

He laughs.

"Nah, I'm not one of those."

"Well, that's good to know"—I smile over at him—"because *that* would've been a disappointment."

His lips spread into a soft grin as he looks out at the ocean.

"I thought the surfing here was supposed to be insane and dangerous, like you see on TV?"

"Oh, it can be," he says. "Mostly in the winter around here, and over at Laniakea. But give it time, you'll see some big waves. I like surfing when the storms roll in, myself."

That takes me a little by surprise.

"Isn't that dangerous?"

He shrugs. "Sure, I guess it is, but I've done all right."

"Don't you worry about getting struck by lightning?"

He chuckles and I feel myself turning red—clearly I know nothing about surfing.

"I'd be more worried about getting my leash tangled on a reef, or getting knocked unconscious and drowning."

I feel my eyes springing open wide in my face.

"Oh, well, yeah, that definitely sounds dangerous—ever been in a situation like that?"

"Nah," he says, shaking his head. "Nothing major."

I nod, taking his word for it, but a faint twinge of uncertainty lingers.

I listen to the waves crashing against the shore and the breeze combing through the trees behind us. I reach up and wipe underneath my eyes again; tiny flakes of dried mascara come off onto my fingers. Suddenly I'm not feeling so confident about how I must look. I could check myself out in the camera on my phone, but to let Luke see me doing it would be embarrassing.

"Sometimes I wish my job was a little more laid-back like yours seems to be," I say.

Luke looks over, his arms dangling casually over the tops of his bent knees.

"What do you do?" he asks.

"Event coordinator," I answer. "Weddings. Parties. All things crazy and hectic and ridiculously expensive."

"You don't like it?"

"No, I like it," I say with a nod. "I must thrive on the chaos, I think." I laugh lightly, shaking my head just thinking about it, because I'm not sure that's true. "And there's no shortage of chaos, that's for sure."

"Yeah, I can see that." He smiles softly, and it kind of melts me a little inside.

"Well, it pays well," I go on, feeling a strange need to justify my job more than I thought I already had, "but...well, it's just been a disaster this time around." I leave it at that. I'm still not ready to think about the other problems I *should* be fixing right now with the Denningses' wedding. I'm having such a strangely pleasant time sitting here with this attractive stranger. On a beach. In Hawaii.

This is how a trip to Hawaii is *supposed* to begin.

He smells good. Not like saltwater or overwhelming suntan lotion, but like soap and toothpaste and heat. To keep from looking at him longer than I should, I gaze down at my toes buried partially beneath the sand, my painted toenails poking through against the tiny grains.

I hear him sigh lightly next to me and I worry that it's because maybe I'm boring him. But then he glances briefly toward the hotel and I get the feeling he's got somewhere he has to be soon—that's better than boredom, I suppose.

"How long are you here for?" he asks.

"The wedding is tonight and I have a plane to catch tomorrow afternoon back to San Diego."

The softness of his face fades a little. He nods.

"That's too bad," he says, not looking at me.

He glances over with a smile but doesn't look at me for long. Then he stands up. He reaches his hand out to me, and this time I accept it without reluctance and he pulls me to my feet.

"It was nice meeting you, Sienna, but I need to get back. I've got an appointment in ten minutes."

My gut is twisting. I don't know why, but I don't want this to be good-bye. It's too soon.

I nod shortly and with disappointment, but I try not to let it show on my face. In just a few minutes I was able to push all of the disastrous problems and the stress caused by them down into

THE MOMENT OF LETTING GO   39

a place where it had no control over me. And I'm not ready to part with that power yet.

"Hey," I say suddenly, "what did you mean earlier when you said to let it go? I mean, it's self-explanatory, I guess, but why did you say it?" He could've easily just said what most people say: *I hope you feel better*, or ask me if I'll be all right just before he walks away, but he didn't, and it intrigues me.

Luke pushes his hands down into the pockets of his shorts, his tanned, muscled arms stiffening against his sides as he draws his shoulders up. The wind moves through the top of his tousled hair as he looks at me, quietly at first. I get the feeling he doesn't want to leave as much as I don't want him to.

"If you decided to stay longer," he says, "I could show you."

I blink, vaguely stunned by his words that, once again, intrigue me to no end.

"*Show* me?"

"Yeah," he says, his face beginning to brighten again. "It's one of those things that can't really be explained." He shrugs.

And here I thought I was just asking him to tell me mostly for the sake of conversation, to keep him around a while longer. I never anticipated anything thought-provoking from such a simple thing.

I sigh. "Well, I wish I could"—I *really* wish I could—"but after Hawaii, it's off to Jamaica for me."

"Wow," he says, "you must do a lot of traveling; it's a shame you can't enjoy the places you see a little more."

Understatement of the year.

"Yeah, I admit that'd be ideal, but at least I get to *see* the places. Most people never do. I can't complain."

He shrugs again, and I get the feeling he disagrees with that statement but doesn't feel right about admitting it.

Then he looks up momentarily in thought.

"Hey," he says, "if you get any free time before you have to head out, come find me on the beach and I'll give you a free lesson."

Stepping up closer with my shoes dangling from the fingers of one hand, I smile lightheartedly. "Don't I have to schedule an appointment first?"

He winks with a playful grin and it makes my heart leap.

"Nah, I think I can fit you in," he says.

My face flushes with heat, my eyes straying downward momentarily.

"All right," I say, "if I can break away long enough, I'll take you up on that offer." In my heart I know the chances of that happening are slim, but it's the thought keeping the smile on my face. "But no dangerous stuff," I add sternly yet playfully.

He puts up his hands. "No way," he says with a big smile. "I'd take care of yah."

I smile back at him.

Luke says good-bye, his hazel eyes—same color as mine—bright with warmth and sincerity and mystery. And as he walks away, I stand paralyzed with confusion and regret. Confused by a strange need deep in my chest that wants to know him more, but regret for accepting that I have to ignore it. He drifts farther away over the white sand beach and back toward the ocean and out of my life. And with his absence, as though I've awoken from a dream, the real world comes back with a vengeance, reminding me that I have a job to do and that this wedding must be absolutely perfect. I already feel the anxiety creeping up at the possibility that it won't be.

FIVE

Luke

*D*oes she have a friend?" Seth asks with a hopeful grin.

I step out of my running shoes and make my way into the kitchen, opening the refrigerator door.

"Not *with* her," I say, leaning over into the fridge in search of my leftover pizza from last night.

"What about the girls she was with?"

"She's just here for a job. Did you eat my pizza?" I rise from behind the refrigerator door and look at Seth expectantly.

"Yeah, but I didn't think you wanted it."

"Why wouldn't I?"

I close the door with a package of smoked turkey in my hand instead and take it with me to the counter, where I get to work on a sandwich. I haven't eaten since this morning, and here it is at sundown and my stomach aches with hunger. I usually get a bite to eat at the resort, but I couldn't risk running into Sienna again.

That's not a good idea: She's beautiful and sweet and motivated—exactly the kind of girl I could get myself in a world of trouble with, especially since she also seems the cautious and careful type. I consider myself a cautious and careful kind of guy, but not every aspect of my life follows those rules.

"Sorry, man," he says. "Next pizza's on me." He always says that.

I leave it alone and finish making my sandwich and then begin to scarf it down standing up.

"She doesn't seem like your type though," Seth says, sitting at the bar with his feet propped on the spindle of a bar stool.

"How do you figure that?" I ask with my mouth full.

Seth reaches up and rubs his hand against the back of his shaved head. "She just seemed kind of ... full of herself. Hot, sure, but I don't think I've ever seen you with a girl like that."

I look at him oddly.

"You know what I mean," he says. "She just isn't the kind of girl you usually go for."

Confused by his judgment of Sienna, it takes a second to realize why.

"I'm not talking about the one who walked up to me," I say and swallow down another bite. "Sienna's the one she was talking to after she stomped off. Long, dark reddish-brown hair. Rockin' body. Carrying a camera."

"*Oh.*" Seth nods. "That makes sense, then. I was startin' to wonder about you, bro." He laughs. "But you'd probably be better off hookin' up with the stuck-up one anyway, considering your predicament."

I take a water bottle from the fridge and move past Seth through the kitchen. He follows as I make my way outside onto the lanai. I sit down at the little round table and set my water on top of it.

"I don't have a predicament."

"The hell you don't." He laughs again and sits down in the empty chair. "I'd say denying yourself the simple pleasures in life because of your conscience is a predicament. Have some fun once in a while. That's the one way we're different, Luke—*you* care. *I* don't."

Now it's *my* turn to laugh. "There are a lot of ways we're different, Seth," I correct him, sporting a grin. "Don't make me crack the list open again."

Stretching my legs out before me, I slouch my back against the wicker, my arms resting along the length of the chair arms with my hands dangling over the ends.

Seth shakes his head, a big close-lipped smile stretching his features. I don't elaborate. He knows as well as I do that we are as different as night and day when it comes to women. And life in general. But I used to be just like him. I don't regret it, but I don't miss it, either. Most of it, anyway.

"So what are you gonna do?" he asks.

"Nothing," I say. "I shouldn't have even talked to her at all, to be honest. It opened a door I probably shouldn't have opened."

Seth looks at me from the side. "Then why did you?"

"I don't know," I say, thinking on it. "Maybe I was just *looking* for something to be wrong with her—makes it easier."

"Yeah, *that's* healthy," he quips. "And did you find anything? I bet you didn't—there wasn't anything wrong with her from where I was standing."

Absently I shake my head no, chewing on the inside of my mouth, thinking about my brief one-on-one with Sienna. "Not a thing," I answer. "Which is what worries me."

"You are messed up, Luke." Seth scratches his head where his scar has been healing. He had an accident on our last trip to El Capitan, which was a close call. Got staples in his head from the top of his right ear and stretching around the back of his scalp. Now he just keeps his head shaved because he says he likes the look.

"Hey, I agree with you to some extent," he says, "but if you can't get close to a girl you like, then at least allow yourself a piece of ass every now and then." He puts up his hands briefly, palms forward. "Not tryin' to be in your business, bro, but if I was in your shoes, I'd have carpal tunnel in my right hand by now."

I laugh lightly and put the water bottle to my lips again.

He slumps forward and then props his elbows on his thighs.

"Maybe you should check out this girl from the resort," he says. "Who knows. You might be disgusted by her and then everything'll be all right." He chuckles.

I shake my head, smiling.

"Well, if you change your mind, let me know." Seth stands up and raises both arms high above his head, stretching. "I'll find someplace to go if you want the house to yourself for a while. Anything to get my best friend laid."

"You'd even move out?" I jest, just before swigging down the last of my water.

Seth's eyebrows draw together. "I don't love yah *that* much," he says and laughs his way back into the house.

Then he pops his head around the corner. "I almost forgot," he says. "Kendra will be over early in the morning—thought I'd warn you."

I raise my index and middle fingers from the chair arm in response. "I'll be sure to lock my bedroom door tonight."

The screen door cracks lightly against the wood frame as it bounces closed behind him.

Kendra. Love her to death, but the most obnoxious alarm clock I've ever had the displeasure of being awoken by.

Gazing back out at the ocean, I let the scene with Sienna from earlier today play though my mind again. I see that long, flowing skirt clinging to her petite form and her soft hair draping her shoulders. Her cute feet covered by those not-so-sand-friendly heels. Her dimpled smile and the mascara smudged all over her face that I didn't have the heart to point out to her—it didn't make any difference to me anyway. She's a beautiful girl, and sweet enough and with just the right amount of confidence, from what little I know about her, that she could have spinach in her teeth and I'd still find her beautiful.

But maybe Seth's right. Maybe Seth's lifestyle with women isn't so bad after all. I try to tell myself that from time to time, in times just like this when I'm trying everything in my power to convince myself that I need to back off. I always think about *why* Seth is the way he is and I can't help but agree with his philosophy. He shut himself off completely from relationships when his fiancée dumped him. He loved that girl, and she loved him, but all of us—me, Seth, Braedon, Kendra, and Landon—knew it would happen. Because it always does with guys like us: Most girls who don't share our lifestyle of extreme sports can't handle it and usually take off in the other direction, the safe, "normal" direction, the second they find out what we do.

I tilt my head back and shut my eyes, inhaling a deep breath. What if Sienna goes looking for me tomorrow on the beach? Damn, I wish I hadn't talked to her because now I'll feel like shit if she does look for me and I'm not there. I don't want to come off as a dick by standing her up.

Defeated by my even stronger conscience, I accept the facts: It'll never work with a girl like her, and I'd be *more* of a dick to pursue it.

———

There's a far-off pounding muffled in my head, like the sound of a hammer drilling a stubborn nail into a wooden beam. I groan and roll over, covering my head with a pillow. My mouth is dry and I can taste my breath, hot and sour and fetid. *BAM! BAM! BAM!* The pounding is getting louder. And then a familiar voice follows: urgent, a little rough, though tinged with femininity.

"Luke, I need my green backpack!" I hear from the other side of my bedroom door. "Have you seen it?"

I wake up fully, grabbing the pillow and pressing it firmly against my face as a low, guttural groan of protest rumbles through my chest. With my eyes closed, I see a visual of where I last saw that green backpack and then want to kick myself for not taking it out of my bedroom yesterday when I thought about it.

"Luke?" Kendra calls out again. "Come on, I know I left it over here. We can't find it anywhere in the house."

A swath of cool air brushes my face as I pull the pillow to the side. My eyes crack open a slit at first, instinctively wary of the possibility of blinding sunlight beaming through the curtain on the window above the bed. But it's still early, the sun just barely making its appearance in the sky, bathing my room in a soft gray hue. My eyes open the rest of the way, but my body is having a hard time catching up.

BAM! BAM! BAM!

"All right! Hold on a sec!"

I toss the sheet off and crawl out of the bed, scanning the floor in search of my boxers. When I find them, I stumble trying to put them on in a rush.

Kendra's backpack is sitting on the floor beside the door, mocking me. I snatch it up by one of the straps and open the door, holding it out to her.

"How did it get in your room?" Kendra asks, standing in the doorway. She slides it off my fingers and hangs it on her arm at the elbow.

"You put it here," I say, still trying to wake up. "When you came in to complain about your roommate."

I keep my position blocking the doorway, hoping she doesn't try to come in. I just want to go back to bed.

"You don't want to come with us?" she asks, frowning.

"I can't. I've got stuff to do today."

I raise one arm, propping my hand above me on the door-frame. Kendra makes a face when my eyes reopen after a long, drawn-out yawn.

"Gah! You need a Tic Tac," she says, wrinkling her freckle-sprinkled nose.

I reach out and fit my hand at the back of her blond head, pulling her toward me; the top of her ponytail pushes through my fingers. I press my lips to her forehead. She smiles, but pushes me away playfully.

"You stink," she says, grinning. "Come on, get up and take a shower and come with us. You never hike with us anymore. I hate it."

"That's not true," I say. "I've been three times in the past two months."

"But still," she argues, her plump lips pouting, "you don't go often enough and that's just like never to me."

"Sorry." I smile weakly because I'm still too tired and it's all I can manage. "I'll go next time. I promise."

With the backpack dangling from the bend of her arm, she crosses her arms tight over her stomach and cocks her head to one side with a disapproving smirk.

Kendra is a cute girl, and a tomboy at heart. At first glance one would think she's just another pretty face who might enjoy walking in the dominant shadow of a strong, attractive guy. But when one gets to know her, they realize quickly that she carries a dominant shadow of her own and few men in this world can keep up with it.

Only *one* could equal it—Landon—and he's long gone, so she's in the same kind of limbo as I am when it comes to relationships.

"Heading over to the resort today?" she asks.

Seth walks past, making his way to the bathroom. "Yeah, he's got a date with disaster," he chimes in with laughter, and then the bathroom door closes behind him.

Kendra looks at me curiously.

Not wanting to get into *any* conversations with her—because I'd rather be sleeping—I brush off Seth's comment altogether.

"I've got a few appointments over at the school," I tell her, "and then after that, I'm free. Too bad you two aren't heading out later in the day."

"It's an all-day hike," she says. "We *have* to leave early."

I nod, yawn with a little less open-mouth, and go to close my door. "Well, I'm going back to bed," I say. "Two more hours and I have to get up."

The door stops at the halfway mark when the palm of Kendra's hand presses against it.

"Luke, you're starting to worry me." All traces of a smile or a playful, nagging attitude are gone from her face. I witness it from time to time, and it always prompts a conversation with her that I don't want to have—one she *knows* I don't want to have.

"Kendra," I say exasperatedly, running a hand through the top of my disheveled hair, "I just want to go back to bed, all right? There's nothing wrong with me." I can never seem to get that through Kendra's thick skull.

"I miss him too," she says, and it stings the hell out of me.

Inhaling a deep, aggravated breath, I tilt my head back and let my eyes slam shut. The last thing I want to do is talk about my brother—it's the one thing I don't like to talk about, even on a small scale. I'm constantly having to avoid it around my friends and my family: *How are you doing?* they ask. *How are you holding up?* they ask. And sometimes people I don't even know—new friends of Seth or Braedon—ask, *How did it happen?* Knowing damn well how it happened because Seth or Braedon already told them, and they don't know what else to say, but feel like they have to say *something.* How about nothing? How about leaving it the hell alone? How about not constantly reminding me to open my eyes to my brother's fucked-up, horrific death that was my goddamn fault?! How about that?

My fist clenches into a rock at my side, then the other, until I slowly let out a long, deep breath and feel the calm wash over me and my fingers uncoil.

"You *have* to stop doing this," I tell her as my head comes back down. My eyes lock on her sad brown ones, which seem flecked with insult. "*Everybody* misses Landon," I say carefully. "But you're—"

Seth comes out of the bathroom with a knowing look in his eyes and saves the day.

"Let's go, Ken-doll!" I hear a loud *pop* and see a flash of yellow behind Kendra's head. A rubber band falls onto the linoleum floor at her feet.

"Owww!" She reaches behind her, cupping her hand over the back of her neck, her round, doll-like face scrunching up like a head of lettuce. "You *ass*hole!" A thud resonates through the confined hallway space as her knuckles make contact with his chest. Seth jerks forward and both arms instinctively come up to defend the area. They both laugh.

Covertly, I thank Seth with my eyes.

Kendra, still rubbing the back of her stinging neck, turns to me. "Next time you're *going*," she says, pointing a finger at me. "I'm holding you to that promise." Then she points at Seth. "And *he's* my witness."

I put up both hands in surrender.

"I always keep my promises," I say, and that stings too, because it's a lie and I feel guilty playing that card—my brother wouldn't be dead if I kept my promises.

Finally they leave me to my room, where I hurry and close the door before Kendra thinks of something else to say. I hear the screen on the front door slam against the house as they walk out, and then their voices carrying on the air as they move past my bedroom window.

Falling against my bed with my arms raised above my head, I stare up at the water-damaged ceiling, where swirling patterns of brown have eaten away at the material in spots. The damage was there when I bought this house seven months ago, and I've yet to do anything about it. Or with any of the other multitude of things wrong with this *rare gem of a fixer-upper with a stunning ocean view!* Those were the real estate agent's exact words when she showed me the place. She was laying the bright personality on thick to prepare me to hear the price. *It's not the house you'd be buying, but the view,* she had said.

That was all that mattered to me, really. I needed a beautiful view, something to help smother the image of Landon's closed-casket funeral, the blue and white flowers that covered his grave; the photo of us together with our mom and dad when they vacationed on Oahu that I buried with him. I needed to get out of the old house that I had shared with him because I woke up every morning expecting him to be crashed in the living room instead of his room, and it killed me when I saw that sofa empty. Every single day.

This new house doesn't smother the images of the funeral—nothing will ever do that—but the house is different, the sofa is different.

My head falls to the side, and the numbers on the clock on my bedside table glow blue amid the slowly brightening light of the room. A breeze pushes through the open window, deftly touching the thin white curtain covering the screen. I shut my eyes and hope to drift back to sleep, but minutes later Landon's face is still haunting me.

I thought I'd be used to this by now, seeing his face everywhere, but just like the memories of his funeral, it'll always be there, torturing me, haunting me.

After a long time, and after suffocating myself with the pillow again to blot out the light, I'm still awake and I know I will be for the rest of the day.

Then suddenly, it's Sienna's face strolling through my mind, instead of my brothers. I had hoped to have forgotten about her by the morning. That's pretty much what happened to the last few girls I took more than a sexual interest in.

But not this time.

I spring up from the bed, resolving to end this before it starts. I shower. Eat. Brush my teeth. Sit outside on the lanai and look out at the ocean. Then finally I call Allan at the resort and ask if he can fill in for me today. When he confirms that he can, I dress not to surf, but to hike, and set out to catch up with Seth and Kendra.

SIX

Sienna

*H*e's not coming.

God, I feel like an idiot—I really wanted to see him again.

Pushing down that uncomfortable feeling of being stood up, I rise to my feet and take my beach towel with me, tossing it over my arm without even shaking out the sand. Clumsily I step into my flip-flops and then shoulder my beach bag. I feel like I can't get away fast enough, as if everyone on the island is looking right at me, whispering about the dumb girl who got stood up by the hot surfer; my stomach swims with embarrassment. And utter disappointment.

There's a small group of people on the beach learning to surf, but this time Luke's not among them. Maybe he got sick and couldn't come today. Or maybe he's just running late.

It doesn't matter. I have to get ready to catch my plane.

Without looking back, I leave the beach in a very dry bikini covered by a pair of white shorts and head toward the hotel.

It's for the best anyway. After today I'll be back at home in San Diego and there's not one good thing I can think of that I'd get out of spending an hour with Luke. If anything, I'd end up liking him enough to want to spend more time with him and I'd have to leave Hawaii more disappointed than I already am.

I saved the wedding from Veronica, Destroyer of Weddings. The caterer showed up as planned. The original band was a no-go when I finally contacted them. They said they'd already booked that time slot with someone else. But the guy took pity on me—after I'd apologized profusely for what Veronica had done—and made some calls. Turns out Veronica decided to fire them because they said they might be ten minutes late—*unbelievable*. At the last minute, just when I thought Mrs. Dennings's angry gaze was actually going to set me on fire this time, I got the call. The new band showed up with just minutes to spare and everything else went smoothly the rest of the evening.

Mrs. Dennings never actually said thank you, but she didn't call Cassandra and manage to get me fired, and I figured that was the best she was willing to offer.

Paige comes around the side of the building just as I'm walking up, a relieved expression settled over her features. Her pink-tinged cheeks blow up with air before letting it all out slowly like pinching the opening of a balloon.

"I'm so glad *that's* over," she says.

I don't agree or disagree, but instead I look beyond her, afraid to meet her eyes. Because I'm not particularly good at this boss thing, especially when it comes to my best friend—another lesson learned.

"Are you ready to pack up and hitch a ride off this rock?" she asks, smiling now, having no clue about what's plaguing my thoughts that have everything—well, mostly—to do with her. Luke is still kinda there, floating around in the back in my subconscious, uninvited.

I sigh, looking down at my feet.

"Paige, I need to talk to you."

Her expression goes slack in an instant.

"Yeah, what's up?" She waits impatiently and then softens her features when I look back at her, almost as if trying to help me out. My shoulders fall into a slump and I let out a deep breath, dropping my beach bag and towel on the concrete as I sit down on the low brick border surrounding the landscaping. Moments later, she sits beside me; I can smell her fruity passion perfume.

"Paige," I begin, gazing out ahead at the palm trees on the side of the building, "you're great at what you do and you help me tremendously, but—"

"You're *firing* me?" Strangely enough, her face softens even more, when I most expected it to shrivel up and make me feel awful.

"What—no!"

She smiles. "Don't worry about it." Her hand touches my shoulder. "I was actually going to put in my resignation." She gestures her free hand and adds suddenly, "It has nothing to do with you, girl, so don't think that for a second."

"Wait—you're *quitting*?" Blindsided, it takes me a second to get anything out. "Paige, I wasn't going to fire you. I just wanted to apologize for snapping at you—it's not as easy being your boss as I thought it'd be."

Paige chuckles. "I can tell," she says, and then lays her head on my shoulder for a brief second. "But I meant what I said about never putting you in a bad position. I think it's better I find another job before I get *you* fired."

"So you're really quitting?"

She nods and her hands fall into her lap. "Not right now," she says. "I mean, I'll definitely stay on board until Cassandra can find someone to replace me, but I'm just not cut out for this stuff. I don't have the patience for it—well, for people like *that*." She laughs lightly. "I have to admit, if it weren't for you, I might've told that bitch off."

I smile faintly.

"So what are you going to do when you leave?"

She pauses and says, "I've got something lined up—not that I've been *planning* to quit, but you know me. I'll manage."

This is true. Paige doesn't really need to work to live like most of us do; she comes from a wealthy family in the real estate business and wouldn't have to work a day in her life if she didn't want to. But Paige *likes* to work. It keeps her busy and off the Lazy Citizens of America list, as she calls it. But mostly it gives her more of a reason to spend ridiculous amounts of money on clothes and shoes and all things expensive and in style.

I nod, a small smile tugging my lips—this is all such a relief. Sort of. I hate to see her go. But I understand.

"So then you're still on for Jamaica?"

She smiles. "Yeah," she says, "but I was hoping my first time there would be more"—she twirls her index finger in the air, a concentrating look in her eyes—"*enjoyable*. I was excited about Hawaii, but it didn't quite turn out like I envisioned it."

"Yeah," I say simply and look out ahead again as the rest is cut off by my sudden deep thoughts. "I guess I can't blame you." My voice is distant.

"It's gettin' to you, too, I can tell."

I look over. "What—" I smile to show her that she's wrong. "Oh, no, I'm just tired. I'm always like this after an event." This is only half true—this time I feel much worse.

She hooks her arm around my back, her hand around my arm, and pulls my shoulder against her side.

"We're gonna go on a real vacation sometime," she says. "We can go anywhere. Just name the place." She points at me briefly and interjects, "Of course, it has to be someplace sunny where I can wear my bikini—nothing cold and no deserts or anything like that."

I chuckle. "We'll figure it out," I tell her with a smile in my voice.

Paige stands up, her small frame hardly shielding me from the sun.

"We should get our stuff packed," she says. "I can't miss this flight. My family reunion is tomorrow. My mom will kill me."

I stand with her, taking up my towel and beach bag and repositioning them on my arm and shoulder. As I walk alongside Paige toward the hotel, from the corner of my eye I see a tanned, athletic figure in navy cargo shorts and a red T-shirt tramping through the sand toward me. Squinting in an attempt to get a better visual, I put my hand up above my eyes to shield my face from the sun. And when I see that it is, in fact, Luke, my face breaks into a smile that I instantly try to conceal from my best friend.

I turn to Paige, stopping her on the sidewalk.

"I'll catch up with you in a few minutes," I say.

Paige, without asking any questions, agrees and heads inside the hotel lobby without me.

I meet Luke halfway, stopping in the sand, glad that I'm wearing flip-flops this time and can stand up on my own. Luke appears out of breath, his feet like fifty-pound weights on the ends of his muscled legs, burrowing into the sand nearly to his ankles with every difficult step. His back is hunched over, his hands propped on his bent knees when he finally comes to a stop in front of me. The more I look at him, the more confused I become—surely he's not serious? Everything about his demeanor seems overly dramatic and... strangely humorous.

"Sorry I'm late," he says between quick, unsteady breaths. "I ran all the way here. You'll never believe what happened." He takes a few more fast breaths, his hands still propped on his knees to hold up his weight, the muscles in his arms hard and defined. "I was on my way this morning when a bicycle came out of nowhere and clipped me as I was crossing the street." My eyes widen and I feel the warm, salty air hit my teeth as my lips slowly begin to part. "And I hit the asphalt hard—"

"Are you OK?" I look him over, seeing no visible injuries.

He nods heavily, rapidly, and tries to catch his breath some more.

"I lost consciousness and woke up in some house—weird beads and shit were hanging from a doorway, and it smelled like incense." My forehead wrinkles as I try to put the odd scene together in my head. "My wrists and ankles were tied to a chair." He points at me briefly. "You know those fancy patio chairs with cushions that you wonder about leaving out in the rain?" *Huh?* "It was that chick on the bike. Somehow she got me to her house and tied me up. I thought: OK, this feels a little like *Misery*—you've seen that movie, right?" He points at me again.

Knowing now that he's full of shit, I cross my arms, crushing the beach towel between them, and narrow my eyes.

"No, I can't say that I have," I answer with a smirk.

I catch him grinning, but he recovers quickly and continues with the charade that I find both ridiculous and charming.

Luke falls down in the sand, lying with his back against it and his knees bent, his hands resting on his chest, the right one crossed over to lie flat against his so-called rapidly beating heart.

"And just what did this girl do to you?" I play along.

He gazes up at me as I hover over him—he looks so serious.

"She wanted me to teach her how to surf," he says matter-of-factly.

I try not to laugh, pushing the urge down and putting on my own serious face.

"So what did you do then? Did you teach her?"

Luke's head moves side to side against the white sand. He swallows and looks into the clear blue sky, recalling the "event." "No," he answers distantly. "I told her I couldn't, that I was booked for the day." He looks at me with concentrating eyes. "I said I had a very important, *beautiful* client today that I couldn't reschedule under *any* circumstances."

My cheeks feel like they're on fire.

"The look on her face when I told her that, it scared the hell outta me."

"It must've been *so* awful for you," I say dramatically, pressing my hand to my bikini-covered chest. "I just can't imagine."

"I know, right? But I managed to get my hands free from the rope and then untied my legs. I was about to jump out the window when she came back into the room and saw me. A tray with chips and a sandwich fell from her hands to the floor. She lunged"—his hand juts out in front of him, his fingers arched into a claw—"like a cat." He bares his teeth and makes a hissing sound—my serious face has vanished and I can't stop smiling. "I leapt at the window, crashing right through the screen, and then rolled when I hit the grass outside. I ran all the way here."

He stops and releases one last quick breath from his lungs. And then he just looks up at me.

"What kind of chips were they?" I ask.

"Tortilla," he says without hesitation.

I nod. "Well, at least she was going to feed you."

Luke smiles, a shadow cast by me standing over him covering his face. I purposely step to the side and a burst of sunlight beams into his eyes, causing him to flinch. He laughs and springs to his feet.

Suddenly his expression shifts, the playful look disappears, replaced by apology and sincerity. I can't stop looking at his eyes. They're so kind and devoted and passionate.

"I almost didn't come," he finally says with honesty.

"Why not?" I'm not sure I really want to know the answer to that.

Luke pushes his hands deep into his pockets, his arms tightening to reveal the hard, defined muscles running along them.

"I guess I just thought if I spent an hour with you before you had to leave, I'd probably like you enough that I'd be more disappointed you couldn't stay longer."

Wow—already on the same wavelength and we barely know each other. This is kinda freaking me out. In a good way.

I look down, trying to tame the heat in my face.

But all too soon reality rears its ugly head and the moment is lost.

I switch shoulders with the beach bag and look back at the hotel where Paige waits for me inside. I sigh quietly. Less than five minutes with Luke and already I like him enough that I wish I could stay longer. I can't be completely sure, but it kind of scares me a little to think what a full hour with him might do.

"Well, I really do have to go." I step away from him. "My plane leaves at one and I still have to get all my stuff together."

Luke fishes his cell phone from his pocket and glances at the screen.

"Fifteen minutes," he says. "At least give me that much time to make up for being late."

Yes! That sounds awesome.

"No," I say, shaking my head disappointedly. "I really can't. There's just not enough time. It's nearly an hour drive to the airport. If anything, I should *leave* in fifteen minutes."

"Then miss your plane," he says simply.

I blink with surprise.

He steps up to close the space I created when I started to walk away from him. I can't find my voice—not sure what to say to something like that.

"Come on," he continues, a smile slowly etching into his features. "Unless you have somewhere you absolutely have to be the moment you step off that plane in San Diego, it's not going to hurt you to miss this flight and catch the next one." His smile broadens and he gestures a hand casually amid the space in front of him. "People miss their flights all the time: woke up late; got stuck in traffic; got clipped in the street by a crazy, bike-riding chick who feeds her victims tortilla chips before she tortures them—pick any excuse and go with it."

I chuckle lightly, a tiny burst of air pushing through my lips. But I still can't bring myself to respond, because I'm not sure how. I know what I *want* to do, but like so much in my life, it doesn't at all feel like I *should*.

He gives me puppy-dog eyes.

Seriously?! Puppy-dog eyes? You think that's actually going to work?

"OK," I say, caving to some mysterious forces at work here that I need to have a serious talk with later. "Let me call the airline and see if I can get a later flight. My assistant is going to think I've lost my mind."

Beaming, Luke nods and takes a step back as if to give me some privacy. I dig my phone from my bag and unlock the screen. I quickly look up my flight info online and call the airline to find out if there's a later flight out today. There is, and I book it without even thinking about the extra charges for making a last-minute change.

"I bought myself three hours," I tell Luke, taking into account the hour it takes to get to the airport. "How are we going to spend it?" I drop my phone inside my bag and suck in a deep, nervous, crazy breath—what am I *doing*? This is nuts! And why does it feel like my face is about to split in half?

Luke grins back at me.

He steps up to me. I hear the sand crunching underneath his flip-flops. His closeness makes me intimately aware of my own heartbeat. I don't know why. I don't care that I don't. I just know that I don't want it to stop.

"I'm going to show you," he says.

"You're going to show me what? How to surf?"

His smile broadens, enhancing the light in his hazel eyes. He starts to speak, but then it seems that just before the answer leaves his lips, he stops. He thinks on it some more, maybe choosing his words carefully? I can never know, but that's what it feels like. I just watch and wait patiently, the light in my own eyes never dimming, the smile on my lips never waning.

But *his* wanes. Just a little.

"What three hours in a place like Hawaii is *supposed* to be like," he finally answers.

I think it was far from the answer he had wanted to give.

"I trust you're a good guide," I say, grinning. "You *should* be, being a local and all."

"Oh, I'm not a local," he says.

"Really? I assumed you were."

"Nope." He crosses his arms over his chest. "I've only lived in Hawaii for a year and a half."

"Where did you move from?"

"Sacramento," he answers and then holds out his hand, giving his head a quick jerk backward. "Come on, we can talk on the way. Three hours isn't much time."

I look down at his hand, wanting to take it, but at the same time feeling that it's too soon. But maybe it isn't, because everything inside of me wants to take it and to throw the too-soon rules right out the damn window.

I reach into my bag instead.

"Wait a second," I say as I retrieve my cell phone again. "Let's take a picture first."

Luke looks vaguely surprised.

"All right," he agrees. "Selfies are doable, but none of that duck-lips stuff."

I laugh lightly as he steps up beside me and drapes an arm around me from behind.

I snap the shot of us together, step to the side, and type Paige a text message that reads: **Change of plans. I booked a later flight out. His name is Luke Everett. He works at the surf school. If anything happens to me, he's the one to look for.**

I hit send. She'll probably be bummed we won't be on the same flight home, but she's always telling me I need to live a little, so I'm sure she'll be happy for me too.

Standing behind me, Luke's light laughter fills the air.

"Worried I'm going to kidnap you and tie you to a chair in a room with beads and incense?"

"Not really," I say, smiling over at him, "but just in case—are you offended?"

He laughs. "Not at all. Kind of impressed, actually."

Paige responds saying she's worried that I've lost my mind, but she hopes I'll have fun, and that she'll make sure to tell the cops if she has to. Then I drop the phone back inside my bag.

Moments later I hear Paige's voice calling out over the sound of waves pushing against the beach.

"Sienna!" She's running toward us, quite ungracefully through the sand, her flip-flops getting stuck and nearly causing her to trip.

Luke looks at me. "Your assistant?"

I nod. "Yeah, and my best friend. Prepare yourself—she bites."

He laughs under his breath.

Then he stands taller, interlocking his hands on his backside, puffing out his chest a little and raising his chin. He looks like he's preparing to meet my dad, and it's adorable. Completely fake, but adorable—the smile gives him away.

Paige stops in front of us and, while catching her breath, she eyes me as if to say, Daaaaamn, *Sienna.*

She looks right at him, all joking aside, her pretty blue eyes narrowed with severity, her thin arms crossed loosely over her chest.

"What's your full name?" she asks him.

"Luke Michael Everett."

"Where were you born?"

"Sacramento."

I'm trying not to laugh—they look so serious!

She twists her bottom lip between her teeth in contemplation.

"You work at the surf school in the hotel?"

He nods. "I sure do. Part-time. And the other part-time I work at Big Wave Surf Shop."

"And someone in the surf school can verify this?"

He nods again. "Yep. Ask for Allan. I work there three days out of the week and I give surfing lessons here whenever he has them to give and I have the free time to take them."

Paige's eyes narrow even more, her head turning a slight angle. Luke's lips continue to gradually turn up with that smile of his.

"How old are you?"

"Twenty-four," he answers right away.

Paige looks at me, then back at him. He beams at her with white, straight teeth. She's about to crack up now, I can tell, but she manages to hold it in a little longer.

I stand here with my lips pressed together, unable to contain the humor in my expression.

She looks down at his feet.

"What size shoe do you wear?"

My eyes bug out of my head and I look at her with a big, hard gaze that says, *You* didn't *just ask him that!*

Oh, yes, I absolutely did, her grinning gaze says in return.

"Paige," I cut in, "meet Luke. Luke, this is my best friend and *former* assistant, Paige."

She smiles with teeth this time.

"*Former* assistant?" Luke asks, looking between both of us.

She nods. "Yeah, I quit today." She hits me lightly on the arm. "This girl is a tyrant to work with; I just couldn't do it anymore." She shakes her blond head, but her grin never fades.

I laugh lightly. "It's a long, boring story, but I'm *not* a tyrant."

Luke's lips smash together, suppressing laughter.

"OK, look," Paige says to Luke. "I love this girl"—she shakes her finger at him—"and if anything happens to her, just know that I will hunt you down; you got me?"

Luke's eyes fall on me from the side without moving his head.

"Yes, ma'am," he says with a nod and an almost frightened kind of smile. "I'll take good care of her."

After a moment, once Paige is satisfied, she drops the serious act and grabs me by the elbow, pulling me off to the side.

"We'll be right back," she says, holding up a finger to Luke.

"Take your time," he says and waves us on.

"I want to stay so bad," she says in a harsh whisper, her fingers digging into my arm. "He is gorgeous! Does he have any friends?"

My eyes catch Luke's, and he's grinning—he definitely heard what she said.

"Well, then, why don't you stay?" I tell her.

She sighs and the smile slips right off her face. "I wish I could. I missed the last family reunion. I can't miss it this time, or worse than my mom killing me, my dad might cut me off."

I laugh lightly. "Then you'd have to work with me longer."

Her little nose wrinkles around the edges and her hand falls away from my elbow.

"Seriously, though," she says, "just be careful and call me every now and then to let me know what's going on."

"I'm only staying three hours," I say with laughter in my voice.

"I know, but still."

"All right," I give in. "I'll text you at least. Have a safe flight back." I lean in and hug her tight.

"Well, I better go," she says, her fingers slipping away from mine. "See you when you get home."

As she's walking away, she raises her index and middle fingers on one hand, pointing them at her hard, narrowed eyes and then

at Luke, back and forth a few times as if to say *I'm watching you.*
Luke laughs under his breath and raises his hands up at his sides in
surrender. Paige gives him—and then me—a big smile just before
she turns her back to us and starts to walk away. Covertly she looks
at me from the side, spaces her hands many inches apart, glances
downward as if at his feet, and mouths something like *his feet are*
huuuuge, and I choke trying to hold my laughter inside.

"Some best friend you've got there," Luke says as she walks
away, clamping his lips together. "I like her."

With my lips pressed in a hard line and my face fiery red, I say,
"Yeah, we look after each other."

"I take it she's the mean one?"

My laughter fades into a grin.

"Actually, we're just alike in that aspect."

"Oh really?" He seems a little nervous. Smiling, but nervous.

I nod. "Yep. If she was the one leaving with some strange guy,
I'd be the one threatening him with bodily harm."

Luke grimaces.

I smile sweetly and pat his shoulder. "No worries," I say, letting
my fingers linger there for a moment until I realize what I'm doing
and pull away. "Maybe she *is* a little meaner than I am." I squint one
eye and hold my index and thumb a half inch apart. "But just a little."

He smiles.

"So I'm some strange guy you're leaving with, huh?"

"I like strange."

Our eyes meet briefly, soft smiles permanent on our faces,
it seems.

He jerks his head back. "Come on," he says, "not much time left."

"Where are we going?" I ask, walking away with him through
the sand.

"I said I'd give you some surfing lessons, didn't I?"

"Yeah, you did. But you don't have a board."

He shrugs and glances at the hotel.

"I can borrow one."

We walk together toward the building and I can't stop smiling the whole way there. I admit, I'm kinda nervous about my first surfing lesson, but I think I'm even more nervous—in a good way—that Luke is the one giving me that lesson.

I hope I don't embarrass myself…

SEVEN

Luke

I've always been a risk-taker—actually that's a huge understatement—but for all of the things I've done, all of the risks I've taken in my twenty-four years, something tells me that this one is by far more dangerous than any of them.

And maybe more worth it.

I had been on my way to catch up with Seth and Kendra on the hike, and I was alone. Knowing they had only about a thirty-minute head start, I could've called Seth and told them to wait for me. But I didn't. Instead I began to slow down. Just as I stepped onto the mouth of the trail and the lush greenery engulfed me on all sides, I began to think of my brother and a conversation we had a few weeks before he left for China eight months ago:

"I wanna say I don't know what the hell your problem is," Landon argued, standing behind me as I sat at my office desk staring at my laptop, "but I do know, and I can't believe what I'm seeing, Luke."

Clicking the mouse, I moved on to the next page, refusing to turn around and look at him. I wasn't in the mood for this. I had work to do.

"I'm not doing this with you today," I told him.

Click, click, scroll. *I typed in my password and hit enter.*

"Goddammit!" *He moved from behind me and stood to my left. I heard him breathe in deeply, trying to calm himself.* "Look, I know the business is important, but we have people to take care of these things." *He motioned his hands.* "We don't pay Derrick to sit on his ass while you do his job."

Finally I looked up at him, his hazel eyes, which looked just like mine, were hard around the edges, his mouth slightly pinched amid a rigid jaw.

"Just because we hire people doesn't mean we can sit back on our asses," *I pointed out.* "I'm just making sure that things stay running smoothly."

"At what cost?"

My expression hardened. "What do you mean? I think it's more costly not to stay on top of things. What the hell would we do if it all came crashing down, Landon?" *My voice began to rise with every word.* "Do you want Dad to go back to cleaning fucking toilets, or you tearing tickets at the movie theatre? Shit, why don't we just give it all up and go back to renting since rent in California and Hawaii is so cheap? We can pawn all of our stuff to pay the bills, eat potted meat sandwiches every day, and hope we have enough gas in the tank to get us to work every morning."

Landon threw his hands up at his sides.

"This is bullshit and you know it," *he said.*

I turned back to the screen. Click, click, scroll.

"I promised I'd go to China with you," *I said in a calmer voice.* "I don't know why you're so worried I'm going to back out of our plans."

*"Because you're leaving everything else behind," he said
with dejection and it prompted me to look up at him again.
"You're not you anymore. And it's scaring the hell out of me."*

He succeeded in making me feel bad, as I knew he would.

*Lowering my eyes momentarily, I swiveled around fully
on the chair to face him and only him, dropping my hands
between my knees.*

*"I'm still me. Nothing is more important to me than you
and our plans. It's always been you and me, Landon, and it
always will be." I paused to catch his gaze, and when he looked
into mine I added, "Nothing will ever come between us or our
plans, not this business—nothing and no one, and you have to
believe that."*

*Landon gave up, but I knew only for the sake of not want-
ing to prolong the argument. I felt like he wanted to believe
me, but it was getting harder and harder for him to do.*

*"Are you afraid?" he asked suddenly, and it caught me
completely off guard.*

I felt my eyebrows knotting in my forehead.

*"Afraid? What are you talking about?" He couldn't be
serious.*

*Landon grabbed ahold of another desk chair and rolled it
closer to me, where he sat in it backward, propping his arms
atop the backrest.*

He looked at me thoughtfully.

*"Let's be real here," he said. "I'm afraid to go through
with it—it's a big jump—but I think you, me, Seth, anyone
would be stupid to not be afraid."*

*"I'm not afraid of it," I told him, but then backtracked.
"I mean, yeah, I've got the natural fear, but if you think I'm*

doing all of this stuff"—I waved my hand at the desk and the laptop—"just to get out of China, you're wrong. It has nothing to do with it."

He looked disappointed.

Silence ensued.

"What?" I finally asked, growing confused. And irritated.

He shook his head.

"I guess I was kind of hoping that's all it was," he said, "that you were just afraid and didn't know how to deal with it." He sighed heavily and rose into a stand, giving the chair on wheels a gentle push out of his way. "But if that's not the case, then I guess I really am losing my brother." He started to walk away, and just as he made it to the door, he turned and said, "I've never known you to run away from anything, Luke, not since you got over your fears. And I never thought I'd see you throw away the things that make you happy for things that only pretend to make you happy—it's bullshit, bro," and he walked out, leaving me with my thoughts.

A minute later, I was right back to scrolling through important business emails. And two minutes later, I'd forgotten everything my brother said.

I stopped on the trail on the way to meet up with Seth and Kendra and looked up at the blue sky peeking through the thick canopy of trees, thinking about Landon's accusation.

He was right—I never ran away from anything. I was unstoppable. But then the business came along and I was so afraid of losing what we'd accomplished that I ran from everything else—including my brother and the free-spirited life we had shared for so long. I pushed away anything that had the potential to make me happy, anything that could take me away from our business—family, love, everything.

But I don't want to do that anymore; I don't want to be that guy—it's slowly killing me inside. Maybe meeting Sienna was the push I needed to heed my brother's words; maybe I've been waiting around all this time for someone like her to come along—who I can't stop thinking about no matter how hard I try—to finally make that change in my life; to get back to being…me, the guy that got lost somewhere along the road to success; the guy who my brother noticed was lost before I even did.

I eventually went back the way I came, hoping Sienna hadn't already left for the airport. And on the way, there were two things I couldn't escape: Landon's voice. And Sienna's face.

When I finally met up with Sienna, I really had been running a little. I was so sure I was already too late, but I picked up the pace when I got closer to the resort, not wanting to end up one of the unlucky dumbasses who misses the girl by merely seconds. I was surprised by how hugely I was smiling when I saw her—I don't even know the girl, so my reaction to knowing I made it in time confused me.

But this feels right. I'm not exactly sure why yet, but it does, and despite what my conscience is telling me, that she might not be able to handle my lifestyle, I'm not going to run away.

I'll never know unless I try.

———

After I borrow two boards from the school—and have Allan in the gift shop put a new pair of swim trunks on my tab—I take Sienna farther down the beach, away from the hotel and most of the tourists. I've been trying not to check out her body in that pink bikini top and tight shorts too obviously, but when she starts to peel the shorts down over the bikini bottom, I find it much harder to pull off.

I turn away and pretend to be checking out the waves, skirting her a little with a sideways glimpse, because, well, I just can't help it.

"So I take it you've never been surfing before?" I ask, just to be sure.

"Nope," she says with a little squeamish expression that I find extremely cute. "And I've not spent much time in the ocean, if you wanna know the truth."

"Really?" I say, surprised. "You live in San Diego and you've not been in the ocean much?" I prop the surfboard in the sand, keeping it upright and balanced with one hand.

She picks hers up and does the same; her fingers fidget nervously around the edge of the board; her lips are drawn in on one side as she nibbles on the corner of her mouth. *I* would like to nibble on the corner of her mouth.

"Wait, just how old are you, anyway?" I joke.

"Twenty-two," she says. "And I guess I just never cared much for swimming in the ocean."

I smile inwardly. Two years younger than me—perfect.

"But you like to swim, right?" I hope it's not that she *can't* swim—I wouldn't mind teaching her that either, but we'd need to skip the surfing lessons.

She shrugs. "Well, yeah, I guess so. But I prefer pools."

"Is it the salt? Or maybe you're afraid of sharks." I point upward, believing I'm right. "That's it, isn't it?"

Sienna looks downward and begins to shuffle her painted toes in the sand. "Jellyfish," she says so quietly that I have to ask her to repeat it.

"Sharks are pretty scary, but jellyfish freak me out," she says in a more audible voice, looking right at me. "I got stung twice when I was a kid. Ever since then, I've always preferred pools."

"You'd rather swim through urine than get stung by a jelly-fish?" I laugh under my breath.

"Actually, I would," she says matter-of-factly. "And people pee in the ocean just like they do in pools—I think they'd be more *likely* to pee in the ocean than a pool, if you really think about it."

"You have, haven't you?" I ask, grinning at her.

"I have *what*? Peed in a pool? No, that's disgusting!"

I laugh out loud.

"No—*thought* about it," I say, but I realize that still doesn't sound right. "It just seems like you've given it a lot of thought, about pee versus jellyfish and all that." I shrug and position the board underneath my arm, still with amusement on my face.

She looks at me in a thoughtful manner for a moment—maybe she's trying to figure me out.

"And besides," I go on, "if you got stung by a jellyfish I'd have to pee on you anyway."

She chokes out a laugh, cupping her long, delicate fingers over the top of her mouth.

"OK, you got me there," she says. "I just overthink things a lot, to be honest. It's one of my *many* flaws."

"Oh?" I jerk my head back, indicating for her to follow. "What are some of your other flaws?"

She steps up beside me. The smell of her freshly washed hair and lightly perfumed skin does something to me.

"You want to know all of the many things that are *wrong* with me?" she asks with laughter.

"Well, yeah," I say. "Might as well get all of that stuff out of the way now so we won't be disappointed later." I don't know why I said that, as if there will even *be* a later.

Sienna smiles, her eyes drifting from mine and toward the sand again. The breeze catches her long brownish-red hair, pushing it against the front of her chest and crossing over her lips. Instinctively I want to reach out and move it away from her mouth with my fingers, but I don't.

"Oh, where do I start?" she finally answers dramatically. "I thought this was a surfing lesson?"

"It is," I say and drop my board carefully on the sand.

She looks at it curiously for a moment and then at me.

"Before we go out there," I say, "I'll teach you a few things here." I strip off my shirt and drop it next to her bag.

"All right, you're the trainer." She smiles and drops her board the same as mine, and I catch her checking me out.

"Fins go in the back." I point, trying not to crack a smile. "Turn it around." I move my finger around in a circular motion and the blush reddens in her cheeks. I crouch to bury the fins in the sand so they don't get damaged.

I show her a few basics on land: paddling, how to pop up on her board, and the proper positioning of her body on the board. I help her with the leash around her ankle, not because it's difficult, but because like taking it upon myself to help her with her shoes yesterday, I *want* to—and just like yesterday, she doesn't seem to mind.

"Remember your feet," I tell her when she lies flat across it again. "Your toes need to be at the edge of the board, but don't hang your feet off like that."

She scoots up a little, wincing when her skin makes a squeaking noise as it scrapes across the board. For the next several minutes we go through the basic steps and she does really well, except for that feet thing. Twice I have to tell her not to hang her feet off the back of the board.

Once the quick lessons on land are over, we head for the ocean.

"Your turn." Sienna looks at me with a cute lopsided smile, holding her board underneath her arm. "What's one of *your* flaws?"

We get closer to the water until finally making it to where the sand is wet and more compact beneath our feet. I stop and turn to look at her as a small wave pushes ashore and crawls up our calves before retreating back into the ocean.

Looking upward in thought, I rub the tips of my fingers around my chin for added effect.

"I'm a backseat driver."

"Really?" she says. "Backseat drivers drive me nuts."

"Yep, that's me." I smile with a shrug. "I don't trust anyone's driving but my own."

"So you're a control freak," she says, grinning under that sun-kissed skin.

"Nah—it's just a trust thing is all."

"So then you have trust issues."

I blink back the surprise and grin at her.

"I guess another one of *your* flaws is that you're quick to judge," I say in jest.

Her face falls.

"No, no, I didn't mean anything by it."

Just when I think I've offended her, a grin sneaks up at one corner of her mouth.

"Ah, I see." I start to walk into the water and she follows. "So we're the Overthinking Manipulator and the Control Freak with trust issues."

"I guess so," she agrees without argument.

"Well, I hope we can stand to be around each other for three whole hours," I say. "Sounds like a lot of work."

Neither of us comments on the likelihood of that, I guess because we both already know that, well, three hours together isn't going to be enough.

"What else?" she asks, and I get the sense that maybe she's looking for something a little more serious. "I mean, surely there's something about you that you, or someone you know, might consider a real flaw?"

Now I'm the one chewing on the inside of my mouth.

Sienna tilts her head to one side thoughtfully, waiting.

"Well, sure there is," I say, though I find myself trying to word it right. "I've known a few…people…in my lifetime who think I'm too much of a risk-taker." When I say *people*, I mean *girls*, but at the last second I thought it might be better not to bring up my past girlfriends and failed relationships.

Her ears perk up and she looks at me contemplatively. "Oh? A risk-taker, huh? In what way?"

I take a deep, but unnoticeable, breath.

Then I point out at the waves and say, "Like with my surfing, for example." I laugh lightly. "Even you seemed a little anxious when I brought up the whole surfing in stormy weather."

She smiles, drawing her petite shoulders up around her. Then she shrugs.

"OK, yeah, I guess I didn't hide that too well," she admits. "But what else do you do that *people* consider risky?"

Hmm, did she catch onto the hidden meaning behind that, or was she just reiterating?

I shrug, too. "A few things: rock-climbing, cliff-diving, hang gliding, skydiving—I love the thrill, the sense of freedom." Quietly I search her face and her eyes and her posture for any signs of retreating, but all I see is interest and maybe a bit of confusion. But so far, she doesn't seem put off by the things I do.

Of course, that never means anything right away—my ex hung around for nearly six months before she decided the stuff I was into was just too much for her.

Maybe that's why I'm not telling Sienna everything yet. Then again, she's only here for a short while, so why worry about even getting into it?

"What about you?" I ask. "Anything worse than overthinking, and manipulating poor unsuspecting guys?"

She reaches out and gently hits me on the arm; the playful gesture and red in her face give me the urge to grab her around the waist—this holding back shit for the sake of being a gentleman is excruciating work.

Sienna looks up at the sky, pursing her lips contemplatively, and then she says, "I'm kind of a neat freak, and I tend to overdo things because I don't like to be caught off guard."

"Hmm," I hum through my closed lips, nodding. "I dunno; I don't think that's much of a flaw."

"Well, neither do I!" She laughs. "It's something Paige apparently thinks is a flaw—she reminds me on a daily basis. But I like being neat and in control and prepared."

"And I like doing 'risky' things," I say, our smiles matching.

We head out into the waves and all I can think about anymore is how short three hours really is.

EIGHT

Sienna

*R*ock climbing. Hang gliding. Cliff-diving. Skydiving. These are things I know I could never do—my fear of heights pretty much makes it impossible—but there's nothing wrong with someone else doing things like that. It seems dangerous, sure, but most people probably wouldn't do it if it was *too* dangerous.

I don't think too much more about it—I'm having too much fun surfing—but it lingers quietly in the back of my mind.

After two and a half hours of failing miserably at my first time surfing, I'm already beginning to dread the last thirty minutes before I have to leave. I don't want to go. I want to stay with Luke. I want to run back to the hotel and grab my camera and snap so many shots of this beautiful island that it makes my head spin and drains my battery. I want to see waterfalls and whales and professional surfers ride big waves and I want to lie against the sand and look up at the stars when night falls.

I don't want to go home. Not yet.

But I have to.

I fall off my board again, sinking beneath the water and sucking more saltwater into my nose.

Luke's strong arm hooks around my waist from beneath the water as he helps me to the surface. My eyes have been stinging for the past hour and I know they must be red-rimmed and bloodshot.

"You're doing awesome," he lies, but I think it's adorable.

"Thanks!" I yell over the sound of a few crashing waves around us. "But I think I could do better."

"You've done better than a lot of people their first time," he says, steadying himself back on his board in an upright sitting position. "Caught six small waves—that's pretty good."

"But I still fell." I laugh and crawl on top of my board to sit like him, straddling my legs on either side.

"Falling is inevitable for beginners," he says, "but catching six waves isn't—give yourself some credit." He smiles, the sun beaming off the droplets of water lingering on his tanned face and dripping from the hair pushed back away from his forehead.

He looks incredible, I can't stop myself from glimpsing him when he's not looking. My stomach flip-flops every time he touches me, whether to help me get back on my board, or to pull me from underneath the water, when he places his hands on my hips, gently helping me with my form—all things that I can really do myself for the most part, but couldn't bring myself to protest. I actually look forward to it each time.

And sometimes I find myself instigating it.

Gah! I'm like a little girl with a crush!

Once again, reality rears its ugly head and ruins the moment.

"I'm not looking forward to going back to work," I say, gazing across the water at the hotel a pretty good distance away.

Luke paddles over a little closer to where the sides of our boards touch.

"You don't seem happy with your job," he says.

I shake my head slightly, still looking toward the hotel. Flashes of the wedding ceremony and of Mrs. Dennings and her evil spawn of a daughter dance through my mind.

"It's a good job," I say distantly.

"What's so good about it?" Luke asks, and I finally turn away from the hotel to look at him sitting on his board right next to me.

"It pays great," I answer.

"Is that all?"

I think on his question a moment, digging inside myself for his reasoning behind it, because I get the distinct feeling there is one.

"I guess that's the most important thing," I say. "I mean, I love the creative side of my job, but the money is why we work to begin with."

Luke smiles softly and gazes across the water. He says, "A wise man once said, *Why work for a living if you kill yourself working?*"

I purse my lips thoughtfully and nod. "Pretty sound advice, I guess. Who's the wise man?"

"Clint Eastwood," Luke answers.

I chuckle. "He said that, did he?"

"Yep. He did—well, it went *something* like that, anyway."

"Good advice," I repeat, "but not exactly advice half of the working population can heed, unfortunately."

"Oh, I don't know," he says, shaking his head. "I think it can be done."

A wave pushes us forward, almost knocking me off my board, but I manage to hold on and stay upright. We've been drifting closer to the shore for the past few minutes.

Once the water calms again, I look back over at him and say, "I'm all ears."

Another wave comes toward us, and this time Luke gives me

that look, telling me I should try to catch this one. With only a little time to spare, I lie forward across the center of my board and start to paddle until the wave comes quickly up from behind. I brace myself, popping my body into a near-perfect stance. The wave carries me nearly all the way to the shore, where I finally jump off one side into shallow water. Luke is right behind me.

An enormous smile stretches my face so wide that the muscles in my cheeks hurt. I never imagined that something as simple as riding waves on a piece of fiberglass, or foam, or whatever these boards are made of, could be so exciting. I probably thought about being stung by a jellyfish only once the entire time I was out there. It was like the waves and the sun beating down on my head and Luke's encouraging smiles and gestures blocked out everything else. My eyes are burning from the salt, but I don't care; my legs and arms are a little sore from all the paddling and such, but I welcome it—I feel exhilarated!

"That was awesome!" Luke says as he takes his board up and positions it underneath his arm. "A few more private lessons and you'll be surfing with the locals." He winks.

I know he's just joking around about that part, but I admit, I did pretty good just now and I'm quite proud of myself.

"Too bad I can't stay." The ball of excitement burning behind my ribs suddenly begins to lose its warmth and become something cold.

We leave the water and walk toward our stuff lying on the dry sand farther away. He sets his board down and bends over, taking off the leash around his ankle, and I check him out quietly from the side: tall, tanned rock-hard body, muscles thick in his arms and his calves. I look down at my ankle quickly and take off my leash, too, when he raises his eyes to me.

I shake out my beach towel and reposition it on the sand, sitting down on top of it.

"People work for money," Luke begins, "and it seems logical that it be the most important thing about having a job, but focusing on the money is usually what makes the job suck, I think."

Luke sits down next to me on the towel. He draws his knees up, propping his forearms on top of them, letting his hands dangle freely. I cross my legs and sit Indian-style, resting my hands within my lap.

"But it's kind of hard *not* to focus on the money," I say, glancing over, "when that's the only reason you're working to begin with."

"True." He nods. "But maybe you should like your job first and think of the money it gives you as an added benefit—makes having a job less like an obligation."

"Easier said than done!" I scoff and then cover it up with a laugh. "I don't see how anyone can *like* flipping burgers or dealing with rude customers on a daily basis or mopping up puke at a bar— *so* much easier said than done."

Just when I think he's got some real flaws after all, he says, "Oh, trust me, I know. You're absolutely right."

"I'm confused," I say out loud when really I hadn't meant to.

Luke reaches down and picks up a handful of sand and lets it fall slowly through his fingers. Once the last of it falls into a tiny mound between his feet, he smiles over at me.

"It's hard to explain," he says. "And we don't have much time left together. I think I'd rather use what's left of it to know more about *you*. What do you enjoy? And I'm not talking about what your favorite television shows are, but what do you really love to do?"

Although I do want to know his philosophy on work and listen to him explain himself out of that one, I don't press the issue. Instead his question about what I love doing excites me.

"Photography," I tell him right away. "I love finding the best angles, the most emotional shots, capturing moments with my lens that tell a thousand stories." I pause, lost in the imagery. "I got my first camera as a birthday present when I turned ten. Been doing it ever since."

"Then why aren't you doing that instead of"—he waves his fingers dismissively—"whatever that is you do that *almost* makes you cry?"

My smile fades and I pick up a handful of sand, letting it fall into a little mound in front of my crossed legs.

"I was going to," I say, "but there's not much money in free-lance photography—at least, it's not guaranteed, anyway."

"It's guaranteed for those who kick ass at it, I bet."

"Maybe so," I say with the gentle shrug of my shoulders, "but when you have bills to pay, you tend to do what you have to rather than take unnecessary risks."

Luke nods but doesn't say anything.

He dusts the palms of his hands together and then gazes out at the ocean. For a long moment neither of us speaks—I'm thinking about how much I'd like to stay and how in just a few minutes I need to be leaving. I wish I knew what Luke was thinking, staring so intensely into the ether. With a gaze like that, there's always something important going on behind it. Something profound. I feel so drawn to him, so fascinated by him. His way of looking at the world, how everything he says intrigues me and just makes me want to know more about him. He seems so free-spirited, so positive, so alive. Our conversations, although few, *mean* something, even the little things—most guys who have ever tried to get to know me have been either too shy and nervous to open up, or too focused on trying to impress me to have any kind of intelligent conversation. Luke is gorgeous and confident and intelligent and everything every other guy I've ever met, isn't. And I've never had so much fun! Just in the short time I've spent with him on this beach, I can't help but wonder what other exciting emotions I've got locked away inside of me that he could easily draw out.

Snapping out of my thoughts, I stand up and fish my shorts from my bag. But the thought of leaving begins to weigh heavier on my heart the closer it comes time to go; a pang of disappointment settles in my chest, and I find myself struggling to do the simplest of things: stepping into my shorts, buttoning them closed, finding the right words to say good-bye—there are no right words, I quickly realize.

Luke is still staring out at the water.

After shuffling my feet into my flip-flops, I reach down and take up my bag, shouldering the lighter weight of it without my towel inside.

Luke is *still* staring out at the water.

I pause, thinking more about how to say good-bye until I realize how ridiculous something so simple is and then I say with reluctance, "Well, I guess I need to head back. I enjoyed—"

"Stay," Luke says, looking up at me at an angle. "Why don't you stay for a while longer? Just a few days." The serious look in his face takes me aback; the determination, although subtle and soft, makes my throat dry up in an instant.

"I-I—Luke, I can't." Yeah, I can't *stay* and I can't *fathom* what made him say that to me, or why every part of me *wants* to.

He rises to his feet, and the intensity of his gaze sends a shot of warmth through my belly and rushing into my heart.

I'm so confused … so—

"I know this sounds crazy," he says, stepping even closer. "I mean, it even sounds crazy to *me*, but I want you to stay."

Suddenly his hazel eyes light up as if an idea just flashed in front of them.

"Hey," he says with a bright face, "you could even give me some pointers on setting up a charity art event at the community center I'm helping organize." His mouth turns up on one side teasingly. "You could show me some of those mad event coordinating skills you have—I'll even pay you for your time."

I start to smile back at him because that grin of his is infectious, but then I just shake my head. "Luke, I really . . . I mean, I'd love to help out, but—"

He takes both of my hands into his and his eyes soften, but with such sincerity and determination. I look down at his hands, his strong fingers curled around mine. I can't fight the feeling his touch compels, and I tighten my fingers around his in response to it.

Oh God, what's happening? Where is this *coming* from? And why is it not making me want to take off running in the other direction?

The soft touch of his fingers against the skin of my arms makes my whole body shiver. But I keep my head on straight and take a step away from him.

He frowns, and I can't help it—so do I.

"I . . . I really can't," I say and hate that it's true. "Maybe we can exchange phone numbers."

He shakes his head and buries his hands in his pockets, looking past me, sifting through his thoughts, it seems.

"I know I probably overstepped my bounds," he says. "I'm not a freak, I swear, but I just thought I'd take a risk." He laughs lightly, trying to cover up his slight embarrassment.

The smile finally returns to my face and my eyes soften on him.

"I don't think you're a 'freak' at all," I say, stepping closer. "It did catch me by surprise, but...well, it wasn't scaring me away, if that's what you're worried about."

He blushes and his gaze strays from mine momentarily. He's ridiculously adorable.

"But I'm curious," I say, and he looks at me again, waiting, those hazel eyes swimming with something magical I only wish I could figure out. "What made you say it?"

He looks past me on both sides again, a knot moving down the center of his throat.

"I'll tell you what," he says as a small smile tugs the corners of his mouth, "if I tell you why I said it, will you give me your word that when you go back to San Diego you'll at least think about spending more time with your camera?"

Surprised all around, at first I can't do much but look at his tall height and hard shoulders and the perfectly sculpted bone structure of his face and wonder where he *really* came from and why he was sent to cross my path, because everything that comes out of his mouth manages to intrigue and excite me and make me feel like I *need* to stay here.

I think on his terms for a moment, pursing my lips in pretend contemplation.

"I give you my word," I agree with a quick nod.

His smile lengthens.

"Good," he says, and then draws his shoulders up, tightening his arms at his sides with his hands still buried in his pockets. He hesitates as he prepares the answer. "OK, being completely honest, what made me ask you to stay is because I know that if you get on that plane I'll never see you again."

I smile gently.

"Why do you think you'd never see me again?" I ask. *And why are you worried about never seeing me again?* My heart sings behind my ribs like a finch in a cage.

Maybe it's to distract me, but instead of answering, Luke leans over and picks my beach towel up from the sand. He shakes it out and holds it out to me. Slowly I take it into my fingers, absently stuffing it inside my bag hanging from my shoulder.

He smiles and buries his hands inside his pockets again.

"Look, I really enjoyed hanging out with you today," he says. "And if you're ever on Oahu again, look me up."

Oh no, is this good-bye? What about your phone number? Do I offer mine? Would that seem desperate?

My phone rings inside my bag, breaking me out of my thoughts.

"Well, I've gotta go," Luke says and walks away, kicking up sand in front of him as he moves through it.

I just stand here, frozen, confused, and wanting to toss the distracting cell phone into the ocean so I can think! And Luke just gets farther and farther away. Then he stops and turns around. He points at me and shouts across the beach, "Remember what you promised me! You have to give it some real thought!"

I hesitate, but finally raise my hand and wave good-bye. "I promise!" I shout with a big bewildered smile.

And Luke keeps on walking.

When the numbness finally wears off, I leave the beach and go back to the hotel to pack.

NINE

Luke

That was probably the most embarrassing thing I've ever done, even more embarrassing than waking up naked the morning after a party, on the front lawn of Seth's parents' house. The neighbors got an eyeful that day.

I smack my palm against my forehead, at first because of making an idiot out of myself in front of the first girl I've ever met that *made* me want to make an idiot out of myself. But then I realize I left the surfboards and my phone on the beach. Make that *two* stupid things I've done today, all because of a girl.

My brother would be so proud.

I turn on my heels and head back to the spot where I left them. Sienna is long gone; I look out at the beach toward the hotel and my shoulders slump with a heavy sigh. I run my hands over my face and then just fall against the sand in a sitting position.

Sitting between the surfboards, I gaze at the ocean, thinking about the girl who got away and the brother who went away. I think about China and then again about the girl who got away. I can't get Sienna out of my head. I text Seth to see if he's still hiking with Kendra even though I know he is—they probably won't be back until this evening. I decide to just go into the shop and hang with Allan, and see if he has any appointments for me today after all.

When I get up and turn around, I freeze, seeing Sienna staring back at me.

"Aloha," she says in the meekest, cutest voice, her freckle-splashed face smiling gently.

"Aloha," I say back, and my stomach does shit it's never done before—it feels warm and mushy and I will never admit that to Seth, lest I become more like a girl to him than Kendra.

She approaches me, and I find myself just looking back at her, immobile, still surprised that she came back. Her smile is so beautiful, and the way her hair is blown gently against the side of her face makes me want to reach out and move it away just so I can touch her.

"I know I don't know you," she says, stopping two feet in front of me, "and this is the craziest thing I've ever done, but I *want* to know you."

I'm still speechless.

Sienna steps a few inches closer. I still haven't moved.

"Have you ever had that feeling," she goes on, "when you know deep down that you should do something? Like if you *don't* do it, you'll regret it for the rest of your life?"

I nod. "Yeah, when I asked you to stay," I answer honestly.

She steps up another few inches, not with a beach bag or a towel, only herself this time. She smells incredible, like soap and sunshine.

"Well, I felt it as I was packing," she says.

She grins and shakes her finger at me. "Now, don't think I'm *that* into you," she warns, still smiling. "I'm just giving in to the curiosity, Luke Everett, so don't get the wrong idea."

I laugh out loud, shaking my head at her.

"Same here, *Sienna Murphy*—I'm not into you at all," I lie through my teeth, "but I just feel like we might have…things to learn from each other."

She nods with a serious face as if to second that motion, but I think she's as full of shit as I am right now.

"But I thought you had to go back to work?"

"I did," she says, "but I had a talk with my boss."

"And?" I raise an inquisitive brow.

"Well, I have two weeks of vacation saved up that I never got around to using. I wanted to take my parents somewhere nice, but they'll never go." She crosses her arms and tilts her head to one side. "So I asked my boss if I could take it now since I'm already in Hawaii."

"And your boss agreed?"

She shrugs and purses her lips. "She was hesitant to let me take it at such short notice," she explains, "but after I saved the Oahu wedding yesterday, she agreed to let me have the time off now."

"Just like that?" I hear every word Sienna is saying to me, but behind all that I really can't focus on anything but the strange turn of events and how glad I am that she came back.

She bobs her head once and says, "Yep. Just like that—granted, she was worried about my event in Jamaica, but she has other employees at her fingertips to take over for me. And I know Paige will cover for me."

A bit surprised, I say, "You turned down a trip to Jamaica to stay here?" *With me?* I want to add, but feel like it might be overkill.

Her freckled face flushes pink and then she shrugs as if it's no big deal.

"Yeah, I guess I did."

Knowing that I'm about five seconds away from being unable to stop myself from kissing that perfect mouth senseless, I smack my palms together loudly, breaking the tension. Sienna jumps a little. God, she's so damn cute.

"So two weeks in Hawaii," I say. "That's a lot better than three hours."

"Definitely."

Who needs the sun with a smile like that?

A moment of silence passes between us. I can't stop staring at her.

"Oh, and I'm happy to give you pointers for your event," she says, "but I won't take your money."

Shaking my head, I say, "Forget I even said anything about that. You're not here to work, remember—I was just getting desperate. I would've said just about anything to make you stay."

She chuckles.

Finally I decide to let go of all my hesitations and all of the uncertainties and just be myself for a change.

And it's liberating.

I reach out and take Sienna's hand in mine—my heart leaps when it touches her hand—and I start to walk with her across the beach.

"So where to first?" she asks.

"To jump off some cliffs," I say with a grin.

Her hand tightens within mine, but I get the feeling it's not because she's trying to keep up—I think maybe jumping off cliffs wasn't what she had in mind.

Sienna

I think my heart just dropped down into my stomach—between his brazen decision to take my hand and him saying the words *jump* and *cliffs* in the same sentence, I was done for.

We stop at my hotel for a few things first, mainly my black

canvas bag and my digital camera. Then Luke and I catch a bus to head out to a place about twenty-five minutes away.

It finally feels like a vacation. It feels *real* and exciting and liberating. I'm snapping photos out the window and even inside the bus of whatever looks interesting, nearly the entire ride. I can't remember the last time I felt this free, or even if I ever really have. I feel like most of my life since college has been about work and securing the best possible job and future. And I think I lost myself somewhere amid all that.

"You weren't kidding," Luke says, sitting next to me, his thigh pressing against mine. "I think you've taken a hundred shots since we left the parking lot." He chuckles.

I snap another one and then look over at him.

"These are what I call just-in-case shots," I explain. "Not a lot of thought put into them, but I take as many as I can of anything and everything just in case I end up with something good."

I snap another one.

"Kind of like how some of the best photos of people are the unplanned ones?" he says.

"Exactly!" I turn the lens on *him*, snapping a few unplanned photographs. He doesn't seem to mind at all and even crosses his eyes for one.

I laugh and snap one more before opening my canvas bag.

"But this isn't what I usually shoot with," I say before putting the camera away inside the bag and zipping it up.

"I was going to ask about that," he says, his hazel eyes slanted with curiosity. "I thought all the 'serious' photographers"—he makes air quotations with his fingers—"had huge cameras with fancy lenses and all that extra stuff. Like that one you were sneaking photos of me with on the beach yesterday." He grins.

I can feel myself blush hard. "Hey, it wasn't like that!"

Bumping his knee against mine he says, "I know."

Conscious of the tiny gap between our legs on the seat, I glance down at his knee, glad to see that he hasn't moved it away. I smile to myself, thinking about it, and fold my arms down on top of my bag on my lap. "Well, I don't know about all the other 'serious' photographers out there"—I make air quotations with my fingers, too—"but I do have bigger cameras—like the one you saw—and my fair share of gear."

"Why didn't you bring any of that?"

"Well, you said we're going to jump off cliffs." I shrug. "Didn't think bringing my expensive gear with me would be very safe."

"Oh, so you're going to jump?" His grin just got bigger.

"No!" I answer right away, shaking my head for added effect. "I don't do heights, much less plunging to my death from them."

Luke throws his head back and laughs.

"The cliffs aren't that high," he says.

"I don't care." I wave both hands in front of me. "I'm afraid of heights more than anything, and there is nothing in this world that could make me jump off a cliff."

"But you don't even know how high it is." He chuckles and crosses his arms over his chest.

"It's a *cliff*," I stress, "not a rock or a bucket or a poolside diving board—cliffs are called cliffs for a reason."

Still laughing lightly, he gives up because he knows he really can't argue with that.

"Well, how did you get to Hawaii, then?" He raises a brow. "Please tell me you didn't take a ship all the way over here."

"No. I flew," I say. "But anytime I fly, it's always a traumatizing experience."

"Seriously?" He seems genuinely surprised.

I'll never understand how people who aren't afraid to fly can't understand how frightening it is for people like me. Sometimes I feel like saying—

"Hey! Don't give me that how-can-you-be-afraid-to-fly crap." I say it anyway because I'm on vacation and I can be myself! "It's terrifying. You may not be afraid, but—"

He puts up both hands, surrendering.

"No, I understand," he says, always with a smile. "I used to be like you, believe it or not."

"You were afraid of heights?" I do find it hard to believe, though I'm not sure why.

He nods and rests his back against the seat.

"Yeah, up until I took the bungee plunge off the Perrine Bridge in Twin Falls, five hundred feet above the river."

My eyes grow wide in my face as he tells me this with too many scary details.

"I was sure I was gonna die that day," he goes on. "But I was more tired of being afraid of everything than I was of dying. It was like I was already dead, letting fear ruin what life I had." He shakes his head with disbelief as he recalls the memory. "I was afraid to ride the roller coaster when my parents took me to Six Flags. My brother—well, let's just say I never heard the end of it. And I used to be afraid of camping." He laughs at himself, as though looking back on it now, he finds it ridiculous.

"Camping?"

"Yeah. Camping—I had a bad experience on a camping trip with my dad when I was nine. Messed me up pretty bad."

"What happened?"

With the back of his head resting against the seat, he leans it to one side to face me, sitting with his fingers interlocked over his stomach, his long, tanned legs fallen apart.

"I went out with my brother while my dad was fishing, and Landon got lost in the woods." His smile fades as he recalls, and his head moves back so that he's looking at the back of the seat in front of him rather than at me anymore. "Took two days to find him, but while I was sitting back with my mom watching the news about the lost seven-year-old boy in the forest, and listening to my mom cry, I thought for sure he was dead and it was my fault. Turned out that when they found Landon, he was perfectly fine. Said he wanted to see if he could survive alone in the woods. He did it on *purpose*— the asshole!" He laughs. "Landon always was the crazy one. The one not afraid to take risks even when he was a boy."

He looks over at me again.

"But that *one* incident made me afraid of just about everything," he says, and slowly his smile is beginning to resurface. "Camping. Heights. Every time my mom, my dad, or my brother would get into a car just to go up the street a few miles, I was so afraid they'd get into a wreck and die. It was all I could think about until they came home safely."

Luke tries to laugh it off, make it seem like it was just something stupid and that he can't believe he ever had these fears. But I'm not laughing, and I find them more heartbreaking than humorous.

"Landon got all the girls when we were growing up. He wasn't afraid of *anything*."

I allow my smile to return now that it feels the right time for it. My gaze sweeps over him suggestively when I say, "Well, if your brother got all the girls when you were growing up, he must look incredible to get more than *you*." Wait. What? I can't believe I went there! But for some reason I'm feeling good enough right now and comfortable enough with him that I'm not afraid of blatant flirting.

But when I see a sort of forced look in his eyes, something misplaced that he seems to be trying to hold down, I can't figure out if he's turned off by my open flirtation, or if something I said offended or hurt him.

I look away and toward the window that I'm sitting beside, and quietly shrink inside myself, hoping he doesn't take notice.

Before the quiet moment turns irreversibly awkward, I try to save it.

"So jumping off a bridge with a giant rubber band around your leg cured you?"

"Pretty much," he answers, his eyes clearing, and that charming smile is back in place

"And you think something like that'll cure *me*, too?"

He grins mischievously. "It might."

"No way."

"We'll see," he says, and the grin deepens.

My mouth falls open and I nudge him in the ribs with my elbow. He does a half double-over, pretending that it actually hurt.

"No way in hell am I jumping off a cliff."

TEN

Sienna

An hour later I'm standing on the edge of a cliff overlooking the ocean, my painted toenails like little blue people hanging on for dear life as I tower over them, looking down into the water as it taunts me.

"I can't do it!" I take another step backward, trying not to let the vertigo cause me to stumble and fall off the edge anyway.

Luke's hands hook about my sides, keeping me on my feet.

"You'll be all right; I'm right here, and I won't let anything happen to you," he says, but I can't open my eyes. "The fear is all in your head."

I back a little farther away from the edge, not realizing at first that I'm pressing my body into his—I just want to get away from the danger zone. He doesn't seem to mind, and his hands are still like permanent fixtures on my hips, which I don't mind, either.

Luke takes my hand and walks with me a few feet to one side and we sit down together on a rock bathed by the bright sun. Just as we step out of the way, two darkly tanned guys make a short run for it and leap off the edge of the cliff at the same time. The one with short blond hair does a front flip into the water, and they land with a splash. My hands come up instinctively, the fingers of one hand dancing on my lips, the other hand touching my heart as it pounds furiously behind my rib cage.

I shake my head.

"I'm just too scared," I tell Luke. "I'm sorry. I can't do it."

His hand tightens around mine and then he pats it, afterward releasing it softly on top of my knee.

"It's all right," he says. "Don't worry about it."

I feel like a baby, and it doesn't help any that there are five other girls out here besides me, all jumping into the water without a fear or worry in the world. I feel weak and small and forgettable.

"Hey," I hear Luke say with concern in his voice. He moves off the rock and crouches in front of me. "Are you OK?"

I didn't realize I had been so obvious—I certainly wasn't trying to be.

I force a smile and nod. "Yeah, I'm good, just a little freaked out."

Luke pushes himself into a stand and reaches out his hand for me. "Come on," he says. "We'll walk down and go swimming for a bit."

I take his hand and he pulls me up from the rock. I don't know why, but he makes me feel safe, even when just holding my hand. I secretly hope he doesn't let go.

And he doesn't.

"At least you tried," he says, smiling.

Luke leads me back down the rocks and onto lower ground, where a friend of his is sitting watching over my bag—Alicia, girlfriend of his friend Braedon.

"It's a no-go, huh?" she asks as we step up.

"No," I say glumly. "After ten minutes of almost jumping, I was pretty sure it wasn't gonna happen."

Alicia smiles with a bright set of perfect white teeth. Long black hair drapes her olive shoulders.

"Maybe you'll do it next time," she says, reaching over and patting me on the back.

Luke, sitting on the other side of me with his knees drawn up, says with kind eyes, "Well, she has two weeks to conquer the fear."

"Two weeks in Hawaii," Alicia says, "now *that's* a vacation."

I glance over and smile at Luke next to me.

"Yeah, I guess it is," I agree. "I like my job, but I'd take Hawaii over it any day."

Alicia nods, beaming. "I'd take Hawaii over *any* job," she says. "What do you do?"

"Sienna's an event coordinator." Luke speaks up for me, which I find cute and not at all intrusive.

Alicia perks up a little. "Oh?" she asks, looking between Luke and me with a curious—and maybe even hopeful—expression.

I hadn't forgotten about Luke bringing up that charity art event earlier; I guess it just got lost in the excitement of staying in Hawaii and how crazy and thrilling and spontaneous the whole thing was. Besides, when he said to forget he said anything about it, that he would've said just about anything to get me to stay, I thought he was joking about the event.

"And a damn good one from what I saw," Luke says.

My face reddens a little. "Thanks." I'm not sure how much of my work he actually saw, but I don't probe. I just take the compliment.

Alicia sits up on her knees on the sand and smiles at me eagerly.

"Maybe you could help out with the charity event we're having over at the community center in a couple months," she says. She presses her knuckles into the sand on each side of her to hold up her petite weight.

Luke shakes his head. "Well, I did sort of ask her," he says, "but I feel weird about it now."

"Weird why?" I ask, looking over at him.

He shrugs. "Just that you're supposed to be on vacation and getting *away* from your job. I'm not going to put you to work." He laughs. "But hey, a few pointers here and there would be awesome—but no working." He shakes a finger playfully at me.

"Well, I'd love to check it out," I say. "I'll do whatever I can to help."

And really I don't mind at all. Somehow, no matter what it entails, I don't see it making me feel like I'm at work. It could be fun!

Alicia looks relieved.

"I've never done anything like this before," Luke says. "Melinda—she runs the community center—hosts these charity art events once a year."

"And she's been planning them and setting them up for…I don't even know how long," Alicia says, twirling a hand in the air beside her. "But she wanted to do something fresh and exciting this year"—she glances at Luke—"so she put *us* in charge."

"We have plenty of time to get it all organized," Luke says. "So don't think about it too much—you're here to kick back and have fun."

"Well, count me in," I say, beaming at them both.

Alicia looks toward the cliffs, probably eager to take her turn.

"Hey, we're having a barbecue at our house later," she says, "if you two wanna come—you can ride over with me."

Luke looks at me briefly.

I shrug as if to tell her, *Sure, why not?*

"Yeah, sure," Luke says. "Just let us know when you're ready to head out."

Alicia stands up and dusts sand from her hands.

"Are you OK to sit with your stuff?" she asks, pointing briefly at my bag.

"Oh yeah," I tell her. "Thanks for bag-sitting."

"No problem," she says brightly and then heads toward the cliffs.

I pull a clean beach towel from my bag and go to unfold it.

"Don't you want to go swimming?" Luke asks.

"Definitely," I say and lay the towel over my bag to conceal it the best I can.

"I'd tell you not to worry about it," Luke says about the bag, looking around at the many small groups of people all hanging around the area, which according to Luke is a pretty popular place. "But I don't know even half of these people—most are tourists."

"How do you know?"

"They're not hard to pick out of a crowd, really," he says and points briefly at a group of girls who just climbed to the top of the cliffs. "Two of them look like they don't spend much time in the sun. The other two have taken probably thirty selfies each just in the past five minutes, duck-lips and all." He points at a man and woman who just walked up. "And no locals who come out here wear running shoes and socks in the sand, or big floppy hats and jewelry."

I stifle a giggle.

"Well, I must really look like a tourist, too, then, shooting a hundred photos on the bus on the way over here, or that rookie mistake of trying to walk in the sand in heels."

Luke laughs.

"Well, you don't look so much like one right now," he says. "Though most locals who come out here aren't afraid to jump off the cliffs, either, so you're walkin' the line."

My face gets warm, but then disappointment in myself steals my good mood away all over again. I sigh, drop the towel the rest of the way over my bag, and look out at the ocean, crossing my arms over my chest.

"Hey, I'm sorry if I—"

I shake my head. "No, it's nothing you said. Really. I mean, it is kind of, but not what you're thinking."

Luke tilts his head to one side, a curious and somewhat confused look in his eyes.

"Do tell," he urges me.

Hesitating, I look out at the ocean again and think on how much I want to tell him, or if I want to tell him anything at all.

"Hey, no holding back," he says and pokes me in the ribs playfully with his knuckles. "Come on, spit it out. And no sad faces allowed in Hawaii, especially while you're on vacation."

He got the smile that he had been trying for out of me easily. But it wasn't hard because the last thing I want to be is a mood killer.

"It's what you said on the bus," I tell him. "About how you used to be afraid of everything." I pause and then say, "It's not just heights that I'm afraid of." I point at him briefly and quip, "But I'm *not* afraid of camping—that's just crazy."

He grins, letting me have that one.

"So what else are you afraid of then?" He sits down on the sand and pats the spot next to him.

I sit down, too.

"Well, I'll be honest—"

"You better be," he jokes, bumping my bent knee against his.

"It feels strange not to be working right now," I say.

"You're joking, right?" he says, looking over at me. "You're in Hawaii. On vacation. And it hasn't been a couple of hours and already you're stressin' out over a job that you're *supposed* to be leaving behind for two weeks—not to be nosy, but is it a paid vacation?"

"Yeah. I'm just not used to *not* working."

"Shit, tell me you're not one of those who works seven days a week and never calls in sick even when you're on your deathbed."

"No, no," I say, shaking my head and my hand, "I'm not that bad—"

"Yet," he interrupts.

"No, not yet," I go on, "but I started my first job when I was old enough to get a work permit—worked at Subway for two years, then a shoe store for a few months, and after that, when I started college, I worked part-time in a café until the day I got my job at Harrington Planners."

"So what are you afraid of? Not working twenty-four-seven?"

"No, I guess I'm just worried that Cassandra will find someone better than me while I'm here in Hawaii soaking up the sun, and when I go back I'll find out that I'm expendable after all."

"Well, first off," Luke says, "I really doubt that'll happen"—he taps his head with his fingertip—"again, it's all in the mind. But even if it did, Sienna, there are a million other jobs out there."

"Not that pays what *this* job pays me," I say. "Event coordinators in general don't make the kind of money that I make. I got lucky landing my job. I just don't want to lose it."

Luke smiles and shakes his head.

"A lucky fluke landed me this job; it's always in the back of my mind that an unlucky fluke will also take it away."

"A lucky fluke?"

"Yeah," I say. "I could only go to college long enough to earn an associate degree. And when I got out, I was prepared to spend years working my way up from the bottom somewhere. But a friend knew a friend who knew a successful friend—my boss—who needed an assistant immediately. I met Cassandra and she liked me enough to offer me a job and I took it without hesitation. Within six months I was already near the top of the Harrington Planners ladder—a total lucky fluke."

"Well," Luke says, pursing his lips, "I doubt luck had everything to do with it; you had to be doing something right." He smiles and I return it in thanks.

Then he gets up and grabs my hands from the tops of my bare knees, pulling me to my feet.

"We're going swimming," he says. "And we'll talk more about this later . . . like on the day your vacation is over and you're standing at the gate in the airport about to kiss me good-bye."

"Wow, you really think highly of yourself, don't you?" I can't keep the laughter from my voice.

"Damn straight!" he says and pulls me along beside him. "Before these two weeks are over, I can guarantee you three things." He holds up three fingers as we continue onward toward the water. "One"—he holds up one finger—"you'll never want to go back to San Diego once Hawaii is done with you." He holds up two fingers. "Two—that photography love of yours will start to take the place of everything else in your life. And three"—he wiggles three fingers and we stop on the beach where the water can pool around our feet—"you'll kiss me at least once before you go home."

I blush hard and it feels like my eyes are bugging out of my head. "I might peck you on the cheek or something, but—"

"No," he says, smiling and quite serious, "it'll be a full-on, tongue-dancing kind of kiss."

I smack him playfully on the arm—something is fluttering around inside my belly.

"Geez!"

Luke grabs my hand and pulls me out to the water with him, where we swim and hang out on the cliffs until late in the afternoon. People come and go throughout the hours, sometimes leaving us with Alicia, Braedon, and a few of their close friends to have the area to ourselves for a while before more people show up in intervals.

"Backflip!" someone says just before Luke jumps into the water for probably the twentieth time.

And every time he does it, it ties my stomach up in knots. But there's something about him that I can't quite figure out when I watch him leap off the edge of that cliff; it's not overconfidence or showing off or recklessness, but something deeper, more profound. Maybe it's a sense of freedom, or a natural high that consumes him while he's in the air, as if he had been born with a pair of wings that only he can see. But the more time I spend with him, the more intrigued I become. Sure, he's gorgeous and funny and polite and all the kinds of things—so far—that would make my mom love him to death. But what intrigues and excites me more is how he kind of makes me want to jump off that stupid cliff regardless of how scared I am of it.

ELEVEN

Sienna

*A*fter nightfall Luke and I head to the barbecue at Alicia and Braedon's place. It's a tiny house just minutes from the beach, and apparently someone else other than them live here as well, because I can smell the food already cooking from the back-yard as we walk up. Voices carry around the side of the house, laughter and conversation that may or may not be accompanied by alcohol.

"Luke!" a voice calls out when we step outside into the back-yard from the back door of the house. A girl, about my height but maybe a little shorter, springs to her feet from a lawn chair and falls into his arms. She has blond hair pulled into a ponytail at the back of her head, and she's really fit, like she works out regularly; little knot-like muscles flex in her biceps as her arms hang about Luke's neck. She's cute, more tomboy than girly girl, but not so tomboy that I feel like I have nothing to worry about when it comes to Luke—she's actually kind of adorable.

I stand next to him, coiling my fingers together down in front of me, my eyes straying from them and toward the fresh-cut grass, instead. But then suddenly Luke's hand hooks around my waist and he pulls me closer.

"Kendra, this is Sienna. Sienna, this is my good friend Kendra."

She smiles at me close-lipped, her brown eyes studying me for a brief, secret moment that usually only other girls can detect. She glances at Luke once, and something passes between them before she looks back at me.

"Hi, Sienna," she says, her smile slowly lengthening.

"Hi. It's nice to meet you."

We don't shake hands, but it doesn't seem necessary. And I don't detect any territorial vibes from her. I take that back—actually I do, but I can't place it. It doesn't feel like jealousy, but something else.

With his hand still at my waist, Luke walks with me down the steps and to the concrete patio laid out in a circle shape over the top of a large portion of the grass. A red grill with a dome-shaped lid just like the one my dad always cooked on during the Fourth of July holiday stands on four legs on one side of the patio. Delicious-smelling smoke billows from the vent at the top and from the sides. A dozen other lawn chairs are set here and there and all of them are occupied.

A guy with a shaved head that has a painful-looking scar running along one side of it raises his arm in the air at Luke. He gets up from his lawn chair with a beer bottle wedged between the fingers of one hand. He's wearing a pair of black cargo shorts and a pair of black flip-flops and has several black hemp—or leather, I can't tell—bracelets around his wrists.

He steps up to us and he and Luke do that weird man-shake where they bump fists and whatnot.

The guy looks at me with a big, close-lipped smile, and then back at Luke—there's an awful lot of inner dialogue going on around here and I'm starting to feel seriously out of place.

"Sienna, huh?" the guy says with a grin and reaches his hand out to me. "I'm Seth, Luke's best friend and roommate—he wouldn't know what to do with himself without me." He looks between us, still grinning.

Luke play-punches him against the arm.

"Yeah right, man," he says, smiling and shaking his head. "I think it's the other way around." He looks right at me. "Really, it *is* the other way around. I rescued this guy from a very troubled time in his life and now he owes me."

I chuckle.

Seth laughs and takes a quick swig from his beer, balancing the bottle neck between his thick, rugged fingers. "You're so full of shit," he says.

Luke looks at me—his hand has not only remained on my waist, but it just squeezed me tighter—and smiles. "We've been best friends for about six years," he says. "And Kendra, she's part of our family."

Kendra, who has been standing with us the whole time, smiles hugely. She has a lot of freckles, just like me, splashed across her nose and cheeks.

"Your family?" I ask Luke.

"Yeah, that's one way of putting it," Kendra says. "So how long are you in Hawaii for?"

I was hoping she'd elaborate.

OK, so everything about me screams tourist. *Great.*

"Two weeks," I answer.

Luke is beaming standing next to me. "I had to talk her into it," he says, and Kendra and Seth exchange a look.

Then they look at me.

"Did he manipulate you?" Kendra says in jest. "He's good at that. You gotta be careful around this one." She grins at me.

"All right now," Luke says and walks with me to the patio. He leans toward my ear and whispers, "Don't let them get in your head; they're worse than they try to make *me* out to be," but it was hardly low enough they couldn't hear him.

"I'll keep that in mind." I smirk up at him.

Braedon comes walking from around the side of the house looking like a linebacker with four more folded lawn chairs in his hands. Luke's hand finally slips away from my waist and he takes two of the chairs from Braedon, unfolding them with a snap and setting them side by side on the patio. Some other guy comes walking down the back steps and goes straight over to the barbecue grill, lifting the lid with a giant spatula in his other hand; smoke billows in big puffs into the air as it escapes the confines of the lid. The meat on the grill sizzles and pops as he begins flipping the burgers over.

I hear the shuffling of ice inside a nearby Igloo chest as Luke reaches inside and pulls out two bottles of beer. He pops the lid on one and holds it out to me.

"Thanks."

He pops the lid on one for himself and we sit down at the same time in the two empty chairs.

"So are you not here with anyone?" Kendra asks in her chair across from us. "I mean, in Hawaii," she clarifies.

"I was," I say. "Actually I was here on a job, but after the job was over, I decided to make a vacation of it." I glance over at Luke sitting next to me and we smile at each other. "He *did* kind of talk me into staying," I admit, and then with a smile, I add, "Not that it was very hard to do."

Kendra and Seth catch Luke's eyes again, but I pretend not to notice. Pressing the bottle to my lips, I take a small sip.

Music plays from a stereo inside the house, funneling through the screens on the open windows, but it's not obnoxiously loud, and none of the people here are obnoxiously drunk. It's more a social gathering than a wild party and I'm glad for that—I'm no angel and like to party every now and then, but with Luke, I just want to hang out and keep things cool.

Luke and Seth start talking about some guy on Kauai who just bought a new hang glider, but he makes it a point to keep me from feeling excluded by interjecting a comment to me about it every now and then. Really, it's not necessary, but I think it's sweet of him to worry about me like that and want to make sure I feel comfortable. All of us talk for a long time—though I talk less than anyone because I'm not from around here, am not familiar with surfing or hang gliding or hiking the Pipiwai Trail or even with the everyday conversations, but still, Luke makes sure I never feel excluded. At one point, his hand finds its way to my thigh, where he pats it for a moment, smiling over at me, and then moves it away.

I don't want him to move it away, but I guess it's too soon to be suggesting something like that, especially in front of other people, two of whom—Kendra more than Seth—happen to be watching Luke and me with overly curious glances that make me more and more uncomfortable as the evening wears on. I'd much rather have Alicia as my company, but she's been pretty busy playing casual hostess and sitting on Braedon's lap since we arrived.

The guy doing the grilling takes the burgers off the fire and stacks them in a large mound of steaming meat on a platter. Without him having to sound the dinner bell, everybody gets up in intervals to make themselves a plate.

"What do you want on your burger?" Luke asks me, standing from his chair.

I start to get up, too, but he stops me. "No, I'll make it for you."

"Just ketchup," I say, smiling up at him.

"Potato salad and baked beans?" he asks.

"Just potato salad—thanks," I tell him, and he smiles and goes off to make our plates.

"So where are you from?" Kendra asks once Luke steps out of the way.

"San Diego. Lived there all my life. What about you?"

"I was born in Hawaii," she says. "Honolulu. But I've lived most of my life in California. Haven't even been in Hawaii long enough to call myself a local." She chuckles lightly.

A bout of silence fills the space between us for a moment.

I sip on my beer just to be doing something.

"So," she speaks up, "did you and Luke meet over at the resort? That's where he usually meets girls"—she sort of chokes down the beer she just swigged from the bottle and waves her hand in front of her face rapidly—"I didn't mean that how it sounded."

Actually I think you did.

I look at the grass, my feet, the strange little insect crawling across the patio beside my shoe, and then back up at her. I swallow nervously and place my beer between my thighs, glancing across the patio at Luke standing next to a table where the bowls of beans and potato salad and bottles of condiments are placed.

Finally Kendra leans her back against the chair with a long sigh.

"Look," she says in a low voice, "let's just forget I said that. It totally came out all wrong." She laughs lightly. "So is Luke going to take you hang gliding?"

My eyes get big.

I laugh a little. "Uh, definitely not," I tell her, shaking my head. "He couldn't even get me to jump off the cliffs when we went swimming earlier."

That seems to have silenced her, though I don't know why. She just stares across the short space at me with a sort of surprised yet vacant look.

Luke walks up then with a plate in each hand. He hands me one carefully and I place it on the top of my legs and thank him with a smile.

"What, are you afraid of heights, or something?" Kendra finally asks as Luke is sitting back down next to me.

I notice them glance at each other again—that's starting to annoy me a little, not to mention making me very uncomfortable. But this time the look that passes between them is something more serious. Kendra's eyes are slanted with confusion and maybe concern—if I knew her well enough to decipher her expressions, that's what I'd call it: concern.

Luke looks as though he wants her to stop talking altogether.

I dig a plastic fork into my potato salad and poke it around in there to distract myself, until finally they look back at me with smiles as if no secret conversation had just passed between them right in front of me.

Finally I answer, "Yeah, actually I am pretty afraid of heights. Planes. Bridges. Ferris wheels. If it's more than ten feet off the ground, I'm uncomfortable with it."

Kendra stuffs the edge of the burger into her mouth, and I get the feeling it's more to keep her from saying something Luke doesn't want her to say. She chews happily, a big smile plain on her face as her jaw moves around.

Luke does the same, but he's not smiling so much as he is beginning to look as uncomfortable as I *feel*.

I notice Seth, from the corner of my eye, talking to a dark-haired girl standing next to the back door. He tucks his index finger behind the elastic of her bikini bottom, just below her belly button, and snaps it back. She giggles flirtatiously and pulls away. My player radar is still working at least—I was beginning to think maybe it stopped somewhere between seeing Luke through my lens and meeting him for the first time. Could Luke be playing *me*? I had started to think that, but decided that he just doesn't seem the type. But this Kendra girl—I'm convinced that something at least *used* to go on between the two of them, and I may not be Luke's girlfriend, but it doesn't make me any less anxious, or feel any less out of place.

I stand up and set my plate in my chair.

"Mind if I use the restroom?" I ask, looking down at Luke.

He gets up immediately, setting his plate in his chair like mine, and he takes my hand.

"Yeah, let me take you inside and show you where it's at."

We leave Kendra on the patio and I feel like I can't get away from her fast enough. Luke's hand tightens around mine as he leads me up the lanai and into the dimly lit house.

"I'm sorry about Kendra," he says as we make our way through the kitchen and into the hall. "She's harmless though, I promise. Just ignore her if she starts talking too much. That's what *I* always do."

Did you two used to have a thing? I want to ask, but feel like it's not really any of my business.

"It's all right," I say, and we stop outside an open door. I hear the toilet running faintly inside. "I do want to get back to my hotel before it gets too late though, if you don't mind."

Luke's face falls and his shoulders rise up and down with a sigh. I step up and place the palm of my hand on his hard chest and gaze into his eyes. He looks down at my hand and is just as surprised that it's there as I am.

"I'm having a great time," I try to reassure him. I let my hand slide away. "I'm just really tired after surfing and swimming. Honestly, I haven't had this much excitement in one day in a long time."

A grin passes over his lips. "I find that hard to believe with that crazy job of yours."

I smile and press my back against the wall, trying to put some space between us. The smell of some kind of air freshener from the bathroom rises up into my nose briefly. I don't like it. I'd rather be smelling Luke.

"Work excitement and vacation excitement are two entirely different things," I say.

He squeezes his lips in thought, nodding in agreement.

"Well, I'm glad you're having a good time," he says.

It gets quiet then and a moment lingers between us as we just stand there in the hallway, together and *alone*. It feels more like we're quietly feeling out the other, wanting to try the one thing we're both afraid it's too soon for. We both know it. We can both see it in the other's eyes—I want him to kiss me and he wants to oblige, but neither of us is willing to go that far yet. But the attraction is undeniable. Yes, I *want* him to kiss me. My skin tingles beneath the surface with his closeness and I can't stand it. I mean I can. I quite like it. But I can't believe the effect Luke is having on me so soon. He's like a magnet and I can't pull away from the attraction fast enough.

I look at the bathroom door, stirring the silence, and say, "Well, I need to…go in."

He nods, his eyes softening as he steps away.

"I'll be outside waiting for you," he says. "And remember what I said about Kendra, all right?"

"All right." I smile and slip inside the restroom. The second the door closes behind me, I let out my breath I didn't realize I'd been holding.

Luke

Kendra is on my ass the second I walk back outside and sit down with my food, as I knew she'd be.

"What are you doing, Luke?"

"Leave it alone, Ken-doll—"

"Don't call me that," she snaps. "Seriously, what's going on with you?"

"Jesus, Kendra, leave the guy alone," Seth says as he walks by with a hot brunette latched to his side. "I'll see yah later, man. I'm heading back to the house." He squeezes the girl's waist and pulls her closer, his way of telling me she's going back with him.

I wave him on and swallow down a bite of burger. "All right. I'll see yah later—hey, leave the pizza in the fridge alone!"

He nods and slips around the side of the house.

Kendra hasn't taken her hardened gaze off me long enough to blink. Finally I look right at her, because she's starting to piss me off, and I say, "You really need to back off. I'm not joking, Kendra; I love you and all, but last time I checked, your name wasn't on my birth certificate." I take another bite.

Her small face falls under wounded wrinkles, and instantly I feel like an asshole. Shaking her head, she spears her fork angrily into her potato salad and moves it around to keep from looking at me.

"I'm sorry," I tell her. "Look, she's only gonna be here for two weeks. I don't see her getting involved with me knowing she can't *stay* here."

Kendra looks up.

"What about the other way around?" she asks with accusation in her voice.

She got me on that one, I can't deny...to myself, anyway; to Kendra is another story.

"I'm not going to get involved," I tell her. "And even if I did—damn, Kendra, it's none of your business."

She looks hurt again, but this time I don't relent.

"Well, it's the truth," I go on. "And what makes you think I haven't decided to turn to the Seth side and I'm not just taking her home for a night?" That felt odd and sour coming out of my mouth. Because it couldn't be further from the truth, but I don't know what else to say to get Kendra off my case.

She guffaws, catching me off guard, and then drops her head and says, "Yeah *right*. You're not cut out for the *Seth side*. Not anymore anyway. And that girl isn't the one-night-stand type, and you know it."

I look away and poke at my food.

"I'm just looking out for you," Kendra says, dropping the humor. Then she leans forward awkwardly so her loose white tank doesn't fall into her food. "She's afraid of heights, Luke. *Heights*, of *all* things. If it weren't for that blatant fucking red flag I wouldn't be saying shit to you right now." She pulls back and sits upright again.

Kendra makes a very valid point. She knows, I know, we ALL know relationships never work out with someone who doesn't get our lifestyle, but I refuse to let her know I get it.

"I'm not getting involved," I say simply and go back to my meal just as Sienna is coming down the steps of the lanai.

I reach over and move Sienna's plate from her chair as she approaches, holding it for her until she takes her seat again. Her eyes pass over Kendra, but her beautiful smile remains in place and it only makes me like her more. I know she's probably wondering what's up with Kendra exactly, maybe even if Kendra and I used to go out or something, but I guess this isn't the time or place to get into those kinds of details.

Sienna looks over at me. I smile back at her and notice her glance at Kendra once more. I'm starting to wish I hadn't brought her here, and I probably *wouldn't* have if I'd known Kendra was going to be here too.

"I really need to be getting back to my hotel," Sienna says kindly. "I'm exhausted."

I nod and get up with my half-eaten plate of food in my hand.

"Yeah, sure, not a problem. I'll take you back now."

Sienna said in the hallway that she was having a great time, but I think for the most part she was just being nice. In fact, I know it. And I feel like a total dick for bringing her here and making her feel uncomfortable.

But I still have time to fix this.

I take Sienna's plate and stack it on top of mine.

"It was nice meeting you," she says to Kendra.

Kendra smiles in return. "You, too," she says and I'm glad there wasn't any underlying meaning behind her expression that Sienna might've detected—at this point, I think Kendra knows better than to push me any further than she already has.

We leave and head for the bus station.

While on the bus I look over at Sienna and say, "I just want you to know that Kendra is just a friend. Well, she's more than that—she's like a sister to me, but that's it."

Sienna smiles softly and I'm not sure if she believes me or not.

"It's all right," she says. "Even if she was ever something more, it's none of my business anyway."

She doesn't believe me. *Dammit!*

"I'm serious," I tell her and lean forward from the seat so I can get her full attention. "I know she seems—"

"No, really," Sienna cuts in, "it's OK. You don't have to explain anything to me."

"Actually, I *do*," I say right away.

She blinks, but says nothing.

"Look, I don't want you to feel uncomfortable, and if anyone I know can pull that off, it's Kendra, but I didn't know she was going to be at the barbecue." I pause because I realize I'm just jumping around the point, and then decide to do what I always do—be vague. "She was my brother's girlfriend." I pause again, because I don't like to talk about it and every time I *start* to, even when at first I feel like it's going to be OK and that I can get through it, I realize that I can't.

I fall back against the bus seat, resting my head and looking up at the fiberglass ceiling.

"Are you OK, Luke?" Sienna's voice is so sweet and caring that I wish it were closer—she's not even touching me and I feel like her arms are wrapped around me in solace.

My head falls to the side and I look at her.

"I'll be fine if you tell me that you'll spend the entire day with me tomorrow." I smile softly and brace myself because all I want in the world right now is for her to say yes.

Slowly, her lips spread amid her delicate freckled face and my insides begin to warm just looking at her.

"I had hoped that's what I'd be doing the whole two weeks," she says, and my heart stops beating for a moment.

She blushes and starts to look downward—she does that a lot, I've noticed, and I think it's adorable. I reach over and fit my fingers underneath her chin, keeping her gaze on me.

"Are you blushing?" I ask with a grin.

She blushes harder.

Damn, she needs to stop doing that! I like it a little too much...

My hand drops from her chin and I raise my back from the seat, propping my elbows on my legs. "I had hoped the same thing," I admit, and then top it off with some humor. "I mean, come on, I didn't try to talk you into staying in Hawaii just so you could spend all your time alone."

She smiles, but then again, she never really stopped.

"But what about your job...or jobs?" she asks. "I guess I didn't think about that," she adds apologetically.

"Hey, don't you worry about that," I tell her with a wink. "Let's just say I've sort of got vacation time of my own saved up—I can work around it."

She seems to be pondering, her lips in a cute little pucker.

And then she gives in. "OK, but no more barbecues," she says. "I'd rather see where you live than your friends."

That takes me by surprise, but naturally I feel compelled to screw with her head. I grin and say, "Oh, so you wanna see my place? So soon?"

Her hazel eyes widen and she bumps my knee with hers.

"You are unbelievable," she jokes. "Well, if that's what you think, then you're more full of yourself than I thought you were."

I laugh and leave it at that.

When we arrive back at the resort, I walk her as far as the lobby, where we stop among the grandeur laid out in marble and expensive furniture and strategically placed plants. Tourists come and go from the nearby elevator. Sienna stands with her bag draped over one shoulder, her fingers interlocked down in front of her. Her long, dark auburn hair hangs loosely over her shoulders, dropping just below her breasts, and her bangs are cut short just above her eyebrows. Even unbrushed and a little rough at the ends from being in the ocean all day, it still looks soft enough I'd like to run my fingers through it.

"So what's on the agenda for tomorrow?" she asks, beaming at me.

I raise a playful brow, cross one arm over my stomach and rub my chin with the other hand in pretend contemplation. "Hmmm," I begin, "how about I pick you up at ten—is that too early?"

She shakes her head. "No, ten is perfect."

"Awesome. I have to stop by the community center not far from here," I say. "And then after that, I'm all yours."

"Is that where the art event will be?"

I nod. "Yeah, but we won't stay long," I say casually. "I just need to check on a few things. I promised Melinda that I'd stop in—she's like fifty, so don't get any ideas." Sienna blushes again, trying her best not to smile too broadly.

She thinks on it for just a fraction of a second.

"I look forward to it," she says. "And I don't mind how long we stay, for the record."

"Great." I can't stop smiling.

Neither can she.

A hotel guest walks by carrying a cup of coffee in his hand and we both glance at him momentarily, probably for the same reason, just to stir the silence between us.

"Well, I guess I'll see you in the morning then," she says.

Damn, I want to kiss her. It's killing me!

She takes a step back, and even though I'm not exactly sure that's a sign she doesn't want me to, I don't take any chances and I bury my hands in my pockets instead. Then I pull out my phone and run my finger over the screen.

"Want to give me your number?"

Her eyes light up, and that makes me smile.

I tap in her number as she tells me and I send her a text message. I hear her phone inside the bag on her shoulder alert her of the message and she reaches inside. I try to smother back my smile. I couldn't help myself.

My stomach is a ball of nerves—I've never been this nervous around a girl before. What the hell is wrong with me?

Sienna looks down into her phone and her skin flushes.

"I'll see you tomorrow at ten," I say, and leave it at that, walking away with my hands in my pockets, a permanent smile on my face, and *her* face permanently etched in my mind.

TWELVE

Sienna

*Y*ou're staying for *two weeks*?" Paige's voice on the other end of the phone is almost loud enough to be unpleasant. "I'm at a loss. Seriously! Who *are* you and what have you done with my best friend? Y'know, workaholic Sienna Murphy who wouldn't even go out to Sage's Steakhouse last month with Alex Miller, sex on legs and rich to boot?!"

"There's something about Luke," I tell her, holding my cell phone against my ear with my shoulder drawn up near my face to free my hands as I paint my toenails. "I can't explain it, but I just feel...drawn to him."

"*Drawn* to him?" I can picture Paige's face all scrunched up in her head. "What, like pheromones or something?" She laughs. "Hey, I admit the guy is delicious; you'll get no argument from me, but I'm worried."

"What's there to worry about—oh *dammit*!" I look down to see turquoise nail polish soaked into the stark white bedsheet where a glop had fallen from the end of the brush before I could catch it on the rim of the bottle. "*There's* another charge on my credit card. Just *great*." I set the nail polish aside on the night-stand and get up from the bed, still with the phone held against my ear by my shoulder, and I walk awkwardly across the room on my heels.

"It's just not like you," Paige rambles on. "I've tried to hook you up with several guys, but you usually had an excuse not to go, or you'd never see them again afterward if you did."

"OK, but I don't get what's got you so worried."

I set the phone on the bathroom counter and run my finger over the speaker icon and Paige's voice appears—should've done that while trying to paint my toenails on the bed.

I hoist my right foot on the edge of the counter.

"Well, we haven't even gone on *our* vacation yet," Paige says, her voice funneling from the tiny speaker into the confined space. "If you take the plunge and fall in love at twenty-two, you'll be bare-foot and pregnant by the time you're twenty-four, living in a trailer somewhere with ugly wallpaper, waiting for your boyfriend who works for minimum wage to come home so you can bring him a beer while he sits on his ass and watches *wrastling*."

I laugh out loud, holding a cotton ball doused in nail polish remover over my big toe.

"What's so funny, Sienna? I'm being *serious* here. Bitches get serious with guys and it's like parts of their brains stop function-ing. You don't *care* anymore if there's no condom, or if you forgot to take your pill, and you blame getting knocked up on the heat of the moment—life ruined!"

"Wrastling," I say, still with laughter in my voice.

I carefully dab the cotton ball around the edge of my toe to clean away the nail polish where it's not supposed to be.

"Are you making fun of the way I talk?"

"Paige," I say seriously, "I'm not going to even *have* sex with him, much less be having his babies. It's just a vacation. One I think I've earned. We'll still go on vacation together soon, I promise." After inspecting my toenails, I drop the cotton ball in the toilet and my foot back on the floor.

"Why are you being so uptight, anyway?"

She sighs. "Honestly?"

"Well, yeah," I say. "Out with it!"

"I'm jealous! There, I said it!"

My laughter fills the bathroom.

"Jealous I might get knocked up and move into a trailer with ugly wallpaper?"

Paige snorts when she laughs.

"No! I just wish I was there on vacation with you. Stupid family reunions!"

We laugh together.

I take the phone from the counter and head outside on the balcony. I hear live music coming from below, faint in the distance. Drums and voices pounding and echoing into the night. The orange glow of fire is cast against the black backdrop of the ocean under the night sky. I want to go out there and see what's going on, but I know I need to get some rest. I want to be well rested for tomorrow because I have a feeling Luke and I will be running around all day. And I'm excited and eager and so many things I never knew I could be all at the same time. And *he's* all I can think about.

Maybe Paige is right—this is very different from any other guy I've ever been involved with before, and we're not even going out.

In a way, it kind of scares me too.

"Paige, I need your opinion on something." I pick the phone up from the table and turn the speakerphone off, putting it to my ear instead, as if I need the privacy.

"That's what I'm here for," she says eagerly.

Hesitating for a moment, I look out at the black ocean, listening to the waves crash underneath the stars, and I think about what happened earlier tonight.

"Well, Luke took me to a barbecue with some of his friends, and there was this girl there—"

"Uh-oh," she cuts in, already not liking where this might be going. "Was she pretty?"

"Adorable," I say. "She seemed kind of tomboyish—"

"Lesbian?" she interrupts again, this time with a little hope in her voice.

"No. I doubt it. Luke said she was his brother's girlfriend. But she just seemed kind of...I don't know—"

"Jealous?"

"Maybe. But not really." I hate how difficult this is for me to explain, or rather to understand myself.

"Either they used to go out," she says right away as if she's an expert, "or they've been friends with benefits. Or she has a thing for him. You say she's tomboyish—y'think she could kick your ass?"

"Uh, I don't know, Paige," I say with confusion. "Besides, I didn't get that kind of vibe from her. It wasn't like that."

"Well, my question would be why would he take you around a girl like that in the first place? It's like he's showing off or something, letting you see how other girls like to fawn over him."

"No, it wasn't like that at all, either," I defend. "She was already there when Luke and I showed up. He even apologized when we were alone and said he wouldn't have brought me if he knew she'd be there."

"Aha!" I picture her index finger shooting upward.

"What?"

"He wouldn't have brought you if he'd known," she repeats, preparing to make a point. "Proof right there that *something* has gone on between them and he knew the girl might be a problem. Think about it—if she was *just* his friend, she wouldn't have any reason to make you question what kind of relationship they have. After he met *me* on the beach did he ever ask you if we've ever been more than friends?"

My nose crumples between my eyes. "No." I laugh. "Why would he ask *that*?"

"My point exactly," she says. "I didn't give him any reason to think that, and that's why he never asked. He slept with that girl. You can bet your ass on it, Sienna."

I feel a pang in my stomach.

"Well, that doesn't mean anything," I say, still trying to defend Luke, but finding it harder to do. "*So what* if they've slept together. That doesn't mean they're still doing it, and it's not really his fault if she still has a thing for him."

"Maybe not," Paige says, "but you could be setting yourself up for some drama regardless, that's for sure."

I cringe over that word. Drama. I hate it and fear it like the Dennings family probably hates and fears having to drive through the projects.

"Just watch yourself," Paige adds. "See, I should be there with you. Just in case."

I laugh and bring my legs up, propping my bare feet on the table.

"Oh please," I say. "I can take you down, so I don't really need your backup."

A burst of air sounds in my ear.

"Hey!" she says with humor and pretend offense, "I'll remember that next time you need help!"

"Yeah, too bad you're not here in Hawaii. Soaking up the sun. Hanging out with me and Luke's hot friends." I *have* to mess with her.

"He has *friends?*"

"No, Paige, he's a loner who lives in the mountains. Didn't you see his knee-length beard?"

She laughs.

"I hope you have a good time," she says, setting all jokes aside. "I really do. You're right, you deserve it." She pauses and then adds, "Who knows, maybe he won't turn out to be an asshole and be perfect for you. Just don't forget to keep in touch—tourists are often targeted, y'know. I worry about you."

"I'll keep in touch," I tell her just before we say good-bye and hang up.

After a quiet moment, I look down into the phone and bring up the text message Luke sent me just before he left. ***kisses your cheek*** glows on the screen and my face flushes with heat every time I look at it.

Everything about this guy feels right. I'm not even sure what *right* means at this point, but I'm not giving up until I find out. As I stare at the screen, letting not just everything he's ever said to me run through my head, but the three simple words on the screen itself, and I can't help but wonder what Luke's doing right now.

Finally I decide to take a leap, not caring if it makes me seem too forward, and I touch the screen just as the light is beginning to fade, and I begin to type:

What are you up to?

My heart is beating furiously now. Maybe I shouldn't have texted him, after all. What if he doesn't respond? I swallow nervously and sway my crossed feet side to side on the table.

Just lying here.

My heart skips a beat when I see his reply and my face spreads into a smile.

What about you?

I think about it for a moment, wanting to be as vague and simple as he's being.

Just sitting on my balcony, I finally reply.

Luke: It's a nice night.

Me: Yeah it really is.

There's no response for six extremely long seconds.

Luke: I can't wait to see you tomorrow.

Did my heart just melt? I think it seriously just melted.

Me: Me too. : -)

Luke: You can't wait to see you tomorrow?

Me: You know what I mean. :-P

Luke: Come on, throw me a bone and just say it. You can't wait to see me.

Now the six-second response time is all on me.

Luke: *pouty face*

Do I do it? No! I shouldn't. We've not known each other long and he might think I'm easy or vulnerable or naïve or desperate.

Luke: Sienna?

Me: *kisses your cheek*

Six more long seconds.

Luke: : -) See you tomorrow.

Me: : -) Good night.

I don't care if Kendra is threatened by me or if the two of them used to have a thing. The past is the past. The only thing that worries me is the future.

I have to go home sometime.

THIRTEEN

Sienna

*T*he alarm on my phone wakes me to the sound of crickets the next morning. My eyes open a slit to see the clock on the nightstand glaring eight a.m. back at me. Immediately, I leap out of the bed, nearly tripping over my shoes. I'm going to be late for work—I'm always up at seven to get ready. My heart is racing something fierce by the time I realize that I don't have work today, or tomorrow, or the day after that. Letting out a long breath, I press my palm against my heart.

"Get a grip," I tell myself.

I walk over and open the long curtains on the windows to let the sun shine through. Then I hop in the shower and shave again even though I showered and shaved last night. I don't want even a millimeter of regrowth anywhere on my body. Not that I plan on letting Luke feel me up, but…well…he might touch my knee again, or pat my leg like he did yesterday. Or, take it upon himself to remove my shoes, which, in turn, means he'll touch my ankles.

OK, I think I'm losing it. Why do I feel like a high schooler with a crush on the quarterback?

My room is a mess before I even halfway figure out what to

wear. Clothes are strewn all over the bed and the floor and the chair by the wall.

I don't want to over- or underdress—why didn't I ask him last night if I should dress casual?

I try on several different outfits, mixing and matching this and that, until finally settling on my cream-colored dress, with orange, black, and light blue flowers around the waist and the bottom, which stops just above my ankles. I top it off with my matching orange purse—big enough to carry my larger camera—orange sandals, and gold bracelets and matching earrings. I pull my hair into a cute braided bun at the back of my head and leave a few wisps to hang about my face.

And I'm incredibly nervous.

This feels like a date. Yes, I think that's exactly what this is. I mean, he never *said* it was a date, and *I* never said it was a date, but it really does seem like—

My phone chimes, interrupting my rambling thoughts, telling me I have a text message. I check it quickly, automatically thinking it will be Luke, until I realize it's still pretty early.

Paige: I want details!

I text her back telling her that she'll get the details if there *are* any, which I highly doubt because this isn't a date and—

OK, it's *definitely* a date.

And it's the first date I've ever been on where I felt a little nauseous beforehand. Where I can't think straight and where I actually got up two hours before I'm supposed to meet him, just to get ready. The last guy I dated was lucky enough to get a thirty-minute prep time—I liked to date like any girl, but it was often hard for me because I've always been so focused on my career and helping my parents.

Standing in front of the elongated mirror, I turn left and right and spin around to see the back of my summer dress. I adjust the thin half-inch straps over my bare shoulders and lean over forward to see if my girls are on display and if my strapless bra is doing its job. I look down at my turquoise-painted toenails—if anyone can ever accuse me of having an obsession, it's more likely to be toenail polish than being a workaholic—and I realize they need repainting, light blue to match the blue flowers on my dress.

After that, all I have left to do is wait. I glance at the clock on my phone and sigh miserably—it'll be a whole hour before Luke gets here—and I thought six seconds was a long time.

Finally the hour is up and ... he's still not here.

I check my phone in case he texted me or called at some point, hopeful that he had. Nothing. Fifteen minutes late and I'm starting to feel like the girl who got stood up at the prom by that stupid quarterback.

My phone chimes in my hand, my heart skipping a few beats.

Luke: Sorry I'm late! I'm almost there. Give me about 10 minutes.

Breathing a sigh of relief, I stand up from the bed and go over to check myself out in the mirror again. Already my face is starting to get oily. Or maybe that's from my nerves, or sweat from the summer heat. I pat the area between my eyes and around my nose with a square of toilet paper. Geez! I've never been so nervous in my life!

I grab my bulky rust-orange leather purse from the bed and shoulder it—no need to make sure I have everything because I've already done that about, oh, at least five times: cell phone, wallet, room key, Canon.

I head downstairs to meet Luke in the lobby just as he's walking through the main doors with his cell phone crushed in his hand.

For a moment, as he walks toward me, all I can do is check him out as I've only ever seen him in swimming shorts and T-shirts—or shirtless—before. He's dressed in a pair of light khaki pants with the legs rolled up just above his ankles, and a light blue button-up shirt, loosely tucked behind a belt, with the sleeves rolled tight around his bicep muscles. A pair of casual brown leather loafers dress his feet. A thick brown braided bracelet dresses one wrist. A smile that I find myself becoming addicted to. I swallow nervously; the pit of my stomach swims with a sort of besotted shiver.

I smile brightly to distract from any incriminating evidence of infatuation left on my face.

"Wow," he says, stepping up to me, beaming. "You're beautiful."

"Thank you," I say, unable to hide the blush in my face, and I refuse to waste time trying anymore.

I look him up and down with an investigative gaze. "And look at *you*," I say as my eyes slowly find his. "I'm impressed. Truly I am. Didn't expect *that*."

He grins crookedly and it melts me a little inside.

"What, am I not the Abercrombie & Fitch type?"

"No, I guess I just didn't imagine you in anything—"

"You didn't imagine me in anything?" He raises a brow and his grin appears more devilish. "So you're imagining me in the buff already?"

Yes.

"No!" My hand instinctively comes out and play-swats him on the shoulder. My face flushes and I look at the floor, almost able to see my reflection in it, the tile is so clean and shiny. "That's *not* what I was going to say." Laughter rolls out along with my words.

"Sure sounded like it," he quips. "*I* didn't imagine *you* were such a pervert. Too cute to be perverted, in my opinion."

I can't find it in me to think of a witty comeback, so I just stand here with my hands folded together in front of me and wearing an embarrassed smile that covers my whole face.

He changes the mood by looking me up and down with the explorative sweep of his eyes, which makes me blush harder. "But seriously, Sienna, you're gorgeous."

My smile stretches. "Well, I'd be lying if I didn't say the same about you—*but*!" I hold up a finger. "I think I've witnessed first-hand another one of your flaws," I tell him in jest.

He tries not to smile too broadly, pressing his lips together in a line. "Being late, I know. But in my defense—" He holds up a finger, too, but I cut in before he has a chance to explain.

"Let me guess—the girl on the bike again? She's starting to freak me out a little. What if she sees me with you and comes after *me*?"

Luke laughs lightly.

"No," he says, shaking his head. "I think she's long gone by now. I was late this time because of the public transportation. But you're right, it's a flaw. I'm not always late. To be honest, I'm only ever late to the most important things."

I don't know what to think of that, but I find myself feeling good about it, at least.

"Well, that's a little weird, don't you think?"

He nods, and I grin and go on, taunting him. "I've always heard that people who are often late don't really care about others, or respect their time. They're rude, inconsiderate, and selfish." Actually I'm a firm believer of that observation, but for some reason, I can't put Luke on their level, not because I'm bewitched by him, but deep down I don't think he belongs there. I just hope he has a good excuse to prove me right.

"Yeah, I know," he says, followed by an apologetic sigh. "It's like the more important something is, the harder I try to make it perfect and then I end up forgetting things or—"

"It's all right," I cut in. "I was just joking with you." Then I narrow my eyes. "But if you're ever late again, I'll have to..." I can't think of anything.

He smiles. "You'll have to *what?*" he challenges.

"I don't know, but I'll figure something out."

"All right," he says, "but if I'm on time from here on out and you accuse me of not thinking you were important enough to be late for, I'll have to do something, too." He nods swiftly once, as if to underline his point.

I chortle and say, "I'll try to remember that."

He grins and then steps to my right, arcing his arm out at his side, offering it to me. "Shall we?" he says, pretending to be sophisticated, and I smile, looping my arm through his, and we leave the lobby together.

We catch the bus and ride to the community center not too far away, where we get off and walk the rest of the way. I'm past wondering if he has his own car, and although it concerns me a little, I'm too afraid to ask him about it—I don't want to offend him. But it does seem strange, because I've not once seen him drive, and this is the second time I've left the resort with him and we've either taken a bus, or ridden with one of his friends. If Paige were here, she'd already have drilled him about it by now, not to mention the particulars of his two part-time jobs, and we'd already know where he lives and what brand of toilet paper he uses in his bathroom.

The community center is very spacious, with white-painted brick-like walls and a ceiling of average height, made up of popcorn tiles and long fluorescent lights—it reminds me of the library back at my high school, minus the books.

There are few people here and there, setting up paintings and sketch art and even beautiful photography on prints as tall as me. Dozens of tall display easels—most of them empty—are set amid giant portable partitions that separate one artist's section from another.

Several black-and-white photographs of an old woman's weathered hands catch my eye instantly, and I want nothing more than to get closer and check out the sharp detail and the gray and black tones that make up the shadows. But the next thing I know, Luke is leading me away from the display floor and in the opposite direction.

"You'll like Melinda," he says, pulling me along gently beside him with his fingers collapsed around my hand. I feel like I have feathers in my stomach and a tiny fire burning behind my pelvic bone.

We approach a set of wide steps that lead not onto a second floor, but a platform floor of sorts that overlooks the art display area. As we make our way up the carpeted steps, a woman with curly black and gray hair, and wearing a pair of black slacks and a pretty white blouse, sees Luke and her eyes light up.

She makes her way over without hesitation.

"I'm so glad you came," she says sweetly, taking him into a hug with her thin, frail arms. She pulls away and smiles over at me and instantly I like her; there's warmth and honesty in her that reminds me of my mother.

Luke introduces us and she shakes my hand.

"Looks like things are coming along," Melinda says, glancing out at the display room. "I didn't expect the artists to start bringing in their pieces this soon, but if you need space to set up, you can have it all moved into the room down the hall."

"Yeah," Luke says. "I told a few they could go ahead and start bringing it in if they needed a place to store it—especially the larger pieces."

Melinda nods and looks between us both, beaming; her hands are clasped together down in front of her like a little basket.

A few more people ascend the stairs, and Melinda makes note of them right away, as if preparing to have to mingle with them next.

"Are you going to hang around for a while today?" she asks Luke.

"Not for too long," Luke says, and I feel his eyes on me briefly. "I've got a day planned with Sienna. She's only here for two weeks and there's a lot to show her."

"Oh, well, that's wonderful," Melinda says sweetly. "Where are you vacationing from?"

"San Diego," I answer.

"I've been there," she says. "Nice place."

"Nothing like Hawaii," I say.

She purses her lips and nods. "Yes, I guess I have to agree with you on that one." She smiles softly.

"Too bad you can't be here for the event," she says, looking between me and Luke.

"Yeah, I go back home on the twenty-first," I say, beaming at them both, "but I'd *love* to stick around and help set up."

Luke squeezes my hand. "Hey now, remember what I said—"

"Yeah, I know," I interrupt, squeezing his hand back.

Melinda's face brightens.

"Perfect," she says. "I think it's really going to be our biggest event yet—I do it every year, but this year I decided to hand over the reins to my two favorite people." She looks at Luke, indicating he's one of them. "Luke is a special young man," she says, and instantly I notice his face flush under his tanned skin.

"Oh, I wouldn't go *that* far," Luke cuts in respectfully, a blushing smile covering his whole face. He looks at me with a grin and says, "Melinda is just biased because she's practically adopted me."

"Hey, if I could *really* adopt you, I certainly would," Melinda says.

"Well, maybe you and my mom can work something out," Luke jests.

I find their kind banter adorable, especially the way Luke is with her.

Melinda smiles.

The people who had just come up the stairs approach us, and Melinda's attention begins to split between us and them. Luke decides it's our cue and then he says, "I'm going to show Sienna around for a few before we head out."

"OK, dear," she tells him and takes him into another hug. "Let me know if you need anything." She looks right at me now. "Hang around for as long as you'd like. There are drinks and snacks in the kitchen—Luke can show you the way."

"Thank you—it was nice meeting you."

"You too, honey," she says.

Melinda greets the other people while Luke takes my hand again and leads me back down the steps.

"So is this another one of your part-time jobs?"

"No, not really," he says as we descend. "It's just something I do on the side. Sometimes I even answer phones."

I get the feeling he's being purposely vague; either that or he's messing with me and I'm too enamored by him to tell the difference.

"What do you do exactly?" I inquire suspiciously, playfully.

Back on the ground floor, the first things I see are those striking black-and-white photographs of the old woman again, and I let my hand slip from his and I go right over to them. He follows. While I'm studying them up close and admiring the detail, I glance back at him and continue. "I don't know why, but I just can't see you doing office work."

He looks at me with a small, disbelieving smile. "Why not?" he asks. "Dressed like this I look like I'd fit right in an office."

I turn from the photograph to him. "Well, sure, you could easily *look* the part; I just don't see you as the sit-down-all-day-at-a-desk type."

One side of his mouth and his eyebrow lifts curiously, as if to say he can't argue with that.

I look at the second photograph, focusing closely in on the beaded necklace draped over the woman's gnarled knuckles, and the black fur of the front of her coat the way it appears to make her aged hands look softer pressed against it.

"This is an amazing shot," I say, unable to take my eyes off of it for a moment. "It was dressed up with a filter afterward to make the black and grays so rich, but even I use filters on a lot of my shots—I think a lot of photographers probably do."

Finally I look away from it, my gaze scanning a few other photographs on display and I start to feel dizzy with inspiration and envy. I pat my purse hanging from my shoulder just to feel the contours of my camera inside. I'd love to break it out right here and start snapping photographs of photographs, but I don't feel right about it.

It takes me a long moment to realize that I've been walking

down this lengthy row, taking in the details of every single shot, and that Luke has hardly said a word.

I stop and turn to him.

He's smiling; his golden-brown hair is tousled in the front, framing a striking face full of regard and mystery that I want more and more to solve.

"I'm sorry, I—"

"Don't be," he says. "I like seeing this side of you—you really are passionate about photography."

"It's always been there for me," I say as we continue on down the aisle. The photography begins to thin out and paintings begin to replace it. "Some hobbies come and go, but I think everybody has one that sticks with them all their life; you know, it's a part of them, like an arm or a leg. Photography is mine. I really can't imagine a life without it." We stop in front of a large canvas painting displayed on an easel of a bird's nest with four little blue speckled eggs amid the sculpted twigs. I want to reach out and feel the raised texture of the paint under my fingers, but I refrain.

"You'll have to show me some of your work sometime," Luke says. "You should've brought your camera today."

My face lights up. "I did!" I say and pat my purse again. "And I have a website. Some of my favorite shots are on it. I'll give you the address and you can check it out later."

Luke tilts his head to the side and says, "Or *you* can show me yourself later." Then he points to my purse. "For now, why don't you take your camera out and get a few shots of the place. You know you want to." His delicious mouth lifts into a grin, his hazel eyes shimmering under the fluorescent lights.

He has no idea how badly I want that.

"You don't think anyone will mind?"

"Not at all," he says.

After hesitating, looking around at other people walking the aisles slowly and taking in the details of so many talented pieces of art, I slide the zipper open on my purse and pull out my camera.

"That has to be heavy carrying around on your shoulder," Luke says, glancing down at it.

I shrug. "A little," I say as I adjust a few settings. "But I don't carry much else."

"So no makeup drawer in there?"

"Nope." I chuckle, then snap a shot of him.

We make our way down several rows of art and I begin to notice that the farther we go, the larger the paintings become. There's a canvas painting of Kilauea that is almost as tall as me, but small in width. A stunning landscape so wide I could stretch my arms out to my sides and still not touch the edges. Easels have long since disappeared, replaced by the actual walls of the building because the paintings here are too large for easels. But there is still a lot of empty space, where I'm sure more art will be added over the next couple months. And as beautiful as all of the paintings and photographs that are here *are*, I can't help but notice how there's no real method to how things are being laid out—being in the business that I'm in, these kinds of things are hard for me to ignore. But eventually I pass it off as it just being too early, and that it will all come together in due time.

Finally, when we get to the last row, there is one giant wall with the most beautiful paintings I've ever seen, tall in height and enormous in scope; some of them could take up half a wall in my apartment back in San Diego.

"*Wow*," I say, craning my neck as I look up. "This is gorgeous.

Just *gorgeous.*" But so is the one next to it, and the one after that, and after that. I begin to see a pattern in the styles, like all artists have, and realize that a few of these were painted by the same person.

"Well, are you ready to go?" Luke says from behind. "There's so many places I'd like to take you."

My head snaps around, and I'm confused by his sudden disinterest in the paintings. But now that I think about it, he started to seem disinterested a few rows down. I didn't think anything of it before, but now with his sudden suggestion that we leave just when some of the larger paintings are actually taking my breath away— Oh . . . wait a minute . . . *no way.*

I search his eyes and his face for the answer. He appears uncomfortable, though trying hard to suppress it.

Just the thought of it being true takes my breath away a little. My eyes move from Luke and the painting next to me, and back at Luke and then the painting again. Finally I decide only to look at the painting, the rich, dark sky with rolling gray and purple and red clouds. The vast, endless field of high dry grasses, stroked with yellows and browns, their tops leaning in the same direction as if a strong wind is forcing them over. A woman stands tall amid the grass, her long, blond hair blowing in the breeze, her black dress clinging to her form and blowing briskly behind her in a graceful tail of silken fabric. It looks so real I feel like I can walk right into it and join her.

The painting beside it is just as stunning and lifelike, even frightening. A great wall of rock climbs a thousand feet into the sky, blanketed by lush greenery that crawls the stone like millions of fingers, gripping and tearing their way to the top. Down below, at the base of the mountain, a tiny valley of rolling green hills covers the surface, and a pencil-thin pathway made by man snakes along in one direction as it spreads out into the center of what looks like the bottom of the world. At the top of the ancient stone wall, I spot four tiny figures sitting on rocks perched over the edge, and other tiny human figures standing at the bottom looking up through beams of sunlight and large swaths of shadow cast by the scaling rock above.

I look again at Luke, but he's no longer looking back at me; he seems lost in the painting, but also just…lost. His smile is gone. That bright, playful personality I've grown so easily captivated by, seems shadowed by some kind of darkness.

"Luke?"

He snaps out of it and the smile returns quickly as if nothing at all had just invaded his mind.

"Are you ready?" he asks again.

I shake my head slowly. "No," I tell him and turn to the painting again. Glancing in the far right corner, I see initials, *Luke's* initials, I realize when I think back to his full name, which Paige had pulled out of him—Luke Michael Everett. LME stares back at me, so small I might never have seen it if I weren't precisely looking for it.

"You painted this, didn't you?"

FOURTEEN

Sienna

I can hardly believe this; I mean I can, but it's so... No, this is *unreal* to me. I feel my lips spreading across my face, my eyes getting brighter. Absently, I reach out my hand and touch his wrist underneath my fingertips.

"*Tell* me," I urge him, feeling like I'm going to burst with impatience. "Are these *your* paintings?"

He smiles gently and nods. "These two are"—he points to my left—"and that one is. A few smaller ones you already saw are mine."

"Why didn't you say anything?" I'm just so absolutely floored by his talent, and the fact that he didn't tell me right away, that I'm beside myself over it.

"Well, I don't really like people to know. I mean, it's not a *humble* thing, per se." He laughs. "It's just that painting is very personal to me. I don't do it much anymore. Not like I used to. But this here"—he waves a hand about the room, palm up—"being on display like this, it makes me uncomfortable."

"But *why*?" My fingers are still on his wrist. "These are... I can't even... Seriously, Luke, you have a gift."

Suddenly his hand turns over and his fingers lock around mine tightly. I can't breathe all of a sudden.

"Why, thank you," he says and raises his chin, grinning, trying to inject a little humor in the moment. "But really it's just a hobby."

My chin draws back, and I shake my head at the absurdity of his comment. "Oh, this is more than a hobby, Luke. You don't just wake up and paint something like this with this much detail and passion. No, *this*"—I point at the painting of the woman in the field and then at the one of the bottom of the world—"*this* is a part of you, like an arm or a leg, and you can't convince me otherwise. How long have you been doing this?"

"Since I was nine," he says, and instantly I begin to make the connection, but I let him explain it anyway. "Shortly after my brother got lost on that camping trip, somehow I picked up painting and it became my escape when I was afraid of everything else."

I squeeze his hand this time, feeling awful for what he must've gone through even though it was so long ago. I have a personal relationship with fear and I can relate and understand what he went through. But hearing it come from someone else—especially from Luke—makes me wonder if sometimes I use photography to escape my own fears.

"So then what are these paintings doing here if it makes you uncomfortable?" Something dawns on me as I ask that question and then I glance up at the price tag dangling from a little piece of string taped to the canvas. Subconsciously my mouth falls open when I see $1,500 scribbled in blue ink on the little white tag.

"I sell them every now and then," he says, and then nods in the direction of the platform floor where we stood earlier talking to Melinda. "Not usually this large, and just a few here and there.

When I—well, *we* actually; Alicia's helping too—agreed to organize the event, Alicia thought I should sell the larger ones, too." He
shrugs. "I thought, why not?"

My eyes grow wider as I look up at his paintings again.

"But why didn't you want me to know?"

His smile fades a little. "Well, it's not really that I didn't want to
show you, but—" He stops abruptly and instantly I get the feeling
he's going over in his mind what kind of answer he wants to give,
even if it's not the truth.

I step around in front of him and look at him with all the interest and curiosity and consideration that I can manage because it
feels exactly like a moment in which it's needed.

"Well," he says, burying both of his hands deep in the pockets
of his khakis, "if you knew they were mine you probably wouldn't
tell me if you thought they sucked."

I throw my head back and laugh lightly.

"You're kidding, right?" My hand shoots out and I press it gently to the center of his chest and give him a playful shove. He teeters
a little on the heels of his loafers and cracks a smile.

"Pu-lease!" I roll my eyes for added effect. "You know as well
as anybody that these paintings are far from 'sucking.'" I laugh
again, and my purse strap begins to fall off my shoulder, bringing
my dress strap down with it. Luke reaches out and catches the
strap of my dress with his finger and slowly slides it back into place.
The touch, although light, sends shivers up my arm. I swallow anxiously and my eyes begin to wander. Toward the floor, to his feet,
then to his shirt and his tanned, muscled arms pressed against the
rolled-up blue sleeves, and then to his neck and ultimately back into
his eyes again.

With my camera still in hand, I step over to Luke's side and say with a really bad English accent, "Mind if I photograph you with your masterpiece?"

Immediately he begins to shake his head. "Oh no," he says, waving a hand at me. "I really don't think I—"

"Come on, just a few quick shots," I urge him.

Still he doesn't look convinced.

"Pleeease?" I say with all the sweetness I can muster and top it off with a smile. It must be infectious because now he's smiling back at me and I find a heat in it this time that I've never felt before.

"All right." He gives in, and I feel my face light up like a Christmas tree.

Luke steps up to the painting of the Bottom of the World and stands in front of it with a shy awkwardness, his hands buried in his pockets again, his shoulders stiff with uncertainty. Dropping my purse on the floor beside my sandaled feet, I shake my head at him and wave my free hand.

"No—crouch down in front of it"—I step up and point out the perfect spot with the tips of my toes—"right about here."

When I step out of the way, Luke does as I instruct and crouches, the top of his shoulder overlapping the base of the painting.

"Just look natural," I go on, "and don't look at me, but off in the distance. And don't smile."

Luke sits crouched on the pads of his feet, his heels raised from the floor, with his elbows resting on the tops of his thighs, his hands dangling stiffly between them. I move several feet away and stand at an angle so that I'm not directly in line with him and the painting and I start snapping shots. Six, twelve, eighteen, as many as I can and all in different angles.

Finally I put the camera away and Luke pushes himself up on his toes.

"So, um"—he waves a hand about the vast room—"you got any event planning pointers?" he says distractingly, changing the subject, and it's so cute I can't help but smile.

I pucker my lips, cross one arm over my stomach, and raise my other hand to my chin, pretending to look professional and contemplative.

"Hmm," I say and look to my left, and then my right, taking my time. "Well, do you have a theme?"

Luke reaches up and nervously scratches the back of his neck.

"No, not really," he says. "Unless Community Charity Art Event is considered a theme?"

I smile warmly. "Well, I mean more along the lines of"—I purse my lips in thought and then point at him—"think about a prom; there's always a theme: a masquerade, Mardi Gras, *Alice in Wonderland*—there are so many things to pick from."

Luke looks upward in thought, slowly nodding his head.

"That's a good idea," he says, and his eyes meet mine. "But there's not a big budget for the setup. Honestly, Melinda never actually gave me a dollar amount, but I know that whatever it is, it's not going to be a whole lot."

I nod and think on it another moment, chewing on the inside of my mouth gently. I'm used to money being little to no issue when it comes to events, and now that I think about it, since this is a charity event, it's counterproductive to spend a lot on a setup when that money could go toward the charity itself.

"OK, how about you find out Melinda's budget," I suggest, "and we'll go from there. We'll keep it simple. Depending on what we come up with, I might have to order some things online, but I know all the right places to look and can even talk to a few people I've worked with before to pull us a few strings."

Luke looks at me in a suspicious sidelong glance.

"Us?" he asks with implication and a grin. "No working, remember?"

I grin back at him broadly, and with a shrug of my shoulders, I say, "It's not the same, trust me. I would really love to help. To be honest, I'm actually kind of excited about it—my mind is already buzzing with ideas."

Luke doesn't appear convinced.

"You sure it's not just that work addiction of yours?" he asks. "I refuse to enable you."

I laugh lightly. "No, it's nothing like that at all," I say, stepping up closer and tilting my head a little. "I *really* want to help. I think it'll be fun and it's for a good cause; I can't think of any reason *not* to."

"Are you sure, Sienna?" His strong hands fall softly on my upper arms, sending a trail of shivers up the back of my neck.

"Definitely." I smile.

We gaze into each other's eyes for a moment until finally he gives in, nods, and says, "OK. If that's what you want, that's what you'll get." The palms of his hands rub up and down my arms.

I can't help but think there's another, more tender meaning behind that comment, accompanied by the warmth in his eyes. I wish I could explore it further, crawl inside that beautiful head of his and listen to his thoughts because I feel like right now every single one of them is about me—I've never felt so... special.

"And no stressin' out, yah hear me?" he says with narrowed eyes. "The second I sense it feels like work to you, I'm pulling you outta there; I'll throw you over my shoulder, kickin' and screamin' if I have to."

"All right," I say with laughter in my voice.

"Of course, that's not the only thing you'll be doing while you're here," he points out. "I'd like to have you all to myself most of the time."

My face feels like it's on fire. I swallow nervously, excitedly.

"It's a deal," I say.

He takes my hand and walks with me out of the building and into the sunshine.

———

He won't say where he's taking me next. I practically begged him when we first got on the bus, quietly so the people sitting nearby wouldn't hear how whiny I might've sounded, but Luke was impervious to my feminine charms this time. And I have to say, I'm glad for that because I like a guy who puts his foot down every now and then and who isn't *so* sweet that he *always* lets me have my way. What fun is there in that? But I've been looking for it. Since the day I met him on that beach, I've been waiting for the one thing about him that's going to turn me off and make me run in the other direction to rear its ugly head. Because it always happens. A guy can be as perfect as a guy can be. I can check the boxes off my little list of requirements from top to bottom and even add a few things I never imagined any guy could have all in one personality, but eventually that hideous sore will pop up out of nowhere and turn a prince into a troll. It's one of my other flaws, but I'll never tell Luke that. Paige says it's because I'm afraid to get serious, because I'm so wrapped up in my career that in the back of my mind I know that getting *too* serious with someone will threaten it. Paige also says I'm "too fucking young to be worried about stuff like that," but she and I are different in that way—I think the younger I solidify my life and career, the better. I look at my parents and how much they *might've* had, the things they *could've* done, the time they *could've* spent together, if only they hadn't had to struggle financially as much as they did. I love them, but I don't want to end up like them and go through what they went through. What they're *still* going through.

But Luke is someone I can't easily brush aside and I *know* it, even if my feelings for him could one day threaten to change my life, veer it off course, turn it in a direction that I've never experienced before. It's frightening to think about the possibilities; my life has, for the most part, stayed on one straight course, never risking unfamiliar roads, rarely contemplating change—but Luke makes me feel like I can, that it's somehow safe to take a chance on something unknown. It's frightening, yes, but it's also exciting, and that's just not something I think I can ignore.

Still, that ugly sore could show up right now as I'm sitting close to him on the bus, our thighs touching even though there's room enough they don't need to, and I know it would take a lot to scare me away. I'm not afraid of getting closer to him. I don't feel a nervous ball in my stomach that makes me want to clam up on Luke. I don't feel the sudden urge to take a step back and slow things down. I'm not afraid of getting serious with him, but instead, I feel like I'm running *toward* him with open arms and I don't care how fast my legs are taking me there. No, I'm definitely not afraid of getting closer to him.

I think I'm afraid of the reverse.

Paige was wrong—I was never really scared of getting serious with a guy. I've just been holding out for the *right* guy.

"Wait," I say, looking out the window when I suddenly realize where we are. "Why are we at the airport?"

Luke's smile borderlines mystery and encouragement and I don't think I like it.

He pats the top of my thigh covered by the fabric of my dress. "You said you wanted to see where I live."

"Yeah, but—" All I see are images of me on a plane, and the same images I always see that take five years off my life.

He takes my hand and leans toward me; the smell of his freshly washed skin and the heat coming off his body almost...*almost*, calms me down a little. "I just work on Oahu," he says. "I *live* on Kauai. You'll be OK. It's only about a thirty-minute flight."

My heart sinks like a stone and my mouth feels like a dry riverbed—I don't even have my earbuds with me to listen to my rain MP3s. I want to protest—well, the *fear* in me wants to protest—but I can't get the words to leave my mouth.

He smiles warmly and tugs on my hand as the bus comes to a stop in front of the terminal.

OK, I can do this. It's not like I've never been on a plane before. My heart is banging against my rib cage and already I'm feeling sick to my stomach when usually that doesn't happen until I sit down on the plane and prepare for takeoff. I think what's different about this time is that I'm afraid of embarrassing myself in front of Luke, of all people. All three times I've been on an airplane without at least my MP3s to distract me, I've had small anxiety attacks. Once, on a flight from San Diego to Dallas, we flew through a thunderstorm and the turbulence was so frightening that I came unglued and the anxiety attack that I had was more than small.

"Luke, I don't know...Isn't there another way across? I mean, if it's only a thirty-minute flight, surely there's a boat that can take us over."

"Not anymore," he says, holding my hand as we enter the tall glass doors of the airport. "There used to be a ferry, but now the only way over is by plane or private boat, and that'd take a while."

"Nothing wrong with a while." I laugh under my breath uncomfortably, finding no real humor in it.

"Do *you* have a private boat?" he jokes. "Because *I* don't."

Luke stops and moves around in front of me, placing both of his hands on my upper arms. He looks into my eyes with a softness that I can't help but surrender to. People walk past us in all directions. The tapping of shoes on the bright tiled floor, the squeaking wheels of suitcases, and the hum of voices carry throughout the vast space. The sound of the intercom speakers in the high ceiling crackles before a voice comes on to make a general announcement that I can't pay attention to, not with those hazel eyes gazing in at me, claiming all of my attention.

"I'll be right next to you," he says. "Look at me."

I didn't realize my eyes had begun to stray.

I swallow hard and look back at him.

"Now, please just listen to what I have to say," he begins; an intense look rests on his face, which initially puts me on edge. "I know you're afraid. I understand that fear because I was there once, but I promise you everything'll be OK. I'm not going to tell you what everybody else tells you, all that stuff about how being in a car is more dangerous than flying, or give you statistics, or whatever—that's cookie-cutter bullshit advice that people give because they think it's what they're *supposed* to say." He shakes his head. His hands are still fitted about my upper arms. I can smell his minty breath and feel my heart beating in my arms underneath his strong fingers. "Most people never let their feet leave the ground," he goes on. "Whether they're afraid of heights, or afraid of hospitals, or they stay in the same place all their life because they're afraid of change—so many people go through life on the ground and die without ever knowing that they can fly."

My mind hangs on every one of Luke's words, as if he were some kind of remarkable mystery; I feel like I want to say something, but my heart wants to just listen.

"Where did your fear of heights come from anyway?" His hands slide away from my arms as he gazes at me with focus.

I have to think about it for a moment. I've been asked this question a few times, but I've never been able to give anyone a solid answer.

"Was it a bad experience like I had with my brother on that camping trip?"

I shake my head absently. "No…it's not because of anything like that…" I stop to ponder, never sure of the only answer I've ever been able to come up with. "The second I step on a plane, I'm handing my life over to the pilot, and once I'm in the air I can't change my mind. I can't tell him to pull over and let me out." My mind begins to drift, and my gaze strays from Luke's.

"*Fear* will kill you," he goes on. "A natural fear is good, but the kind of fear that *you* have, Sienna"—his hands squeeze my arms gently—"it's the unhealthy kind, the terminal-disease kind." Then he raises his chin importantly; a playful manner swaps with the serious one. "And as of today I'm making it my mission to cure you of it."

"Terminal diseases have no cure," I tell him smartly.

"Every disease has a cure," he comes back. "They're just waiting to be found is all."

How does he do that—make me question my own stubborn thoughts?

Finally I begin to nod slowly. "OK, I'll go. I mean it's not that big a deal—I've been on a plane several times."

"But have you ever been on a plane and not been afraid the whole flight?"

"No."

"And have you ever sat by the window and looked down at the landscape without feeling like you might faint?"

A nervous knot moves halfway down the center of my throat and it takes me a moment longer to answer him because it wedges there stubbornly.

"I've never sat by the window," I confess, "or looked out of one while the plane was in the air."

Luke's left brow rises just a little and he looks at me in a searching sidelong glance.

"Never? Not once?"

I shake my head slowly and switch my big orange purse onto the opposite shoulder.

"Then today will be your first time," he says.

My heart falls into the pit of my empty stomach, and now I feel more nauseous than ever.

"No, Luke, I really can't do that." I take a step back and sit down on a nearby plastic chair to catch my breath. "I-I can get on the plane and fly over to the other island with you, but"—my head is still shaking, I realize—"but there's no way I can sit in the window seat or look out... That's a really bad idea."

He sits on the edge of the empty seat beside me, his body turned at an angle so he can face me, our knees touching.

"Why is it a bad idea?" He looks thoughtful, concerned.

"Because, seriously...it's just...Luke, really, I draw the line right there. I'm sorry."

He peers in at me, ensnaring my unsteady gaze; his eyes are so sincere and comforting and I want to give in to him, but I know that this time I can't. I just can't.

His hand cups my knee.

"Sienna, you can do this," he says in a quiet voice so as not to draw the attention of anyone walking nearby. "Fear is an illusion. A hallucination. And all you have to do is make yourself believe that by defying it *once*"—he holds up the index finger from the hand on my knee and then lets it drop back down—"just once, and after that first time, you'll start to see that all along you've been lied to, and then you'll begin to take control of your own life."

"That's not entirely true," I tell him right away. "The first time I got on an airplane, I was so terrified. But I forced myself on that plane anyway, and I sat in that seat and cried for two hours, my hands gripping the armrests until the bones in my fingers ached. And when that plane landed, I couldn't get off it fast enough. That was about"—I count in my head briefly—"oh, maybe fifteen flights ago. And since then, I've been afraid of every flight I've taken."

Luke regards me quietly for a moment, his hand smoothing the top of my knee in consolation, and then he says, "That's because you weren't telling the fear to piss off." His hand slides away and he rests his back against the seat, stretching his arm behind me over the top of mine. "You got on that plane that day because you forced yourself. And I bet"—he nods at me once—"you told yourself that you just had to get it over with, didn't you?"

I think back on it, but I don't have to for long because those particular words had run through my head a hundred times in preparation of that first flight and it's not easy to forget.

"Yeah, I did say that," I admit.

"That's not fighting the fear," he tells me. "That's being submissive to it, accepting it as a part of your life that you can't control. And I'm sorry, but I just don't take you for the type." He shakes his head, a teasing look hidden behind his eyes.

"What type would that be?"

He shrugs and leans farther back in his seat, bringing his arms up and interlocking his fingers behind his golden-brown head, his long legs, bent at the knees, fallen open before him. I turn around on my seat, dropping my purse in the space between us, and just look at him, waiting for his answer as I chew on the inside of my mouth.

"I just think you're stronger than that," he says and then turns his head to lock eyes with me. "Everything I know about you so far tells me that although sweet, you're a no-nonsense kind of girl. You're set in your ways and you don't want your life dictated by anything you can't control—why else would you work so hard at your job?" His eyes smile at me, but the smile only faintly touches his mouth. "You work your ass off because you want to secure your financial life. You don't want *not* having money to control any part of it."

Is that truly the answer? Control?

Luke's comforting smile pulls me back in; I think maybe he knows I've taken the first step to understanding a deeper part of myself.

Suddenly he pushes his body forward and away from the back of the seat, leaning over with his elbows resting on his legs. "But that's getting off the subject," he says. "Look, I'm just saying that you're stronger than you give yourself credit."

He stands up and reaches out his hand to me. Hesitantly I take it.

"Just try it," he says as he helps me to my feet, "this one time—if you step off that plane on Kauai and don't feel even the slightest bit liberated, then I'll leave you alone about it and eat my words."

After turning it over and over inside my mind, a long moment that feels like forever, I swallow down the rejection I had prepared and I give in.

"OK."

Luke shakes his head as if I were already making a mistake and he needs to quickly correct it.

"You can't do this for me," he points out. "You have to want to do it for yourself. Just take a deep breath and think about how afraid you've always been and set it straight in your mind that you don't want to be afraid anymore." He smiles and adds, "To be blunt, Sienna, just tell the fear to fuck off and *you* take the control. Seriously. Grow a set of balls—I'll loan you mine if you need them."

I guffaw, drawing the brief attention of passersby. Then my laughter falls under a red-hot face.

Slowly my lips spread into a grin and I look toward his crotch, holding out my hand, palm up. "All right, then loan me your balls."

Judging by the stunned look on his face, surrounded by a broad smile, he probably didn't expect that.

He sighs dramatically and says, "Oh, all right," and then moves his hand down in front of him, makes a *really big* clawlike fist—I chuckle uncontrollably—and pretends to remove his balls, afterward placing them in my open hand. "Be careful with them. I'd like to extend my family name somewhere down the road."

Unable to suppress my grin—and just barely my laughter—I pretend to drop his balls inside my purse.

"I'll be very careful," I say, patting the side of my purse deftly.

He cocks a curious brow, looking to and from my purse and my eyes as if to complain about where I put them.

I laugh out loud. "Come on," I tell him with sarcasm, tilting my head to one side, "girls don't really carry them there—surely you knew that already."

Grinning, he shakes his head and takes hold of my hand. "Let's get our tickets," he says. "And don't worry. I'm paying for yours."

"No, I can—"

"I got this," he says sternly, shutting me up in an instant.

He smiles and pulls me along beside him as we head to the ticket counter.

FIFTEEN

Luke

*S*he sits down nervously and places her bulky purse on her lap, her back stiff, her eyes looking at the back of the seat in front of her. I feel compelled to tell her to loosen up some, but I don't want to push her.

I've been here before, where Sienna is:

"You can do this, bro!" Landon said as the wind hit the bridge and made his semi-long brown hair whip about his face. "And hey, if you die, you'll be there on the Other Side waiting for me when it's my time to go!" The wind was so strong on the bridge, elevated five hundred feet over a river, that he had to shout over it. Laughter followed.

"You're an asshole, Landon!" I told him.

He smiled. "Yeah, I know, but I learned from the best, big brother!" He shook his finger at me, grinning like a devil.

With the bungee cord secured around my leg, I stepped out onto the perch and looked down at the river snaking its way through the earth, and the hundreds of green-topped trees that looked like little pieces of broccoli set about in clusters. It was so far down that standing where I stood, that close to the edge, would make anyone with an immobilizing fear of heights piss themselves. I wasn't as afraid of the height as much as I was afraid of the way down, deliberately leaping to what could potentially be my death. But in my mind, it was the only way I could release myself from the fear. And if I died trying, then at least I died trying. I was tired of merely existing in a life that I was supposed to be living.

I looked back at my brother, just in case it was my last chance to do so, and I did what any brother would do—I flipped him off and leapt off the bridge.

And I lived.

No, I was reborn.

Sienna's hands are trembling against the armrests. I reach over and cup her right with my left.

"Look," I say, "you don't have to do this if you're not ready. I won't try to guilt you into it. But I can guarantee you that once you land, you'll be glad you did it. You'll feel more in control. Do you want to switch seats?"

I can't force her, I know, but I have to give her the option; otherwise she'll *feel* forced and this will all have been for nothing.

She hesitates and finally shakes her head. "No, I *want* to do this."

"And why do you want to do it?" I quiz her.

"Because I don't want to be afraid anymore."

"And why don't you want to be afraid?"

"Because fear is like a vampire," she says, still looking at the back of the seat in front of her. "And I'm tired of letting the bastard suck the life out of me."

"Hell yeah." I smile proudly.

When the plane takes off, Sienna's fingers dig into the armrests. The back of her head has been shoved against the seat as though the plane were a fighter jet and we took off at an unimaginable speed. Her hazel-colored eyes are as wide as my fists underneath her short bangs.

The plane levels out and soon after we're surfing the clouds hanging over the Pacific.

"Sienna?"

Frozen in her seat, she won't even move her head to look at me next to her.

"Yeah?" she says with a nervous tenor.

"You're terrified right now," I whisper, leaning toward her. "And I gotta say, I'm a little embarrassed."

Her head falls to the side and her eyes wrinkle at the edges with confusion.

"*You're* embarrassed?" she asks with disbelief.

I shrug. "Well, yeah, I mean you have my balls in your purse and they really don't seem to be helping much." I shake my head solemnly. "It's kind of hurtin' my ego, y'know?"

A smile sneaks up on her features, and the freckles splashed across the bridge of her nose and her cheeks seem to soften with the glimmer in her eyes. It's what I was shooting for, that smile. I wouldn't mind framing it on my nightstand so I could see it every morning when I wake up. I smile back at her, close-lipped, trying my best to contain the true measure of it.

Then slowly her fingers loosen on the armrests. Her chest

begins to rise and fall with a steadier pace. Her shoulders melt from the ice and begin to relax.

"Remember," I whisper softly, "this isn't about getting it over with. It's about *wanting* to do it." I lean in so close that I can smell her shampoo and I point toward the window next to her. "Tell yourself that this flight is *nothing* and you're not afraid of it. Smile to yourself and just let it go." I spread my fingers toward the window as if I were releasing a butterfly into the air.

Sienna

I don't know what has come over me, but I suddenly begin to feel freed, like I've finally crawled from underneath a thick, suffocating blanket and am tasting the cool air for the first time. I look toward the window, but not out it yet, and I see the baby-blue sky filling up the glass, unmoving, even though we're traveling fast through the air. I begin to feel like I shouldn't think about how I'm doing this to get over a fear, but instead I'm doing something as natural and as common as walking outside to check my mailbox. This is *nothing*, I tell myself. And I start to believe it.

Finally I lean toward the window and without taking a deep breath or any other beforehand preparations, I just do it. I look through the small oval glass and down at the massive ocean and it takes my breath away. At first I'm breathless because of the fear as it tries digging its talons in me, but I force it at bay and watch with a breathless awe instead, letting the experience fill me from my head to my heels—it's terrifying, but exhilarating just the same, like how a rush from the world's tallest roller coaster must feel. My heart beats with a rapid fervor, making the blood around my eyes feel thin. I don't think I've blinked in several long seconds. My lips are parted just a sliver, letting me suck in the air as it dries the inside of my mouth. And for what feels like forever, I can't look at anything else but the sky and the ocean and the thousands of feet between them.

"What's your opinion on Norway?" I hear Luke say.

Confused by the question, I look over at him. He's staring down into the pages of a magazine.

"Norway?" I ask curiously. "Well…I don't really have an opinion," I tell him. "I've never given it much thought, I guess. What do you mean exactly?"

He glances over at me. "Oh, I just mean if you've ever been, or have you ever thought of going there?"

"Nope, never been. And I can't say I've ever thought about going, either."

Luke flips a page of the magazine and then rests his hand on the text.

"I'm going there in a month," he says. "I guess you can call it a vacation."

Crossing my arms over the top of my purse, I adjust my back against the seat so that I'm sitting at an angle, facing him somewhat.

"I thought since you do so much traveling for your job," he goes on, "you might've visited Norway—could've given me some first-hand insight."

"Nah," I say. "I've never traveled outside of the United States. Jamaica was going to be my first really big trip."

He smiles and closes the magazine on his lap. "Well, I'm glad you decided to hang out with me instead."

"Me too."

Silence ensues.

"Why Norway? Though I admit, it'd be awesome to see the fjords."

Luke shrugs and glances at the magazine cover briefly, then back over at me. "It's just a place I've been planning to go for a couple of years with my brother and our friends. Part of a multi-stop trip. China, then Norway, then Switzerland..." He stops and gazes out ahead of him. A sort of sadness rests in his pensive features. "...well, I didn't make the China trip, but I...well, I just had too much work to do and it wasn't a good time to be taking a vacation."

He rests his back against the seat and crosses his arms over his stomach. I can't put my finger on it, but it I get the feeling there's far more to his story than what he's letting on.

I rest against my seat, too, and decide to change the subject, only because it seems like the thing to do.

"So does your brother—Landon is his name, right?—does he live with you on Kauai?" That might explain why I have yet to meet him.

A knot moves down the center of Luke's throat, and for a moment he doesn't answer. Then finally his head falls to the side and he says with a gentle expression, "Nah, Landon went to China as planned and never came back." He laughs bitterly and his smile lengthens. "I guess he liked it too much."

The smile fades as his head moves to face forward again, where he stares off in front of him and says no more. I get the feeling he's not OK with his brother's choices; that shifty smile and the dark undertone of his voice bled sarcasm.

"I bet you miss him."

He looks over, quiet and mysterious at first, as if contemplating, and then his eyes soften on me, and his mouth begins to turn up again. "Yeah, I do, but I'd say right now you're giving him some real competition."

My heartbeat quickens; I press my lips together to keep from smiling.

I have dozens of questions about Luke and his brother, Kendra and his other friends, and about the trip to China they were all supposed to take together, but this seems like sensitive territory to me even though he's the one who brought it up.

Reluctantly I ask, "Well, do you still talk to him?"

He hesitates and then nods, but doesn't look at me. "Yeah, every now and then."

He says nothing more on the issue. And neither do I.

If Luke wanted me to know more he'd tell me. So I decide to leave the questions alone and stick with my hunches: There's some bad blood between Luke and his brother; of this I'm pretty sure. And since Kendra used to be his brother's girlfriend, there's definitely something more to the story regarding her and Luke, or maybe Seth.

As if time went by quickly as a favor to me, the next thing I know the plane is preparing to land, and the flight, which was supposed to traumatize me and make me never want to travel by air again, is about to end.

"That wasn't so bad, was it?" Luke asks, a knowing grin manipulating his delicious mouth.

And it suddenly dawns on me, all that random talk about Norway that came out of nowhere was his way of helping calm my nerves and making me forget that I was on a plane at all. I never would've thought that simple conversation could achieve such a feat—and in the past, it never worked—but here I am, thirty minutes later, watching out the window with just an infinitesimal amount of lingering fear, as the plane lands.

"I don't know how that happened," I say as we're heading toward a long-term parking lot to find his car. "Actually, I'm kind of baffled."

He looks over, tugging on my hand as we continue weaving our way through parked cars.

"I've tried everything," I go on. "Therapy, medication, trying to trick my brain into not being afraid, but nothing ever came close to making me feel as relaxed as I did just now." I laugh. "Paige *hates* flying with me, says I'm a crazy person. And my mom, she flew with me once on a job just for support so I wouldn't be alone, but with her there, I think it was worse. All I wanted to do was curl up beside her until the plane landed." I squeeze his hand and playfully add, "Maybe you should start up a business; fly around with people who have a fear of flying."

He laughs, and I hear his car beep twice somewhere to my right as he presses the button on his key chain.

"You were more relaxed," he says, "because I wasn't paid to tell you not to be afraid. I'm not your best friend, who, despite being your best friend, thinks you're just being a crazy person. And I'm not your mom, who's probably the first person you want to cling to when you're afraid because she's your mom. No matter how old we get, when we get scared, we can become ten years old again just like that"—he snaps his fingers—"when Mama walks through the door." We approach his car, a shiny blue Hyundai. "I dunno," he goes on. "I think a lot of people who have debilitating fears need more than a therapist telling them why they're afraid, a friend telling them not to be afraid, and a family member telling them that it's OK to be afraid." He opens the passenger door for me. "You need someone who understands the fear, who makes it their priority to help you overcome it because they genuinely want to and not just for a paycheck, and someone who approaches it in a way that comes from the heart instead of a list of stereotypical responses."

I smile warmly. "So I guess you're that person, huh?"

He smiles back at me and we just gaze at each other for a moment.

I take him into a gentle hug. It surprises him a little, but he pauses only a second before wrapping his arms around me.

"Yeah," he answers in a soft voice. He nods, his eyes glowing. "I think maybe I am that person. If you want me to be."

My insides are mush.

"I can't think of anyone else I'd rather," I say with a thankful smile and then get into the car.

"And a gentleman, too," I add, adjusting on the seat. "You're full of surprises."

He waits until I'm fully seated, propping one muscled arm along the top of the door, the other on the roof, and then peers in at me and says, "Hey, I'm just a guy who happens to be starving. How about some lunch?"

I beam up at him wordlessly. His tall, tanned height dressed in khakis and a blue button-up shirt, adoring me with a gorgeous crooked smile as persuasive as it is mysterious.

Luke Everett is dangerous.

He's more dangerous than flying in a plane or jumping from a cliff into water or from a bridge attached by a giant rubber band or getting lost in the forest. Everything about him screams *change* and *the unknown* and *if you let him in, your meticulously planned life will never be the same again.*

But still I refuse to run away and I feel my legs running toward him faster, the muscles in my thighs hurting intensely with the kind of pain that a runner welcomes every day after that last lap. My heart is banging against my rib cage, my lungs gasping for air. But I can't stop. I refuse to stop. I'm determined to see what's at the finish line.

SIXTEEN

Sienna

*I*t's raining by the time we get to a small strip of tiny shops and a farmers' market. It was like the sky just opened up and dumped buckets of rain on the streets, so heavy I can't see ten feet in front of the windshield.

"How can you see where you're driving?" I shout over the raucous pounding on the roof of the car. Both of my hands are fixed to the edges of my seat, and my head is pressed against the headrest.

"I can't!" he says, and I swallow a lump. "I just remember where the roads curve and whatnot!"

"You better be lying!" I tell him, gripping the seat tighter. "The roads may not move, but I highly doubt the people and other cars on them stay in the same places, y'know!"

He laughs and turns right at a stop sign and pulls into a small nook that I'm not even sure is an actual parking space, and then shuts off the engine.

"Don't worry about it! I could see just fine!" Before he even finishes the sentence, the rain just...stops, leaving his voice booming through the small, confined space inside the car. We both look at each other for a stunned second, and then laugh. God, he's beautiful when he laughs.

We get out of the car and start to stroll down the wet street, stopping at a few places along the way as I break out my camera and get a few interesting shots of locals in their everyday life with tourists.

By the time we sit down to eat outside at a little restaurant, the clouds have moved off and the sun is shining again. The blacktop glistens with leftover moisture. I hear a constant dripping to my left, where water steadily falls from a roof into a little puddle. Voices hum all around, and there are sounds of the shuffling of shoes and the snapping of rubber against bare heels and the rolling of tiny wheels on baby strollers.

"Other than the obvious," I say across from Luke at a small round table, "why did you move to Hawaii?" I take another bite of my food.

Luke swallows a mouthful down and then drags a napkin across his mouth.

"Seth would be to blame for that," he says with a smirk. "I met him years ago when I came here on vacation. Been best friends ever since." He takes another bite, holding his head over his plate in case any of it misses his mouth.

"Is he from here?" I take a quick sip of my soda.

Luke nods with food in his mouth and then he swallows. "Yeah, Seth is a local, like Alicia and Braedon."

I pause, taking another sip, reluctant to ask my next question, but decide to anyway.

"Not to be nosy," I speak up, trying not to be obvious as well, "but does Kendra also live with you and Seth?" God, I hope not.

He shakes his head rapidly. "Definitely not," he says, and I quietly breathe a sigh of relief. "She used to when she and Landon were together, but after China..." He pauses briefly, almost inconspicuously, but I still make note of it. "She got a place of her own with a friend not far from Seth's and my house." He laughs under his breath. "She's a good friend, but I lived with her long enough when she was with Landon. Too long. She drives me nuts sometimes. We get along a lot better now that we're not under the same roof."

Well, that's a relief.

I take another bite, but offer no comment.

After lunch, Luke takes me to some other places around town, where I buy a few small souvenirs for my parents, which I tuck away inside my big purse. But it's when I notice that I'm literally the only girl walking around this place in a long dress that I regret not having packed a pair of shorts and a top, and I decide to buy a new outfit.

"There's nothing wrong with your dress," Luke tries to convince me. "It's a summery dress—not like you just left church in it, or anything." He grins, looking me over once. "And besides, it's sexy on you."

I blush hard—all that's missing are my shoulders drawn up around my cheeks.

"Well, thank you," I say all fancy-like, stepping past Luke holding the door open for me and into a shop that sells all things cute and touristy. "But I'll feel less out of place if I'm in shorts and flip-flops like everybody else."

The glass door closes behind Luke, the jingling of a bell fixed to the top, sounding around us. There are surfboards and surf-this and surf-that just about everywhere in this tiny place. Surfboards are mounted on the walls and hanging from the ceiling. Surf accessories are placed here and there, leaving little room for the more normal summertime stuff, which is what I need. Migrating to a small T-shirt rack, I sift through them in search of my size.

"How about this?" I hear Luke say from behind.

An ugly button-up Hawaiian shirt with a loud flowered print dangles from a hanger on the end of his finger.

I wrinkle my nose at him. "Seriously?" Then I lean in closer and whisper, "I think that's for old men."

Luke laughs under his breath—because he totally knew that—and places the hanger back on the metal rack behind him.

"Tryin' to make me look like a tourist?" I accuse in jest and go back to sifting through the shirts on a more fashionable rack. "Might as well find me a muumuu and drape a lei around my neck, too."

He points and says, "I think the muumuus are on the back wall, but I, uh, wouldn't go that far." He almost looks scared.

Shaking my head and trying not to laugh, I quickly find a suitable outfit: a simple white scoop-neck tee, a pair of light pink shorts with two white stripes down the sides, and a pair of white flip-flops—Paige would not be proud. Five-minute shopping, to Paige, is reserved for things like a quick run into the drugstore for a box of tampons.

Luke breaks out his wallet when we step up to the register.

"No, I don't think so," I protest sassily and reach inside my purse, but before I can fish my wallet out from underneath my camera, he slaps a credit card down on the counter.

I lean toward him and hiss low under my breath, "Luke, seriously, I can pay for my own stuff."

"Yeah, so what," he says in a normal tone, not caring that the cashier can hear us, "and so can I. As your host here on the best vacation you'll ever take, I'm paying from here on out. I talked you into staying; it's the least I can do."

The cashier hesitates, looking between us, and then reluctantly slides his credit card from the counter and goes to run it through the little device attached to the side of her computer screen.

I just look back at him, baffled.

"You won't win this argument," he says, "so just save your breath." He smiles charmingly with teeth, and I don't know whether to play-pop him on the arm and tell the girl *not* to use his card, or smile at him in return and let him have his way. But I get the feeling he'll have his way no matter what, so I don't argue with him.

The bell on the door jingles again as we make our way back outside into the sunshine. Walking side by side down the length of the sidewalk, I glance over at him and say, "Maybe I'll just find a bunch of really expensive stuff then. Make you pay for that, if you wanna play that game."

He grins, looking over at me briefly.

"Like what?" he asks.

I shrug. "I have a professional shopper and fashion guru for a best friend, just so you know"—I nod heavily once, one eyebrow arced in a dramatic fashion—"and she taught me everything I know about shopping and fashion."

"Oh, she did, did she?" Luke's grin seems to deepen; I halfway expect something clever to come out of his mouth any second now, but it's like he's biding his sweet time.

I cross my arms. "Yeah, she did. I didn't really have much of a sense of style before Paige got ahold of me. And by the time she was done, I fit right in on Rodeo Drive with the best of 'em."

He purses his lips. "Wow, that's really interesting," he says smartly. "But y'know, I gotta be honest; I think your best friend is probably better at it than you."

Shocked, I stop on the sidewalk, turning to look right at him, not knowing how to take what he just said, but knowing that it stung.

"What's that supposed to mean?"

Luke smiles softly, tilting his head to one side.

"I guess that came out wrong," he says. "I just mean that you don't seem wasteful."

Still unsure, but feeling a little better, I just look at him, waiting for him to go on, and we both begin walking down the sidewalk again very slowly.

"I used to buy stuff like that," he says, and now I'm even more confused. And intrigued. "For about two years I blew every dime I earned on clothes and cars and you name it"—he looks over—"but now I'm back to being me. And I prefer me."

Wait...cars, plural?

"Wow," I speak up. "Do tell."

Unlike the enigmatic topic of Kendra and his brother, I don't feel at all hesitant to probe for answers this time—and I hope he doesn't keep them from me, either.

We make our way back to his car.

"Landon and I used to own a business," he says, opening my door. "It started out fairly small, like most businesses do, I guess." He closes my door and picks up where he left off after he hops in on the driver's side. "Truthfully, we never expected anything to come from it. Made a few bucks here and there online—wasn't enough to put gas to last two weeks in the car we shared." He laughs and starts the engine. "But then the sales picked up, the money started rolling in, and next thing I knew, we each had a million in the bank."

Silence. From me anyway—I can't seem to figure out what to say, much less get my mouth moving again to say it.

As soon as we leave the makeshift parking space, the sky opens up again as if the sun had never shone.

Finally I manage to say, "You made a million dollars?"

Luke keeps his eyes on the road, driving slowly through the downpour.

"By the time it was all over," he goes on casually, "we had to split millions three ways—me, Landon, and, of course, Uncle Sam." He laughs out loud, his voice filling the car with bitterness and irony. "Uncle Sam is a greedy, thieving bastard—everybody knows that—but I didn't know just how much until I was out of the poorhouse and had to write seven-figure checks to him. But don't get me started on government and politics or the IRS—they're my least favorite topics."

Millions? I must've heard that wrong. No, I'm pretty sure he said millions. I am so completely surprised, it takes me a moment to get my next question out.

"W-what...well, what kind of business did you have?"

He looks over. "Well, it started out with apps," he says and then begins to reminisce. "I think Landon was born with a chip in his head—a technological genius, my brother." He smiles distantly. "We played a lot of video games when we were younger, obsessed, like any kid, spending hours upon hours every day in front of the television until our parents thought it was time we started doing more things outdoors." He glances over briefly. "So enter that camping trip I told you about—anyway, later, when my parents finally let us on the Internet, our game obsession intensified when we discovered our first online multiplayer role-playing game. We felt like *gods*." He laughs out loud again, demonstrating how ridiculous he thinks all of that was, and then turns left onto another road, the car now zipping through the rain instead of crawling through it. "Eventually, Landon—being more into the creation process than the game playing itself, like I was—abandoned the games and started creating his own. I thought he was crazy, and in a sense he probably was, but before he turned eighteen and graduated, he was offered a full ride to two different colleges and eventually a job at one of the most successful gaming companies in the country."

"Wow, that's huge."

"Yeah, he thought so too, until after the first year, and he dropped out of college and never took the job."

We turn onto another blacktop road and the rain is beginning to die down to a drizzle.

"Landon hated being…suffocated," Luke says sketchily. "I was surprised he even graduated high school. He *hated* school. He hated working in the same place for too long." Luke shakes his head and flips on his blinker. "He just didn't like being tied down to anything—with the exception of Kendra, of course, and a couple of girls before her." He laughs. "No, Landon enjoyed being tied down when it came to women, but that's another story. A really boring one."

Luke is different when he talks about his brother—he seems really proud, but despondent and even bitter at times. I feel like he's holding something back, and I'm still not sure yet if it's OK for me to probe.

Ultimately I leave it alone. I don't want to risk making too much of his business mine.

Finally we pull onto a concrete driveway shrouded by trees and bushes on either side, creating a canopy of lush green over it like an arch. A little blue house sits off in the distance amid more trees and bushes, and just beyond it, down a sloping, grassy hill, I can see the beach and then the ocean. Luke shuts the engine off and leaves the keys in the ignition. He looks over at me. "But to answer your question," he says, "we owned a business called Trivium Studios. A few failed smartphone apps eventually led to one successful one, which led to our own online multiplayer game, which led to a few other things, which put a lot of useless money in our accounts and eventually drove a wedge between my brother and me." He smiles faintly, maybe to bring the light back into what had briefly become darkness, and then he opens the door, the smell of rain filling my senses. "But that's also a boring topic," he says, and I get the feeling that boredom has nothing to do with why he doesn't want to talk about it anymore. "And you're not here for that." His smile turns into a grin.

"Now, I haven't had a chance to clean," he says, unlocking the front door. "Oh, and for the record, I don't have roaches like the nasty ones over on the mainland, but Hawaii is notorious for these large, freakish cockroaches and you might see one from time to time. Oh and centipedes. Just a warning."

I know I must look pale all of a sudden—maybe he's just screwing with my head. Or exaggerating.

God, I hope so.

He grins and says with a gesture of his hand, "Let's get inside before it starts raining again."

SEVENTEEN

Sienna

*L*uke's place isn't at all what I imagined on the ride over here, at least not since he told me about the money he and his brother made. When I step through the front door, I'm surprised to be standing in something kinda small with dingy white walls that need a serious paint job and a ceiling pockmarked by discoloration from water damage. The linoleum floor is old and beyond repair and the only thing that could do it justice would be to rip it all up and replace it entirely. But it's only cosmetic, I see right away, as the house overall is livable and quaint in a bachelor pad sort of way.

Before I step farther in I take my sandals off at the door.

"Nah, you don't have to do that," he says, but I do anyway. "This isn't exactly a palace, as you can see."

I can also see a hint of slight nervousness hidden behind his eyes and that innocent smile of his, as though he's quietly worried about what I might think of him now that I'm seeing his house. I don't really know what to say. I want to say, *If you had that much money, why didn't you buy something bigger and more updated?*

Because that would be an obvious first question. But I don't want to offend him. So I say nothing at all and continue to act as though I'm not bothered by it. Because, in truth, I'm really *not* bothered by it—I lived in a tiny two-bedroom trailer in a mobile home park for a long time growing up and I'm no stranger to the less extravagant things in life. In fact, I'm more familiar with it than any other lifestyle.

Luke leads me into his living room and his nervousness only seems to grow. Maybe it's because I haven't said anything at all.

"I thought you said you didn't have time to clean?" I finally think of something. My gaze sweeps the area lit only by the gloomy outside light filtering in through the open windows on the far side of the room. I sniff the air. "And it smells like some kind of lemon disinfectant, so somebody's been cleaning." I grin at him, and his expression falls under a shroud of blushing guilt.

He did clean this house, that's a definite, and now all I can envision is Luke running around with a mop and a broom, cleaning the way I think most guys do, by sweeping everything out the front door and stuffing dirty clothes in various hiding places all confused and panicky-like. And the visual is hilarious.

"So you're one of those," I accuse in jest.

"One of what?"

"When you know your house is clean, but a guest comes in and you wave your hand about the room"—I wave my hand to demonstrate—"and then say, 'Please excuse the mess.'" I roll my eyes for dramatic effect.

Luke smiles and shakes his head. "OK, you got me. I did clean a little last night."

"Where'd you sweep the dirt?" I ask.

He points behind me. "Out the front door, of course."

I laugh. "And I bet your dirty clothes are stuffed under a chair somewhere."

"Nah," he says. "I'm super-organized when it comes to laundry."

That takes me by surprise—now I'm visualizing him folding laundry in a precise manner, turning his washcloths into perfect little squares and rolling his boxers up like fancy dinner napkins, and this too is hilarious. And adorable.

Luke gestures toward his very gently used navy sofa. He still appears a little nervous, but he's shedding it quickly.

"Sit down wherever you want."

I take a seat on the center cushion without any hesitation. With a smile, I look around some more. Up at the ceiling and then the walls and then the large flat-screen television mounted across the room from me, surrounded by a small entertainment center with two speakers on either side, and a stereo, movie player, and satellite box underneath, sitting atop an oak stand. Two framed posters stare back at me from different walls, one of the biggest moss- and grass-covered cliffs I think I've ever seen surrounded by a yellow-orange mist and a mountain backdrop. Two figures sit atop the cliff looking out at the world. The other poster is of a guy in some kind of sports gear that I can't recall having ever seen before. It looks like an oversized ad of sorts.

The entire space is airy with all of the windows open and the breeze pushing through the screens. I see that just beyond the open kitchen area there's a screen door that opens out onto a lanai, which overlooks the beach a few yards away. The house might need a lot of repairs, but being that close to the ocean more than makes up for it.

"I've got beer, water, and V8 juice," Luke calls out from the kitchen. "The V8 is Seth's, but if you like that kind of stuff you're welcome to it."

I shudder at the thought of drinking a bunch of vegetables. "Water is good."

He comes in carrying two bottles of water and hands me one. "So I know you're probably wondering about the house," he says, sitting down next to me on the sofa.

"No...not really," I lie and take a sip just to fend off the awkwardness.

Luke grins, takes a drink from his water, and sets the bottle on the coffee table stained by years of wet-bottomed glasses. "So you're one of those," he says, getting me back for earlier.

"One of what?"

"Itching to ask certain questions, but afraid to offend."

I shrug and take another sip.

"Hey, you can't offend me," he says. "Go on. Ask."

My eyes stray toward the bottle in my hands, until finally I work up the courage.

"Well, not that there's anything wrong with your house"—I lock eyes with him to point out how much I mean that—"but if I had millions I might've gone a different way." I take another nervous sip, not feeling very good about how that came out, after all.

"I did in the beginning," he says. "Owned a big house about an hour from here, but later sold it." He pats the sofa arm with the palm of his hand. "This place feels much more like home than the other one did. You don't like it?"

I shake my head rapidly. "No, that's not it at all," I say. "I actually like this house. It's adorable."

He laughs gently.

Then he stands up and takes my hand.

"Let me show you the rest of the place," he says, and I follow.

It doesn't take long to see the other rooms: the kitchen, the bathroom, and then a quick peek into his room, but he doesn't offer for me to go inside, probably because he doesn't want me to get the wrong idea. And instead of letting me see inside Seth's room across the hall from his, he points at the door and tells me whose it is.

The last room he shows me is the biggest room of the three, covered in his paintings from ceiling to floor on every wall and stacked against them on top of one another in disarray, all different sizes and landscapes that each take my breath away. Paint is all over the floor and the walls and even on the ceiling. A few different size easels are folded and propped against the closet door, one easel with a painting half-finished sits in the center of the room. It's easily the messiest room in the house, but also the most inspiring and certainly the most beautiful.

"Luke . . . I just can't get over what you can do to a canvas. These are"—I reach out as if the painting is a magnet to my fingertips and I want so badly to touch it, but I stop just short—"so lifelike."

He steps over a large piece of fabric sheeting covered in paint that lies across one section of floor and bends down behind a box underneath a window.

A laptop hangs from his hand when it emerges. He opens it and walks over to me.

"I showed you mine; now you get to show me yours," he says, wriggling his brows.

I know right away he's referring to my photography website, which I told him about back at the community center.

Luke sits down in the center of the floor Indian-style, placing the laptop on his lap. I look at the floor and then at my dress, white and bound to show every little speck of paint that might get on it no matter how dry—he realizes right away.

"Oh, I'm sorry," he says and starts to get up. "I'm used to just coming in here and sitting wherever. I didn't even think about your dress."

I stop him before he gets up by sitting down with him, my legs bent beneath me. A light beaming in from two horizontally elongated windows washes over the space. I don't care about my dress. It's just a piece of fabric. Luke's face softens and something passes over his eyes that I can't make out, but it makes my heart race.

Reaching out for the laptop, I take it from him and prop it on my own lap. The Internet speed isn't all that great here so it takes a few minutes to bring up my site and for the thumbnails to load, but once everything is there, I turn it at an angle so Luke can see. He scoots over closer to me, his side touching mine, and peers down into the screen. I feel breathless to have him next to me. My palms begin to feel moist and my pulse quickens.

I can't remember the last time I felt so eager to share my photography with someone other than my mom or Paige. It's very personal to me; I may display it on my website for all to see, but this is different. Meaningful. And with Luke, already it feels so natural.

Luke looks at every last photograph on my site, enlarging each one to get a closer look at the details.

"And you say *I* have a gift," he tells me and I smile in thanks. "You definitely have an eye for a good shot, that's for sure. Who is this woman? She's in several photos."

"That's my mom." I point to a close-up of her sitting near the kitchen window waiting for my dad to come home. A shadow is cast across her face by the window blinds, creating a dozen dark lines over her skin. "Dad used to work as a truck driver. For about three years, I think. I was fifteen when I took this one." I pause, thinking back on the moment. "I just thought it was so out of character for my parents—Mom in this case—to miss Dad and to show it like this. I don't think she even knew I was aware, or that I even took this photo. But Dad was gone a lot on the road and Mom would always sit in front of that window when she knew he was on his way home and she'd watch for him." I smile to myself, thinking about it. "And for about three days, before Dad had to leave again, my parents were the happiest people."

"They weren't always happy?" he asks.

I look away from the screen and glance over at him with a forced smile; his expression—the intensity of his hazel eyes, his unwavering focus—is filled with interest.

"Whose parents ever are these days?" I laugh lightly.

He shrugs, smiles faintly.

"Did they fight a lot?"

"No, it was nothing like that," I say. "They just never had much time for themselves. They each worked two jobs when I was growing up. Sometimes my aunt would babysit me until I was old enough to stay at home by myself. I didn't see my parents as much as they didn't see each other."

Luke is quiet for a long moment, a little longer than what I feel is normal.

"Well, believe it or not," he finally says, "I can relate to that one hundred percent."

"Really? How so?"

Luke uncrosses his legs and draws his knees up, balancing the weight of his body on his backside, his right hand clasping his left wrist as he wraps his arms about his knees. The muscles in his arms harden like rocks beneath his tanned skin.

"Same story as yours pretty much," he says. "But we were considered poor."

"So were we," I say. "I lived in a trailer park for a long time before my parents were able to get a loan for a house—nothing wrong with trailer parks unless it was *that* particular one. And welfare wouldn't help us because my dad made sixteen dollars more a month than what was allowed to qualify—just *sixteen dollars*. It was really hard. We didn't starve or go without utilities that I can ever remember, but we didn't see each other much."

Luke nods, thinking deeply, it appears.

"Same here. We mostly lived in one-bedroom apartments. Landon and I slept in the living room. Mom was a waitress usually, or sometimes she worked as a cashier in a gas station. My dad was an underpaid mechanic for most of his life until he lost his job to someone fifteen years younger and who'd work for less money. So then my dad joined the wonderful and fulfilling career of cleaning toilets and mopping floors at a junior high school."

"Oh joy," I say with sarcasm that matches his.

I start to add to his sarcasm, but I'm stopped in my tracks with his next set of words.

"But not having much money is not such a bad thing. Having been on both sides of the fence, I can without a doubt say that I'd choose no money over no passion or family any day of the week."

Taken aback by his admission, I absently set the laptop on the floor and look at him with inquiry.

I agree with most of his views, but I just don't want to struggle. I've seen it and lived it all my life and I can't see not striving for something better.

"What's wrong with having both?" I ask.

Luke shakes his head, his jaw tightening as he stares off at nothing.

"Some people can pull that off," he says, "but I'm not one of them, and I don't think there are really that many people who can. It's true what they say—money really does change a person."

"Is that why you called it 'useless money'?" I point out, and when he doesn't recall right away, I explain further. "Back in the car, when you were telling me about the business. You said there was a lot of useless money in yours and Landon's accounts. Why was it useless?"

He seems surprised I caught that, much less that I remembered such a small and seemingly insignificant detail. "Because it was a trade," he begins. "One that I had no idea was a trade, or what I was trading for. Otherwise I would've dropped my millions like a bad habit and never looked back."

"What was the trade?" I ask with soft caution.

He pauses. "Everything," he answers, and suddenly becomes distant, staring toward the window, lost in his thoughts. "Absolutely everything."

Silence passes between us for what feels like forever, until Luke snaps back into the moment, smiles hugely, and jumps to his feet. He leans over and grabs my hand, pulling me up with him. Next thing I know, I can feel the heat from his body pressed to mine and he's looking into my eyes so closely that I can feel the warmth of his minty breath on my lips. I want him to kiss me. I even find myself beginning to lean in to it, my eyelids getting heavy, but I'm also snapped back into the moment when he starts to walk with me to the door instead, and we leave the room and all of the paintings behind.

"Why don't you change?" he suggests, pointing to the bag on the coffee table with my new clothes and white flip-flops. "Let's go for a walk."

While we were sitting together out on the beach, just before dark, Luke told me more about the money and the trade, elaborating a little on the wedge he mentioned that it drove between him and his brother. "I wanted to keep the money coming," he had said. "But Landon, he wanted to give it all up. Literally *give it up*. I thought he was insane. Who does that? Who is poor all their life, then one day hits the jackpot and never has to worry about money again, but then wants to give it away?"

I just sat there beside him on the sand, yards from his house and listened, feeling the intensity in every word as if he thought Landon were sitting there beside us.

But as always, he seemed to tiptoe around any topic having to do with Landon. He has so much to say, so much to get off his chest, and I feel like he's trying the only way he knows how to take that step, to reach out to someone, but he can't bring himself to do it.

Maybe he needs a nudge.

"Luke?" I ask, now sitting on the lanai at a little round table.

He looks over at me from the other side, the moonlight casting a shadow on his face. He smiles.

"Yeah?"

I hesitate, trying to make sure in my mind that it's OK to open this door to him, and that I'm not making our inevitable separation more difficult by becoming the shoulder I sense he desperately needs.

"What's really bothering you?" I ask softly, trying to be comforting; it hurts my heart to see *his* hurting. "I'm here for you if you need someone to talk to."

Luke's chin draws back, his smiling eyes eclipsed by hardening eyebrows. "Nothing's bothering me, Sienna," he says, and although it sounds entirely believable, I don't believe it.

He pats the table with the palm of his hand and a long, drawn-out sigh bursts through his lips.

"Damn, I am such a clueless dick sometimes," he says. "Seriously, I didn't mean to give you any crybaby vibes."

"No, *no*," I say, shaking my hand at him, palm forward, "you haven't." I follow that comment up with laughter, an instinctive reaction to combat what my question seems to have caused.

And it doesn't go unnoticed to me that I failed miserably at my attempt to open him up on the issue.

Luke laughs out loud, tossing his head back, and then he looks right at me. "See what you've done to me?" He points at me with a crooked index finger. "This is your fault."

My mouth falls open and my eyes get big.

"How is it my fault?!"

His laughter fills the night air.

"You borrowed my balls and never gave them back."

Now I'm the one rolling with laughter.

Luke points to the back screen door. "Go in there. Right now. And get them before I start my menstrual cycle."

I cackle, throwing my neck back over the chair.

"Hurry up!" he shouts and it just makes me laugh harder.

Finally I manage to drop my bare feet onto the wood floor of the lanai and rush into the house, the screen door slapping against my heels on the way in, and I pretend to grab his balls from my purse. And when I run back outside I present them to him in one hand. He doesn't seem to approve, cocking an eyebrow up at me from his chair beside the table. He looks at my hand and then up at me, down at my hand again, up at me again. Realizing, I roll my eyes and bring my other hand up so that it looks like it takes both to hold them, and slowly his grin begins to lengthen.

"Y'know," I say, "this is the stupidest thing I've ever experienced with anyone in my life." I'm trying so hard not to laugh, but the huge smile on my face gives everything away.

He goes through the motions of taking his balls back and then, to my surprise, fits his hands about my waist and pulls me onto his lap. I become breathless. My nerve endings stir and race, sending a tingling sensation like a wave through my limbs. He leans forward and grazes the side of my neck with his lips. My heart thrums behind my rib cage; my mouth feels dry, my lungs empty, my heart full.

"Stupid, maybe," he says and presses his lips against my neck, "but it feels right."

I turn a little on his lap so I can see his eyes and he looks deeply into mine, one of his hands fixed against my thigh, the other fitted at my waist just above my hip.

"I'm glad you decided to stay," he whispers, his eyes lingering on my lips for an intense moment before finding my eyes again.

"So am I," I whisper back.

Luke's lips part mine slowly, and it feels like my whole body sighs as his mouth searches mine, carefully, yet with passion and intent. The heat of his warm tongue tangles around mine, making my insides tremble and shiver. I feel like I'm going to come apart in his arms, lose complete control of my muscles and become mush on his lap. I inhale his breath, feeling like I need it as much as I need my own, and my hands somehow find their way to his neck, where I probe the muscles under my fingertips. Luke kisses me hungrily, one hand fitted underneath my throat, the other holding tighter onto my waist; I can feel the tips of his strong fingers pressing into my flesh, and his hardness beneath me, which practically sends me over the edge with need.

Gasping, I pull away, breaking the kiss, and just stare into his eyes. I can't let this happen.

I could sleep with him. I could take advantage of this vacation and everything it has to offer. There's nothing wrong with a brief sexual encounter every now and then as long as we stay safe about it. But that's not what this is. And Luke's not the kind of guy I could sleep with a time or two on vacation and then never see him again when it was all over.

Luke is different. I knew that from the moment I met him. And I've never been so confused about anything in my life.

"What are you thinking about?" he asks, smiling faintly up at me with a heat in his eyes I've never seen before.

His left hand squeezes my hip once.

I smile back at him. "Nothing," I lie again and lean down to touch my lips to his once more. "But I should probably be getting back to my hotel."

"Why don't you stay here?" he suggests, and then adds. "Y'know, while you're on vacation."

Surprised by how quickly and casually that came out—then again, I should be used to him doing that by now—I can't find an answer.

He pats my thigh. "You can sleep in my room and I'll take the couch. No expectations. I swear." He puts up both hands and his smile is bright and innocent, laced by mischief that I completely expected of him.

"I don't know," I begin. "I mean it'd be kind of weird, don't you think? You have a roommate. He might not think it's such a good idea." I know I'm grasping at straws here and that my excuses are lame, but it's all I've got.

Luke pats my thigh again and then lifts me carefully from his lap so he can stand up.

"Seth won't mind," he says. "Besides, it's my house, not his. And why would it be weird?" He laughs lightly.

I shrug coyly. "I dunno."

He takes my hand and walks with me into the house and through the kitchen.

"Think about how much money you'll save on the hotel alone," he says. "Two weeks in a beachside hotel in Hawaii of all places—what's that costing you, a few thousand dollars?"

I follow him down the hallway toward his bedroom while he continues to go on about all the reasons it would be better that I stay in his house while I'm here. And every single one of them is spot-on and I can find no argument. While I'm standing in his room, checking out his simple little bed with a simple nightstand and a chest of drawers and a clothes hamper pressed in one corner, Luke is stripping the sheets and pillowcases from his bed. He tosses them across the room with ease and hits the hamper almost perfectly.

"But what about when you have to go to work?"

Snapping a clean sheet open, he begins to make the bed, bending over to fit the corners around the mattress.

"I work at the surf school when I'm available, for the most part," he says as he gets on the bed and fits the sheet on the corner against the wall. "If Allan needs me one day, then we can head over and you can hang out on the beach for a few while I do my thing, if you want to. As far as Big Wave Surf Shop, Braedon won't mind picking up my slack for a while—we own the place together."

"Oh, really?" I ask, surprised.

He nods with a shrug. "Yeah, it's nothing like the business I owned with Landon, but I like things simple."

He begins to slide the first pillow of three down into a green case, wedging the pillow underneath his chin.

"So whadya say?"

"I guess that wouldn't be so bad." I'm still trying to convince myself that this is a good idea.

"Then it's settled," he says, and tosses the last pillow down. "You're my guest while you're in Hawaii and you might find your stay at," he waves his hand dramatically across the room, "the Everett House pleasant and relaxing, not to mention free—you'll have to give it a five-star rating on that alone." One side of his mouth tugs into a grin.

I try to hold in my own grin, but I don't do so well.

"Well, how's the service around here?" I joke, crossing my arms and popping my hip. "Will there be a complimentary breakfast waiting for me when I get up?"

He straightens his back, raises his chin importantly, and says sophisticatedly, "Oh, absolutely. I'm quite the cook, too, I should warn you in advance."

"Really?" I smirk playfully. "Why do I need to be warned?"

He smiles with confidence. "Because once you eat one of my dishes, you'll never want to leave."

I kind of already never want to leave . . .

"So what'll it be?" he says. "A hotel crammed full of tourists, a bagel and a tiny carton of orange juice as a complimentary breakfast, and six months' worth of rent just to pay for the hotel? Or a free room steps away from a quiet beach owned by a guy who can make a tire taste good, and not to mention"—his grin deepens and he sweeps his hands from his chest downward—"who looks like this?"

I burst out laughing.

Luke is trying not to, but like me, he doesn't do so well.

I think on it a little longer, looking at the nicely made bed and, yes, the guy standing in front of me who is as sweet as he is gorgeous.

"All right." I finally give in, and his face lights up. "I'll stay here—but no funny stuff!"

He surrenders again, his smile the broadest I've seen it in hours.

"Nope. I'm a total gentleman." The smirk that follows sends a tickling sensation up the back of my neck.

We share a quiet and serious moment together, Luke looking across the room at me now that I've found my way to his bed, sitting down on the edge with my feet barely touching the floor. Slowly he walks over and crouches down in front of me. He looks up into my eyes, and I feel like I'm falling deeper and deeper into them the longer he's there. His lips are wordless, yet an unmistakable array of words flutter within his eyes. Words that I wish more than anything I could hear and understand so that I can once and for all unravel the mystery that is Luke Everett.

He reaches up a hand and touches the side of my face lightly with his fingertips. It's such an intimate gesture that it confuses me slightly, but I want it there and I can't bring myself to do or say anything that would make him pull away.

"Thank you for staying," he says softly and then his hand slowly falls away.

"Thank you for letting me stay."

Luke smiles and pushes himself to his feet.

"I'm going to take a shower," he says. "Do whatever you want. Eat and drink what you want. Watch TV. Play the stereo. Just make yourself at home."

He leaves me sitting on the edge of his bed with my thoughts as he disappears around the corner. I don't know why, but I don't want him to go and I fight my instinct to pull him back.

What is happening to me?

EIGHTEEN

Luke

I spend nearly an hour in the shower, letting the hot water beat down on my skin until it begins to run cool. I always do most of my thinking in the shower, and I always have things figured out by the time the water is cold. But not this time. I have more questions now than I did when I stepped in, and the only answers I have to any of them are the kind you can't be sure are the right ones, or just the ones you want to believe are.

I've never been this drawn to a woman before. I've never met a woman who I want to open myself up to in every way, and who I know—I *think* I know—deep down would accept everything about me no matter how deeply flawed. And I've never met anyone, *no one*, who has ever made me feel this...*content*, just hanging out and doing the simplest of things together. She makes me want to spill my guts, to get everything out in the open so she can make it all better. But I can't. And I can't let her. She tried. The attempt didn't go unnoticed, or fall on deaf ears, but it did fall on a bitter heart that isn't ready to heal and may never be ready. When I lost my brother, I lost a part of myself. Sienna...she scares the hell out of me, and despite that, I feel like I'm only growing closer to her instead of trying to push her away. I *should* push her away—for so many reasons—but I can't. I want to ignore my conscience and see where this goes. Already I feel like...I need her. Just being around her, she makes me forget. Sometimes that's what I want to do: forget. Sienna is the only person I've met since China turned my life upside down who makes me see light at the end of this long, dark tunnel I've been walking through for eight months, while hiding from everyone around me. So I don't have to talk about it. So I don't have to relive it.

It's going to be shitty when Sienna's vacation is over and she has to go back to San Diego. I don't want to think about it. I'd rather think about that kiss out on the lanai.

We stay up way past two a.m. watching movies in the living room until she passes out close to me on the sofa, her soft dark auburn hair like a wave tumbling over the arm of the sofa as her head lies pressed against it. Her perfect little feet with brightly painted toenails are pressed against my leg as she lies curled up with her legs on the cushion. I had hoped she'd fall asleep against me instead of the sofa arm, but close is better than nothing. And I had hoped that when I quietly got up and tried to fit my hands underneath her so I could lift her into my arms and carry her to my room she wouldn't wake up, but she did, and she stretched and yawned and walked herself in there after telling me good night in the sweetest half-asleep voice I think I've ever heard.

And for the first time in eight months, I lie in bed—or rather the couch—staring up at the ceiling with feelings of serenity and stillness, instead of chaos and that merciless, unrelenting feeling of guilt that has haunted me for two hundred forty-three days.

———

"Ahem," I hear somewhere above me as I lie in the realm of semi-wakefulness.

Something is pressing against my hip.

Lying on my back, I moan into the pillow suffocating my face and try to adjust it like I always do because unless it's close to cutting off my breath, it's uncomfortable and I can't sleep. With my arms wrapped tightly over the pillow, I draw it closer and then exhale, feeling the heat of my breath warm my whole face. And needing a toothbrush.

Something nudges my hip again.

"Hellooo," the voice says, and finally it dawns on me.

As I peel the pillow away from my face, my eyes barely open a slit at first as the bright sunlight has filled the living room. It's more than what I'm used to waking up to in my room with just a single window.

"It's almost noon," Sienna says, standing over me.

My eyes crack open a little more, slowly, until they adjust to the light. She's wearing the same white shirt and pink shorts she changed into yesterday, and the same beautiful smile and splash of freckles that I can't get enough of. Girls with freckles drive me crazy, but this girl, with freckles like a work of rare art, makes me mental.

I rub my eyes hard with the palms of my hands, my fingers curled rigidly into claws. *"Noon?"* I'm still not registering, but it's slowly coming to me.

"Yeah, I've been up since nine."

Awareness floods into me like a bolt of lightning. *"Nine?"* Why didn't you wake me up earlier?" I start to sit upright, but a pain shoots through my lower back and I stay put for a second longer.

I can't believe I slept this long, especially on this piece-of-shit sofa. And I don't recall waking up once in the middle of the night even to take a piss, much less to toss and turn, because a good night's sleep has been alien to me for a long time.

"You looked so comfortable," she says. I don't know how she came to that conclusion, but I go along with it. "But I figured if I didn't go ahead and wake you up now, you'd sleep all day. Not to mention," she goes on with a growing trace of sass, "you didn't make my complimentary breakfast and I'm going to have to take one star off when I rate this…establishment." She sits on the edge of the coffee table, facing me.

Shit! I can't believe I didn't get up to make her breakfast. Feeling like a loser, I shoot straight up into a sitting position and drop my legs over the side of the sofa. Grimacing, I reach behind with both hands and knead my lower back with my fingertips, but now the ache has spread upward all the way to my shoulders.

"Hey, I never said what *time* breakfast was around here," I counter with a crooked smile, and she narrows her eyes playfully. "This is Hawaii, remember? We're on an entirely different time scale than the Mainland, and I don't just mean that we're a few hours behind."

She cocks a brow. "So what are you going to do about breakfast, then?"

I try to hide my smile when I catch her checking me out.

I run my hands over the top of my disheveled hair and then raise them out to my sides and stretch until I hear my joints and spine pop and crackle. More pain shoots through my back, and although it's not unbearable and I know I could easily get off this couch and do front flips if I wanted to, I decide I'd rather play Sienna at her own game and use it to my advantage.

"Damn, my back is killing me," I say, grimacing and reaching behind me for my muscles again. "Sleeping on this sofa is brutal."

Sienna's face falls under a little veil of guilt and pity.

"Oh, I'm sorry," she says. "Is it bad?"

No.

"Yeah, it's pretty bad." I groan deeply for added affect. "I should've crashed in Seth's room—would have if I'd known he wasn't coming home last night." Truthfully, I'm not sure of that; Seth might be in his room and I just slept so well through the night that I didn't hear him when he came in, like I usually do.

"Now I feel bad," she says and stands up from the coffee table, her long, lightly tanned legs stretching for miles underneath the thin fabric of her cotton shorts—damn, she is sexy; the things I want to do to her right now. "I'm not really hungry anyway, so don't worry about breakfast. I was just messing with you."

"Nah, don't feel bad." I wave it away like it's nothing, while at the same time still kneading my back with the other hand. "I'm going to make you something...but you could help me out by walking on my back."

"Huh?" Her face scrunches into a cute, confused expression. "You want me to walk on your back?"

"Well, yeah," I say with a nod, suddenly realizing myself how just the thought of her touching me—with her feet, her hands, her lips; I don't even care which—makes my heart ache and my palms sweaty. "It'll work out the kinks."

She smiles ridiculously and shakes her head—I fight the urge to reach out and pull her down on my lap; the image of her bare thighs around my waist, my hands hugging the curvature of her ass...Breathe, Luke...just breathe.

"I'm not walking on your back." She sort of laughs the words out.

"Why not?" I cock my head to one side.

"Well, I think I'm a little too heavy to be walking on your back," she says as if I should already know this. "And because it's weird?" It was more a statement than a question, but something else she thinks I should already know, apparently.

God, she's so fucking cute.

I roll my eyes. "Don't tell me you're one of those girls who wears a size zero and thinks she's fat."

"No! I'm not one of those," she defends. "I just don't want to hurt you!"

I laugh without restraint.

"OK, well, you're not going to hurt me. I can promise you that." I get up from the couch—with pretend difficulty—and step around Sienna and the coffee table and then lie on my bare chest on the floor. "Come on. It'll really help me out a lot." One side of my face is pressed against the rug as I look up at her at an angle. She stands over me with her flimsy arms crossed—I grow even harder beneath my shorts.

"No, Luke." She laughs. "I'm not going to do it."

"Yeah you are," I say casually and wave my hand at her as if there's nothing to it. "The only way you can hurt me is if you jump up and down really, really hard. Now, get on."

"No."

"Please?"

She shakes her head repeatedly, her smile growing.

I break out the big guns.

"It's the least you can do for me letting you stay here for free and have my bed." I grin slightly, which I imagine looks strange with my cheek smashed against the floor.

"No!" She laughs out loud. "I'll sleep on the couch from now on if that's the case."

With me? I want to say—and almost do—but restrain myself.

"No you won't," I tell her sharply. "What kind of guy would I be if I made you sleep on the couch while I was all sprawled out on the comfy bed? Now, step on and start walkin'."

"You're crazy."

Absolutely, one hundred percent, no-going-back crazy for you—I admit it.

I scoff. "OK, then if you won't walk on it, sit down and use your hands instead. You can't hurt me like that for sure."

That seems to have shut her up for the moment. I smile up at her, searching her face for the meaning behind her expression, and come to the conclusion that she's a little embarrassed. That, too, I use to my advantage. Because aside from that whole gentleman thing, I'm an ass sometimes, and I happen to enjoy it.

"It's either walk on my back," I taunt her playfully, "or . . . sit on my ass with your naked thighs straddling my sides and rub with your bare hands, *allll ooover*, until you get the kinks out of all those sore muscles."

Her face would be beet-red if she didn't have a light tan.

I break into a smile, unable to contain it for long.

"All right, fine," she says and steps onto my back carefully. "But if I hurt you, you better tell me." I feel the other foot press into my muscles and my body melts as her weight presses against me and pushes me harder against the floor.

I want to keep up the whole screwing-with-her-head thing, making her laugh and blush and smile, but I'm finding that becoming almost impossible to do anymore. I'm intoxicated by the feel of her little warm feet kneading the muscles in my back, her delicate steps trying so hard to be careful; her small form brings out something primal and protective within me, and it takes everything in me not to roll over and grab her in my arms and kiss her breathless.

"Am I doing it right?" she asks, snapping me out of my thoughts.

"Ah, *yeah*, that feels *awesome*." I moan a little in between words, my eyes opening and closing as if a coaxing hand lies across my lids. "*Mmmm* . . . yeah, right there . . . ah, *yeah*."

"Stop that!" She chuckles, and I feel her weight shift as she tries to balance herself. "You sound like you're about to get off."

Babe, if you only knew . . .

My laugh is muffled and strained, followed by an *oomph!* as Sienna's weight continues to shift unsteadily.

She walks on my back for a few more minutes, losing her balance only a couple of times and causing me to suck in a quick breath and my eyes to bulge. But she could go ahead and hop up and down if she wanted and I'd still want her to stay right where she was.

After a while, when I feel like she's suffered enough, I let her off the hook.

"*Owww!*" I brace the palms of my hands against the floor.

Sienna jumps off immediately. "Did I hurt you?"

"Not with your weight," I say with a grimace, pushing down the grin trying to sneak up on my lips, "but your heels are kind of rough. Felt like sandpaper there for a second."

A burst of air pushes through her lips.

"Shut up!" She laughs and then I feel her toes prodding me

in the ribs. I pretend to be wounded. "My feet are *not* like sand-paper! Trust me, I spend enough time on them so they should be immaculate."

I roll over onto my back and grab one of her feet in both my hands before she can snatch it away. Then I pretend to inspect it, turning it this and that way with my fingers collapsed around the top and my thumbs pressing into the bottom, which is actually quite soft. She hops on one foot, trying not to fall over.

"OK, you're right." I give in and let go. "Must've been something else." I smile up at her.

Then, unable to hold myself back anymore, I bring her down on top of me so that her bare legs straddle my waist. Fitting my fingers at the back of her neck, I pull her gently toward me, touching my lips to the edges of her mouth, the little hollow below her nose, and finally her lips—I feel her warm, soft body melting into mine. I kiss her softly, winding my fingers in the back of her hair.

When she pulls away slowly, her eyes are still closed for a moment. And when they open, she just looks at me, I look at her, and I never imagined that so much could be said between two people without a single word.

Finally the moment shifts and she smiles brightly and jumps to her feet, poking me gently in the ribs with her toe again. I draw my legs up, bent at the knees with my feet flat on the floor to conceal the other part of me that is fully awake this morning, making sure that the shorts I slept in last night are loose in all the right places. But I'm pretty damn sure she felt just how hard I am when she was straddling my waist—must be mostly what that red in her face is all about.

I want more than anything to carry her into my room right now, lay her across my bed, and carefully strip off her clothes—it about killed me when she stood up and broke the moment—but then I realize how much more it makes me want her, not just physically, but in every way, and I find myself trading sexual frustration for patience, and her heart.

I never make her breakfast. She said she really wasn't hungry and that lunch was right around the corner. She let me off the hook this time, but I won't miss the opportunity again.

We set out soon after for Oahu first thing so Sienna can officially check out of the hotel and get her stuff from the room. And on the way over she sits by the window on the plane and looks out every now and then between our many conversations. There's never a dull moment between us. And barely a full minute will go by without one of us having something else to say, or needing to laugh, or me needing to pat her leg or hold her hand when I see that lingering fear of flying try to rear its ugly head again. She's not cured. It'll take more than a few flights to cure her, but she's already come a long way.

And she should be proud of herself. I was of myself when I made that first bungee jump with my brother. It was a powerful feeling—letting go of my fear—that left such a mark on my life that I feel compelled to help Sienna feel it as I did. I'll do whatever I can to help her as my brother helped me.

I want to take it a step further.

I know it's a long shot, but when we get back to Kauai later… I have an idea.

Sienna

The community center looks pretty much the same way it did yesterday, with the exception of a few more tables that have been set against one wall, and several more paintings placed on easels. It's practically a ghost town in here—the lights are dull, not bright like they were before, which tells me they're on dimmers; there's only a few people walking around, carrying trash bags and boxes, and it's so quiet. That is, until Alicia sees us and practically glides across the room to meet us.

"It's good to see you," she says, taking me into a hug. Then she waves her hand about the room, an anxiety-filled look on her olive-colored face. "As you can see, things aren't going so well." She looks right at Luke. "I think we're in over our heads."

"Ye of so little faith." Luke pokes fun at her. "Stop worrying so much; it's two months away"—he looks at me with bright eyes—"and I have a secret weapon."

My face falls under a blanket of heat.

"Ye of so much confidence," I joke. "Keep your expectations of me *that* high and you might be disappointed."

Luke pulls me against him with his arm hooked around my waist and he presses his lips against my temple. "I doubt you could pull off disappointing me," he says, and I melt a little more.

Alicia smiles softly at us, and I admit, it's nice to see a friend of his who's a girl look at us as if she *wants* us to be together, unlike someone else I know.

"So"—Alicia props her hands on her tiny hips and glances about the large room—"any suggestions?" Her long black hair is pulled into a tight ponytail at the back of her head; tiny turquoise teardrop earrings dangle from her earlobes.

Luke's arm falls away from my hip as I take a step forward, cross my arms over my chest and gaze around at the vast, nearly empty space. Contemplating deeply, I let the ideas I've been thinking about since yesterday play through my mind.

Taking into consideration Melinda's small budget Luke told me about on the flight over, I look to them both and say, "Well, I can definitely help you out; I think I have just the idea."

"Really?" Alicia looks wide-eyed and hopeful.

Luke just looks proud, as if he'd never doubted me for a minute. He stands quietly with his arms crossed, his defined muscles making his navy T-shirt tight in all the right places. He's wearing a pair of loose-fitting dark jeans, also tight only in all the right places, with a stylish belt that peeks out from beneath the messily tucked shirt—I've yet to find him unattractive in anything he wears; he just gets sexier.

I begin to walk about the room slowly.

"One question," I say, stopping briefly. "What time of day will the event take place?"

"It'll be from five to nine in the evening," Luke answers.

I nod. "That's perfect," I say and start moving again. "So it'll be a day *and* night event—I can definitely work with that."

I stop in the center of the room, surrounded by empty easels and extension cords running across the gloss-stained concrete floor. I look up, gauging the distance from the ceiling to the floor.

"The ceilings aren't too high," I begin, pointing upward, "so it'll be easy to hang decorations from them." I look right at Luke once and gesture with both hands toward the popcorn ceiling. "I think white tulle fabric would be beautiful streaming from the ceiling in highlighted sections of the room"—the motion of my hands becomes more dramatic as I try to visually describe the idea to them—"like this, in one long, sweeping piece, and with enough that the fabric pools just a little against the floor."

Luke purses his lips, nodding; his expression is thoughtful and absorbed as he takes it all in.

"And then amid the tulle," I go on, "I think strings of white or clear lights would be perfect—simple Christmas lights will do the trick." I gesture my hands again, this time to indicate the top portion of the fabric. "And then white globe paper lanterns can hang in clusters from the top of the tulle—in the daytime it'll all still look really pretty even unlit, but when the night falls, just turn on the lights and it'll give the entire room a beautiful ambiance."

"But won't we have to turn the ceiling lights off for that?" Alicia asks with only a little concern in her voice. "It might be hard to see the art then."

"Not with enough string lights and lanterns," I say. "But you can leave the ceiling lights on." I point briefly at them. "I noticed before that they're on dimmers; just turn them down to about halfway and that'll keep them from flooding out the decoration lights, but leave just enough ceiling light so the room isn't too dark."

"I'm liking this idea already," Luke says, beaming at me. "How would we hang the fabric and"—he waves his hand in front of him, trying to remember—"those lantern things, and the lights?"

"With fishing line," I answer and start gesturing toward the ceiling again. "It's strong and durable so the weight of the lanterns, string lights, and the fabric won't break it, plus it's clear and won't be easy to see."

"That's so perfect!" Alicia says excitedly, clapping her hands together once.

"I told you I had a secret weapon," Luke says, glancing at Alicia briefly and then turning back to me, his proud smile stretching and his bright hazel eyes privately thanking me.

I smile back softly, privately telling him, *You're very welcome.*

"How much of this fabric do you think we'd need?" Luke asks

after a moment, observing the space contemplatively, as if trying to determine the answer on his own.

"I'll have to do some calculations," I say, "but I definitely think with Melinda's budget, you can get all of it that you need and still have the funds for everything else—the tulle and the lanterns will make up the biggest portion of the budget."

I go on to explain to them where would be the best places to hang each decoration, and judging by the easels and partition walls and other contraptions used for hanging art already scattered about the vast area, I begin to put together a method for an efficient way to lay out the floor plan.

After an hour, Alicia leaves us so she can start shopping for certain items—we also decided to hang clear silver and gold balloons in grape-like clusters from the ceiling in other sections of the room. But some things will have to be ordered online—the tulle, for instance; since we need so much of it, it's unlikely it could all be found in any local craft or material store.

Luke comes walking toward me with two bottles of soda in his hand.

He sits down next to me against the wall where his paintings hang just above us.

Breaking the seal on my soda, he hands the bottle to me.

"You really have an eye for this stuff," he says.

He presses his back against the wall and leans his shoulder against mine. I lay my head on it momentarily.

"I love the creative aspect," I tell him, raising my head from his shoulder and then taking a quick sip. I look out ahead of me in thought, the moving figures of a few people walking back and forth blurring out of focus. "But you know...this is different somehow. I mean it... well, this is *enjoyable*. That wedding I did, not so much."

Luke is smiling. I know without having to look over at him.

He brings the bottle to his lips and takes a small drink, then props his arm on the top of his knee, letting the bottle dangle between his bent legs.

"Maybe it's because I'm appreciative of you," he begins. "And, I *dunno*," he says with a perceptive tenor, looking over and catching my gaze, "maybe it's because you feel like you're getting something more out of it than a paycheck."

I nod softly with an appreciative smile. "Maybe you're right."

Luke sets the soda bottle on the floor on the other side of him and then wraps his arm around my bent leg. I set my bottle down, too, and rest a hand on his wrist. We look out at the room together.

"Too bad Harrington Planners doesn't take on more jobs like these," I say. "I can't recall one event I've ever been a part of that didn't involve some kind of negativity. I've worked with a lot of really nice people—most of them aren't like the Dennings family— but there was always some kind of drama." I shake my head just thinking about it all.

"But a job is a job," I say.

Luke shrugs. "Sometimes it is." He turns his body at an angle so he can focus on me better; he's got that look in his eyes, the one he always gets when he's about to tell me something profound yet so simple that I can't for the life of me understand why I didn't already know it. "But if you're unhappy with your job, you have two choices: Find a *way* to be happy, or find one that *makes* you happy." He looks out at the room again. "But never let yourself become a slave to it."

I sense there's more meaning behind his comment than what is obvious—having to do with his brother, I'm sure—but he shifts the mood too quickly for me to explore it.

Raising his back from the wall, he looks right at me with the brightest smile and says with absolute determination, "You know what? I think you should display some of your photography in the event."

A little surprised by his suggestion, I just sit here wide-eyed for a moment.

"You don't have to sell any of it if you don't want to," he says, assuring me. "But even if you did, you could keep your profits—however you want to do it—but I just think it'd be awesome if your photography was on display like my paintings."

I was shaking my head long before I realized I was; I just don't feel very confident. The other photographs, not to mention Luke's paintings, are way out of my league.

"I don't know, Luke," I say, still shaking my head slightly. "Did you see those other photographs over there?" I point absently in the direction of the black-and-white photographs of the old woman. "My stuff is nowhere near—"

"Your photography is fantastic, Sienna," he cuts in and then says, "Hey, I'm up close and personal with those self-doubting demons—as artists we're our own worst critics—but I'm telling you that your photography is some of the best I've ever seen around this place, and I'm not just saying that because I like you."

My whole face is bright and warm.

"I don't know…"

"Just think about it," he says eagerly.

He stands up and reaches out for my hands, helping me to my feet.

"Maybe you could even . . . come back for the event," he suggests in a gentle, smiling voice.

"Oh, is that why you offered?" I ask, grinning; he rubs my arms up and down underneath his warm hands. "Just to get me to come back here?"

He shrugs, his mouth lifting on one side.

"As much as I'd love for you to come back in August," he admits, "I still think your photography is worthy of being on display—don't tell me you have a fear of compliments, too."

I laugh lightly.

He just smiles.

"No, I'm not afraid of compliments—I like them more than I'm willing to admit." I glance downward, feeling weird about saying that out loud, trying to keep my smile to a minimum.

"Well, that's a good thing," he says, and I feel his fingers press gently around my biceps, "because that's just not something I can go easy on you about." He leans in and presses his lips against my forehead, and my heart leaps and does flips and I feel like I want to fall into his arms.

Luke pulls away slowly, letting his hands slide away from my arms with reluctance.

"But as far as that real fear of yours," he says, "I've got plans for it."

I'm not sure I like that subtle look of mischief playing in his eyes.

I swallow nervously.

"Plans for it?" I ask hesitantly, and I'm beginning to wonder why he's so intent on helping me overcome my fear of heights. Not that it bothers me—I couldn't be more grateful—but I still have to wonder where it's coming from, why he's so, dare I say it, exactly what I've needed in that regard.

"Yep." He nods.

I don't wonder for long—now I'm just worried about what he has in store. "What kind of plans?" I ask. Am I grimacing? I'm totally grimacing. I probably look petrified. Luke is unfazed.

He curls his fingers around mine and says, "You'll see," as he walks us out of the building.

Luke

I ask her to trust me and not ask questions about where I want to take her. It's definitely going to be a surprise, but I'm not one hundred percent confident that it'll be a welcome one—I'm leaning toward no, but it's worth a shot. She's been awesome at going headfirst into facing her fear of flying, sitting by the window and looking out, but I can see the change taking shape within her already, the unmistakable confidence, her unbending strength.

I wish I was as strong as her.

I wish I could face my own fear—accepting Landon's death and moving on with my life.

But maybe I *am* finally beginning to find my way again. Since Sienna walked into my life, I've felt lately like...I can *breathe* again. When I'm around her, I forget about everything else: the news from China, the funeral, the nightmares, the denial...but mostly the pain.

"Well, at least tell me if I'm dressed for the...occasion," she says with a fearful tenor in her voice—I come back into the moment, the backs of my eyes burning with tears, and I adjust my expression quickly so she doesn't notice.

She looks down at her outfit: cute blue shorts, pink tee, and white and hot pink running shoes.

"What you're wearing is fine," I assure her.

She's so nervous sitting beside me on the bus on our way to the airport, the way she wrings her hands together on her lap.

"Well, do I need anything?" she asks. "Like maybe a...parachute or something?"

I laugh because it was certainly a joke, told by a beautiful, timid girl who was definitely not smiling in the least bit when she said it.

"No," I say, patting her bare leg and leaving my hand there. "But you've got your camera, right?"

Her face lights up and it makes my stomach feel like a warm ball of, I dunno, something mushy and feminine, and all I'm waiting for now is to see a burst of little hearts shoot from my ears. I shake it off, laughing quietly to myself.

"No," she says, "but we can stop by your house and pick it up first, right?" She looks hopeful and doe-eyed—damn; what this girl is *doing* to me!

As if she really needed to ask. She may not know it, but I am one hundred percent at her service.

"Well, that's really all you need," I say, squeezing her knee. "We'll stop by the house first."

Back on Kauai, Sienna reemerges from my room, pulling her hair into a ponytail.

Minutes later we hop in my car and leave just as Seth and Kendra are pulling into the driveway in Seth's red Jeep, which has seen better days. Pressing my finger on the button, my window slides down as he and I come to a stop next to each other. The doors and roof of the Jeep were taken off months ago and Seth never cared to put them back on. I can smell the mildewy seats that have been rained on countless times.

"Where yah headed, bro?" Seth asks, looking down from his seat at me in my little blue Hyundai.

"Taking Sienna…" I pause, having to be careful. "Well, we'll be gone for a while."

Seth leans over some behind the steering wheel so he can get a better look in at Sienna on the other side of me. "Hey, girl," he says and waves at her with two fingers.

He shaved his head again recently, I notice.

Sienna waves back. "Hello again," she says, beaming.

Seth grins at me like some kind of mad scientist as he rises back up.

"Hey, I meant what I said about finding another place to crash if—"

I wave a hand at him to cut him off.

"Yeah, I remember." Then I give him a covert look, my way of quietly taking him up on that offer.

His deeply tanned face spreads into an even bigger grin and I'm just glad Sienna is on the other side of the car and he's so much higher up that she can't see it.

Kendra just looks at me from the passenger's seat of the Jeep and shakes her blond head with disapproval, her mouth pinched into a hard line. As usual, I ignore her, but *also* as usual, a small part of me just wants to tell her off. Thankfully—and shockingly—Kendra doesn't say a word before Seth and I drive away from each other.

"She doesn't like me much, does she?"

I look over at Sienna, not surprised that she feels that way, but surprised that she actually brought it up.

"That's not it," I tell her with sincerity. "Kendra's just...painfully complicated. She's...well, she's been through a lot: with me and Seth, with my brother, but her heart is really in the right place. I admit, she's not exactly the friendliest person in the world, but she's a good person; she's just looking out for all of us. Don't for a second think that her bad attitude is in any way your fault."

Sienna scoffs quietly. "A girl knows when another girl has a problem with her. Trust me. I know she wishes I were long gone by now."

For the first time, Sienna is letting me know how much this situation with Kendra is, and probably has been, bothering her. And I don't like it. The last thing I want is for Sienna to constantly feel uncomfortable whenever Kendra manages to show up in the equation, an equation she was never invited to and is creating more issues than I need right now.

I have to fix this now before it gets any worse.

Slowing the car down as we come to a big, winding curve, I keep my eyes on the blacktop while also trying to give Sienna most of my attention.

"I'm calling Seth later," I begin, "and telling him not to bring Kendra to the house again unless he asks me first."

Sienna's head snaps around.

"No, no, no. Luke, do *not* do that. I really mean it. I don't care if she doesn't like me, but I don't want to make it worse by doing something like that." She smiles softly and I realize that she's as serious as she appears. "It wouldn't be the first time I got looks like that." She laughs. "It's what girls do."

"Well, if it'll ease your mind at all, I can tell you with absolute truth that I have never kissed, dated, or slept with Kendra." I slash my hand in the air. *"Ever."*

"I believe you," she says, smiling.

I think the conversation is over, but then Sienna catches me off guard when she says, "But she *does* like you, Luke. That's as obvious as Seth telling you with that not-so-secret look of his that he's rooting for you to get laid."

I think all my bones and muscles just turned to cement.

She's grinning hugely when I finally manage the courage to turn my head away from the winding road to look at her.

"I, uh," I stammer, shaking my head. "I swear I do not expect anything like that from you, and—"

"It's OK," she says, gesturing a hand between us, trying to ease my panic. "If I thought that was all you had me here for, I never would've agreed to stay in your house."

That's good to know.

"But Kendra does have a thing for you," she goes on, pointing at nothing. "Can't convince me otherwise."

And I'm not going to try, because I won't lie to her. Kendra has—and maybe she still does; hell if I know, or care anymore— had a thing for me since about four months ago. I can't deny that.

I just can't *explain* it, either.

Because, like Kendra, the situation is painfully complicated.

NINETEEN

Sienna

After a long drive, we pull into the lot of a building with a big wooden helicopter tour sign. My blood becomes acidic and begins to rush through my veins like a raging river. I swallow hard and press my hand to my chest, trying to find my heartbeat, only to realize the reason I can't feel it is because it's beating way too fast, undetected like the wings of a humming-bird. The drive here was filled with conversation and laughter and Luke saying the simplest of things that always somehow managed to make me blush or smile—I was having *such* a great time—but now I'm beginning to wonder if it was all just to prepare me for this moment.

"What are we doing here?" I ask somberly, unable to take my eyes off the sign as we pull into a parking space. It's obvious what we're doing here, but surely he knows that what I'm really saying is, *Are you crazy? There's no way I'm getting on a helicopter.*

Luke shuts off the engine, breaks apart his seat belt, and turns on the seat to face me. As always, his smile alone is enough to calm me down, but this time it's not enough to make me get out of the car.

"Imagine seeing Kauai from the air," he says. "Imagine the

photos you can take that you'll never be able to take from the ground."

"I'm fine with taking photographs from the ground."

He smiles and regards me quietly for a moment.

"You got on the plane," he says to make a point, "and you sat by the window—"

"Yeah, but this is *much* different," I argue.

"You're right, it is," he says. "It's a sight that you'll never forget, and if you do it once, I guarantee you that you'll want to do it again."

I highly doubt that.

I shake my head and face forward, peering out the windshield.

"I got on the plane," I say in a quiet voice, "but this is so much smaller, and I dunno, Luke, but I might feel claustrophobic in something like that and freak out worse."

"*Are* you claustrophobic?"

"No…" I admit.

"Then you won't freak out because it's smaller."

That was an excuse, I know, and he probably does too.

I feel the warmth of his hand on my bare thigh and I turn away from the windshield and look at him, his hazel eyes filled with everything that threatens to make me trust him: protection, unimaginable strength, adoration. A part of me really does feel like nothing could ever happen to me with him at my side, but still it's not enough to quell the fear.

"OK, think about this," he says, switching gears. "Helicopters are safer than planes, in my opinion, because the pilot can set them down just about anywhere with a flat surface. He can lower it to a safer height if he has to. A helicopter can hover in one place. An airplane, although generally safe, can't do *any* of those things." His strong fingers curl around my unsteady ones. "If you can get on a plane, you can get on a helicopter."

What he said makes sense, and I think on it heavily. I think about my camera in the backseat and of the beautiful shots I could capture. I would love to expand my portfolio, to go on to the next level and see and shoot things I've only ever dreamed of. But more than anything, I really do want to break this fear. And for the first time in my life I'm in the presence of someone who *truly* understands it and seems to want nothing more right now than to see me free of it.

His lips fall on the corner of my mouth and my heart pounds against my ribs. I turn slowly to face him, our noses almost touching. I get lost in his eyes as they search mine and then he kisses my lips softly, causing my eyelids to become heavy with a warm, relentless tingling sensation. "You can do this, Sienna," he whispers. "Fear is just the part of you that wants you to fail. It's all of your regrets and your pain and your failures wrapped up into one emotion. It's a weakness, nothing more." Slowly I open my eyes and he's still there, so close I can feel his breath on my lips and it takes everything in me to keep from tasting them. "We're all stronger than our weaknesses," he says. "Sometimes we just need someone else to help us find that strength."

"Who are you, *really*?" I ask.

His eyes soften on me in a curious manner, and his mouth turns up slightly at the corners.

"What do you mean?"

"I don't know...I mean, how is it that you can make me question just about everything?"

He seems genuinely surprised by my confession, so much so that he doesn't seem to have an answer or a comment.

226 J. A. REDMERSKI

"You make me question my job," I go on, trying to grasp my own words as much as he appears to be. "You make me question the amount of time I don't spend behind my lens. I question my future. Where will I be in ten years? What will I be doing? What do I want to be doing?" I laugh lightly. "And every day now I question..."

After a moment, Luke says, "What do you question every day?"

I smile, the kind of smile that borders reflection and confusion, looking down at my hands in my lap. But I can't answer him because I'm still not sure of the answer myself.

"I'll get on the helicopter," I say. "Not because I feel forced, or because I'm trying to do what you want me to do, but because I want to do it for myself. I *need* to do this." It was difficult to say that, but it made me feel a little stronger.

His lips spread into a wide, close-lipped smile.

"That's my girl," he says, and my heart utterly melts into a puddle of hot mush.

The helicopter ride was terrifying at first, with the floor-to-ceiling glass that gave me more of a view than I initially thought I could stomach, but eventually I came around. My hands and legs stopped trembling. The tears dried up from my eyes. A look of awe and fascination replaced the expression of dread that I knew I wore as obviously as my clothes. The scenery literally took my breath away. The multicolored sea cliffs with sharp ridges and deep valleys. The majestic waterfalls and rolling green mountains. I was surprised how quickly I became comfortable with the height, and I don't know if it was because the beauty made me forget about being afraid, because Luke was sitting beside me and I felt safe, or a combination of both, but... well, Luke was right—after I did it the first time, I wanted to do it again.

I thank him all the way to his car: with the actual words; by how tightly I grasp his hand; with the way I can't stop beaming or talking about how amazing it was to be in the air, drinking in the stunning beauty of this island—I never would've done it without his help; I never would've even attempted it.

"Hey," I say as we stop in front of his car, "what is it with you wanting to cure me of my fear of heights so badly, anyway?"

He places his hand on the car door and pulls it open for me. The vanilla-scented surfboard hanging from the rearview mirror tickles my nostrils as I hop inside.

"I dunno," he says. "Maybe I just can't help it." He smiles and starts to close the door.

I stop it with my hand.

"No, seriously," I tell him, looking up at him from the seat with intense eyes. "There's gotta be something more to it than that." That's certainly not a generalized assumption—some people are just that way, ready and willing to help anyone at the drop of a hat, but with Luke, I feel like there's definitely more to it.

He looks out at nothing, one arm propped on the top of the open window.

Then he peers in at me and says, "I guess I'm just passing along something I learned from someone very special." Then he leans into the car toward me, the inviting smell of his clean skin and the heat of his body wrapping around my senses, and then his lips touch mine. "It's not bothering you, is it?" he asks when he pulls only inches away.

But his face is still right there, his warm lips so close I can still taste them—how could I ever say anything but *no*?

I shake my head slowly. "No..." and am now left wondering

if Luke just bewitched me, made me lose my train of thought so I wouldn't press him further for a more detailed answer.

I start to tell myself, *No, I can't be bewitched!*

Until much later I realize I had forgotten all about it.

Two days later, we go back and I can't get on the helicopter fast enough.

Every day that passes, it's a day closer to when my time will be up here. And already I can't imagine a life without Luke in it in *some* way. I would love to pursue a future with him. I want that, actually, but he has become so special to me, rare like my stupid poetic freckles—his word, not mine—that even if I couldn't be *with* him, I would be happy just to always have him as my friend.

———

It rains a lot on Kauai—at least since I've been here it has. Today it rained for an hour straight. We planned to go hiking, but ended up hanging around the house instead.

Luke has been in the kitchen cooking burgers, leaving all the windows and doors open to let out the heat from the stove and let in the breeze. The burgers smell awesome, but I'm worried about having to pretend how good they *taste*. Turns out that Luke isn't all that perfect, after all. Ha! That stuff he told me about how well he could cook—well, he did cook me breakfast on the second day: eggs, biscuits smothered in gravy, and bacon on the side. I give him points for the presentation, but the eggs were bland, the bacon was overcooked, the biscuits *under*cooked, and the gravy was kinda runny. "What do you think?" he said, sitting on the couch next to me that day with a big, proud smile, his cheeks moving around and around as he chewed.

I smiled back as I chewed more slowly, swallowed carefully, and replied, "Oh, it's...really good!"

I was lying through my teeth, but I couldn't bring myself to tell him the truth. He really did spend a lot of time on that breakfast for me, messing up his kitchen, and he put a lot of effort into strategically placing everything on my plate as if he were in front of one of his canvases, creating a masterpiece. But I admit, I'd still take his cooking over the hotel's complimentary breakfast and even the steaks at four-star restaurants. Because no matter how bland or bad it is, Luke cooked it just for me and that somehow makes it taste better.

"I usually cook burgers out on the grill," he says, walking out onto the lanai with a plate balanced on each hand, "but it's gonna rain all damn day it looks like."

He sets my plate in front of me on the table.

I take a deep breath and prepare myself; it's almost like that day when I prepared myself mentally to get on that helicopter. *I can do this. It's OK if blood runs out the side of the meat. Just take a deep breath, bite down, chew with a smile, make an* mmmmm *sound, flutter my eyes, and then swallow. Wash it down quickly with soda and then repeat.*

"You don't like my cooking, do you?"

Shit! Was that whole scenario on my face just now where he could actually see it?

"What?" My mouth falls open and my eyebrows crinkle in my forehead. "No, Luke. Why would you say that?"

He shakes his head, laughing on the inside, and then takes an enormous bite from his burger; the lettuce makes a crunching sound between his teeth.

"Because," he says with his mouth full and then swallows, "you reminded me of my mom when she was driving and a spider crawled across the dashboard. She tried to keep from freaking out and wrecking the car until she could pull over somewhere and deal with it." He laughs.

"I did *not* look like that," I defend, but I know I probably did. "And your cooking is...all right."

He raises a brow. "Oh, so now it's just all right? You've been faking it with me since you got here?"

I take a huge bite so I don't have to answer.

Luke smiles. "Well, then I guess you'll have to cook for *me* tomorrow."

I'm the one laughing now. "I think you cook better than I do." That's not true, either.

"Well, we'll just have to find out, won't we?" he challenges.

Great! Now I know I have my work cut out for me.

I manage to get most of the food down, but it wasn't really that bad, just bland, and bland I can manage better than bloody.

"So other than heights and losing your job and my cooking," he says, sitting back down beside me after taking our plates away, "what else are you afraid of?"

I shrug. "Nothing really, I guess."

"Nothing at all? Are you sure?"

"Nothing that really stands out," I tell him.

"So you have no issues with snakes or snails or anything like that?"

"Nope."

"What about bugs? All girls are afraid of bugs."

He chuckles when I poke his leg with my toe underneath the table.

"That's sexist and stereotypical," I shoot back playfully.

"So then you're *not* afraid of bugs?"

"Nope." I smirk at him. "What's with the twenty questions, anyway?" It dawns on me only slightly how odd he's acting.

Then suddenly he very slowly stands up and goes to lean across the table, reaching his hand out toward my hair.

"Just be still," he says.

I don't.

Freaking out instinctively, like a jack-in-the-box, I come out of my chair in two seconds flat, shrieking when I feel the movement of whatever terrifying creature is crawling in my hair burrowing itself deeper into my long locks.

"Oh my *God*! Ahhhh! What the fuck is it?" I run across the lanai in a frantic, chaotic spectacle, my arms flailing above my head and then my hands grasping at the back of my shirt.

"LUKE!"

I can't see him because my body is spinning, but I can hear him calling out, "Just be still, Sienna, and I'll get it!"

Wings of some sort flutter against my skin as it crawls down the back of my neck and out of reach of my hands—I lose it the rest of the way and scream at the top of my lungs, so loudly and intensely that my eardrums seem to pop. And then I take off running in whatever direction is forward. I hear Luke's voice and laughter somewhere behind me, getting louder as he follows.

"Come here, Sienna!" He laughs between words. "I'll get it out! It's just a roach!"

"A ROACH?!" Did he seriously just say a *roach*? I'd rather have a cobra in my shirt than a *roach*. "GET IT OUT NOW!" I roar, my hands still grasping behind me at nothing because I can't reach back that far.

"I'm trying, babe. Be still."

In the commotion, I feel my ankle bend painfully to one side and I cry out and lose my footing, then go tumbling down the steps. I hit the ground with a big *splash!* and muddy water sprays up into my nose and paints the side of my face. I look down in the disarray to see that I'm lying on my hip in a giant puddle of fresh mud, feeling it cold and gross and soaking up into my *white* shorts and *white* shirt and all the solid *white* undergarments underneath— bleach'll never get this out.

TWENTY

Luke

"Oh shit! Sienna, are you all right?"

I leap off the lanai, missing all five steps, and might've landed crouched like a ninja if it weren't for all the mud—my foot slips instead, and I slide through the mud on my side like a baseball player sliding into home plate.

"Sienna," I say, putting my hands on her shoulders from behind, "are you all right?"

She's sitting upright in the mud, *and* covered in it, her white clothes drenched and stained; her long auburn hair is dripping and matted. She won't look at me, and the little humor I found in watching her freak out like that drains right out of my body. She's looking downward into her lap as she sits with her left leg bent upward and the right one lying against the mud, both hands gripping her ankle partially under the water.

"I'm fine," she says in a wounded, unforgiving voice.

I tried to get it, but I feel like an asshole. Sighing heavily, I place my fingers about the tail of her drenched shirt and lift it to the middle of her back. The bug is nowhere to be found—I think it might've fallen from the back of her shirt before she made it all the way down the steps.

"It's gone," I tell her carefully and then drop her shirt back down. "Did you hurt your foot?" I move around on my knees through the mud to be in front of her.

"I said I'm fine."

I reach out for her foot anyway, taking it carefully in both my hands.

She winces, hissing through her teeth. She still won't look at me.

"I'm sorry. I think you just twisted it. Here, I'll carry you back inside." I start to reach for her when she cackles loudly and then her hand comes toward me, mud flinging in the air between us, before it slaps me across the side of my neck.

Sienna roars with laughter.

Mud covers one side of my face, sticking to the facial hair I need to shave soon and dripping down my neck and into my shirt. I'm too stunned at first, realizing she was playing me for an idiot—and did it so well—until she tries to run away from me and slips twice, scrambling to get to her feet.

"Oh no, you're not going anywhere," I call out from behind.

Her laughter fills the air, along with the sounds of her hands and feet sloshing through the puddle as she tries to crawl her way out and onto the wet grass. In a swift movement I reach out and grab the ankle she was pretending was injured and I yank her backward. She falls onto her back into the water. Slimy mud and droplets of brown water splash outward from beneath her.

"Let me *go!*" she shrieks, laughing so hard that it seems like she might cry.

And then *bam!* The wind is knocked out of me momentarily

when her bare foot buries itself into my gut. Instinctively I release her other ankle. She stops, on her hands and knees, looking across at me with wide eyes, shocked and riddled with guilt.

"Oh, I didn't mean to kick you *that* hard!" She winces.

I growl under my breath, low and guttural, shooting her with the most pretend pissed-off look I can manage, my jaw grinding harshly behind my mud-caked cheeks. Sienna's eyes get wider. *Mine* get meaner. Sienna's lips press together hard. My nostrils flare. And then, just when she intends to crawl over to me through the mud and console me with her girlish innocence, my lips turn up at one corner, my glare shifts, and she knows she's in for it. She takes off in the opposite direction, laughing and shrieking as she tries desperately to get to her feet.

"No! Please!" She chortles, looking back as I'm coming up behind her on my hands and knees.

She flings herself out of the mud and onto the grass, and just as she's clambering to her feet, my hand collapses around her ankle and she's on her back before she knows what's happening, sliding toward me. I'm on top of her in seconds, straddling her with my knees pressed into the grass on either side of her hips, glaring down at her shrinking, laughing face.

"I'm *sorry!*" she cries out, tears in her eyes.

Her arms are stretched out at her sides, my hands securing them against the wet grass.

"You *kicked* me," I tell her.

"You *laughed!*" She cackles, struggling futilely underneath my one-hundred-eighty-pound weight.

"You said you weren't afraid of bugs."

"Yeah, but I don't want them in my *clothes!*"

A quiet calm passes between us; Sienna's laughter subsides, her smile softening. She's so beautiful, even with mud streaked across her face and clinging to her eyebrows.

I've wanted to be with her since the first night she stayed in my house. A part of me hoped she'd initiate sex. I've laid on the couch every night since she's been here, imagining her coming into the living room to get me, or calling for me from my room for something stupid like a glass of water, just to get me in there. But the other part of me hoped she wouldn't, as if I want to wait as long as I can, and I'm afraid that if she gives in to me too soon, I might feel differently about her like I do with every other girl. But if she *were* some other girl, I might've initiated it myself already, and she'd surely be gone by the very next day. But with Sienna it's different. *Everything* is different. I want her more than anything, especially right now as I feel her body beneath me. And I know it must be obvious to her just *how* much I want her, but I don't care. I don't try to hide my hard-on this time. And she doesn't seem to mind.

I lean in closer and study her features with a calculated sweep of my gaze, fighting my growing feelings for her and my ever-present conscience. Her hazel eyes—more green today than brown—the plump heart shape of her lips, and her cute nose and the freckles splashed all over that I want to kiss individually no matter how long it takes. The smell of her skin and her breath and her soft hair makes me ache with need. I grow even harder against her, having never imagined that I could *get* any harder. Leaning over farther, my fingers tightening around her delicate wrists, I press myself eagerly against her below. A little gasp escapes her parted lips and it alone drives me insane. I bite down on the inside of my mouth—*God*, what I wouldn't do to strip off her clothes and take her right here. Or even just to put my fingers inside of her, or pleasure her with my mouth—I'd do whatever she asked me to do.

Sienna

Feeling how hard Luke is through his shorts—I can hardly stand it. My skin is covered in goose bumps, a fluttery sensation swirls around in my chest, and there's an unrelenting feeling of need tugging between my legs.

"Kiss me," I tell him in a soft whisper; I can already taste his sweet breath, and I ache to taste the rest of him.

Without hesitation his lips cover mine, both of his hands moving from my wrists to the sides of my face, where he holds on so tight that I wouldn't be able to move my head if I tried. His tongue is powerful and warm and sweet as he steals my breath away; my eyes flutter blissfully behind the lids. And even though I taste a little mud in our mouths and feel the dirty, watery sensation on my cheeks beneath his firm hands, I don't care and I never want this kiss to end.

Luke breaks the kiss slowly, letting his delicious lips linger on mine before finally pulling away.

I swallow nervously, looking up at him.

The creaking sound of the hinges on the back screen door shake us both from our passionate stupor.

"Ah shit—bad timing." Seth stands at the back door with no hair on his head and an apologetic look on his face.

Luke's chest rises and falls a little deeper than normal, and then he gets to his feet, taking my hand and bringing me up with him. Water drips from us both, down the backs of our bare legs, and for me, in places that make me cringe inwardly, thinking about need-ing a shower. *Stat.*

Seth rubs the palm of his hand across the back of his shaved head. "Sorry to barge in on yah like this," he says. A dark gray T-shirt hugs his muscular form, partially tucked behind a belt holding up a pair of black cargo shorts.

"It's all right," Luke says as we're ascending the back steps. "What's goin' on?"

I get the feeling right away that Luke might have something more harsh to say to Seth if I weren't standing among them. "I thought you were going to hang back for a while?"

"Yeah I know; sorry, man. I had to come over and get some of my gear." Seth looks us over with curious dark brown eyes, finally taking stock of our drenched and mud-stained clothes. "I'm not even gonna say it." He shakes his head, laughing under his breath.

"Yeah, please don't," Luke warns.

Wringing the water from my shirt and as much as I can man-age from my shorts, I do my best not to seem as though I'm inter-ested in their conversation. I'm not, really, but I feel kind of trapped, not wanting to go inside Luke's house and leave a trail of water and mud across his clean floors in my wake.

"Come on in," Luke tells me, holding open the screen door. "Don't worry about all that. I'll clean it up."

Our eyes meet in passing, reflecting the moment we just had, and then I go ahead and walk past him into the house. Luke peels off his T-shirt before he comes in and tosses it over the lanai rail-ing. I try not to look at his tanned, muscled upper body as he walks through the kitchen toward me, but that's not such an easy thing to avoid, I realize quickly. His shorts, weighted down by all the water, reveal a sculpted V-shape between his rigid hips. *Oh my God...*

Finally I avert my eyes.

Seth stands in the kitchen, leaning against the counter with his big arms crossed. It's apparent to me that he probably came here for more than his gear, and the fact that he's not saying much tells me they might need some time alone.

"Mind if I get a shower?" I ask Luke.

As if he feels bad for not offering it to me right away, Luke completely ignores Seth and says, "Yeah, babe. Let me show you where the towels are."

Babe? I'm not going to have a working heart left by the time I leave this island.

I notice from the corner of my eye that Seth seems as surprised to hear something like that coming from Luke as I am.

I grab some clean clothes from my suitcase in his room, and then Luke leads me down the hall to the bathroom after getting a clean towel and washcloth from a hall closet.

"Thanks."

He smiles, and for a brief moment it seems like he might want to kiss me again, but he doesn't, and I shut the door and start stripping off my wet clothes. A moment later, I can faintly hear their voices through the thin walls and it seems like they've moved into the living room.

"This seems serious, bro," I hear Seth say, but at first I don't think he's talking about me. "You sure about her?"

Is he talking about me?

I listen closer, not making any movement and trying not to breathe so I don't miss anything. But then suddenly I'm paralyzed by fear and I change my mind, letting out my breath noisily and fumbling my clean clothes on the counter to avoid hearing anything else. What if Luke tells Seth he isn't sure about me? What does *sure* even mean exactly? What if Luke says something, anything that I don't want to hear and that might change everything I've come to love and enjoy about Luke and my time here? I turn on the shower quickly and close myself off behind the glass door. And all I can think about is Luke. I've never felt this way about anyone before, and I'm not even sure *how* it is that I feel. All I know is that I don't want to leave. I know it's crazy, but I feel like I want to stay here with him forever. But I can't. We live worlds apart and long-distance relationships rarely ever work. And I can't leave my job, or my family. Or Paige.

I've been living in a dream world since I've been here—reality, my real life, will be here again soon enough, and I should be preparing myself for it.

I don't know what I'm going to do from here on out. I think maybe I should've left days ago, before Luke and I got any closer. Before that first kiss out on the lanai. I know I should've done a lot of things differently. But I didn't. And turning back now seems almost...impossible for me.

What have I done?

TWENTY-ONE

Luke

I'm sure that I like her," I answer Seth. "A lot more than I wanted to." I strip out of my shorts and toss them on the floor of the laundry room as I pass by, heading into my room in soaked boxers.

Seth follows.

"Well, I'm happy for yah," he says. "I just hope this one doesn't screw you over, man."

I look back at him. "Seth, my exes didn't screw me over, either," I correct him and turn to my chest of drawers, shuffling open the second drawer.

"Yeah, I know," Seth agrees reluctantly, "but this one doesn't even *live* here."

Shutting the drawer, I keep my back to Seth because I don't really want him to see the tormented look on my face. Seth may be right about getting too close to Sienna—she's afraid of heights (considering my extreme sports lifestyle, a fear of heights is almost a certain relationship killer) *and* she's a tourist (she has to leave Hawaii eventually, and long-distance relationships require more work than most people are willing to put in); our chances couldn't be more doomed—but nothing can change my feelings for her.

I walk over to my closet and yank down a clean T-shirt from a hanger, tossing it over my shoulder. I intend to hop in the shower after Sienna, though maybe if Seth hadn't shown up I would be in there *with* her right now.

Maybe it was for the best that he did.

"Well, in any case," Seth changes the subject, detecting the reluctance in me, "we were just wondering if you were still on for next week. I mean if you're not up to it with Sienna being here, that's totally understandable—might piss Kendra off, but who gives a shit, right?" He laughs, but it fizzles quickly when I don't join in.

"Well, I *don't* give a shit," I say as I walk past him and back toward the living room. "In fact, do me a favor and…" I pause, thinking about what Sienna begged me not to do. "Well, just try to keep her on her side of the fence for a while. Don't tell her I said that, just—"

"I got you," Seth cuts in. "Don't worry about it. But you know she's going to throw a bitch-fit if you back out again."

I slam the palm of my hand against the wall at the end of the hall and whirl around at Seth, my breathing deep and uneven, my jaw rigid. "I'm *not* going to *back out*!" I roar, the memory of my fatal decision to back out of China filling my head, but I calm myself fast when I realize what I'm doing.

A long, deep breath settles in my chest and I hold my eyes closed for a tense moment until I let the breath out and the anger along with it.

"I'm sorry, man," I tell him, my voice coming out calmer.

"Nah, don't be," he says in a nonchalant voice. "I understand. You *know* that. And I wasn't talking about Norway. I just meant—"

"I know, Seth. I know what you meant. I just… reacted."

He pauses, letting me gather myself the rest of the way.

"So it's a no-go next week then?" he asks.

I shake my head and plop down on a kitchen chair, sprawling my mud-crusted legs out before me. "No, I'm not going to do anything without Sienna. I want to spend all of my time with her while she's here. After that, things will be back to normal."

Seth remains silent, though I'm pretty sure of what he's thinking because it's all over his face. He knows I'm not looking forward to when Sienna leaves and things get back to normal. But it is what it is.

"Luke, man," Seth says, looking at me with a concerned face, which is rare for Seth. "Look, you know that getting into your shit isn't usually my thing, but you're my best friend and I'd be lyin' if I said I haven't been worried about you since Landon died."

"I know you have and I appreciate it, Seth, but I'm fine."

"I'm not so sure you are, bro." He cocks his head to one side. "It's not just about you hangin' back a lot when the rest of us go out doin' stuff, but even when it comes to jumping, when you do go with us, it kinda seems like you're—"

He stops and looks behind me instead of at me anymore.

"Like I'm what?" I ask, wary.

His big shoulders rise and fall with a heavy breath of preparedness.

He reaches up and scratches the back of his shaved head and says after a long hesitation, "I dunno. It just seems like you don't enjoy it anymore, like maybe you're doing it out of obligation— sorry man, I'm not tryin' to—"

I put up my hand.

"Don't worry about it," I say with forgiveness. "Like I said, I appreciate your concern, but I really am fine. And yeah, I can see why you'd think I don't enjoy jumping as much, but I've just had a lot on my mind, that's all."

Seth nods, leaving it alone.

"Maybe you can talk Sienna into staying." He changes the subject with a small, suggestive smile.

"Maybe so," I say, wincing as I pick small clumps of dried mud from my leg hairs, "but somehow I don't think she can."

"She may surprise you," Seth says. "You'll never know unless you say something. Shit, man, try it out—imagine how liberating it'll feel!"

I don't share his positive outlook, or his enthusiasm, and I find it odd that he's actually advocating a relationship *outside* of sex with Sienna, seeing as how he's so anti-relationship himself and just moments ago he was telling me to be careful.

"All right." Seth gives up. "I'll leave you to it, then."

"Thanks."

A moment later I ask, "So what's goin' on with you and Kendra?"

His dark eyebrows harden. "Nothin'. Why do you ask?"

I shake my head with disbelief and look away, not putting too much effort in hiding my knowing smile. Seth should be used to it by now—I've been on him for a couple weeks about his secret feelings for Kendra, and he's been denying them ever since.

"Gotta get off my back about her," he says, but he can't look me in the eyes. "She's too wild. I like my women sweet and tame."

I scoff. "Yeah, you keep telling yourself that."

"Whatever, man," he says, and then glances down the hallway as if to make sure Sienna isn't in earshot. He turns back to me with a suggestive grin. "So have you banged her yet?"

"Get the fuck outta here, Seth." I can't help but laugh a little— he can always get one out of me if he tries hard enough.

Seth crumples his nose up tightly, his top row of white teeth pressing over the top of his bottom lip, and he pumps his fist in front of him. "Fuckin' *score!*" He laughs himself all the way out the front door.

It wouldn't have mattered if I told him nothing had happened between me and Sienna beyond kissing, as he wouldn't have believed it anyway.

Sienna

An angry rumble of thunder and the heavy pounding of rain battering the roof wakes me early the following morning. Shuffling the sheet from my head, I open my eyes slowly to the dim gray light of dawn blanketed by clouds. More thunder rolls amid the sky; I can hear the distinctive sound of waves crashing against the shore through the open screened window above the bed.

I get out of bed and slip my bra on underneath my T-shirt before leaving Luke's room.

But Luke is nowhere to be found. The television is off; the kitchen doesn't look or smell as though anything has been cooked in it yet; the running shoes, as well as the flip-flops Luke normally wears, are still sitting sloppily on the floor beside the television; his wallet and car keys are still on the kitchen counter, so I know he can't be far.

I push open the squeaky screen door, making my way out onto the lanai, but he's not sitting out here, either, which was where I expected him to be.

"Luke?" I call out softly from the lanai, my voice smothered by the thunder and heavy rain; a streak of lightning darts across the sky in my peripheral vision, followed by a vociferous crack and roar of thunder—I jump at the unexpected sharp sound; I can feel it move through my feet as the lanai seems to shake. Rain splatters on me in tiny spray-like drops as the brisk wind pushes it sideways amid the storm.

I don't know how it hit me so fast, but suddenly I react on the urge to look inside the house from the screen door, my eyes passing over the wall in the kitchen where two surfboards—Luke's and Seth's—are usually propped, and when I notice Luke's is missing, my heart sinks into my feet.

Before my mind even realizes, my bare feet are carrying me down the lanai steps and into the hammering storm.

I run through the rain and wind and thick wet sand all the way out to the beach, where I stop as if a brick wall suddenly shot up in front of me when I see Luke, a speck of dark, out-of-place movement, riding the violent waves on his surfboard.

Gasping, my stomach tightening, I fling my hand over my mouth. Rain rushes over my head and down my face in heavy streams, but nothing can force my eyes closed, as I'm fixed on the perilous scene, watching Luke surf in the storm.

For a second I'm more mad and disappointed than I am afraid—why is he doing this alone? I ask myself.

But he's not alone, I realize when I find the courage to tear my eyes away from him. Another dark figure, stark against the gray-and white-capped water, emerges from the top of a wave not too far from Luke.

All I can do is watch in awe and in horror—I've never seen Luke surf quite like this, riding big, thrashing waves and very much like a pro, which he told me once he was not. Maybe that's true, but he sure looks like one to me out there. But every time he gets clipped by a wave and disappears under the water, my hands begin to shake and my heart stops and every muscle in my body locks up. Not until I see his head appear from the top of the churning water do I feel like I can move and breathe again.

A long time passes while I stand on the beach in the downpour, before I decide that I just can't watch anymore.

I run back to the house and to the safety of the lanai, where I wait for another thirty minutes, drenched in my clothes, before Luke finally comes back safely.

He looks stunned to see me sitting here when he notices me from the bottom step, surfboard tucked under his arm.

He smiles hugely, looking me over.

"What are you—why are you wet?" he asks with a wrinkled nose, setting his board upright against the side of the house.

I return his smile, but it's not as bright as his.

"I was watching you surf." I tell him the truth—I wonder if he can detect the discomfort in my voice.

He crouches down in front of me on his long, muscled legs, tilts his head to one side, and says, "You all right?"

Great—I guess he did see the discomfort, after all.

My legs drop from a crossed position on the chair and I set my feet on the wood in front of him.

"Yeah, I was just a little freaked out seeing you do that."

He places his hands on my knees; his smile just gets bigger.

"Look, I'm fine," he points out, gesturing both hands at himself, but when he sees that I probably don't look too convinced, he pushes back into a stand and reaches for my hand. "Come on, why don't you get out of those wet clothes, and I'll make you breakfast."

I take his hand and follow him into the house. I change clothes and pin up my hair before heading into the kitchen to the delicious smell of bacon cooking on the stove.

"I'm sorry, Sienna," Luke says as I sit down at the bar. "Last thing I wanna do is freak you out. I shouldn't have gone out there with you here at the house. But I'm fine, see!" He turns from the stove, smiling brightly, and places an empty glass in front of me. "I may do some extreme stuff, but I'm really safe about it all. I never surf like that alone." He reaches over the bar and brushes his finger-tip over the bridge of my nose—it eases me in an instant, and a smile turns up on my lips. "I had Braedon out there with me," he adds.

"Yeah, I saw you weren't alone." I admit that does make me feel a lot better, and I think he knows that judging by the smile of acceptance on my face.

"And I never am," he insists, going toward the fridge. "Orange juice? Milk?"

"Orange juice is good."

He comes back with a half gallon in his hand and pours some into my glass.

Maybe I'm just being overly cautious, as usual, letting my fear of heights bleed into everything else. I've never really been afraid of the risks associated with cliff-diving and storm-surfing and other things like that, but then I've never really been faced with them before I met Luke, either.

Just the same, I don't want to come off bitchy or maternal, tell-ing Luke I think he shouldn't do this and shouldn't do that. It's his lifestyle, and from what I've seen so far he seems to know what he's doing.

We enjoy a breakfast together at the bar and talk for a long time about his surfing and rock-climbing and cliff-diving, where I learn that if anyone is more prone to being injured, out of all of Luke's friends, Seth apparently takes the trophy.

"Nothing can kill the guy though," Luke said. "He's broken

several bones, ruptured his spleen in a motorcycle accident, and almost drowned surfing."

"Geez, what the hell is wrong with him?" I asked.

"Seth is just Seth—he wouldn't know how to live any other way. But he's generally safe, too. He's just accident prone by nature, not reckless by choice."

But the extent of Luke's injuries in the years he's been into all this wild outdoors stuff is a broken toe and some scrapes and bruises.

And this too fills me with a sense of relief.

Not a full sense, but a sense nonetheless.

Luke

We finally get a break from the rain. I take Sienna out to the waves behind my house later, where we surf until the sun begins to set. She's getting better at surfing, but I have to admit, I like it when she falls. It's cute because she's so dramatic about it sometimes, and she screams and laughs and I have another reason to either rush to her side and put my hands on her, or to hang back and make fun of her.

"What's *wrong* with you, girl?" I shout from my board over the sound of the waves. "No giving up early! Pull that bikini out of your butt crack and get back out here!"

She cackles and then flips me off. She drops her board on the sand and plops down next to it. I paddle my way closer and walk out after her with my board secured underneath my arm. I sit beside her on the sand and we watch the sun begin to sink into the ocean.

I think heavily about our conversation this morning—I've been thinking about it all day, in fact—and I feel really good about her acceptance of my lifestyle.

What she knows of it anyway.

"Luke?" Sienna says and I look over. "I just want you to know that just because I'm staying here and all that, you don't have to drop everything else."

"What are you talking about?"

She taps her knee against mine, both of us sitting with our legs drawn up, our arms wrapped around them, hooked loosely by our fingers.

"Come on," she says. "I know it wasn't exactly something you planned, and I don't expect you to set everything else aside that you normally do just to cater to me, you know what I mean?"

I smile and tap her back with my knee.

"I know, but I want to. You're my guest, and I need that five-star rating." I grin and look out ahead and add, "If you rate my services badly, I'll never get another girl to stay here on vacation."

The sound of air bursting shortly from her throat is light. My grin deepens, satisfied I got the reaction I was looking for.

"So is that what you're gonna do when I leave?" she asks suspiciously, playfully.

Turning my head to see her on my left, I just smile and shrug my shoulders.

"I dunno," I tell her. "I mean look how great things are going between the two of us. I could really get used to this kind of company." It was meant to be laced with suggestion.

She drops her bare legs into a crossed position and her shoulders slump forward. Her hands rest in the hollow of her lap. I love that black bikini—a little too much—how it hugs her perfect breasts, which would fit nicely in my hands...

Shake it off, Luke.

"Maybe I want to be your only guest," she says cautiously, keeping her eyes on the fading ball of fire being swallowed up by the ocean. I can tell that was hard for her to say, the same way it's been hard for me to kiss her—it's something I always want to do, but I'm still testing the waters and I'm never sure how she's going to react to it.

"Honestly, I'd kind of love it if you were the only guest."

We barely look over at each other, but as briefly as our eyes meet, it's plain that we're both smiling.

Suddenly I take a deep breath; the urge to take the plunge becomes important and hits me unexpectedly. The need to lay everything out on the table is finally at its peak, forcing me to the edge of the cliff as if for the first time. My heart is pounding, my shoulders feel tense, and my throat is dry. I see the drop-off out ahead, beckoning me. The urge to run to the edge and leap off has never been stronger, but the thought remains in the back of my mind that if I take that plunge I may never come back from it. I don't want that to happen with Sienna, but maybe Seth was right. She *is* different—maybe she'll surprise me.

It's in this moment that I decide to tell her what I've been not only afraid to, but have been trying to make sure if it's even necessary. She likes me enough that I think it is.

"You know what would be awesome?" she asks, snapping me out of my contemplation.

"What?"

"We have a sunset, an ocean, and a beach." She smiles and leans over sideways, laying her head on my shoulder. "All that's missing is a good drink."

"You want a beer?" I ask, agreeing.

"Whatever you have," she says.

I lean over and press my lips to the top of her hair. "Then a beer you'll get." I push myself to my feet and hurry off through the sand back toward the house, leaving her sitting on the beach. A beer is a good idea, if not for anything than just to loosen me up some. Because I'm going to tell her tonight, when I go back out to sit with her on the beach. It's odd, but even though I'm nervous as hell because I don't want to scare Sienna off, I think I'm just as excited.

I smile, thinking to myself all the way back to the house, because I have a really good feeling about tonight.

But then the smile drops from my face when I walk in and Kendra is coming through the front door ahead of Seth, a look of anger—and betrayal—boiling in her face.

Sienna

Luke has been gone for longer than I expected. He seemed kind of excited when he jumped up on those sexy muscled legs of his and jogged his way through the sand to go get the beers.

I start to leave the beach to find out if he needs help with anything—though I'm sure he can carry two beers all by himself— but then I decide against it. I've already invaded Luke's life and home. There is no reason that I shouldn't give the guy a few minutes of solitude.

A few more minutes pass by and I'm lying on my back against the sand, watching the sky darken above me and the stars begin to come alive within it.

Finally I get to my feet and head toward the house.

I hear raised voices as I approach. Luke and what sounds like Kendra. The light is on the kitchen, pooling on the ground outside the back window next to the lanai. I walk closer but find my steps slowing down and my ears beginning to burn.

And then I stop cold in my tracks before I take the first wooden step, and I can go no farther.

Luke

"Do you actually *think*," Kendra shouts at me in a rage, "that when she finds out about us she'll really make some kind of effort to get mixed up with you? *No*! She'll have the excuse she needs to put you behind her when she has to go back to wherever the fuck she lives! This is stupid! You're being stupid!" Her hands are clenched into fists at her sides. She's wearing a white flowered bikini top and a pair of cutoff jean shorts over the bottoms. There's redness in her face, caused by being in the sun all day and probably from her blood pressure shooting through the top of her skull.

Gritting my teeth, I point my finger right in her face. "This has gotta stop, Kendra! I've tried to be calm about this, always overlooking the obsessive attitude you have toward me—"

"Obsessive?!" The word hisses through her clenched teeth, her chin rears back and her brown eyes pop wide open in her angry face. "I'm just looking out for you! I *love* you, Luke! I'll *always* fucking love you! And *I* know bitches!" She points at Seth and then looks back at me. "Seth's the only one of you who's got it right! Fuck 'em and leave 'em so you don't have to go through the dramatic bullshit of *losing* them! Whether they leave or they die; there's no difference if you don't *care*!"

I throw my arms up above me and then lean toward her, roaring in her face, "But it's *not. Your. Life!* It's *mine*! You're fucking insane, Kendra!" She flinches at my words, not afraid of me, but hurt by them and the ones she knows are soon to follow. Moisture begins to form in the corners of her eyes. "YOU NEED HELP!" I bellow, because it's long overdue. "Stop using me as your goddamned crutch and get some professional help!" And then I go in for the kill. "If Landon could only see you now—"

A white-hot flash crosses my vision as her hand falls hard across the side of my face. A hot stinging sensation moves outward across my skin when she pulls her hand away. Before I can even find the words to apologize, the front screen door is slamming against the side of the house and Kendra's headlights are shining in on Seth and me.

Seconds later she fishtails out of my driveway, her brake lights glowing red through the darkness until her car disappears around the bend.

The dark silence left in the house is long and filled with even darker thoughts. I never wanted to treat Kendra that way and I feel like shit about it, but things needed to be said—maybe not that last part, but definitely the rest of it. Running my hand through the top of my hair, I take a deep breath and just watch out the front door for a moment, thinking that Kendra will turn around any second now and come back for another round because it's expected of her.

She doesn't come back.

"I followed her over here," Seth says from somewhere behind me. "I knew she'd be pissed that you weren't going with us on Saturday, but honest to God, man, I didn't expect *that*. I tried to calm her down."

"Don't worry about it," I say distantly with my back to him. Then I turn around. "Look, I don't want to deal with this right now." I walk into the kitchen just a shot away to get two beers from the fridge. "Sienna's waiting for me out on the beach and I've left her out there long enough."

"All right, I'm gone," Seth says. "Just give me a call when it's OK that I crash in my bed again."

"I will. Thanks, Seth."

Seth nods and leaves.

I use this brief moment alone to gather my composure. I don't want to go back out there with the girl of my dreams, oozing left-over chaos and bullshit.

Letting the back screen door close behind me, I start to descend the steps of the lanai, but my heart stops and the air sticks in my lungs when I see Sienna sitting at the bottom of them.

She heard.

For a few long seconds that feel much longer, I can't get any words out. Finally I make my way down the steps and start to sit beside her, but she gets up.

"Sienna, I—"

"You don't have to explain anything," she says kindly, with not an ounce of bitterness or anger or anything that might make this easier—just a lot of hidden pain that only makes it harder. "I-I really would rather if you didn't explain, anyway, OK?"

Disbelief and confusion take over.

I set the beers on the lanai railing and step toward her.

"But I need to explain it to you," I say.

She takes a step back.

Shaking her head gently and looking down briefly at her hands, she says, "Luke, I just want to go back to Oahu, if you don't mind giving me a ride to the airport."

"Sienna"—I gently take her arm, trying to stop her—"I swear to you there's nothing going on with me and Kendra. I know it might seem like that with the way we argue, but—"

She moves her arm away from my hand and my heart falls with my shoulders and my breath.

"Then what was she talking about, Luke?" Pain lies in her face as plainly as I know it does in my own; her eyes are hard and filled with conflict and disappointment, but not with anger or resentment, which makes this so much harder for me. "What did she mean when she said 'when I find out about you'?"

Wounded—Sienna is the epitome of the word and just seeing her like this, it guts me.

"Sienna, no, listen," I start to say, wanting to wash that wounded look off her face before it deepens. I reach out to touch her cheek with the backs of my fingers, but she takes another step back. I sigh and go on. "Kendra wasn't talking about her and me—it's not about that—it's... She was talking about what we do, the part of my life I've not told you about."

I get the feeling she doesn't believe me, but for a moment at least, she's listening. I still have time to fix this.

But then suddenly she blurts out, "No, please, Luke," and stops me again, a hint of pain rising in her voice. "I'm sorry, but I just can't do this. It was never going to work anyway, and I think you know that: you living in Hawaii, me in California; this... whatever it is you and Kendra haven't resolved—I can't be a part of that not to mention the very different lives we live."

I swallow hard.

"It's probably better that we part ways now," she goes on, "before we go too far."

I hear Landon's words in the back of my mind again—*I've never known you to run away from anything, Luke.*

Sienna's words—*it was never going to work anyway.*

Seth's words—*you know better than to get involved with a tourist.*

Even Kendra's words—*whether they leave or they die; there's no difference if you don't care.*

"OK," I say quietly, giving up because I know it's the right thing to do—I knew all along it would come to this moment, and to drag out the inevitable is the same thing as dragging out the pain.

My gaze falls to my bare feet standing amid the prickly, unkempt grass of my backyard. "I'll take you to the airport." I never imagined such simple words could cut so fucking deep.

"Thank you," she says just as quietly.

I step aside to give Sienna space as she ascends the steps and disappears inside the house to pack her things, the sound of the screen door hitting the wood frame lightly, as if she made it a point not to let it slam behind her.

We don't talk on the drive. Not once. I never feel her eyes on me from the passenger's seat, or any indication that she might secretly want me to be the one who speaks up first—exactly the opposite: I get the sense she doesn't want me to say anything, that if I do, it'll only make things harder. The silence is shattering, as if everything we experienced together in her short time here, how close we became, has so quickly become nothing more than a memory. The pain I feel is more than crushing; it's a burden that I know I'll carry with me forever: I knew better than to open myself up to a girl like her—the perfect girl—because it never would've worked, just like she said; as much as I wanted to believe that it somehow could, that Sienna could overlook and accept my dangerous lifestyle, I know deep down that she won't be able to. And so I'll let Sienna go. Against all that's inside of me, all the things I want to say to her to make her stay, I'll let her go. And things will go back to normal.

Normal...I hate normal; the thought of going back to the way things were before Sienna came into my life with her faultless, infectious smile and eyes brighter than the sun—I don't want to think about it.

Maybe hate isn't the word. I *fear* normal.

Not until it's time for Sienna to board her plane do we finally speak.

"Are you sure you don't want me to fly over with you?" It took everything in me to say those words and not all the things I really want to say. My heart is breaking into a thousand unrecognizable pieces; tears burn the backs of my eyes as I force them down; my chest feels heavy like a stack of bricks sits on top of it; my throat is beginning to swell and I can't fucking swallow.

"I'll be fine," she says.

Silence.

I look at the floor. She looks at the plastic seat beside her.

"Luke." She speaks up reluctantly. "I really did have a great time. I'll never forget this... vacation." It seemed hard for her to say that word, as if it didn't feel like the right one. "Or how you helped me with my fear of heights. It really does mean a lot to me. I hope you know that."

I nod and try to force a smile, but I doubt it looks very much like one. Inside it's the furthest thing from a smile.

She reaches out and touches my arm. "Thank you for everything—and please tell Alicia and Melinda that I'm sorry I can't be there to help anymore." She leans in and presses her soft lips to the corner of my mouth, and I'm on the cusp of losing it, but for her sake I keep my head on my shoulders. "I hope everything going on in your life works out," she says as she pulls away.

I hope so too, Sienna... but somehow now that you're leaving, I doubt it will.

"Sienna," I call out as she walks toward the gate.

She stops and turns around.

"Remember what I said about your photography."

I smile a little.

She smiles back, nods, and walks away.

TWENTY-TWO

Sienna

J burst into tears the moment I walk into my new hotel room. I had been holding them in the whole way back to Oahu, from the moment I went into Luke's bedroom to pack my things. Why am I crying like this? Why do I feel like my heart was just ripped right out of my chest? I've never met anyone like Luke before, who seemed too good to be true, and I guess who turned out to be, after all. But what I felt being with him was different from anything I've felt with any other guy before. The way he effortlessly made me laugh, how he could make me blush, how he could say anything to me and I couldn't find it in myself to *not* trust him, or feel comforted by him. I wanted to get lost in him. I *did* get lost in him.

"She actually said, 'when she finds out about us'? Are you sure that's what you heard?" Paige has been talking my ear off for the past five minutes since I called her.

"Yeah, that's what she said."

"Sienna, you were right to leave," she says into the phone, her voice carrying through the room from the speaker. "I dunno, but that whole situation really seems weird to me. Obvious, but weird.

They definitely had a thing goin' on at one point—that's the obvious part." She pauses and sighs contemplatively. "The weird part, well, whatever happened between them, it wasn't normal."

"What do you mean 'normal'?"

"I don't know," she says, adrift in thought, and then she becomes energized. "*Oooh*, maybe she's like his cousin, or something." My face twists with disgust. "Yeah, I mean think about it: You said he told her she needed professional help, and all that stuff about her being obsessed with him—*ewww*, but you said she's his brother's ex, so that would mean—"

"I doubt that's it, seriously." I shudder at the thought. "Maybe you should cut down on the time you spend watching *Game of Thrones*, Paige."

I slide open the balcony door and sit down at the table outside, propping my bare feet on the empty chair. I'm in a room on the opposite side of the building this time and now I know the source of the live music I'd heard before: drums pounding and shouting, voices echoing in the night—Hawaiian fire dancers are performing for the tourists.

"But what else could it be?" she asks and then answers her own question. "Exactly what it seems like: They used to go out after Kendra and his brother broke up—maybe they even broke up because something was going on between Luke and Kendra; that could explain why Landon stayed in China. And it does seem like there's bad blood between Luke and Landon."

I shake my head, listening to Paige ramble on and on. I guess if anybody could figure this out, it'd be my trusty wannabe PI best friend.

"Well, then, I'll say it again. You were right to leave. You don't need that kind of crap in your life."

"I know. I don't." But I still miss Luke enough that if I saw him right now I could easily change my mind.

"But why China?" Paige asks. "That's weird, too. Seems to me like this guy was holding in a lot more about his life than he should have."

"Maybe," I say, gazing out at the swirling fire batons moving rapidly in a circular motion against the surrounding darkness. "But when it came to his brother, it didn't feel like he was keeping things from me because he might be ashamed of them, but more like they were just really painful to talk about."

"Well, did you at least ask for an explanation on the stuff you overheard?"

"No," I say. "He started to tell me—he did tell me some, but I stopped him." I look down at the smoky glass texture in the tabletop, reflecting on the hour earlier. "I was scared to know—but I knew I was going to have to leave Hawaii anyway and I didn't want to get more invested…more invested than I already was. But Luke and Kendra being involved at one point isn't what would've bothered me, Paige; it was him lying to me about it that I knew I couldn't forgive. He swore to me that he'd never kissed or slept with her, and he was pretty adamant about it. I can't stand a liar, Paige. More than anything, I can't stand a liar." I sigh heavily and rest my forehead on my fingertips, my elbow propped on the table. "I was falling fast and hard for him. I liked him too much"—I *like* him too much—"and if it turned out that he'd lied to me about his involvement with Kendra, everything I felt for him would've been a lie, too, and I don't want to give any of that up. I guess I just wanted to leave with the memories intact, know what I mean?"

"Yeah, I guess I understand," she says. "If it were me, I would've confronted them both, but I still get where you're coming from. But what *did* he tell you?'"

"That it was something about their lifestyle," I answer, though with difficulty as I try to understand it myself. "That there was something they were involved in that he hadn't told me about yet."

"Another red flag," Paige points out—I wish she'd stop doing that. "These people could be serial killers or something."

"Paige," I cut in before she goes off on another tangent, "they're good, normal people. That much I'm confident about. I just—"

Already I'm starting to regret . . . everything.

"Like I said," I finally go on, "I knew what we had wasn't going to go further than my two weeks on that island."

Neither of us says anything for a long, tense minute; and for a moment I forget I'm even on the phone with Paige. All I can think about is Luke, and the more I think about him, the more I want to cry into my pillow until sleep gives me some reprieve.

"Things between us felt so real. I just . . ."

"Sienna." Paige says my name as if preparing to scold me. "Don't talk yourself into giving him the benefit of the doubt. Don't you dare. Just leave things like they are, like you said you'd rather do, because you know he's lying. You don't want to believe it, but I think deep down, you know."

Paige is right. I do feel that way deep down—it's the main thing that gave me reason to stop him from lying to me further and to get up the courage to finally end it and leave.

After I hang up with Paige and tell her I'll be heading back home tomorrow, I give my mom a call to tell her how my vacation has been going. I don't tell her as much as I told Paige, but I do tell her about Luke and how he made me feel.

"But what is your heart telling you, Sienna?" my mom asks.

"I'm not sure," I answer distantly, thinking about it. "All I know is what I want it to be telling me, Mom."

"Well, baby, don't you think that's pretty much the same thing?"

My mom always knows the right things to say. But that doesn't mean I've always listened. As I lie in bed, missing the feel of Luke's lumpy pillows pressed against my face, all I can think about are all the things that I knew going into this: We live in different states; Kendra hates me and seems out to make my life a living hell if I trespass on her turf; Luke seems to have a lot of baggage he has yet to unpack and put away.

But what gets me the most, what confuses me to no end, is that even though I'm running away physically from this situation, emotionally I'm not ready to let go. I have to, but it's going to be hard when I get on that plane tomorrow.

———

I slept awfully last night. I missed the quiet peace of Luke's secluded house on Kauai and listening to the rain fall against the earth as I lay in his bed at night, thinking about him being on the couch. One night I came so close to letting him know it was OK to sleep in the bed with me. I don't know if I would've taken it further than that, but the thought of going to sleep with his arms wrapped around me was enough to sustain me probably forever.

But things are so much noisier at the resort. I constantly hear people shuffling by outside my room in the hall, the rolling wheels of suitcases, kids talking loudly, excited to be going swimming. After Luke's house, I never want to spend another night in a hotel again. After Luke, any guy I meet in the future will have a lot to live up to.

Standing in front of the bathroom mirror with a frothy toothbrush in my mouth, I hear what sounds like a knock at my room door. I shut the water off and listen, my head hovering over the sink, toothpaste dripping from my lips. Another series of knocks rap against the door and I spit and rinse quickly so I can go answer it. For a second I assume it's just the housekeeper, but toss that theory quickly when I don't hear "Housekeeping!" following the knocks.

My heart races just knowing that it's Luke, because who else could it be?

I press my eye to the peephole and freeze with my face against the coated wood.

What is *Kendra* doing here? Kendra, of all people.

I move my eye from the peephole and just stand here for a moment, not sure whether I want to, or should answer the door; my arms are rigid down at my sides. She might be here to hack me to pieces or something—crazy comes in many forms and Kendra doesn't seem far from the farm.

I open the door. There's a long pause rife with tension between both of us as we stare at each other.

She breaks the quiet. "Can I come in and talk to you?"

"How did you know what room I was in?" That's the only thing I want to talk about right now.

She seems anxious to come inside, but answers just to get it out of the way. "A friend of mine works at the front desk."

Oh really? Well, if you attack me, that's a lawsuit waiting to happen.

"Sienna..." She sighs and hesitates, looking discouraged as her big brown eyes stray toward the wall. Then she looks right at me. "I just really need to talk to you. I'm not here to give you shit, or to make you feel any more uncomfortable than I already have. Can I come in?"

I step aside to clear a path for her.

She wastes no time getting right to the point.

"Seth tried to call Luke this morning," she begins, standing in the center of the room with her tanned arms crossed over a pink tank top, "and it took forever to get through to him. Basically, Luke didn't want to talk, but Seth got enough out of him to know that you took off last night and that...well, you might've overheard our argument."

I cross my arms, too, and nod slightly, unable to look her in the eyes. "Yeah, I did. I heard enough."

"Maybe you didn't," she says, and my gaze snaps back to hers. "I think if you did—well, what did you hear exactly?"

My eyebrows stiffen and my defenses shoot up around me. "Well, you said some really hurtful things. Called me a bitch in a roundabout way and basically told Luke he's better off screwing me and leaving me"—I snarl at her—"And, well, if there was more, I'm kind of glad I didn't hear it."

I purposely omit the part about if I found out about them, even though I want to know the truth. I don't want to know because of what I told Paige last night, but with Kendra standing here in front of me, I can't help but give in to that desperate need to know all the answers even if they will destroy the memories. Kendra reaches behind her head and tightens her ponytail. Her long blond hair dangles against her back. She has freckles splashed across her face like me, but not nearly as many. She smells of suntan oil and salt and apology and regret.

"Look, I'm really sorry about all of this," she goes on. "It's just been really hard on all of us, mainly me and Luke, since Landon's death. *Really* hard, you have no idea, and I hope you never have to go through it."

"Wait a second." I stop her, waving a hand in front of myself. "What are you talking about? What do you mean Landon's death?"

She stares at me with a blank expression, though behind it seethes an ocean of confusion and shock. She starts to speak, but at first the words only manage to part her lips. The corners of her eyes crease with deepening lines and she shakes her head looking at the floor.

She looks back up.

"He didn't tell you?"

No, he didn't tell me. Suddenly I feel nauseous with grief and guilt. And anger.

I shake my head and move around Kendra to sit on the end of the bed. "I had no idea..." My voice is as distant as my thoughts are.

"Jesus," Kendra says with disbelief. "I can't believe he didn't at least tell you that much." She turns around to face me and starts to say something else, but I cut in.

"How did he die?" My voice feels a little choked.

She gets really quiet and even her demeanor shifts. Before she seemed eager, ready to talk, but now her shoulders appear to have stiffened and she isn't as ready to open up anymore.

"If I'd known that Luke hadn't told you that Landon died, I wouldn't have even said that much. When it comes to you, it's more his story to tell than mine."

"OK, then what did you come over here for?" Now I'm just getting irritated with her, but the pain and sadness I feel for Luke overshadows it.

"To apologize," she says, "and to clear up anything you might've thought you heard."

"Well, I'm ready to hear it." Really, I'm not. I'm terrified. I don't want her to prove me right, that Luke lied about the two of them.

Kendra sighs heavily and then walks over to the table by the window and pulls out a chair. She sits down on it much like a guy would, with her back hunched over, her deeply tanned legs wide apart and her arms resting atop her thighs, her hands dangling freely between them. She's beautiful, but definitely one of the guys.

"Luke needs just as much professional help as he says I do," she explains, "but he's also as stubborn as I am, too, and won't admit it." She slashes a hand in front of her. "But I didn't come here to talk about Landon—I can't talk about Landon." She sighs. "When Seth told me how devastated Luke was that you'd left last night, I felt like shit. I know it's no excuse, but I was only ever trying to look out for him. I didn't mean to hurt him—Look, I just came here to tell you that Luke is an awesome guy. He's golden, Sienna, and if you let him pass you by . . . I just think it's a huge mistake, is all."

"From what I heard last night," I say resentfully, still skeptical of her sincerity, "you don't want me within five feet of him."

"Yeah, yeah, I know," she says, shaking her head again and gesturing her hand. "I totally admit that I said some messed-up shit, things I shouldn't have said. But you've gotta understand that I really do love him like a brother, and he's been through so much and he means everything to me. I know it sounds clichéd, but I just don't want to see him get hurt. Especially right now. It's too soon. He hasn't even come to terms yet with Landon's death and I'm just so afraid that if something else happens before he can find some closure, he might lose his shit, y'know?"

I nod slowly. I *do* understand, as much as I *can* anyway, only being someone looking in at the situation from the outside and not having all of the details.

"Luke is better around you," she goes on. "Since you came here he's changed. He's happier—I dunno, like I said, he's just better around you. I just think you should at least give him a chance to explain."

"If I ask you something," I speak carefully, "will you answer me honestly and not get offended? Because I'm not trying to offend you in any way."

"Sure." She shrugs her petite shoulders and raises her back out of a slouch, resting it against the chair. "As long as it's not about Landon. I don't talk about Landon." There was a harshness in her words this time that I recognize right away as unbridled pain seething beneath the surface—she's at as much risk of losing her shit as she says Luke is; this much is clear to me.

I nod, agreeing, and then prepare my question, but I'm so nervous about the answer that I literally feel sick to my stomach; tiny beads of sweat are beginning to form in my hairline. I take a deep breath and try to compose myself, try to prepare myself for the truth, no matter how deeply it'll cut into my bones to hear it, if I turn out to be right.

Licking the dryness from my lips, I look back at her and say, "Has anything ever happened between you and Luke?"

She looks down at the floor. "No," she answers, surprising me, because I thought her hesitation was all the answer I needed. "But there was a time when I tried." She can't look at me for a moment. She appears ashamed. "But don't worry about me, or feel like I'm somehow a threat. I'm not. And I don't want to be. That's not what any of this is about and it never was. I guess since I tried to hook up with Luke months ago, he can't help but mistake my concern for jealousy. It's understandable, I guess. Frustrating, but understandable."

"But...something you said," I begin. "You mentioned something about if I found out about the two of you." Was Luke telling the truth? And why am I now suddenly feeling sick to my stomach because of the possibility that he was?

She shakes her head and corrects me. "No, I said 'about us,' but I wasn't talking about Luke and me. I was talking about all of us. Me, Seth, Luke, Alicia, and Braedon."

Suddenly Kendra jumps up from the chair, lets out a long, deep breath, and heads for the door. I get the feeling she doesn't want to talk about anything having to do with her and Luke anymore, beyond what she's already admitted.

I feel a sort of panic rising up in me because she didn't elaborate on her explanation. "But...what were you talking about, then?" I ask with faint desperation in my eyes—now that I know Luke was telling the truth, I need to know what the rest of the truth is. "What about you and Luke and Seth and everybody?"

She sighs and shakes her head, looking briefly at the carpeted floor.

"Luke didn't want you to know before," she says, "because he thought it would scare you off. It always does with girls like you."

"But what does—girls like me—I don't understand." I can't decide which question to ask first.

Kendra smiles slimly, but it looks more apologetic than anything else.

"Sweet girls with their heads on straight and their feet firmly planted on the ground," she says. "That's all I mean."

My gaze drops to the floor as I try to take it all in, but I'm just becoming more frustrated.

"What does he do, Kendra?"

"If he didn't want you to know," she says. "then it's not my place to tell you. I really am sorry." She fits her long fingers around the lever door handle. I get up from the bed and approach her.

"About everything," she goes on. "I didn't mean to be such a bitch, and I think you're a really nice person, not like those bitches that Seth goes through like socks." She hesitates, but looks me right in the eyes. "Luke likes you a lot. I've never seen him as happy as he seems to be when he's with you. Not even with any girl before Landon died. And Seth told me that when he talked to Luke this morning he didn't seem himself. And it's all my fault. And I'm just tryin' to make it right by coming here and clearing the air. But Luke is in a lot of pain; not only because you left—that's a given—but because he misses his brother and I worry about him a lot. We all do."

Tears begin to well up in my eyes. I reach up and wipe underneath them. I want to know about this secret Luke has been keeping, this thing he's so afraid will scare me off, but I want to go to him and be there for him, more than anything else. I want to hold him in my arms and let him use me to cry it all out if he needs to; I want to cry with him.

"Just do me a favor," Kendra says at last. "It's all I ask."

I nod rapidly, eager to hear it and to oblige because, despite everything that happened before, I forgive her, and I feel really bad for her. And for Luke. My stomach is twisted in a thousand knots and my heart feels permanently broken, but for such a different reason than it did last night.

"If you decide to see Luke again," she says with profound determination, "and if—*when* he tells you how Landon died, don't let it scare you away. If you really like Luke as much as I think you do, remember *why*, and don't let anything else change that."

I don't think I've ever been so baffled.

I nod, agreeing, even though I have no clue as to what I'm really agreeing *to*.

The door locks automatically behind Kendra after she leaves, and I'm left here alone, standing in a pool of confusion and dread. Why would how someone died scare me away? But mostly what I think about is the ominous feeling in my heart for Luke and what he must be going through. That's what's important right now. Luke lost his brother, and all I can think about is how much pain he must be in, how much he's been in the whole time that I've been in Hawaii with him. I picture his smiling face and his infectious laughter and his vibrant, magnetic personality, and I wonder how he could be that way around me twenty-four hours a day and keep it together.

Then realization sinks in.

My shoulders slump with a long breath and I fall back onto the end of the bed and find myself staring at the carpet until the little specks of color bring weird spots before my eyes.

Luke always seemed distressed when it came to talk of his brother. I see it now for what it really was and I feel terrible for not pushing the issue further. I remember asking him about Landon once, about what was really bothering him, because I knew that something was. But I didn't probe when he said nothing was wrong, and I feel nothing but guilt now. I should've dug deeper. I should've listened to my instincts.

TWENTY-THREE

Sienna

*I*t's raining again when I step off the plane on Kauai, and it rains on the taxi ride all the way back to Luke's house. I pay the driver and step out into the downpour, covering my head with my hands until I make it up the steps, my purse hanging on one shoulder. My heart is beating a hundred miles a minute. I knew I'd be nervous to see him again after leaving the way I did last night, but things are so different now. I have so much to say, but, more important, I hope that Luke will give me so much to listen to.

The windows and doors are wide open like he usually leaves them, letting in the rain-cooled air and the ocean breeze. I hear music playing inside on the stereo in the living room, not too loudly but enough that he probably didn't hear me pulling up in the cab or he might've come to answer the door already.

I stand in the doorway, looking into the living room through the screen, but Luke's nowhere to be found. I knock lightly and wait. He never comes. Finally I open the screen door and let myself inside, feeling a little weird about it but knowing that Luke doesn't mind and might even complain to me if he found out I stood out here and *didn't* let myself in.

Unless he has a girl in there...No, I don't even know why I thought that—Luke doesn't seem the type.

"Luke?" I call out in a normal tone, walking through the living room. I set my purse down on the recliner as I walk by and slip down the hallway in my flip-flops.

A shadow moves along the wall from the room at the farthest end of the hall where Luke keeps his paintings. I step up to the open door to see him inside, wearing just a pair of running shorts, a paintbrush in one hand; a large canvas with familiar scenery stands nearly finished in front of him on an easel. There is paint everywhere—it looks and smells like fresh paint—even on Luke. A few splatters of green and yellow and brown are smeared across his shoulders. Paint streaks run down the backs of his hands as one moves furiously over the canvas; the other hangs at his side, his strong fingers arched. There's paint on his muscled calves, clinging to his leg hairs. Little glass jars filled with paint are set on the floor beneath the easel. One has been knocked over, a puddle of blue pooling near Luke's bare feet.

To see him standing there like this, I don't just see a guy in front of a painting. I see a broken heart in front of a memory. As I study the scenery being created by his brush I quickly begin to realize where I've seen it before. At the community center. The enormous painting of the sheer rock wall covered by green that seemed to reach into the sky forever. A valley below, shadowed ominously, beautifully, by the rock around it. The painting I named the Bottom of the World. I wonder what *Luke* calls it.

My eyes move slowly about the room, the overcast light bathing the other paintings in a somber ambiance, most of which are of mountains and cliffs and the sky and the ocean seen only from above. But most of all, there are paintings of the Bottom of the World. Different sizes. Different angles. Different viewpoints. Some with sunlight beaming in thick, bright rays. Some with yellow trees instead of green. Some with fog. Some with rain. But all of them of the Bottom of the World.

This place, wherever it is it, holds a painful memory for Luke, and it tears me up inside to know that he's still trapped there, that no matter how much he paints it, or how hard he tries to perfect it, it won't relent and give him the closure he seeks. That's what I see as I look at him; that's what I *feel*.

With his back to me, I wonder if he even knows that I'm standing here, but he's working on that canvas with so much passion and intensity that at first I can't bear to interrupt him.

Then I see his strong shoulders rise and fall seconds later, just as his paintbrush falls away from the canvas and rests in his hand down at his side. I sense he knows now that I'm here, but he has yet to turn and face me.

"Why didn't you tell me," I say softly, "about your brother's death?" Tears begin to well up in my eyes, already taking on his pain, but I choke them back.

"Because these two weeks were supposed to be for you," he says in a quiet voice, still with his back to me. Thunder rumbles amid the gray, cloud-covered sky outside. "I wanted it to be special."

With my heart steadily breaking and filling up with guilt, I step into the room and approach him, trying to hold down my tears.

"But, Luke...it *was* special. Everything about being here with you has been...It's been more than I ever imagined it could be."

"It wouldn't have been if I'd laid my problems in your lap, Sienna. I didn't want that. I just wanted you to have a good time. And because—"

He stops.

He still hasn't turned around, and as I draw closer I hear tears in his voice—faint, but I hear them as clearly as I hear my own—and they cut off what he had wanted to say.

I lay my hands on his shoulders from behind, carefully at first, not sure if he's in the frame of mind for such comforts, and when he doesn't reject me, I lay my palms flat against his skin, moving them down the length of his arms, before wrapping them around his waist from behind and resting the side of my face against his warm back.

Then suddenly, as if human touch has triggered a side of him he's been keeping down for such a long time, Luke falls to the floor, sitting on his bottom with his knees bent, and he lets the tears roll right out of him. His strong hands grip mine around his waist as I go down with him. One fierce sob rattles uncontrollably through his body, and that's all it takes to make my own tears rush from my eyes, causing my vision to blur. I hold him as tight as I can from behind, wanting to wrap him up within my arms and hold him here forever, but his strength is more palpable than mine, his hands gripping the tops of my fingers, pressing my arms against his hard body with so much force.

He turns around to see me, his hands touching the sides of my face, and I don't care that I might become a canvas too. I never want him to move them away. He looks deeply into my eyes, his filled with moisture and emotion, my cheeks warm beneath his hands. "I didn't want you to go, Sienna," he says and another repressed sob fights its way through his chest. His hands tighten on my cheeks as he holds my fixed gaze. "I wanted to tell you the truth, to make you understand, but—"

I lean toward him, my knees pressed into the hardwood floor beneath me, and I kiss his sweet, trembling lips softly. "I'm here now, Luke." I kiss him again, and his eyes search my lips when I pull away. "I came back because I want to be here. With you. I don't care about what happened last night, or about what you didn't get to explain. I'm here and I don't want to be anywhere else."

His warm, forceful lips fall on mine and he kisses me passionately with worship and elation, his hands, wet with paint, gripping the sides of my face with fierce protectiveness. I feel the wetness of his tears on my cheeks, mingling with my own, the intensity of his hands and his mouth and his heart encompassing me.

He breaks the kiss, and we're both breathless when he says, "I wanted to tell you about Landon. I wanted to tell you a lot of things, but I knew you had to go home and none of it would've mattered."

I touch his lips with two of my fingers. "You can tell me whenever you're ready. I'm here to listen, and I'm not going anywhere. There's nothing you can say to scare me away. I still have four days left of my vacation and I want to spend them with you."

"I want you to stay."

"Then I'm staying."

"What about after that?"

"We'll figure it out."

He gazes into my eyes, searching for something, longing for it, and I look back up at him, wordlessly giving him whatever he wants. His lips press against mine and he kisses me hungrily. I feel my body being lifted into the air, my legs wrapped around his waist and the air in the room hitting me as he carries me quickly through it, never breaking the kiss. In seconds I feel the comfort of his bed beneath my back and the lumpy pillows I missed so much under my head. His natural scent envelops me, his heat, his warm flesh, the exploration of his mouth, his ravenous kiss, his everything. I'm done for and I know it. I've never wanted to touch or to taste or to feel anything more in my life than this moment, this inevitable crushing, blissful moment when I give myself to Luke knowing that no matter what happens between us, I'll never be able to forget him. And I'll never want to.

We strip each other clumsily—paint from his hands stains my clothes and my skin—and Luke is on top of me before I can even catch my breath. But I don't need my breath when I have his, and his kiss is deep and forceful and it alone makes my body dizzy with need. My insides tremble and shiver, and my rapidly beating heart threatens to burst, or to stop, and I don't care—as long as Luke's eyes are the last eyes I see, as long as his arms are the last arms to ever hold me.

Luke shoves the pillows out of the way and lowers himself on me. I'm breathless and willing, giving myself completely to him. Arcing my head against the mattress, I open my lips partway, seeking air to fill my lungs with as the sensation of his lips moves over my breasts. His tongue snakes a path between them before he finds my lips again.

I gasp when I feel his hardness press against me with intent.

"I imagined this every night you were here," he whispers hotly into my ear, sending shivers down my spine.

He presses harder below me, and all I can think about is him being inside me, sharing his soul with me, becoming one with me.

"So did I," I whisper and push my hips toward his urgently. He pushes back even harder, and I feel like I'm going to die if he doesn't give me what I want.

And as if he'd heard my thoughts, my eyelids become heavy when I feel him inside of me. I gasp, my body trembling beneath his. My legs shake and my fingers dig into the hard flesh and muscle of his back, holding on to him as though I'm afraid to let him go.

"I've never wanted anything more in my life," I whisper onto his lips just before he takes me into another hungry kiss.

Luke begins to move in and out of me with deep, forceful thrusts, and my thighs quiver around his warm body.

I can't steady my breath.

My heart is beating its way out of my chest.

The muscles in Luke's arms stiffen, holding his weight above me as he dips his head lower, the warmth and moisture of his mouth searching mine possessively. "Look into my eyes, Sienna." I hear his low, coaxing voice, feel the heat of his breath on my lips.

Slowly I open my eyes; it feels like a magic hand lies over them, causing them to tingle and resist.

"Look at me," he whispers, thrusting deeply into me in a slow but hard motion that threatens to send my insides into a quivering frenzy.

I peer up into his eyes, seeing them so full of unbridled passion. And intent—it's as if he's preparing me for something, teasing me with only the wonder of what's to come, knowing I'm going to want it again, and again, and again. He drives into me deeply once and holds himself there, never losing eye contact, and I feel myself clench around him in a desperate, lustful fit. *"Luke…"* I whimper his name, barely conscious of having said anything at all.

"Don't close your eyes," he whispers hotly onto my mouth, and then suddenly I feel the palms of his hands pressing on the insides of my thighs, pushing my legs farther apart and toward me and repositioning himself without ever pulling out.

"Tell me you want me," he says in a low, rumbling voice that demands an instant response. "*Tell* me. I want to hear your voice."

"I do want you, Luke," I whisper, my voice shuddering, my lips parted, sucking in the warm air between us. "I want every part of you. Every inch of you." I gasp when he thrusts against me once more, hard. And he stops and holds himself there again, deep inside.

His lips move against mine urgently, aggressively, the vibration of his voice moving through me in a rumbling, hot growl. Each time his hips rock against mine, it's rougher than the last, more determined than the time before it, sending my mind into blissful oblivion. Claiming me that much more. I belong to him. We belong to each other.

He presses his solid chest against my breasts. My eyes slam shut of their own accord as he rocks in and out of me so hard and so deeply that I lose my breath once more. My senses. My self-control. My thoughts. I wind my fingers through his hair, pulling and gripping with no regard for how much it might hurt him. I know it doesn't. It only makes him fuck me harder.

Arcing my neck on the pillow, my mouth open, my lungs and heartbeat frozen somewhere inside of me where I can't feel anymore, I feel a growing fiery, tingling sensation between my legs, spreading outward through my thighs.

"Oh my God...Luke—" My own body cuts off my words.

"I'll only come after you come," he says, rocking against me.

This can't be real...can it? This has never happ—

Just as that thought enters my mind, a tiny explosion goes off inside my belly, heat spreading throughout my hips and thighs and down into my toes. I moan his name, digging my fingertips into his back. My legs tremble and shake as they tighten around his body, and I feel myself contracting around him, over and over, and I feel like I'm inches from passing out.

Luke pulls out and comes hard, and I reach down and help him, collapsing my hand around his. His sweating body trembles atop mine. His kiss is deep and forceful, the heat of his tongue tangling around my own. He moans into my mouth, pinning me against the mattress with one arm.

With my eyes closed, I feel his lips kiss mine more softly now. Tenderly, as if I'm too delicate to be rough with, too important to him not to be cherished.

My eyelids break apart slowly and I gaze up into his eyes.

I smile softly and he does too.

"What?" he asks, his gaze searching my face. "Why are you blushing?" He pecks my lips.

Reaching up with one hand, I trace the pad of my thumb across his bottom lip. "Oh nothing," I say mysteriously. "It's just that... Well, never mind."

He pecks my lips again. "No, tell me," he urges, tugging on my bottom lip with his teeth. "What is it?"

When he lifts his head, my eyes veer away from his for a moment.

"Well, I don't want to bring up my past... you know... *experiences*, right now of all moments, but—"

A sexy, devilish grin spreads across his face. "Just say it. It's all right."

After a moment, I say, "I've just never been able to orgasm that way."

Luke chuckles lightly, plants kisses all over my cheeks and

forehead, and then lies down next to me, pulling me closer. I can feel his heart still beating erratically against my shoulder.

"I'm serious," I say, and I'm telling him the truth. "It's always been fingers or oral for me."

His arm tightens around my body. "Well, I can do that for you too, if you want." A shiver moves up my spine and into my neck as his fingers brush along the bare skin on my waist and down over my belly.

Then his hand moves down. Farther. Farther.

"No, not yet," I say with light laughter, stopping his hand before there's no turning back. "I need to recuperate first."

"All right," he says and lays his hand across my stomach. "Just tell me when and what and I'm on it."

For a long time I just lie curled around him with my head in the crook of his arm, and we listen to the rain pattering on the roof and the sound of the ocean not far away. He runs his fingers through the top of my hair softly as we lie tangled together in silence. A sweet silence that says more than anything I could ever say with words. I never want to leave this bed. I never want to leave his arms.

After a while Luke says quietly, "It was an accident." He's gazing up at the water-damaged ceiling, but I know the only thing he sees right now is Landon's face.

TWENTY-FOUR

Luke

*E*ight months ago we were all supposed to go to China. All of us, including me. We'd been planning this jump for three years." My chest rises and falls heavily beneath the palm of Sienna's hand, my heart beating to the rhythm of guilt underneath her soft cheek. "But I didn't go with them. I stayed behind because I thought the business and the money were more important than being with my brother." I pause, at war with myself internally. "We always checked each other's packs," I say with blame and quiet anger. "But I wasn't there to check his that day and he died because of it."

My body tenses next to hers. She lays the palm of her hand softly on my heart.

"Landon was on his way to becoming one of the best BASE jumpers in the world," I go on, "and would've been if he hadn't died so soon. He had more than six hundred jumps in fifteen countries under his belt, won competitions, had plenty of sponsors. But none of that stuff was what was most important to my brother. It was never about winning with him, or about being the best. He just wanted to drink the sky. He wanted to fly."

Sienna raises her hand from my chest and wipes a tear from her cheek.

"I was so pissed at him," I go on, reliving the events out of order, my body growing tenser against hers. "Landon had everything going for him. He could hack into any system, if he really wanted to. Our business never would've happened if it hadn't been for the things he could do behind a computer. I hated him; I always loved him as my brother, of course, but I hated him for a while because here he was, intelligent beyond my understanding, scared of nothing, and I was afraid of everything and all I could do was paint." I pause to catch my breath.

Sienna moves her hand closer to my heart, and my hand collapses around it, squeezing gently.

"But Landon, being the brother that he was, made it his priority to help me beat my fears. He practically kicked me out of my bed one morning and said, 'Get up, big brother! I've got something to show you!' He took me to Perrine Bridge that day, and after a long drive listening to Landon tell me everything I needed to hear about why I shouldn't be afraid to live, it was enough to make me want to leap off that bridge that day. And I did. And I never looked back."

"You're like him in that way, you know," Sienna says softly, her cheek pressed against my chest. "That drive and passion to help someone overcome."

I squeeze her hand, acknowledging the meaning behind her comment.

"Sienna," I say in a composed, purposeful voice, "when I met you out on the beach that day, do you remember what I said to you? When I told you that if you stayed longer I could show you how to let it go?"

"Yeah. How could I forget?" She raises her head from my chest and props it on her hand so she can see my eyes. "I didn't under-stand it really, but that didn't matter. I was intrigued by your weird-ness." She blushes a little.

I reach out and brush her short bangs with my fingers, the tips of them grazing her forehead.

"There was more to that," I say, and drop my hand back on my chest, winding my fingers around hers. "You were upset that day, all stressed out because of your job. I had this ridiculous idea that I could somehow make you see what Landon tried to make *me* see." I pause, thinking back on my motives that day. "You seemed to be drowning in some of the same shit I was drowning in before my brother died. And it wasn't until after he died, after I lost the per-son in my life I loved more than anyone, that I realized everything Landon tried to make me see, all of the arguments we had about money—I finally understood what he was trying to tell me."

"What was he trying to tell you?"

My eyes fall away from hers and I look toward the open win-dow running horizontally along the wall above the bed. The rain is still falling outside, the waves still pushing against the shore, churned up by the weather. A gray light pours in through the screen on the window, bathing us in the overcast day, and somehow it seems perfect for the moment.

"That I didn't need money to be happy," I answer. "He was try-ing to make me remember who I already was. Before the money, Landon and I were inseparable. We always had been, but when I started BASE jumping with him, and skydiving and surfing, and rock climbing—you name it, we probably did it—that was when we were the closest as brothers. We didn't give a shit about material stuff, or worry much about not having money to keep the electricity on, because we were too wrapped up in life itself to care—he could turn any bad situation on its head. And Landon still played computer games and dabbled in that stuff on the side when we weren't going here and there to find the best places to jump. He had computers. I had painting."

"Sounds like you both lived . . . free," Sienna says.

I nod once.

"That's exactly what it was," I say. "We lived free. And as long as we were happy, nothing else mattered. We had a fucking blast." I smile faintly, looking above me, picturing my brother's smiling face.

Sienna

Luke begins to sit up on the bed and I do the same. He presses his back against the white wall, his knees bent, his arms propped atop them, dangling at the wrists. He looks out ahead of him, deep thoughts running rampant over his unshaven face; paint is smeared on the side of his chin.

I press my shoulder against the wall beneath the window and cross my arms over my naked breasts, not to hide them, but for comfort. And I take in every last word, finally beginning to see what Landon had tried to make Luke remember. And I think about my own life, and my job, and my struggles, and the more Luke talks, the less significant I begin to feel these petty things in my life really are.

"The money blinded me," he goes on. "It changed me. I didn't become a rich prick who thought he was better than everybody else, but I lost the person I was. I no longer had to think about bills, or how I was going to afford my next tank of gas. I could buy anything I wanted. Cars. Houses. Stupid shit that collects dust. I could take care of our mom and dad, who'd struggled all their lives, raising us. I had everything I could ever need or want, Sienna. Except anything left to strive for. I lost my ability to push myself to greater heights. I lost my inspiration and my drive and my passions. I stopped painting because all I could think about was the business. I didn't want to ever fall back into a life of being 'poor.'" He quotes with his fingers; there's bitter sarcasm in his voice. "It terrified me to think that I might ever have to work some shit job for minimum wage again, living paycheck to paycheck, struggling each week to live a halfway comfortable life."

I watch and listen with the utmost attention, absorbing every one of his words as if this is a pivotal moment in my own life. Because it is.

"Sorry for the rambling," he says. "I-I just feel like I've needed to get this out for so long."

"No," I tell him, "don't be sorry, Luke." He's sharing a part of himself with me that he hasn't been able to share with anyone else and I can't find words to explain how much that means to me, how deeply it breaks my heart but also fills it with a sort of tragic joy. I feel special to Luke in so many ways—that he'd trust in me to understand and care about his deepest, darkest feelings, that he'd allow me to be the one to help him carry the burden.

He looks at me, and there's a level of intensity in his eyes that holds my gaze firmly in place. "Landon's least priority in life was money. He gave all of his up, just like that"—he snaps his fingers—"because he didn't need it. He was the free-spirited type, didn't care much about material things, or how much simpler life could be with more of it. But not me. I couldn't let it go and I couldn't understand how he could. And the point of all this is that...because I was weaker than my brother, I let money destroy us, destroy me, and now he's dead."

I scoot across the bed to sit beside him. He puts me between his legs instead. "I do understand why you feel guilty. I do. And I know that if it were me, I'd probably feel the same guilt." I curl my fingers around his and tug on his hand. "But you know you can't do this to yourself because it'll kill you inside. Because you feel guilty, because it hurts you so much, is proof that it wasn't your fault. The truly guilty just don't care."

"But I should've been there to check his pack," he says, pain choking his voice. "If I had been there—"

"If you had been there," I cut in, "he probably still would've died—when it's our time, it's our time. And there's no way you cared more about money than Landon. You may have convinced yourself of that, but I'm not blinded by the guilt you're blinded by, and I know he meant more to you than anything ever could."

His strong arms squeeze me gently.

"How did it happen?" I ask carefully, wanting him to be able to get everything out, but not wanting to push him too far. "If you feel like talking about it."

"I told you I wanted to," he says, and then takes a deep breath. "I told you I'd tell you everything. It happened in China. Tian Keng. The Heavenly Pit. His chute didn't open. He plunged two thousand feet to his death. It hasn't even been a year."

My heart stops for a moment, and it feels like a fist is collapsing around my stomach. It takes me a few long seconds to gather the strength to speak, but I don't know what I should say, and so I just say what everyone seems to say when confronted with something so tragic.

"I'm so sorry, Luke," I begin, but it doesn't feel sufficient enough for me, and I add, "I can't possibly know what you've been through, or what you're feeling right now, but it hurts my heart to know that this happened. To your brother. And to you."

I feel his lips on my hair again and then he traces his fingers along the top of my leg.

"What I feel right now," he says with the side of his face pressed against my head, "is that I'm glad you came back."

I turn sideways, drawing my knees up together and curl my body against his. His skin is so warm and smells faintly of salt and paint and soap. The heavy rain becomes a light shower and though the stereo has been on the whole time, I'm only now noticing it in the background as it carries lightly through the speakers in the living room. But mostly what I hear is the rain and the sound of Luke's heart beating as I lie against him with my head buried in the crook of his neck.

"Sienna?"

"Yeah?"

"You don't know much about BASE, do you?"

I'm sensing something dismal in that question, something I feel like I should prepare myself for.

"A little," I say. "I know it's kind of like skydiving, but more daring."

"More dangerous," he says as if correcting me.

I don't say anything. I'm not sure what I can say. All I know is that already I hate it; I feel like I'm about to carry the burden of having to choose between two things I love most, that to have both is not only impossible, but forbidden. My heart feels lodged in my throat, and I can't swallow it down.

Luke raises my head from his neck and I turn around to see him. The look in his eyes is dark and concerned. It's making me anxious.

"I'm not going to sugarcoat it," he says. "It's one of the most dangerous extreme sports in the world. A lot of people die doing it. My brother is proof of that."

I think of Landon.

Then I think only of Luke and I start to feel a tiny spell of panic in the far recesses of my mind. But it expands so fast, quickening my pulse and stealing my breath. A lot of people die doing it? *Die?* Then why do it? I want to shake him, I want to tell him how crazy it all sounds to me already, but instead I choose to be rational and listen first, try to understand; maybe it's not as bad as that unsettling feeling moving down the back of my neck is making it out to be.

"And you do this all the time?" I ask hesitantly.

He shakes his head. "Not as much as I used to when Landon was around," he says. "But from time to time I go out with everybody and we do a few jumps."

"All of you do it?" I ask. "Kendra and Seth, too?"

He nods. "Yeah. Kendra, Seth, and Braedon are pretty hard-core. Alicia not as much. I used to be on their level. Before Landon died. Before the money. I might've even been more into it than Seth at one time." He sighs and his gaze strays. "But I don't do it so much anymore."

I want to say, *Because your brother died?* but I don't, because I already feel like that might be the reason. Is it because he's afraid that it could happen to him, too, or is it because the void in his heart that his brother once filled has taken away his passion to do it anymore?

I don't want to seem presumptuous or accusatory. I don't want to open that can of worms if I'm right.

"Do you still love it?" I ask instead.

Luke pauses, and as the silence wears on, I begin to wonder if he even knows the answer at all.

"Yeah, I do..." he says, and it surprises me because I think deep down a part of him—the larger part—doesn't believe that.

"It's the most freeing experience," he goes on distantly, and I get the feeling that maybe the things he's saying are coming from his brother. "Euphoria. *Drink the sky,* Landon always said. And I did. I drank it until I was so drunk I couldn't see straight. I was blind and deaf to everything except the experience. Nothing else matters in the world when you step off that edge. Nothing else matters. The feeling is so powerful that you're willing to die for it..."

Luke

Sienna's face blurs back into focus. I realize I was so lost in thought for a moment that I had forgotten where I was.

But I know where I was...I was in my brother's head.

I shake it off fast and focus on Sienna, the only topic that matters to me right now.

Damn...I'm so crazy about her, everything about her. And what just happened between us...I...There's no going back now. I feel so protective of her, even more than I did before, as though her giving herself to me closed the door of my conscience and opened the one to my heart. I want to scoop her up into my arms and hold her forever, beg her to stay here with me, to forget about San Diego and her life there.

In the back of my mind, though, all I can think about is how much of this is going to be OK with Sienna. Because I've yet to meet a girl like her, who doesn't BASE jump, but who can handle me doing it.

I hope she can. More than anything, I hope she can.

"What's on your mind?" I ask her.

She snaps out of her thoughts and smiles at me.

"I was just thinking about it," she says. "I was wondering... Are there many girls who do this stuff?"

Interesting. Is she asking in general? Or is she hinting around at something? Because if she is, I know damn well it's not because she's thinking of trying it herself.

"Some girls do," I say. "I've known quite a few. Dated one for a short time. But the majority of BASE jumpers are guys."

I wrap my arms around her and pull her close. I love the smell of her hair, her soft skin pressed against mine. I'm getting hard again.

"Are *you* a very experienced jumper?" I feel her body tense.

"Yeah," I say. "I've got a lot of experience, have done a lot of jumps. And I'm not one of the reckless ones. Crazy assholes go out there with little training, thinking, 'Hey, I can do this shit. I'm not scared of anything,' and then their family is making funeral arrangements the next day. I'm very careful. In fact, I'm pretty anal about safety. I *always* checked Landon's pack..." My voice grows distant again.

Sienna

I turn around and sit right in front of him, taking more notice of the tiny streaks and flecks of blue and green and yellow paint on one side of his neck and on his chest muscles.

"Hey," I say, reaching out my hand and touching the side of his face, "don't do that." I brush my fingers softly against his skin, just above the stubble, rubbing away a fleck of paint. "No blaming yourself, all right? Do you think I'm a stupid person?"

He blinks back the confusion.

"Umm, definitely not," he says.

I smile and brush the pad of my thumb over his lips.

"Then believe me when I tell you that his death wasn't your fault. Take my word for it because I know what I'm talking about." I lean in and kiss his lips.

Luke smiles faintly and hooks both of his hands about my hips.

"You're an amazing girl," he says. "Everything about you makes me want to be a different person. To be the person I used to be."

I kiss him again.

"But I like the person you are," I whisper onto his lips.

His hands move from my hips to my butt. The tip of his tongue traces a path along my bottom lip.

"How are you even *real?*" His fingers press into my flesh, pulling me closer to his naked lap.

"What do you mean?" I kiss him again.

My legs straddle his lap, his hardness palpable between us, his arms wrapped around my back.

"You're just unlike anyone I've ever met," he says breathlessly between kisses. "You didn't freak out on me last night before you left—it made me feel even worse. You didn't hold a grudge against me about that roach."

I pull away, grinning into his eyes. "What makes you think I'm not holding a grudge about that?"

He arcs a brow. "Are you?"

"Maybe," I taunt him. "You could've flicked it off me a lot sooner."

He squeezes his arms around me tightly and buries his face in my throat.

"So what are you gonna do to get me back?" His tongue moves along my collarbone and then his mouth finds my neck.

My chest begins to rise and fall more rapidly, my skin breaking out all over in chills.

"I don't know yet," I say with my eyes shut halfway. "But paybacks are a bitch."

"Is that right?" His hands squeeze my butt and pull me hard against him. I gasp lightly. "Well, how about this," he says against my ear. "I can make it up to you and *you* can promise to drop your little vendetta. I don't like always having to look over my shoulder." He sucks on my neck and then my earlobe.

I ache with need.

With my arms draped around his neck, I whisper back, "I don't know. Maybe. It depends on what you plan to do to make it up to me."

Suddenly he hoists me off his lap and puts me on my back across his mattress. My eyes grow a little wider, my heart is pounding fervently behind my ribs. I look up at Luke, sitting at my feet, and his hands slide between my thighs, parting my legs before him.

Oh my God...

He just looks at me for a quiet moment, across the landscape of my body. I'm becoming breathless again, just looking at his eyes hooded with passionate, voracious intent. A heat moves through my thighs and travels down into my knees.

His head falls between my legs.

I can't... I just can't—

I claw the sheet with both hands as his mouth sends me into sweet oblivion.

TWENTY-FIVE

Sienna

*I*t takes a lot of scrubbing to get the paint off both of us the next morning. And between the cleaning, Luke has his way with me in the shower, too. And then it's back to scrubbing again. He can't keep his hands off me. I'd be really disappointed if he could.

"Let me do that," I tell him as we're standing naked in front of the bathroom mirror. I take the razor from his fingers and jump onto the counter.

"What if you cut me?" he says, stepping over in between my bare legs hanging over the side of the counter.

"You jump off thousand-foot cliffs and massive buildings, Luke. I doubt my shaving your face is that worrisome." That was meant as a joke, but once I said it, it didn't feel so funny to me, after all.

He laughs under his breath.

"Luke," I say, losing my smile, "why do you still do it? Wait, I mean...I guess the real question is: Why do you risk your life BASE jumping? I guess I sort of get all the other stuff—cliff-diving, surfing in storms, rock climbing; they're not so...deadly—but I don't really understand the risks you take with BASE." When I realize

I'm practically talking in half sentences, I stop for a second to gather my thoughts. "What I'm really trying to say is that...it scares me."

Something unfamiliar flickers in his eyes. Uncertainty? Disappointment? Dread? I can't tell which, but I get the feeling it's not something he wanted to hear me say.

It makes me wish I hadn't brought it up.

Suddenly, as if I'd never said anything at all, Luke's hands grab my hips and he steps closer, lining himself up with me below, a lopsided grin at his lips.

Although it seems like he's deflecting the topic, I give in to him, unable to shake that playful gleam in his eyes.

"Don't even think about it," I warn him, glancing downward, and he makes a pouty face.

Despite my concerns—my fears—for Luke, I try not to think about it, but find that impossible. For a moment my playful smiles are forced and my laughter is only covering up my worry. But I get to work shaving him while trying to keep him in line at the same time, and before long Luke manages to make my smiles real again.

I only nick him once, and he really lays the complaining on thick—more like whining—but he's not fooling me. I threaten to cut him on purpose if he doesn't hush, but the only thing that gets him to shut up is when I kiss him. That always works. But it always leads to more sex. If he's not inside of me, he's touching me with his fingers or his mouth. Just about everywhere except the laundry room and Seth's room. Watching a movie—he can't keep his hands off me. Standing at the stove cooking a *real* breakfast to show him how it's done—he can't keep his hands off me. Swimming in the ocean—he can't keep his hands off me. In his car on our way to hike to a waterfall—he pulls over under a canopy of trees and I return the favor, surprised I can get him almost all the way into my mouth.

"Oh my fucking God, Sienna…"

The steering wheel hits me on the head when he moves his hips in a way that pushes my head against it.

"Owww!"

"No, no, no, don't stop," he says kind of frantically—and hilariously—with his free hand on the top of my head, I know just wanting to push it back down.

I finish him off and complain more about the steering wheel on the way to the waterfall.

He makes it up to me later.

If the thought of having to leave Hawaii was unbearable before, now, after all of our intimate moments together, how he cherishes me in every single way, the thought utterly rips me apart. Every kiss, every touch, every whisper, every time he looks at me with those magical, endearing eyes of his, I lose myself a little bit more: to Luke, to the possibilities of change; I lose myself in ways I never imagined, or would have welcomed before I met him.

After the hike, and a thousand photographs later, we spend the rest of the afternoon near a beach, lying out on a blanket on the grass, looking up at the blue sky. Our shoes kicked off, my camera sitting next to my purse. A couple of sub sandwiches half eaten beside us as we watch some local surfers ride the waves.

"Luke," I say, my voice filling the small space between us as we lie tangled on the blanket, "I've been thinking a lot about Monday."

His long fingers comb through my hair as he gazes into my eyes thoughtfully.

"I think about it every day," he says. "I wish you didn't have to go back."

"Me too." It's all I can say; it kills me to think about it, much less talk about it, but I know we have to.

"I know you have to get back to your job and all that, but I'd like to come visit you. My parents live in Sacramento. I can stay with them and visit you. And I know my way a little around San Diego already."

"I have my own apartment in Ocean View Villas," I say, thinking it might ring a bell. "It's in downtown San Diego. When you visit, you can stay with me." I love the thought of that, but I still can't keep the sadness from my voice. I want to tell him that the thought of a long-distance relationship is depressing, but what can I say? I *want* to be with him. I *want* to try to make this work, whatever this is growing so fast between us, even if it means living six hours apart, separated by an ocean.

There's something else, though, something darker looming in my heart. It bothers me worse than the distance that will separate us and I don't want to think about it: him BASE jumping, and killing himself doing it.

"What's wrong?" he asks, his face just inches from mine.

"I'm just a little overwhelmed," I say, and instantly the smile drops from his lips. I try to bring it back quickly. "I just mean everything that's happened between us. I wasn't exactly prepared for that when I boarded the plane for my job. But I'm overwhelmed in a *good* way." And that's mostly true. Never in a thousand years did I ever think I'd meet someone like Luke and be lying here right now with him underneath a Hawaiian sky, talking about a possible future together. Things this magical only happen by accident. Sometimes only once. Sometimes never.

"Are you sure?" The backs of his fingers brush the edge of my cheek.

I nod, smiling, and lean in and kiss his lips. He kisses my nose and then my forehead and pulls me closer, tucking my head beneath his chin.

"We'll figure it out," he says. "Who knows? You might realize you don't like me as much as you thought you did."

I scoff quietly, because that's the stupidest thing I've ever heard.

"That won't happen," I say and lace my fingers through his on top of his chest.

"Yeah? How do you know for sure?"

Because I think I'm falling for you, and it's breaking my heart to know that in a couple days there will be an ocean between us...And because...

"I just know," I say out loud and choke down the pain of my inner thoughts.

"You were right," I speak up after a long time.

"About what?"

"About at least two of the three things you said would happen before I went home."

"Oh yeah?" There's a huge smile in his voice. "Which one was I wrong about?"

"That photography would take the place of everything else in my life."

We lie together for a long time, talking about our families and our firsts: first kisses, first time we had sex, first bad breakup—his first kiss was age thirteen, mine age fifteen. He lost his virginity at sixteen. I lost mine at seventeen to a football player who I liked a lot, until I had sex with him. Probably had something to do with the weird noises he made when he was on top of me. Luke laughs at the expression on my face as I tell him about it.

"Now I know how to get you good if you ever piss me off," he says. "I'll make sounds like a hippo giving birth when we have sex." He laughs hard.

I smack him on the knee. "You better not!" My eyes are wide and I'm trying not to smile. He grabs me and kisses me hard and then makes a weird noise into my mouth that makes me choke with laughter and play-kick him right off of me.

We didn't even realize when the clouds had started rolling in and then without warning the sky opens up true Kauai style and sends us scrambling to get our stuff off the ground.

"My camera!" I shout over the rain thrusting into the ground like a million tiny marbles.

Luke scoops my camera up and covers it with his body until I can get my purse open and make room for it. Then he grabs the blanket and the rest of our stuff from the grass and we run to his car parked a few yards away in a parking lot. The drive back to his house is gross and uncomfortable. We're drenched right down to our underwear, and our clothes soak the fabric of the car seats. I just feel icky and want to strip off my clothes right here, but I refrain. I don't want to pull into the drive at Luke's house and be naked if Seth happens to be there already.

Sometime today Seth and Kendra are coming over. Now that things have been cleared up between Luke and me, I wanted Luke to know that I thought it was important he invite Kendra over. So that's what I did just before we got rained on. I like her now that I know more about what's going on. And I know she's an important person in Luke's life and they need to make up.

Luke comes back with some beer, and I'm trying to clean the place up before they get here—old habits. I wash our dishes and wipe off the counters. The stereo is on low in the background, playing a mix of my favorite stuff.

"What time are they supposed to be here?" I ask as Luke is putting the beer away in the fridge.

He steps up in front of me and kisses me hard.

"With them you never know," he says, rubbing his hands up and down my arms. "They're the most unpredictable people I've ever met." He fishes his wallet from his pocket and tosses it on the counter. Then he begins to sift through the cabinet. "Seth has to meet Allan over on Oahu at the surf school. It might be six o'clock before they get here." He points at me. "Want some?"

I glance at the package of Nutter Butter cookies and shake my head, making a face. He breaks apart the package and shuffles out a few.

"I kind of like Kendra," I say. "I don't know her very well, and we got off to a bad start, but she seems like a really good friend to you and I'm a little worried about her."

Luke holds a cookie near his mouth and asks, "Why?" before biting it in half.

I cross my arms and lean with my hip pressed against the counter.

"I don't know. I just am." I pause and then say, "She tried to get closer to you because you're the closest thing to Landon, didn't she?" It was both a question and a statement because I'm confident I already know.

He stops chewing for a second, looking at me thoughtfully, then finishes the cookie and swallows it down. He nods.

"Yeah," he says, and then pulls out a chair from underneath the tiny kitchen table. He puts the other cookies down. "Like I said, we've all taken Landon's death really hard. Him being my brother; her fiancé. They were together for four years. It was crazy how much they loved each other. Everybody used to give 'em shit about it. All in good fun." He stops, takes a deep breath and shakes his head. "She was pretty messed up when he died. Seth and I thought she was being reckless on purpose. I swear she wanted to die jump-ing a few times because when she did it, she walked away alive and well, but she seemed disappointed." He looks right at me under hooded eyes. "And no one is *ever* disappointed after a jump. So even though I was trying to deal with my own demons, I tried to help her too, because I thought that if someone didn't, she'd be next."

"What about Seth?" I ask.

"Nah," he says. "Seth loves her and all, but he's not the helping type. Not that he doesn't care or try to help. He just doesn't know how. Anyway, I tried to help her, and we got closer, and I think she started seeing me as my brother's replacement."

I nod, understanding.

"Well, I think it's natural that she'd feel like that toward you," I say. "Especially after something like that. You and Landon must've been a lot alike."

Luke smiles, a reminiscent look passing over his features.

"In more ways than not, yeah, we were a lot alike." His eyes meet mine and then he laughs lightly. "All except for the hair."

Luke gets up from the table and takes my hand, walking with me into the living room. Mild excitement has filled his mood, a per-manent smile at rest on his face. Just seeing him like this makes me smile too, and I can't help but make note of how devastatingly gor-geous he is, even more so when he's happy.

He guides me to have a seat on the couch and then goes over and crouches down in front of the television. He switches off the stereo.

"We recorded a lot of our jumps," he says, looking through a pile of DVDs, reading the words scribbled across the front in black Sharpie until he finds one he's looking for. "This one was a blast. After the jump, the ten of us camped out on the site. Landon got kind of drunk and..." Luke's words fade into the DVD.

"No, man, Kendra gets first jump this time," a guy same height as Luke, same hazel eyes and tanned skin and dazzling white smile, says, standing next to Kendra.

Landon had longer hair than Luke, but not too long, and it was done up in dreadlocks that he kept pulled back behind him.

There were several people standing on top of a cliff in a desert, all wearing thick black harness straps over their shoulders, across their chests, and between their legs, bunching the fabric of their jackets. Packs were mounted on their backs, containing their parachutes. Helmets on their heads, some with built-in cameras mounted on the front. Landon's dreadlocks poked out from beneath his helmet.

I never considered dreadlocks attractive on a guy before, but Landon Everett owned the look and I can't help but find him as gorgeous as his brother. Luke sits down next to me on the couch with the remote in one hand, his eyes fixed on the flat-screen where his brother still lives and breathes and smiles and jokes around like they had always done.

"All right," Luke says. *"I guess we have to give her one on account that she's a girl!"*

"Hey! Shut the fuck up, Skywalker!" Kendra says.

"Control your girl, bro," Luke tells Landon, grinning.

Landon puts up his hands. *"Hey, I don't control her. If anything, it's the other way around!"*

"WHIPPED!" Seth yells from the side.

"WHOOP!" some other guy shouts.

Landon laughs when Kendra play-punches Seth on the shoulder.

"Hey! No abuse until after the jump!" Luke says as he straps on his helmet.

The jumpy video went on for a few minutes while all of them

checked each other's packs and hardware and things I couldn't begin to name or understand what function they serve. There was a lot of laughter and Luke and Landon were exactly like I always imagined close brothers would be. And although Luke was right about him and his brother looking and being so much alike, it's a surreal and heart-wrenching experience to finally place the face with the name of Landon Everett, who I've heard so much about and who has been such a force in all their lives.

Kendra jumps off the edge of the cliff and I absently dig my fingers into the sofa cushion.

And then Landon jumps and my heart sinks into my toes when the edited video switches to his head cam and shows how fast he's free-falling toward the desert landscape below.

And then Seth jumps and does a front flip on his way down; his camera view seems so close to the sheer rock wall that my hands begin to shake.

And then Luke jumps...

My stomach swirls with panic as the ground comes up so fast toward him. He's shouting his excitement all the way down, and all I can think is, *Please pull the parachute, please pull the parachute, hurry and pull the parachute,* and, *I hope the parachute opens,* even though Luke is sitting right next to me, alive, and this video is old. As I watch him fall to the earth and the blue sky spin around his body, I can't help but be terrified he won't make it.

Then Luke pulls his chute and the canopy opens up above him with a snapping sound that fills my heart with relief. He hits the ground softly, on his feet as if he'd just walked right out of the sky, and the camera wobbles and jumps until he comes to a stop. The bright yellow canopy falls like a giant windblown blanket off to the side of him.

Luke shows me several of these videos, and I can't understand how I can feel so afraid and inspired at the same time. I *can* see how Luke can say that BASE jumping is the most freeing experience, just by watching them do it. A part of me, a part so small yet so powerful wishes I were that brave, because I'd love to *drink the sky* and feel what they feel, but I know I never could.

"No disappointment," Luke says beside me.

"Huh?" I glance over, snapping out of my spinning thoughts and back into the moment.

"Kendra"—he reaches out and presses stop on the DVD—"there's no disappointment in that girl after any of those jumps."

"Definitely not," I say. "She seemed as happy as the rest of you."

Seth's bad brakes whine briefly, sharply, as his Jeep pulls into the drive out front.

Luke turns the television off.

"Don't say anything about those videos with Kendra here," he suggests. "She'll want to watch them. I told her I got rid of them." He crouches in front of the television again and puts the DVDs away, sliding them back in between other clear, square jewel cases.

I get up from the couch.

"Maybe she needs to watch them," I say. "It might give her some closure. You can watch them and he was your brother; maybe she can handle it, too."

Luke pushes himself to his feet and looks at me, a somber expression in his eyes.

"Kendra watched my brother die, Sienna."

I gasp sharply, quietly, and my heart stops.

"She was at the bottom," he goes on, "not experienced enough to make that jump in China herself, but she was there, standing two thousand feet below him, waiting for him. When he hit the ground she saw and heard everything." He says this all so casually, with absolutely no emotion, as though he's worked very hard toward being able to explain without breaking down, despite working even harder to never have to talk about it at all. This I find incredibly sad, that Luke would ever have to work to suppress such emotion because he knows it'll kill him if he can't.

Seth and Kendra's voices move toward the front door, and seconds later there's a knock.

I can't move, or breathe, and I'm trying so hard to force down the tears burning their way to the surface of my eyes. I feel as if I'm looking through Landon's eyes, seeing the ground, two thousand feet beneath me, coming up to meet me in the most violent way imaginable. I can't fathom what he must've been thinking, the terror in his heart, knowing that he was about to die—he faced my worst nightmare.

And I picture Kendra, looking up at him from the bottom, knowing something is wrong—the horrific sight and sound of his body hitting the ground. My God, how can she hold herself together? I can barely hold it together just imagining it.

My breath finally releases in a shuddering exhalation; my hand flies up, pressing against my breast.

TWENTY-SIX

Sienna

*S*eth lets himself in after the second knock, peeking his shaved head around the corner of the door, the scar running along the side more prominent in the light. I wonder how he got it, if it was from this crazy stuff they all do.

"Knock, knock," he says with a big grin. "Get your clothes on!"

"Come on in," Luke says and reaches out to grab Seth's hand. They bump chests and let go.

"Feels odd knocking, bro," Seth says.

Kendra comes in behind him, long blond hair pulled into a ponytail, tanned skin stark against the white tank top and red ball shorts she wears. Seth is like a gorgeous, bald-headed giant standing next to her, with buff bronzed arms and strong calves rippling with muscles underneath his knee-length cargo shorts. When my eyes fall on Kendra's for the first time since I saw her last in the hotel, mine aren't holding as much of a smile as I had wanted. There's more sadness in them, I know, but I try my best not to let it show.

Stepping up, I pull Kendra into an awkward hug—awkward because she apparently isn't much the hugging type, but she doesn't push me away, and pats my back and says, "Yeah, uh, it's good to see you too," and then she chuckles.

I can't imagine what's going on inside of her, what she's been keeping down, the nightmares she must wake up to in a sweat at night, the replay of Landon's horrific death going over and over in her mind, all while at the same time putting on this brave face and pretending, every single day of her life, that she's OK.

Kendra is anything but OK.

I take a step back and look between her and Luke. Seth walks past us all and goes straight into the kitchen.

"Please tell me you have beer," he calls out.

I decide to follow, to give Luke and Kendra a moment alone, and I pass Luke a soft smile as I walk by, which he returns.

"Yeah, he just got back with beer," I tell Seth as he's pulling the fridge door open.

That makes him happy, but then again, Seth always seems happy. Nothing much ever seems to bother the guy. "Awesome," he says and pulls two bottles out, wedged between the fingers of one hand.

I sit down at the table after Seth gives me a beer. He joins me in an empty chair, slouching his tall height against the back, stretching his long legs out in front of him.

"So you're afraid of heights, huh?" Seth laughs lightly, his broad shoulders bouncing as he puts the bottle to his lips, but he's not at all making fun of me. "I guess asking you to go skydiving with us tomorrow is out of the question, then." He sets the bottle on the table.

"Uh, well, yeah, I'd say that's not gonna happen." I take a quick sip, making a slight face as the beer sours on my taste buds. "But Luke has really helped me out a lot with my fear of heights."

"He's good like that," Seth says with a nod and winks at me. "I guarantee you that if you give him a few months, you'll be jumping out of planes and shit."

I laugh corrosively and choke a little on my beer.

"That'll never happen." I point at him, shaking my head.

He grins and takes another drink.

I leave it at that because something tells me Seth is the type of guy who believes what he wants, confident beyond my understanding, but not in a conceited way, just a positive way. And if he's ever wrong, he laughs it off, sucks it up, admits it, and just tries to be right about the next thing. Seth is a strange one, I admit, but I can't find a single thing about him that I don't like. Not even his habitual brief encounters with girls, which anyone who's never even officially met him can see a mile away. I picture him as the type who tells them up front that it's a one-time thing. It's their own damn fault if they ignore that and think they can change him.

I notice the scar running along the side of his head again, though it's kind of hard *not* to notice.

"How did you get that?" I don't have to point at it for him to know what I'm talking about. "BASE jumping?"

He chuckles. "Nah. If I got it BASE jumping, it probably would've opened my head up the rest of the way." He laughs and swigs a quick drink—I *don't* laugh, I just swallow nervously. "Got this one rock climbing. Misjudged the terrain, grabbed some loose rock, and one about the size of my fist"—he makes a fist with a rather large hand—"came off with it and knocked me unconscious. If I hadn't been secured in my harness, I would've fallen about three hundred feet."

I wince.

Just as I start to ask Seth more about BASE jumping (because the comment he just made about it planted another dark seed in my brain), Luke and Kendra walk into the kitchen.

Luke comes straight over, leans down behind me and kisses me on the cheek, his way of thanking me without words for insisting they make up.

Kendra sits in a chair on my right.

"So we're cool," she announces. "He's still an ass because he won't go skydiving with us tomorrow, but"—she grins at me—"since I like his girlfriend, I'll let it slide."

I blush and smile back at her. Girlfriend—I like the sound of that.

Luke gets two beers from the fridge.

"I'll go next time," he says. "While Sienna is here I'm spending all of my time with her."

"She could go with us and watch," Kendra says. "It'll be fun."

Luke hands Kendra a beer, and then instead of taking the empty chair on my left, he helps me out of mine, sits down on it, putting me on his lap.

Already I'm shaking my head, rejecting the skydiving idea.

"She won't be able to see much," Seth points out.

"No," Luke says, "I don't think that's her idea of fun—don't let them talk you into it; there's plenty of other stuff to do."

I swallow nervously and speak up.

"No offense, but Luke's right," I say. "It's just not my idea of fun; sounds really terrifying, to be honest."

"Well, you don't have to jump or anything," Kendra says.

My expression darkens a little and I shake my head. "I'm just not into that BASE jumping stuff—sorry."

Kendra waves a hand at me, brushing my comment off. "Nah, it's not like BASE. Skydiving is really safe; you see eighty-year-old ladies out there doing it." She looks over at Seth quickly. "Remember that one lady who jumped like three times?"

Seth and Luke laugh, nodding and pointing their beers at each other.

"I remember her," Luke says.

"That was pretty insane," Seth adds.

Luke rubs my leg with the palm of his hand.

"Skydiving is safe," he says, "but don't worry about it; I want to do whatever you want to do, all right?"

I begin to contemplate it: OK, it's not BASE jumping, so maybe I should go and at least watch; they say it's really safe, and if eighty-year-olds can do it, then it must be. Besides, maybe watching them will help me a little more with my fear of heights.

"I don't know. I guess it wouldn't hurt to go." I can't believe I'm saying this. "I-I mean, not to jump, of course, but I think I'd like to go and watch."

Kendra looks at Luke and then at Seth. Seth looks at Luke and shrugs and swigs his beer. Luke's hand squeezes my waist again.

"Sienna, if you don't—"

"No, I'm really OK with it," I cut in. "If you want to go, I'm all for tagging along." If that's true, why do I still feel this dread in my heart?

Come on, Sienna, you can do this, I tell myself. I know I'll probably never accept the BASE jumping, but I at least want to be supportive in the other things Luke loves to do: cliff-diving, a little dangerous surfing every now and then, skydiving—I want to make an effort to accept these things, because Luke's worth it. And I have to remind myself that when it comes to heights, my fears are more irrational than most people's.

"I think we have a verdict!" Seth says.

Kendra beams across the table at me.

"You're all right," she says, her way of thanking me not only for wanting me and Luke to go with them, but for everything else, too.

Luke's lips fall on the side of my neck.

"I guess it's settled then," he says and he can't mask the excitement in his voice.

It's not until they start talking about Norway that I become the quiet one, sitting on Luke's lap, listening, and trying to take it all in. They go on and on about it—things I sort of get, most of it I don't: Equipment. Gear. This and that. Jumping off the Troll Wall. July ninth. And more about Landon.

Finally, when I can't sit silently any longer, I ask, "Why is July ninth so important?"

The table gets quiet.

"It would've been Landon's twenty-third birthday," Luke says.

Kendra speaks up, all traces of excitement from before gone from her face. "It was something Landon wanted us all to do after China."

"To honor Landon," Luke says as he combs his fingers through my hair, "we agreed to go ahead with the plans and jump in Norway on his birthday."

"Oh," I say.

"And then next year," Seth joins in, always with a smile, "we'll be heading to Mexico and Australia, baby!" He leans his long arm across the table and bumps fists with Luke. I smile and laugh... No, I *fake* smile and *fake* laugh. Then Seth drinks down the last of his beer and heads toward the fridge. Kendra, without realizing it, saves me from having to explain the look creeping up on my face, the one I know is akin to another kind of fear—fear for

Luke's life. She jumps up from the table, trying to get to the fridge before Seth.

"Hey! Back off, Ken-doll!" He puts his big arm out and easily holds her at bay.

"Stop calling me that!" she growls, grabs him around the waist, worms her way past his giant form, and snatches the last two beers right out of his hand.

"Those are mine!" Luke calls out, and Seth and Kendra both freeze in their steps. "You want one?" he asks me quietly.

I shake my head. "No. I'm good."

"Have at 'em," he says, and their bodies reanimate as they scuffle a moment, only to end up with a beer each in the end.

I often wonder why the two of them aren't together because they really seem into each other, but maybe they are holding everything back for the sake of friendship; I don't know. I'd probably ask them about it right now, put them on the spot and join in on their fun, but this whole Norway thing in a couple of weeks is too heavy on my mind.

Luke tightens his arms around me.

"You sure you want to go with us tomorrow?" he asks.

His smile and those beautiful eyes that regard me with emotions I can't begin to explain are enough to erase my newfound fear. Even if only for a little while.

I lean in and kiss his lips. "Yeah, definitely," I say. "I look forward to seeing some of this world above the clouds that makes you the way you are."

He presses his lips to my forehead.

"I can't wait to show you," he says, and I get lost in his smile.

It's important to me that Luke know I'm not in his life to *change* his life, and I don't want to be the reason he doesn't go out with his friends and do the things that make him happy. I like him the way he is and I respect his close relationship with his friends. But another part of me is so afraid for him, for all of them; a part of me, as much as I want to be supportive, makes me feel like I don't know what I'm getting myself into, and more than that, I don't know if I can truly handle it.

Later I lie curled up next to Luke, listening to the steady sound of his breath as he sleeps, the thrumming of his heartbeat against my cheek, and I don't recall ever having so many profound thoughts running through my head all at one time. So many decisions that I have to make. So many unavoidable consequences of each and every one of them.

I want to stay here with Luke, but I can't. I want to prove Seth right about Luke's persuasive abilities and be stripped of my fear once and for all so I can experience the things they experience no matter how reckless and dangerous, but I won't. I want to shake Kendra and tell her that she'll be OK and in order to let Landon go she should *talk* about him, but I'm afraid. I want to stop spending all my time working and start photographing more, but I'm conflicted. I want to be able to know Landon Everett as closely as Luke and Seth and Kendra because he was so loved by them all and seemed like such an extraordinary person, but I know that's impossible. But most of all, I want to stop feeling this strange darkness inside of me, this looming sense of fear and worry for Luke, and even Kendra and Seth, because of what they do, but I have a feeling that darkness will never go away.

"Why are you crying?" I hear Luke's voice in the darkness. I hadn't realized he was awake.

He rolls over and drapes his arm over my chest, wiping the tears from my cheeks.

"Ummm..." I can't find the right words.

"Sienna?" He nudges his head closer to me. I can feel his warm breath on the side of my face, exhaling from his nose. "Tell me what's wrong."

I sniffle and wipe my tears.

"I uh...well, I was just thinking about your brother."

"What about him?" he says softly, the pad of his thumb moving deftly across my chin.

Silence fills the space between us. I'm still unsure of what to say.

"I...just can't get over how he died." My voice is quiet, distant. "It's just really sad."

It was true: I was thinking about Landon, but mostly I was thinking about Luke. Seems there's something now I fear more than heights or losing my way in the financial world: I'm afraid of losing Luke the same way he lost his brother. I want to tell him— I tried to the morning after we slept together the first time—but something tells me it's the one thing he doesn't want to hear. That wounded look on his face, that air of dread and disappointment. I don't see me being able to hold this in forever. I won't be able to hold it in for long.

Luke

Sienna is a special girl—my special girl, the one I think I've been waiting for all my life. I knew it before. I knew she was the one long before this moment. I *knew*. With her here, in my arms, I feel peace again that I never thought I'd feel.

But there's also something there that threatens that peace— Sienna's worry over my BASE jumping. I can take it from my past girlfriends, but not with Sienna. I need to make her understand how safe I am about it, how OK I'll be, before she decides she can't be with me because of it. I *need* to make her understand. I hope that I can. Sienna is different; I have to believe that she can accept it.

No, I *do* believe it.

I refuse to believe otherwise.

"I'm sorry," she says. "I know it's hard for you to talk about it."

I roll carefully on top of her and take her into a kiss, cupping her face firmly within my hands. The kiss breaks and I look down into her eyes, searching them through tears and conflict and the sweetness she harbors as naturally as I harbor risk.

"You're an angel, Sienna Murphy."

She smiles, and I lean in and kiss away the tears lingering on her cheeks. And then I make love to her before letting her fall sleep in my arms.

"I drank the sky *and* brought an angel down with me," I whisper into the darkness. "Not bad, huh, little brother?"

I shut my eyes and sleep the whole night through.

TWENTY-SEVEN

Sienna

I haven't breathed since we got here, in this giant field surrounded by rolling mountains and ocean, with nothing but blue sky above us. I've been holding my breath since we all got out of Luke's car. And I've sat on the grass, out of the way, watching everybody get their packs, or parachutes, or whatever, ready. A small plane sits on a black landing strip not far away, waiting for them all to get on.

"Do you usually jump with them?" I ask Alicia, who is sitting on the grass next to me with a broken leg, stiff in a cast from her thigh to her ankle.

"Yeah," she says with a frown, "and it sucks that I can't do much of anything for the next six weeks." She knocks on the top of the cast with her knuckles. "Kind of ironic—I jump out of planes and off cliffs, but I break my leg falling down three steps." She laughs sardonically and holds up three fingers to me. "*Three*— would've been less embarrassing if it were a whole staircase, or somethin'."

I laugh with her because she has a point.

Luke raises his hand from afar and waves at me one more time before heading toward the plane. I wave back, my smile fighting against the nauseous feeling in my stomach.

"You could fly tandem with Luke," Alicia says.

"Huh?" I look over, having barely heard anything she said because I was so fixated on watching Luke get into the plane. Finally her words catch up to me. "Oh, no, I couldn't do it. I have a fear of heights."

Alicia nods. "Understandable, but the best way to get over it is to face it head-on." She makes a weird face while sticking a straw down into the cast to scratch her leg on the inside.

"If only it were that easy," I say.

"I hear yah," she says, steadily scratching. "But skydiving is really safe. If you ever decide you want to try it out, Luke is the best guy for the job. I actually jumped with him my first time."

"Really?"

"Yeah," she says, pulling the straw out and focusing more on me. "Me and Braedon went out together our first time. I jumped tandem with Luke, and Braedon went with Landon. It was great. After that first jump, it became an addiction."

I gaze back out at the plane as it goes into motion across the landing strip, getting ready to take off. I think of Luke, of him being on that plane right now, and that darkness grows inside of me again when I imagine him jumping out of it.

"Seriously though," I hear Alicia say, "for people like you, who are afraid of heights, or just anything really, something like skydiving can change your life. I actually feel sorry for people who've never done it at least once."

"Why's that?" I ask, looking over at her.

Her black hair pulled into a ponytail glistens in the sunlight.

Her dark brown eyes are full of kindness and are set in a small oval, olive-colored face with not a freckle or blemish or line anywhere to be found.

A thoughtful look appears. "It's just something I think everybody should get a chance to do," she says. "Explaining the experience itself wouldn't do it justice, though. I think it's a little different for everybody—kind of like a personalized brush with God, or whatever it is you draw your spirituality from." She smiles and leans back, holding her petite weight up on her arms, her hands pressed flat against the grass.

The plane lifts off the ground and buzzes into the sky, becoming smaller and smaller as it flies higher into the blue ether.

I really do wish that I wasn't so afraid. I've been afraid all my life and there comes a point when all you want to do is be free of it, when you begin to actually see yourself doing things you never thought you'd do. A year ago, I never gave a *first*, much less a *second*, thought to something like sitting in the window seat of a plane and deliberately looking out, or riding in a helicopter. But right now, as I sit on this grass under the bright sun, watching that plane become a little black dot in the sky above me, I *can* see myself doing it. And it's not just because of Luke that I feel this way; I feel like I want to be able to do it for myself, so that I can beat this fear and finally know what freedom feels like. But I know that if I'd never met Luke, or Seth, or Kendra, or even Alicia, I'd still be doing the same thing I was doing two weeks ago in my comfort zone, and not being inspired by any of it.

"What about BASE jumping?" I ask Alicia, my mood growing dimmer all of a sudden.

"That's a whole 'nother ball game," she says. "Skydiving, like

I said, is really safe. BASE jumping, on the other hand, is…well, there's a saying: 'It's the next best thing to suicide.'"

I swallow tensely and what was left of my smile fades in an instant.

"What's the difference?" I ask. "I mean, both are jumping from extreme heights and landing with a parachute."

"Well, there's a *huge* difference," Alicia says. "With skydiving, it's all in the wide open and there's nothing around for you to hit. Plus you go much higher up—twelve, fourteen thousand feet or more, and have plenty of time to pull your chute. With BASE, you're jumping from much lower heights—an average of a thousand feet or so. And you're jumping from cliffs and buildings and bridges and towers—all kinds of stuff you can hit on the way down."

I grimace, thinking about it.

"Why do *you* do it, then?" I ask.

Alicia smiles over at me. "Nothing makes you feel more alive than being that close to death."

I say nothing.

After a few moments staring into the sky, Alicia says, "I'm starting to wonder about Luke though."

I look over.

"What about him?"

She shrugs, her gaze still peering into the encompassing blue.

"I dunno, but I'm thinkin' maybe his heart isn't as into BASE as it used to be."

I feel a little guilty for thinking it, but this news, if it's true, makes me hopeful.

I sit quietly, looking right at her, and she finally returns the gesture.

"I think he just feels really guilty," she goes on. "But what do I know?"

I smile back at her, but it's totally forced.

"Though I have to say," she adds, "Luke may not be feelin' it anymore, but ever since you came around, he seems a lot"—she shrugs, contemplating—"I dunno, happier, I guess. Landon's death really messed him up. But it's been almost a year, and instead of getting better, he just seemed to be getting worse up until recently." She smiles in what I perceive as a thankful manner. "Maybe you're just what he needed."

Somehow her comment doesn't make me feel like I desperately want it to: happy and warm inside. I'm not sure what it is I feel exactly, but it's strange and dark and I don't like it and I wish it'd just go away.

"Are you two gonna see each other after you leave Hawaii?" she asks.

"I hope so."

"Yeah, well, I hope so, too," she says, shaking her head and gazing back out at the sky. "I hate to see Luke falling back into that dark place once you're gone." She beams over at me. "Besides, I like yah; his past girlfriends, not so much."

The only thing I hear is: *I hate to see Luke falling back into that dark place once you're gone.*

That strange, dark feeling that doesn't have a name—just go away!

Is Luke latching on to me for the right reasons?

Or have I become something he needs for all the wrong reasons?

The devastating answers—if they're the answers I don't want them to be—are sitting heavily in the bottom of my heart.

Luke

The roar of the wind makes it hard to hear one another and I've yelled so much my throat is sore. The plane moves through the air at about twelve thousand feet.

"I TOLD YOU!" Seth shouts at me over the roaring wind and the plane's engine. "SHE SEEMS TO BE HANDLING IT JUST FINE!"

I nod happily while a guy does one last check of my parachute and then my harness.

Seth steps to the door of the plane, a red helmet much like mine stuck to the top of his shaved head.

"THREE MONTHS TOPS!" he says. "SHE'LL BE UP HERE JUMPING WITH YOU!"

"I DOUBT IT!" I shout back at him, adjusting my helmet. "BUT I'M OK WITH THAT!"

He grins at me, displaying his teeth, and then jumps out of the plane—it looks like the wind just snatched him into the sky.

Kendra, wearing a hot pink helmet and with a little black skull-and-bones sticker stuck to the left eye of her goggles, steps to the door next. Her blond hair, braided behind her, whips about her back as the wind hits it.

"SEE YAH AT THE DROP ZONE, SKYWALKER!" she says to me and jumps out.

I laugh out loud and shake my head.

I hate it when she calls me that, but I guess I deserve it since I was the one who started up the Ken-doll nickname she hates so much.

When it's my turn, I waste no time and jump right out of the plane, free-falling, looking down at the ocean and the earth, so vast and endless, yet so small beneath me. I succumb to the moment and think of my brother.

It feels like I'm flying forever. It's so breathtaking. Every bad experience I've ever had, every bad memory, every failure, every regret, it all just leaves me, and I'm filled with something I never imagined a person could feel before I started doing this: absolute freedom from every kind of darkness.

Nothing can touch me up here.

Nothing.

Except Sienna...

Her face enters my mind, the softness of her hair, her adorable freckles, the heavenly taste of her lips, the brightness of her smile—I could fall in love with her so easily.

I know she worries about me and that she may fear for my safety, but I still believe that she'll understand, that she's the one and that she'll be able to accept my lifestyle. But I don't want her to worry for me; I don't want her to constantly have that fear of me getting hurt digging in the back of her mind—I wouldn't want to put her through that; I care too much for her. But I believe we can get through this. Together. I just *know* it.

All too soon I feel a hard jerk as I pull my chute and my body jolts upward for a few seconds.

I take hold of the parachute toggles and float toward the earth for several long minutes and I continue to take in the view. Not of the sky, but of Sienna's face. And it's in this moment when I realize that nearly the whole time I was up there, I thought about her. I thought not about the experience...but about her, and somehow—though I never knew it could be done—it made the experience even more breathtaking.

The ground is getting closer, and the closer I get, the faster it seems that it's rushing up to meet me. My feet hit the ground first and I slowly run into a stop.

"Woo-hoo!" I hear Seth scream out.

Seth and Kendra run up as I'm unhooking my harness.

"Shit, man, that was awesome!" Seth says.

"Perfect day for skydiving—wasn't it beautiful?" Kendra is euphoric.

I nod my head underneath my helmet.

"Yeah," I say distantly, thinking about Sienna, "it was definitely beautiful…"

Sienna

When Luke and everybody come walking back up after their jump, I try not to think too much about the things Alicia told me. In fact, when I see Luke again, walking toward me safely on the ground, enormous, beautiful smile lighting up his face, I tuck the conversation away easier than I thought I'd be able to. But it's still there, lingering in the back of my mind, along with other things I'm trying so hard not to think about. Like me having only two days left in Hawaii. Two days left with Luke that I want to make the most of.

———

"I'm surprised it's not raining," Luke says, tangled with me in a hammock tied between two trees in his backyard.

His fingers brush through my hair, one arm wrapped around me. Our legs and feet are bare, our shoes kicked off on the ground beneath us.

"Yeah, me, too." My head lies on his chest, his other hand atop mine just above his stomach. His body is so warm. "But I like the rain. I mean at home it just gets in the way of everyday life, but here, I dunno, it just fits."

His lips press into the top of my hair.

"Have you thought any more about what we're gonna do when you go back?" he asks.

The waves lap the beach out ahead, more calmly than usual. The sun is out, but we're shaded heavily by the palm trees above us.

"I've thought about it a lot," I say. "Haven't come up with any solid plan or anything. All I do know is that I don't want the day after tomorrow to be the last time I ever see you."

"It won't be the last time you ever see me," he whispers onto my hair. "We'll start out with the visiting plan like I talked about. I'll visit you, and you can come visit me."

Trips back and forth to Hawaii aren't exactly an easy thing to do, but I can't think about that right now.

"Can I ask you something personal?"

"Sure," he says. "You can ask me anything you want."

He kisses my forehead.

"I'm curious about what happened to your business."

I feel weird asking that kind of question; I've been curious about it for a while but didn't want to come off as a gold digger by asking about it, about how much money he makes. But maybe now it's OK to question. Does he still have access to any of the money the business generated? Is that what he plans to use to make these trips back and forth to see me?

He squeezes me gently. "The business still draws in revenue every year. Not nearly as much as when it started out. Landon gave his share up one hundred percent, about a month before he died." He looks upward at the trees in thought, the smile gone from his face, replaced by something more profound. "He set up a fund, and after Uncle Sam got his share, the rest went into this fund. It still does to this day. Anyway, Landon intended to take that money at the end of every year and split it up among a few different charities. He still worked at the Big Wave Surf Shop until the day he died, and that's the only income he lived on. It's all he needed."

"And now that's what you do," I say, knowing.

He nods and rubs my arm from shoulder to wrist underneath his palm.

"Well, I co-own Big Wave now, of course," he says. "But it certainly doesn't bring in the same kind of income. Anyway, after Landon died, I gave up my share of our business to his fund and have been doing it ever since."

"And you intend to break into it to fly to and from Hawaii?" I'm not sure I feel right about that.

"No, babe," he says. "I'll only break into it if I absolutely have to. But I don't intend to have to. I'll work some extra hours, or even get another job if I need to. It'll be worth it."

My heart is melting.

"Well, you know what," I say, lifting my head a little from his chest. "I'm going to do the same. Whatever it takes."

"Really?"

"Yeah," I say. "I can't imagine not being able to see you."

He raises my hand to his mouth and kisses the tops of my fingers. "Me either," he says, kissing another finger. "We do have a lot of fun together, don't we?" His warm lips brush across my knuckles and the top of my hand—I suddenly feel incredibly light-headed, and my skin tingles from the nape of my neck down into my knees.

"Yeah...we do...have a lot of fun," I say in a quiet, unfocused voice.

I feel his lips move downward near my ear, and the heat of his breath trails along the side of my neck. "So...what do you wanna do the rest of the day?" he whispers as his free hand slips beneath the elastic of my shorts and into my panties.

"Umm..." I gasp when his fingers find me. "I, uhh..."

"Don't think about what I'm doing to you," he says as his hand pushes my legs apart. "Just answer the question."

Is he kidding? No, I don't think he's kidding...

A series of shivers runs up my thighs, and my mouth parts, sucking in the warm, salty air.

"We could go swimming," he says softly, his fingers moving in and out of me; our legs are tangled in the hammock, my left leg fallen to the side to give him access. His free hand combs through my hair. "Or maybe go on a hike. What do you think?"

"Well, umm"—oh my God, I can't fucking breathe—"I-I uh—"

I can't. I just can't.

"Sienna?"

"Y-yeah?"

"Do you want me to stop?" His voice is so calm, so quiet, so deliciously irresistible.

"No," I say quickly. "I-I don't want you to stop."

I gasp when he pulls one finger out and moves it around in a circular motion against me.

"Then answer the question, babe." He kisses my head again, his lips lingering within my hair.

My whole body shivers from the inside out.

"OK...um, maybe we could go hiking..." Inhale, exhale. "I-I think that'd be fun."

"Then what?"

I swallow hard. My legs are trembling.

Silence.

"Sienna?"

"N-no...umm, let me think." I can't think of anything else right now!

I get really quiet. His hand stops.

"Luke...seriously, I-I don't want to think about that stuff right now."

"What do you want to think about, then?" he whispers, two of his fingers now pressing firmly against me, moving a little faster in a circular motion.

I gasp, my back arcing a little, my chest heaving.

"I want to think about what you're doing to me right now," I say breathily. *Oh my God...*

"Don't close your legs, baby," he whispers. I didn't even notice I had tried.

"OK..." He doesn't have to tell me twice.

He pushes my leg over the side of the hammock, where it hangs at the bend of my knee.

Every muscle in my body begins to tense. I feel like I need to raise my arms above me and grab on to something, but we're too tangled, lying in the hammock, closely compacted together, preventing much movement.

My mouth falls open and my breath comes out in a shudder. "Oh my God...Luke...seriously."

He manages somehow to get his mouth near mine and his tongue touches the corner of my lips. I try to roll to the side to kiss him, but it's nearly impossible. My chest rises and falls with a deep, unsteady breath.

"What would you do if I stopped right now?"

"I'd cry."

"You'd cry?"

I gasp and moan, digging the tips of my fingers into his abs. "Yes, I'd probably cry—please don't stop."

"But what if I stopped and took you inside," he says with his mouth still near mine and his fingers still moving below, "and I laid you out on my bed and stripped off all your clothes and spread you open and finished you off with my tongue?"

My eyes roll into the back of my head.

My body goes rigid underneath his hand, my neck arcing over the side of the hammock, and Luke's warm, wet mouth falls on my exposed throat. I let out a moan as a tiny explosion goes off inside of me, my legs shaking, my hands gripping on to something—I don't even know *what* at this point. He drags his teeth gently down my throat, and then his tongue, a low growl moving through his lungs. As my body slowly calms and my breathing begins to even out again, his fingers move more slowly until finally he pulls his hand from my panties. We lie here quietly together, looking up at the blue sky peeking through the green palm leaves above us.

He kisses me.

"I'm going to miss you, Sienna."

"I'm going to miss you too."

I feel like crying. Maybe it's the overwhelming emotion I always feel after an intense orgasm, but I know it's not *only* that—I don't want to leave.

I shake off the tears and choose to make our last few moments together more fun and memorable than sad and dark. Carefully, I try to roll over on top of him, but it's not an easy thing to do in a hammock and it sways precariously side to side, threatening to spill us both. But he catches me, wrapping his arms around me, steadying the hammock and us within it, his long, tanned leg dangling over one side.

I kiss his lips. He smiles.

"I think since I have to leave soon," I say with a coy grin, dragging the tip of my index finger over his bottom lip, "maybe we should spend what time we have left in bed."

He grins.

"That is so tempting," he says, grabbing my butt with both hands and squeezing.

"Well, the offer still stands," he says and kisses me again. "Let me take you inside—unless you want to do it out here. I don't mind either way."

My cheeks feel hot. "No, let's go inside."

After very carefully finding our way out of the hammock without falling out of it, Luke carries me piggyback up the steps of the lanai and into the house. And instead of hiking, we spend the entire day in bed. Sometimes napping. Sometimes lying curled up next to each other listening to the rain patter on the roof. Sometimes having sex. But mostly what we do with our time left together is talk. We talk about everything. And the more we talk, the more we feel like we've known each other forever and the more we know that my leaving is going to crush us both.

TWENTY-EIGHT

Luke

*W*hy didn't you tell me before about the BASE jumping?"
Sienna's lying against my stomach, her cheek pressed near
my navel; her long, soft hair is splayed outward against the mattress,
tickling my side. I reach down and comb my fingers through her
short bangs and trace the curvature of her jaw and chin with the
edge of my thumb.

She had asked this question before, the night she came back
from Oahu and found me painting, the first night we slept together.
I know she didn't forget that she'd asked, so this must be about
something else.

"I didn't think any of that mattered at first," I say. "No reason
to drop a shitload of drama on your lap if you were only going to be
here for two weeks and we wouldn't see each other again."

The palm of her hand is warm against my stomach muscles.
Her eyes stray from mine and she looks off at the wall, seeming lost
in thought. I get the feeling she's all of a sudden rethinking the topic
altogether.

"What is it?" I ask curiously. She seems nervous, off in her
own world.

Finally she looks back at me and smiles warmly, the tips of her fingers brushing my abs.

"Nothing," she says. "I was just thinking."

"About what?"

"I dunno," she answers timidly, looking away from my eyes again. "I guess I just imagine it might be difficult for you to be in a relationship with a girl who doesn't...do the things you do."

Oh, now I see what this is all about.

I smile and brush her jawline again with my fingertips.

"Sienna," I say, and she looks right at me, "I'd rather be with a girl who doesn't BASE jump—granted, if you were into it I'd still have a thing for you. Seriously, you couldn't be more perfect the way you are."

Her smile is faint, but it's there. I touch the tip of her cute freckled nose and then her lips.

"But why don't you want to be with a girl who BASE jumps?"

I pause and then just tell her the truth.

"Because I'm selfish. And I'm a hypocrite."

That surprises her; faint lines of confusion appear around her eyes.

"Because BASE jumping is dangerous, Sienna," I begin to elaborate. I sigh deeply, her head rising with my stomach. "It makes me sick with nerves when I know my girl is going to jump because I just don't trust her to"—this isn't coming out like I planned—"well, it just scares the shit out of me. I know *I'm* safe— well, as safe as I can be, considering. I'm OCD when it comes to packing my gear and making sure that the tiniest thing has been checked three times. I'm really careful, and it's why I'm still alive. But not everybody is as careful as I am, or takes safety as seriously as I do. You wouldn't believe how many people get into this sport thinking it's just another sport and think they're invincible. Well, it's *not* just another sport and *none* of us are invincible. I just don't want to be with a girl I have to worry about every time she steps off the edge."

She just looks at me, probably not sure what to say.

"Hypocritical and selfish—I admit it. Maybe that's my biggest flaw of all."

Her faint smile brightens a little and her lips fall on my stomach briefly.

"What about the other stuff?" she asks. "Skydiving and rock climbing and all that?"

"If you ever decided you wanted to skydive, I'd support you and be there for you." She raises her head from my stomach and props the side of her cheek in her upraised hand, her elbow pressed into the mattress on my other side. "But don't ever think I'd be disappointed that you never wanted to do it," I go on. "I may be helping you out with your fear of heights, but I don't ever expect you to do anything that your heart's not into. I happen to like you just the way you are."

She smiles.

"Come here," I say, reaching out and grabbing her arms, pulling her on top of me, where she lies down fully across the length of my naked body, resting her chin on the tops of her hands lying flat against my chest so that she's looking right into my eyes.

"There's something important I want you to know," I tell her as I brush her hair behind both ears. "I never want you to feel like you have to be someone you're not. Not for me, not for *anyone*. Do you understand?" I hold her face in my hands firmly, peering deep into her eyes. "Never change who you are, Sienna." I know in my heart that she's too strong for that, to change who she is for someone else, but I still want her to know how I feel about it, that I'd never expect it of her.

A profound smile warms her eyes.

"Y'know," she says as my hands slide away from her cheeks, "I don't think I ever really *knew* who I was... I still don't completely, Luke, but since I met you, for the first time in my life I've begun to find myself."

I smile thoughtfully and let her go on, needing to hear this as much as I know she needs to say it.

"I majored in business, even though I had no idea why— no interest in it whatsoever. All I knew was that I needed to find a good job so I didn't have to struggle the way my parents did. And I wanted to help them." She laughs lightly with a hint of sarcasm, looking off at nothing. "And I did get a good job and I make enough that I can help them now, and my parents won't even accept it."

"I can relate," I say. "My parents were like that, but you know what I did?"

"What?"

"I paid for their shit anyway," I say. "Behind their backs. I did what I had to do by getting them back on their feet before I gave up my half of the money."

She looks deeply in thought.

"But finish what you were saying about finding yourself," I tell her.

She reaches out and traces my eyebrow with the tips of her fingers.

"I've never really stopped long enough to think about what I want out of life—not a career, but *life*," she says. "Of course, I've always been into photography. It's my passion. But I've never let it go further than a hobby because...well, I guess I just never have time for it anymore. My job is demanding, but maybe I'm a little addicted to the ladder of success, too—do you know what I mean?" Her eyes harden with reflection, as if she's going through all of the answers in her head for the first time, learning something more about herself that maybe she kind of always knew, deep down, but is finally admitting. "When I actually have a day off," she continues, "I jump at the opportunity to fill in for someone else. I'm always on the go, looking ahead, wanting to prove not just to Cassandra, but to myself, that I have what it takes to be successful. I have this incessant drive, this need to climb higher and higher—but for what? What am I going to do when I get up there, y'know? Work some more and never have time to enjoy my life?" She pauses in thought, her eyes lit by self-realization, acceptance, even discouragement. Then she says, "I really admire Paige. She works hard even though financially she doesn't have to, but she never lets work—or anything for that matter—get in the way of life. She always finds time for herself. And when something threatens to bring her down, she gets rid of it and moves on."

We sit in silence for a moment, her expression hard and concentrating, her eyes looking at the wall behind my head, but probably seeing something entirely different than the dingy white paint.

"I just want something more out of my life," she says distantly.

"We all do at some point," I respond, reaching out and taking her hand into mine. "And when we realize that, we have to accept that some things have to change in order to get it. You have to be willing to take that first step to making it happen." I press my lips to her knuckles. "And I think yah kinda have."

Sienna's smile is thoughtful and curious. She tilts her auburn head to one side. "How so?" she asks.

I grin and place her arm down on my chest, rubbing the palm of my hand over her smooth, warm skin.

"You finally used up that vacation time," I say with the curve of my lips. "I have to say, I feel all special 'n' stuff"—she giggles—"especially now, knowing about how you rarely ever take a day off. But here you are, spending two whole weeks with me. Either I'm a very convincing, charming, remarkable, and devilishly handsome guy"—I grin playfully at her, pursing my lips on one side while she tries to hold her laughter in—"or you know more about what you want than you think you do." That last part I actually meant, and judging by the thoughtful smile in her eyes, she's well aware.

She wants to be with me—we want to be together.

Sienna rises a little and moves closer, a teasing look lurking in her face.

"Nah," she says, scrunching up her pink lips and freckled nose. "I'm just as clueless about all that as I was yesterday."

"You don't know *anything* you want?" I ask suggestively, trying to conceal the playfulness in my face and failing miserably.

I reach out with both hands, carefully hooking them underneath the backs of her upper arms, and I pull her toward me.

Sienna smiles faintly and close-lipped, then leans in and touches her lips to mine, her soft breasts pressing against my chest.

"No," she whispers. "I do know *one* thing I want."

I kiss her nose. "Oh? What do you want?" Then I kiss the edge of her mouth.

She smiles and says, "A really good massage—wouldn't happen to know anyone with magic hands, would you?"

I laugh out loud and roll her over onto her stomach on the bed, straddling her, and although I'm as hard as a rock, and her cute, round little butt is...seriously right there—*Jesus Christ*—I ignore the easy access as much as I can and knead my hands into her back for nearly an hour—and then I put myself inside her.

She falls asleep in my arms later, the same as the night before.

I'm going to miss this.

I'm *really* going to miss this.

————

"You sure you're OK to hang around here by yourself?" I ask, coming into the kitchen and opening the fridge. "Braedon will understand."

"No, you go on," Sienna says, sitting at the bar eating a bowl of cereal. "I'm a big girl. I can stay by myself."

I grab an orange juice from the fridge and come around the counter toward her, leaning down and pressing my lips to her forehead.

"I'll only be gone a few hours," I say. "Do whatever you want. Eat and drink whatever you can find. Hell, you can even trash Seth's room for fun if you get bored—I'll tell him I did it."

She laughs quietly and swallows her food before speaking up.

"I'm more likely to clean his room than to trash it," she says.

"I'm sure he'd *love* that," I tell her in jest and kiss her lips. "I'll be back soon."

"All right," she says and kisses me back. "I'll be making myself at home."

Yeah, babe, you do that...I smile thoughtfully, kiss her one more time, grab my keys from the counter, and head out the front door.

Braedon needs me to work at the shop today, and since I've pretty much been on vacation since Sienna came here, I didn't want to let him down.

On the drive to Big Wave Surf Shop not far from my house, I crank up the radio and sing like a loud idiot all the way there. Damn, it's like I'm love-struck or something. And the funny thing is I'm not ashamed of it and feel like I could sing outside of the car, in the middle of the street in front of everyone and not give a damn that I suck.

This girl has made me crazy. Good-crazy. The kind that makes you want to do dumb shit and forgive all your enemies and *not* flip the guy off who cut you off on the highway. I can't stop smiling. It really feels like my face is sort of stuck like this. I try to *not* smile and it only makes me smile bigger. What the hell?

I have the urge to paint all of a sudden. But with brighter colors. Sunlight. Blue water instead of gray or black. A breeze instead of a storm. A drizzle instead of a downpour. Sienna is a light in the darkness that my life has been since Landon died. I hoped that one day I could see it again, the light—I guess I just never knew how bright it could be.

TWENTY-NINE

Sienna

*I*t's so quiet here with Luke gone, quiet in the sense that I can hear everything else: the ocean, the breeze brushing through the trees, the birds. But mostly what I hear are a hundred thoughts in my head, trying to get my attention. I hear a few of them screaming, and I know they're there, but I'm not sure what they're trying to tell me, and a big part of me doesn't want to know. I settle with the thoughts that make me smile. The ones of Luke and me and the amazing two weeks we've spent together, and the future I *hope* we spend together.

Eventually I go out onto the lanai and look out at the ocean for a little while. I text Paige and my mom to let them know how I'm doing. And then I decide to clean the place up, though I stay away from Seth's room—it scares me to think of what might be in there. After an hour I've run out of things to do, and I go into the living room and sift through the DVDs stacked in and around the small entertainment center. Running my fingers over the titles, I eventually come to a section of jewel cases that have no labels on the spine and one by one I pull them out and read the Sharpie text scribbled across the front.

They're all BASE jumping DVDs.

I shove them back down into a neat stack, along with those thoughts in my head that suddenly started screaming again.

Then I come to a small section of documentaries and stuff that originally aired on the History and Discovery and National Geographic channels. One in particular catches my attention—*Journey to the Center.*

When I first look at the plastic cover, something heartbreaking washes over me, something familiar—a great wall of rock climbs two thousand feet into the sky in a deep tunnel-like formation, blanketed by lush green that crawls the stone, gripping and tearing its way to the top, where beams of bright sunlight pierce the shadows cast by the scaling rock above. And at the top, three figures hang from a cable that stretches from one side to the other.

The image is the same as the giant painting of Luke's that I saw on the wall at the community center, with just a few differences— the men on the cable the most noticeable. It's also the same image as the one I saw Luke working on the night I came back here, and as many of the other paintings in that room just down the hall. Different angles. Different lighting. Different weather. Many differences, but all of them of the same thing, the place I privately called the Bottom of the World.

My heart sinks into my stomach.

It all becomes clear to me in an instant—I think all along most of it was there, digging through my subconscious, but I haven't truly seen the full picture until now: the paintings of this fateful place where his brother died; how he fell back into their darkness and their colors and their power the moment I left him and went back to Oahu; Kendra telling me, *Since you came here he's changed. He's happier...He's just better around you,* and Alicia telling me, *Ever since you came around, he seems a lot happier... Instead of getting better, he just seemed to be getting worse up until recently,* and *I hate to see Luke falling back into that dark place once you're gone.*

That strange, unfamiliar, dark feeling I had before finally has a name—punishing bereavement—and those questions finally have devastating answers:

Is Luke latching on to me for the right reasons?

No.

Have I become something he needs for all the wrong reasons?

Yes.

A deep, burrowing pain, like a fist in my chest, drills its way into the depths of my heart. I know it's true, that Luke may care deeply for me; he may want to love me unlike he's ever loved anyone—but not more than his brother. Because he hasn't made peace with his brother's death; he hasn't forgiven himself, and until he can, Luke will live in darkness.

Tears stream in rivulets from my eyes, but I'm too lost in the truth and this moment to gather the strength to wipe them away.

I feel like I should be disappointed, that I should feel somewhat betrayed, or even used, but I don't. There's no room in my heart for that right now because of the sorrow I feel for how lost to the world Luke really is, and because I know I'm not the answer to his pain. I want to be. I want nothing more than to be, but I know that I can't be.

Will Luke's guilt ultimately kill him?

Finally I reach up and wipe the tears, my chest shuddering with a million more.

I flip the DVD case over to look on the back. And I read. And the more I read, the more broken my heart becomes. China. Tian Keng, the Heavenly Pit. The place where Landon died.

The place where Luke died.

The thoughts are so loud now in the back of my mind that I can *almost* hear the words. They're so strong, so relentless, that I know I can't ignore them for much longer. I can't push them down and think of things that make me smile anymore. They're winning.

I pop the DVD of *Journey to the Center* into the player and I don't even make it to the couch. I sit down on the floor in front of the television. And I hit play. And I don't take my eyes off the screen for the next hour while I reluctantly go along on the journey with three world-renowned BASE jumpers who made this jump in China. Three who lived doing it, whose passion to make the jump terrifies me on levels I don't understand.

And when it's over, I wipe the tears from my cheeks and absently watch the credits roll, but all I can hear are those screaming thoughts. And I hate them. I fucking *hate* them.

I open a web page on my phone and immediately begin googling BASE jumping. And for another hour I read story after story, and my life comes falling apart around me, bit by bit, piece by painful piece.

A BASE JUMPER DIES AFTER CRASHING INTO A CLIFF FACE.

. . . LEG SEVERED AT THE HIP AFTER CLIPPING A BRIDGE

The Deadliest Extreme Sport in the World
Another BASE jumping death—Troll Wall, Norwegian West Coast

. . . her parachute failed to open.
"If you're not ready to die BASE jumping, you're not ready to go BASE jumping."—FROM THE SNAKE RIVER BASE ACADEMY'S READER

Welcome to Death Camp

... BOTH LEGS NEARLY SEVERED BELOW THE KNEE ...

A Sport to Die For

HORRIFIC 2,000-FOOT PLUNGE TO DEATH

"The next best thing to suicide."—Tom Aiello
"After identifying his body, it took me a long time to remember
   what he actually looked like."
"Our friends started dying off one by one—that's the reality of
   life and death in this sport."

I can't read anymore.

I leave my phone on the floor and push myself shakily to my feet, my hands running through the top of my hair, tears wet on my face, my heart exhausted.

Don't let it scare you away. If you really like Luke as much as I think you do, remember why, *and don't let anything else change that.*

Now I understand what Kendra meant when she said those words to me.

I can't do this.

I rush quickly out the back door, letting the screen slam shut behind me. And I stare out at the ocean from the lanai, just like I did before, but now with a heavy heart and a thousand screaming thoughts inside my head, whose words are unmistakable: *You weren't cut out for this kind of life, Sienna,* they tell me. *You* know *there's no way you can be with this amazing guy, always worried that he's going to die too soon,* they torture me. *You knew this the second you learned about it, but you chose to ignore it because you're falling in love with him,* they remind me. *This sport will kill Luke just like it did Landon, and you* know *it, Sienna,* they haunt me.

I run down the steps and out onto the beach, falling against the sand on my bottom and crying into my hands.

"And I could never ask him to change who he is for me," I say aloud to myself, recalling what he said to me just yesterday.

It's in this moment that I know what had started as a vacation and became something so much more is over.

THIRTY

Luke

*T*he first thing I notice when Braedon walks into our store after my short shift is his arm.

"Is that another tattoo?" I ask as he walks up in a black T-shirt where a colorful Mad Hatter peeks out on his right biceps.

"Yeah, man, whadya think?" He lifts the arm of the shirt away from the ink.

"That's sweet," I say, examining it closer. "When did you get it?"

"Yesterday after we went skydiving," he says and drops the arm of the shirt back down.

The bell above the door chimes as a customer walks in—a regular, who comes in once a month. Braedon and I both wave at him from across the small space. He waves back and heads over to the surfboards on the back wall.

"Are yah ever gonna tell me about that girl you got stayin' in your house?" Braedon grins faintly amid a tanned face framed by dark hair.

That unrelenting smile attacks my whole face again, and when Braedon sees it, his grin just gets bigger.

"Ah shit, man, seriously?" he says, knowing the whole scenario without me having to explain it to him. "She must be somethin'."

He steps around behind the counter and punches buttons on the register.

"Yeah...she is."

"She seems sweet," he says and closes the register after putting a few twenties inside. "Cute as hell, too. But afraid of heights." He glances at me briefly.

"Yeah, but we're workin' on that." I lean on the counter, my arms lying across the top. "But I don't think it's an issue this time. Sienna's different from other girls."

Braedon doesn't say anything. I know what he's thinking, but he's the opposite of Seth and doesn't care to speak his mind. Braedon has always been the laid-back one of us, never offering much in the way of advice even when you ask for it. He prefers to let people find their own way because, in his words, *they're going to anyway.*

"She's different," I repeat, though I think I said it more to myself than to Braedon this time, as if *I* need the reassurance.

I brush off that brief bout of doubt and let the dopey smile take over again.

The customer walks up and I step aside.

"Well, I'm gonna head out," I say.

"All right," Braedon says. "Can you cover for me Tuesday?"

"Sure thing," I call out as I make my way to the tall glass door. "See yah later!"

The door closes behind me with the jingling of the bell.

I feel like I can't get back to see Sienna fast enough.

———

Sienna's been acting strange today. Ever since I got back from the shop, she seems a little distant. When she smiles at me it feels like there's something else going on behind it. When I kiss her she kisses me back, but it just doesn't feel the same.

I think I know what's wrong; the same thing that's wrong with me—she's going back to San Diego in the morning.

I'm determined to make her last night with me memorable.

For the rest of the day, even though I feel as shitty as she probably does inside, I keep a smile on my face. I mess with her head as normally as I would any other day. I take her surfing and we walk along the beach together before sunset. And I get the smiles out of her that I can't get enough of. But in a small way, it somehow feels…forced: the smiles, her kisses, her laughter. I just want to cheer her up, make her feel better about having to leave, let her know that nothing will change and that we'll see each other again soon.

Finally, just before sunset, she begins to seem herself again. She curls up next to me in the hammock and we talk for a long time about her family, and later I tell her about the many odd jobs I've had—she laughs when I tell her I used to wear a chicken costume and stand outside a restaurant flashing an advertisement sign.

"Hey, you wouldn't think so," I say, "but several chicks walked up just to talk to me when I was sweatin' my balls off in that costume."

"Nuh-uh," she says, wrinkling her freckled nose. "There's nothing sexy about that."

"That's what *I* thought," I say with a shrug.

She crosses her arms, sitting on the other end of my sofa across from me, our legs tangled in the center.

"You got laid, didn't you?" She smirks and her playful jealousy is cute as hell.

I shrug my shoulders again, pursing my lips and looking off toward the television.

She makes a short breathy noise and her mouth falls open.

"Oh no, you *did*!" She throws her head back and laughs. "You got laid in a chicken costume!"

"HA! HA! No, not *in* the costume, but I did pick up a few girls when I worked there."

She presses her toes, painted all kinds of weird colors, into the side of my thigh.

"That's hilarious," she says, shaking her head. "I see people dressed up in all kinds of strange costumes, dancing on the side of the road holding up signs, but I have *never* thought to pull over and hit on any of them. It's an unfortunate, *un*sexy job." She chuckles.

I poke her back with my foot in her thigh.

"Apparently not for all of us," I say with a grin.

Every now and then, in times like this one, Sienna seems back to her playful self again, forgetting about having to leave. But she always slips back into that seemingly depressed state of mind that bothers *me*, even though she tries really hard not to let it show. I don't want her to go. Hell, I'm crazy enough about her that if I didn't think it'd be crossing some kind of line too soon, I'd tell her I want her to stay here with me for as long as she wants. But I know it wouldn't be that simple. It wouldn't be like it was that day two weeks ago when I asked her to miss her plane. Or when I told her to stay for two weeks. Sienna has a family and a job and a life in California. And I have all of that stuff here.

No, it wouldn't be that easy.

It's just an hour after dark and Sienna is inside taking a shower. The second she got in there, I went into my bedroom and dug through a box in my closet where I keep the holiday stuff I haven't used in two years. It takes me five minutes to unravel a string of solid white Christmas lights. I plug them into an extension cord and take them outside, stretching the cord across the yard as far as it'll go. I string the lights around the base of a palm tree.

I step back and cock my head to one side, looking at my work. *Damn.*

OK, it kinda looks like shit—this crafty chick stuff really isn't my thing, but I continue with it, going around the front of the house to get the other stuff out of the trunk of the car that I picked up from the store on the way home from the shop.

It doesn't turn out at all like it was supposed to.

I feel like an idiot.

Sienna

I have to tell him. I've been avoiding it all day, both because I didn't know how to say it, and also because I've been trying to force myself not to see it that way. I had hoped that maybe my mind would change and I'd be able to accept it, his dangerous lifestyle. Because it's true—I care about Luke enough that I want desperately to just accept it. But the longer I thought about it, the more he held me in his arms, kissed my lips, made me smile and laugh and feel unlike I've ever felt before about any guy, the more it became clear to me that it would hurt a thousand times worse to lose him.

It would *kill* me to lose him like that.

So the only thing I can do is let him go like this, now, before we get so close that nothing can separate us other than death.

I blow-dry my hair and pin it to the top of my head before putting on a tank top and my ball shorts.

Luke isn't anywhere inside the house, so I go out onto the lanai to see if he's sitting at the table. He's not. I start to go back inside, but then I notice an out-of-place arrangement of white lights and flickering flames out ahead in the short distance closer to the beach.

I follow the light, tiptoeing my way through the prickly grass in the dark in my bare feet. Soon the grass becomes sand and the flickering lights become brighter and the steady lights become more apparent. A string of white Christmas lights have been wrapped around a palm tree, illuminating the sand and the grass poking up from it. A blanket has been laid out over the sand beneath the tree, surrounded by a few Mason jars propped in the sand, glowing with little white candles inside.

After I've shaken off a little of the surprise and I see Luke standing there smiling back at me, all I want to do is smile and cry at the same time—smile because he did this for me and cry because he's made it that much harder to tell him what I need to tell him.

He waves a hand, palm up, at his handiwork, a blush in his face he's trying so hard to hide. "It looked better in my head," he says and then reaches behind and scratches the back of his neck nervously.

I smile, shaking my head, looking to and from Luke and the most thoughtful thing a guy has ever done for me.

"No, it's really perfect, Luke." I smile and then laugh gently. "I didn't know you were so crafty."

He shrugs and buries his hands in his pockets, still nervous, and I think it's adorable—big, strong, death-defying BASE jumping guy more worried about what I'll think of his craft skills than killing himself jumping off a cliff.

"Well, technically I'm not." He chuckles. "I, uh, kinda got the idea from one of those binders you brought with you."

Wow . . . he really put a lot of thought and effort into this whole thing. It's the sweetest, most thoughtful thing anyone has ever done for me before. I almost want to cry; a tightening sensation grips the center of my chest, threatening to bring tears of happiness, as well as tears of sorrow and regret, to the surface, but I retain my bright smile and try to hold them down, deflecting the pain with humor.

"You read my binder?" I ask accusingly.

He winces. "I'm sorry. I just—"

I smile and step toward him, making my way around two flickering glass jars. "I'm just messing with you," I tell him and lay my head against his chest.

It wasn't like he had to dig through my stuff to find that binder; I had left it out on the floor beside my suitcase for days. Besides, I looked through a photo album I found of *his* on a shelf in the living room while he was at work today, so I guess we're even.

"You did pretty good your first time," I say. "I should hire you on as my new assistant."

His arms tighten around me.

"I doubt we'd ever get any work done," he says suggestively.

After a quiet moment, Luke tells me to sit down and he goes into the house and comes back minutes later with a few Coronas in a wooden ice bucket with a handle. And we sit together on the blanket, surrounded by little lights and little flames illuminating a small space around us. And we drink and we talk and he tells me more about his trip to Norway soon with Seth and Kendra, still oblivious to how I really feel about it.

"It's really important to you to go there, isn't it?" I ask, looking up at the stars with my head lying on his arm where it joins his shoulder.

He's looking up at the stars with me, his free arm bent upward and propped behind his head, his bare feet crossed below at the ankles.

"Yeah," he says. "Landon wanted it to be his birthday jump. Since he can't be there to do it himself, I dunno, I'm glad to be able to do it for him."

I say nothing for a while.

"What about after that?" I ask. "Seth made it sound like you'll all be doing a lot of traveling."

His arm that I'm lying on tightens a little around me. His thumb brushes the skin on my wrist as it rests against my stomach.

"Hey," he says in a soft voice, "if that's what's bothering you, let me say right now that you can go anywhere with me that you want. Mexico, Australia, Switzerland, even Norway in two weeks if you want. I'd love for you to go with us."

"Oh, no, I don't think I could do that...I mean"—*why can't I just tell him? I need to tell him*—"I just have to get back to work and I won't have another vacation for a while." I swallow a nervous lump and feel nauseous and heartbroken.

"Well, no matter where I go," he says, "we'll definitely keep in touch."

For an even longer time than before, I say nothing.

Then finally: "Is going to all of those places really important to you?"

I feel him nod. "Yeah," he says distantly, as if he's off somewhere else. "It was important to my brother and that's why it's so important to me."

Privately, I lower my eyes in sadness.

Sadness. It's unmistakably how I feel inside. Because I know I can't help Luke the way he needs to be helped; I can't be the one who heals his pain; I can't be his crutch.

But still…I say nothing. Because it hurts too much to think about it, about what I know I have to do.

Suddenly I realize why I've waited so long to say anything, why I've put off telling him that I can't pursue a relationship with him, why I haven't tried harder to change his mind about jumping or express my feelings about it: because I know that right now, at this dark point in his life, nothing I say will register with him. He will take my concern and only try to make it better by bandaging it, rather than seeing it for what it is. He will kiss me and smile at me and tell me that everything'll be OK, that I shouldn't worry about him.

But also I fear that Luke will be able to somehow shake my resolve not only about his jumping, but more so about having to leave him…for good. Because I don't want to. I want to stay here with him forever. Already, right now, as I sit here with him on this beach under the stars, surrounded by his thoughtful hard work that has softened my aching heart, I'm at risk of becoming putty in his hands. If I'd told him yesterday that I just can't be with him, or the day before, I fear he'd already have changed my mind by now, despite what I know I *should* do.

That's why I have to do it in the morning, just before I have to leave.

He won't have time to shake my resolve then.

He won't have time to change my mind.

Later, after Luke blows out the candles in the jars and unplugs the lights, we head inside to go to bed.

"I'm going to miss you like crazy," Luke says, moving in and out of me slowly. "I think I already do."

He kisses me hungrily, pushing himself deeper inside of me.

Later, like I've done nearly every night since I came here, I curl up in his arms and listen to his heart beating as he sleeps. I stare up at the ceiling, the shadows cast by the trees outside the window dancing along it in a slow, swaying motion. But it isn't until hours after Luke has fallen asleep that I begin to drift off myself, accompanied by the sound of rain pattering on the roof and Luke's steady breathing.

And those thoughts about knowing what I have to do lingering in my head, cruel and victorious.

THIRTY-ONE

Sienna

*L*uke gets me up on time at nine. My flight leaves at eleven. I sit up in the bed, feeling like a bundle of frayed nerves, just as he's coming around the corner with a mug of coffee in one hand and a smile on his face. I can barely look at him at first; my rapidly beating heart sits deep in the pit of my stomach; my hands are trembling against my bare legs; my mouth is incredibly dry and I know that no amount of water in the world can moisten it.

"I ran out of sugar," he says, leaning against the doorframe. He takes a sip and makes a face. "I don't know how Seth drinks this shit black."

"Luke," I say and then pause, looking down at my hands wedged between my thighs.

He steps farther into the room.

"You want some coffee?" he asks, even though he knows I always say no.

I look up at him.

"You...Luke, you said something to me the other day that I can't stop thinking about."

He places the coffee on the nightstand and sits down next to me. "What did I say?"

I sigh and look down at my hands again, my fingers tangling nervously.

"That you'd never want me to change who I am for you or anyone else."

"And I meant that," he says, all traces of the good morning he was trying to maintain before gone from his voice—he knows something's wrong.

And I know I can't linger on this anymore.

Finally I raise my head and look over at him next to me, pain and regret at rest in my eyes. I know because I feel it in every part of my body.

"Well, I'm a firm believer of that," I say, "and I'd never want you to change for me, either—I wouldn't let you."

He waits for me to go on, but the sudden look of realization in his eyes tells me that he wishes I wouldn't.

A tear rolls down my cheek. I reach up and wipe it away quickly.

"I watched that documentary on Tian Keng yesterday." His jaw hardens as if he's fighting to suppress emotion. "I-I didn't make the connection until I saw it: your paintings, the ones at the community center, the ones in that room at the end of the hall"—I look right at him again—"the one you were painting when I found you that night."

"What are you saying, Sienna?" He stands up from the bed and begins to pace.

I stand up, too.

"Luke," I say, meeting his eyes, "I know you're going to Norway to honor your brother, but...do you really, down deep inside of you, feel like it's going to help make his death OK?"

He shakes his head. "Nothing will ever make his death OK."

"I know, but"—I'm struggling to find the words; this is all so much harder than I expected, and I expected it to be excruciating—"but do you really have jump off that rock?"

His eyes crease with confusion.

"Have to?" he says. "I—well, I *want* to. Landon and I were going to do it together. On his birthday. We made plans. And I—"

He stops and stares at the wall, struggling as much as I was moments ago. When he looks back at me, there's even more pain in his eyes. More guilt. More heartbreak. More of everything that makes me want to take back everything I've said.

And I feel every ounce of it, burning me from the inside out.

"I was supposed to jump with him in China," he says, angry with himself, and although he's said these things aloud to me before, I feel like this time he's repeating them only to himself, condemning himself with the memory, over and over again. "I was supposed to be there. I was supposed to check his pack like I had always done. I was supposed to *be* there." Tears fall from his eyes and it's breaking my heart—and taking everything in me not to reach out and comfort him. But I can't. I can't keep being his crutch. "But I didn't go. After all that planning we did, all of the excitement, I was too busy with work to keep my promise, to stay true to my brother. Too busy with my bullshit life"—he slashes his hand in front of him—"to go with him and make sure he was going to be OK."

He looks beyond me, his jaw hardening, his eyes focused and wet around the edges. His hands clench into fists at his sides.

"He's dead because I was supposed to be there!"

The sharpness of his voice quietly stuns me. But I'm not afraid of him—the anger he's projecting is only at himself.

But I know finally, looking back on my two weeks with him, hearing his friends tell me how much me being here has changed him, witnessing his anger seconds ago, the turmoil inside...I know now that I'm not what he needs right now, that this isn't something anyone else can help him with.

"I feel better when you're here with me," he says, but he can't look at me. "I haven't felt at peace with anything since he died. Nothing. My life just stopped. I might as well be dead, too. But here I am. And he's gone. And it should've been me because Landon was *good*." He swallows. A tear rolls down his face. He wipes it away angrily with the back of his hand. "*I* was the older brother, but I was the one learning from *him*. He was the one helping me overcome my shit. He had his head on straight. He knew what was important in life, what really mattered. But me, I lost my way and forgot *everything* that mattered, and I didn't listen to him when he tried to make me see it."

He pauses and looks back over at me. "Sienna, you're the first thing that has made me smile since Landon's death."

I choke back the tears.

"But, Luke," I say softly, compassionately, "I can't replace him."

Silence.

"I...I want to help you," I say, stepping up to him, his eyes red-rimmed and glistening with moisture. "But I think you're so scarred by the guilt that you have to make this kind of peace on your own. Covering up the pain with me won't heal it. I...can't replace Landon."

Luke sits back down on the edge of the bed, defeated, his legs apart, his hands dangling between them.

"This isn't just about my brother, is it?"

"No," I say softly and sit down next to him. "I know that this jump is important to you. I understand why, and as much as I want you to change your mind about it, I can't ask or expect you to change who you are. I know that BASE jumping is part of your life...but the thought of being in love with you and losing you the way you lost your brother...I, well, I just can't put myself through that. Not now. Not ever."

He looks down at his interlocked hands, and I can't escape the feeling that, judging by the wounded look on his face, he expected this, he knew it would end like this even though he tried so hard to have hope. And it just makes me feel that much worse.

After a moment I add, "But, Luke, I think more than anything, bigger than me, bigger than *us*, you need to find yourself again, find your way again and your peace with Landon's death, before anything else."

He glances over but doesn't meet my gaze. He knows that I'm right.

"Y'know," he says, "I would say that I shouldn't have let it go this far, this thing between us, but I don't regret a moment of it. Maybe I'm being selfish again, but even though I knew the day I met you that it probably wouldn't work out, I don't regret taking it as far as we did."

I smile softly. "Neither do I." I reach over and take his hand. "You did something for me that no one has ever come close to doing—my fear of heights, of course, but you did more than just try to help me overcome it. You helped me see everything else with a whole new perspective: my career; my family and financial priorities; my future." I pause and look off at the wall. His fingers slip between mine, over the top of my hand.

"Landon may have been good, like you said," I say, meeting his eyes, "but something tells me he learned it from you. Little brothers always look up to their big brothers."

I stand up and step in between his legs. He gazes up at me and takes both of my hands into his.

"I want you to promise me something," I say.

A brief moment of quiet passes between us.

"Anything," he says, tugging on my fingers.

"When you go to Norway, before your feet leave that rock, promise me, Luke, that it'll be for the *right* reasons."

"The right reasons?" he asks, confused.

"Yes," I say softly. "Luke, you can't do something like this, take such a risk with your life, unless it's for the right reasons. You can't go through with this if you're only doing it because you feel guilty, or because you're holding on to"—I pause and take a deep, uneasy breath—"holding on to something you had with Landon that's no longer there." Mentally I hold my breath, hoping that my words don't hurt him and that he won't take offense to them.

For a split second, I see his jaw harden and a flash of pain shoot across his eyes. But he recovers quickly and pulls me closer, wrapping his arms around my waist and laying his head against my stomach. I spear my fingers through the top of his hair.

Then he raises his head and answers, "Yeah...I *am* doing it for the right reasons," and that's all the answer he gives.

Disappointment, thick and heavy, floods me. My shoulders fall with my breath, my heart with my hopes.

I want to believe that he's lying to himself—I want to believe that I'm right—but if he won't, or can't, admit it to himself, then he can't admit it to me. Maybe I'm wrong. Maybe I'm too blinded by my feelings for him and wanting nothing to stand between us being together, and he really and truly loves this dangerous sport. But if that's the case, if that's the truth, then I can't stand in his way.

And I can't stay with him, either.

I could never in a million years ask him to give up something that makes him feel alive and free. It would be the same as him asking me to give up photography.

"You know I have to do this, Sienna, don't you?"

I nod, holding back my protest.

"And you know I'll be OK, right?"

I don't answer—he can see the answer in my teary eyes.

"I've been doing this a long time, so don't worry about me."

"I will *always* worry, Luke. Nothing you can ever say will ease my fears or change my thoughts on this."

He sighs and then stands up from the bed with my hands still in his and he smiles. "Sienna, you have to know that you're important to me." His hands grip mine more firmly with emphasis. "I never imagined I'd meet someone like you. I want you to be a part of my life. I want to share everything with you. Look, I understand completely why you can't put yourself through this. But I know what I'm doing. I'm careful. I'm precise. And although I know there's truly no such thing as a safe jump, I minimize all the risks by taking the safety measures that I take."

"But you could *die* doing this, Luke. At the end of the day, safety measures or not, you could die."

"I could die walking out the door, babe," he says with emphasis, squeezing my hands. "Death can happen at any moment. Life is finite, Sienna. The one thing we're all destined to do, no matter what, is die. I don't want to be someone always afraid of it. I want to live what life I have left to the fullest and have as much fun as I can while doing it." His eyes soften on me, his head tilting thoughtfully to one side. "I'll be fine. I promise."

No you won't, Luke. Nothing you can ever say . . .

I want to say these things to him aloud, but I can't. I can't because I know Luke is still in a place where guilt and redemption have such a strong hold on him that it will take much more than my words to convince him of it. This he has to do on his own. This he has to realize on his own.

I look away.

"I . . . I just can't do this."

His hands fall away from mine.

"I'm not giving you an ultimatum, Luke. That's not the kind of person I am. And even if you said to me right now that you'd give up BASE jumping to be with me, I wouldn't change my mind. I wouldn't because I know you can't ask someone to give up something they love. Ultimatums come with consequences. And resentment. You might be happy with me for a little while, but sooner or later you'd miss what you gave up to be with me, and then you'd resent me for it."

Luke takes a step back and puts up his hand. He shakes his head, looking downward at the floor, struggling to find words.

Then he looks at me.

"Sienna, please don't say that." A knot moves down the center of his throat. He takes a deep breath as if to compose himself. "Don't say you wouldn't change your mind either way—that means you're giving up on us."

"No, Luke, it—"

He moves toward me, cupping my face in the palms of his hands. Seeing the devastation in his eyes feels like a fist is collapsing around my heart, another one about my throat, choking me to death slowly.

"I want *you* to be in my life, Sienna." His hands tighten against my cheeks. "Before you, my brother was my life—"

"And I said I can't replace him," I remind him. "Luke...I know you're not doing it on purpose; I know with all my heart that you don't see what you're doing, but—"

"What am I doing, Sienna?" He looks wounded—it kills me inside.

I swallow hard.

"Instead of making peace with yourself," I say, my hands trembling, "you're ignoring what happened, ignoring the pain, the guilt you feel, and using me to forget about it—Luke, you have to face this." I lower my eyes, sniffling back the tears. "And I wish I could help you—I want that more than anything—but I can't do for you what you have to do for yourself, all on your own." I just hope he understands.

He looks away.

Finally I say, "I think it's best we just go our separate ways." I swallow down my tears—it's so hard to say these things without breaking down in a weeping mess. Because I don't want to say them—I want to *be* with him.

His face falls, the sudden surge of determination becoming devastation in an instant.

Then suddenly he rounds his chin as if to gather himself, and his expression shifts to something more casual, but to me it feels like denial. He nods a few times, licking the dryness from his lips.

Then he looks me in the eyes, takes a deep breath, and says, "I'll prove it to you then. After Norway, I'm not jumping anymore. I *will* give it up for you. And I'll wait for you, Sienna."

Shaking my head, I take a step to the side and away from him; his hands slide away from my elbows.

"I told you…it can't be like that." I stop with my back to him, my arms crossed tight over my chest. I can't look at anything but the floor. And I treat this as if his answer were true, that he's jumping for the right reasons—there's no other way I *can* treat it at this point. "This is your life, Luke. It was your life long before you met me." I turn to face him. "I'm not going to take you away from your life, from your friends, your passions. I won't be the cause of that."

"Norway will be my last jump," he repeats, growing more desperate, more hurt. Then he steps up to me again, cupping my cheeks within his large hands. "I'll leave you alone and I'll wait for you to come to me. I'll let it be your choice to come back to me, but if you do, if you decide a year from now that you want to be in my life, you'll see that I'm still here and I was yours the whole time we were apart."

Tears tumble down my cheeks, my lips quiver, and my hands tremble down at my sides.

He presses his warm lips against my forehead.

"I don't know what else to say other than I'll wait for you."

I want to fall into his arms, but I don't.

I want to throw my beliefs and my code out the window and embrace consequence. I want to forget about what my conscience is telling me and listen only to my heart.

We ride to the airport mostly in silence. We don't talk about Landon or Norway or our very different lives or what could've been.

Seems we laid that to rest before we left his house. On the outside, at least. On the inside, I know it's an entirely different feeling. My heart hurts. My stomach is twisted in knots. Tears burn the backs of my eyes constantly. And the more I think about leaving him, about never seeing him again and going back to my stressful, unfulfilling life in San Diego, the more I want to suck it up, strap a pack to my back, and jump into the sky just to be with him.

This is the hardest thing I've ever had to do: letting him go. But there's something much darker looming in my heart and it grows tremendously the closer we get to the airport.

A part of me knows deep down that he's going to die in Norway. It's just a feeling. Maybe I'm just being fearful and paranoid, but I can't shake the terrible feeling.

He's going to die...

"Sienna?"

I snap back into the moment.

He's standing in front of me with my elbows in his hands, that beautiful smile and those warm hazel eyes looking in at me, breaking my heart into a thousand pieces.

"I'm glad I met you," he says and his lips move against my forehead.

"Me too." It's all I can say—I feel like if I try to say too much at one time I'll burst into tears.

"Remember what you promised me back on that beach," he says, smiling.

I nod slowly and smile back at him.

"My photography," I say. "I promise."

I fall into his arms and he squeezes me tight. Then he pulls away and kisses me lightly on the lips.

As I walk away from him through the small crowds of people in the terminal, I want to look back not only because I feel his eyes on me, but because I'm not ready to let go. Because I'll *never* be ready to let go. And as I slip around the corner and out of his sight, in an instant I feel his gaze disappear. Tears stream down my cheeks all the way onto the plane. And when it takes off, I look out the window, not with fear but with a broken heart.

THIRTY-TWO

Sienna

*Y*our father is really upset, Sienna," my mom tells me as she comes into the living room with an envelope in her hand three days later.

She sits in her recliner and places the envelope, tattered at the top indicating it's already been opened, down on the end table between us. With my legs drawn up on the sofa, I glance over at her casually, my eyes skirting the envelope.

"I know he is, but he'll get over it."

"You know how your father is," she says, "and I can't say that I disagree with him. You should've come to us first."

"I did," I tell her. "A few times actually, Mom, and you both always shoot me down when I try to help."

"Because our bills are *our* responsibility," she says. "How do you think it makes us feel, Sienna? We worked so hard to give you a good life, saved up every extra penny we earned to put you through college. We didn't spend our lives working so hard just so you can spend your savings to pay *our* bills—we don't want you to struggle like we did."

I glance over.

"I appreciate everything you and Dad did for me, but if you want to know the truth, you gave up too much."

Her brown eyes slant with confusion behind her thin golden glasses.

I sigh heavily and turn around more on the sofa to face her fully, dropping my feet on the floor.

"Mom, you and Dad never saw each other. My childhood was nights with Mom and days with Dad. The only time I ever remember seeing you two together was on a holiday every now and then." I lean forward on the sofa, interlocking my fingers and dropping my hands between my knees, my elbows propped on the tops of my legs. "I love you both for giving up pretty much everything for me—I couldn't ask for better parents—but you and Dad missed so much of *each other*. Even now, when you don't have to support me anymore, you still struggle to pay your bills, and when I talk to either of you on the phone, or in person, you sound...tired. I'm gone and you still never see each other."

I stand up and begin to gesture my hands as the gravity of their situation hits me harder.

"How often do you and Dad go out on that boat?" She starts to answer, but I cut her off because it wasn't so much a question as it was the beginning of me making a point. "Once, twice a year, maybe?" I say, pacing the carpeted floor. "Uncle Stevie talked Daddy into buying that boat. Took you five years to pay it off and he hardly ever uses it—talk Daddy into selling the boat, Mom."

"But he likes to go out on the water, Sienna," she says from the recliner. "When we do get a chance to use it, what will we do when we don't have it anymore?"

"Rent one for a day," I tell her without flinching. "You could sell that boat and pay off the car at least, and then that once or twice a year he wants to go out on the water, rent a boat for a day—if it's not something you do *every* day, you don't need it."

She shakes her head with uncertainty, already knowing that getting my dad to agree to sell the boat will take a lot of convincing.

I'm no expert, but it doesn't take much to see that my parents need financial counseling. When they finally got on their feet and paid off their house after years of struggling, they thought, *Hey, now that we've paid off the house, we can take out a loan for another vehicle so we don't have to share one between us.* Then later they went on to say, *Hey, since we only have one large payment to make every month, why don't we take out a loan to get that boat we've always wanted?* And so they did. And then my dad's health started failing and the hospital bills began to mount, and then, because they had no other choice, they refinanced the house to pay them. And now they're stuck with more large payments every month and they've driven themselves right back into financial despair.

I take a seat on the sofa again, looking right at my mother with all of my adamant attention.

"I want you and Dad to be happy for once," I say. "I want you to go on a vacation somewhere—and I don't mean Texas. I mean somewhere you've never been, somewhere beautiful. And I want you to spend what life you have left *enjoying* it. Doing things you love. And spending time *together*. Because you deserve it more than anyone I know."

My mom smirks. "What life we have left together?" she says in jest. "What are you tryin' to say?" She chuckles and adjusts her glasses on the bridge of her nose.

"Mom, that's not what I mean." I smile at her, shaking my head, and then bring the importance of the moment back. "This money-is-the-most-important mind-set is an illusion, a scam. Half the stuff you work so hard to pay for, you don't need as much as you and Dad need each other—in the end, having each other is all that matters and will be all that *ever* mattered." Luke's words, in a roundabout way, coming out of my mouth.

I pick up the envelope from the end table and retrieve the folded invoice from inside. It's for one of two of my dad's hospital bills I paid off with part of my savings. If Dad is upset about that, he'll really be upset when he finds out I also paid his car payment for next month.

But it is what it is.

"Do you want to talk about it?" my mom asks suddenly, and I know right away she's not on the financial subject anymore.

I barely look up from the invoice to see her; her long auburn hair, which is just like mine, is pinned behind her head by a black hair clamp; her small hands are folded down on her lap, glistening with the lotion she smoothed on them recently. Freckles are splashed across the tops of her fingers and hands and wrists—she's where I inherited mine from.

I don't answer. I look back down at the invoice, now only using it as a distraction.

"Sienna," she says gently, "you haven't been yourself since you got back from Hawaii; why don't you tell me what's on your mind?"

The room gets really quiet for a long time; all I can hear is the clock ticking on the wall above the sofa and the occasional bird chirping outside the screened window by the front door.

I didn't tell my mom too much about Luke when I was in Hawaii. I've always been able to tell her anything, but when it comes to guys, I tend to be vague. I never knew why until now: I've never really been serious about a guy before like I was with Luke, and unless a guy is important to me, I guess there's little reason to involve my mom.

Finally I look into her eyes and say with a heavy heart, "You know that guy I met that I told you about?"

She nods slowly.

I pause, steady my breath, and say, "I wish I'd never left Hawaii."

And then, unable to hold it together any longer, somehow hoping my mom can make it all better, I break down in front of her. *And I'm not your mom, who's probably the first person you want to cling to when you're afraid because she's your mom. No matter how old we get, when we get scared, we can become ten years old again just like that— he snapped his fingers—when Mama walks through the door.* Luke's spot-on words turn over in my mind as sobs roll through my body.

"Oh, Sienna, what is it?"

And through a thousand tears, I tell her everything, from the moment I met Luke on that beach, to the last time I saw him and the last words I said to him, and everything in between.

I hardly noticed when she left the recliner and sat down next to me on the sofa, wrapping me up in her arms.

"I shouldn't have left," I say with a tear-filled voice. "I should've tried to make him stay, begged him not to go to Norway—I should've been there for him and tried to help him cope with Landon's death."

"No, baby, no," I hear her whisper; she tightens her arms around me. "You did the right thing; as hard as it is to accept, to believe, you did the only thing you could do."

I lift my head from her chest and wipe my tears, but more fall in behind them.

"Look at me," my mom says as she raises my chin with her thin fingers. "You were right, Sienna: Making peace with his brother's death was something he needed to do on his own. Sure, there's absolutely nothing wrong with being there for him and helping him cope, but it sounds to me like he was going about it the wrong way—you said he still wanted to go to Norway even after you expressed your feelings about it?"

I nod, confirming.

"Well, from what you told me," she goes on, "you tried to make him understand how deeply you felt about it or how much it scared you, but he just didn't quite understand—or want to believe it. And he sounds like an intelligent young man, so the only thing that would make him not see that is being blinded by the guilt he feels for his brother, his unwavering need to do whatever he thinks it will take to make it right."

She hugs me and adds, "He wants you in his life—that much is clear to me—but forgiveness for the guilt he feels is the most important thing in the world to him right now, and nothing you or anyone else can do or say to him is going to change that."

I stare at my hands in my lap, letting my mother's words sink in. Because she's right, and as much as I harbor my own guilt for leaving, I know she is.

We sit together for a long time in the silence. I feel like maybe she wants to say so much more to me, but in a way, like I needed to let Luke figure things out on his own, she's doing the same for me in this moment.

Finally I feel her hand on my knee, patting it gently, and then she says with a smile in her voice, "I'll make a deal with you."

I look up into her smiling brown eyes.

"If you promise me that you'll stop spending your hard-earned money on us, I'll talk your dad into selling the boat and I'll take your advice and start making some changes so that we can spend more time together."

A little smile manages to break through my sadness.

"That sounds like a deal," I say. "But you have to promise me that you'll go on a vacation by next summer"—I shake my finger at her—"and going to Oregon to see Aunt Jana doesn't count."

She nods. "I promise."

Then she takes me into a hug.

"I just want you to be happy, Sienna," she says, pulling away. Then she tilts her auburn head to one side and adds thoughtfully, "I think you may be onto something—I don't regret working hard to give you a decent life, but I do miss your father; maybe now's the time to change that."

My smile slowly gets brighter.

She pats me on the leg once more and gets up from the sofa, taking the hospital invoice from my hand.

"But no more of this," she says with an air of demand as she tosses it on the coffee table. "Got it?"

"Yeah, I got it."

I leave that afternoon feeling a little better than I felt when I went over there, not wanting to be alone in my apartment and needing the comfort I knew I could get from my mom. And although nothing can lessen the fear and despair I feel in my heart knowing Luke will be in Norway soon, I at least feel better about my decision to leave him, because I know it was the right decision.

———

Cassandra knocks lightly on my office door before pushing it the rest of the way open and letting herself inside. My boss is dressed in a black pencil skirt and a crimson silk blouse; her breasts are pushed up to show cleavage where the top two buttons have been left undone. A thin silver necklace with an infinity pendant dips between them. Long, dark hair sits like a wave of chocolate behind her shoulders and down her back.

She steps up to my hardly ever used desk and places an itinerary printout and a brand-spankin'-new credit card in front of me.

"The Bahamas," she announces with a proud smile and an air of tamed excitement. "You leave next Friday."

But I don't share her enthusiasm.

Glancing down at the itinerary, I think about the plans I already had for next weekend, the off days I put in for nearly two months ago so that I can go with my mother to visit her sister in Oregon.

"But…" I start to say, pause and look at the paper again, then back up at my bright-eyed boss who—hopefully—must've simply forgotten. "I'm supposed to be off next weekend," I say carefully.

Cassandra waves a manicured hand in front of her and purses her lips. "Oh, I know, Sienna," she says as if what she's about to say next will make it all OK, "but I think the commission you'll make from this job will easily change your mind."

I set the itinerary on my desk and just listen to her talk—because it's all I can do at this point.

"You'll never guess who the client is," she says, gesturing her hands. "Trent Devonshire"—my eyes pop open a little more, hearing that I'm supposed to be planning an event for a big-time soap opera actor—"and you'll be pleased to know that it's the best kind of job: Money is no object."

Normally that might make me excited about planning an event because then I could go wild with ideas. But this time I'm not the least bit excited. And I'm not as enthused as Cassandra probably expected me to be that my client is *the* Trent Devonshire. He would be my first celebrity client.

"Cassandra, I'm sorry, but I really can't work next weekend."

Her smile is beginning to fade, just a little, but enough that I know she's not pleased.

"Oh, Sienna," she says, tilting her perfectly made-up face to one side to appear thoughtful. "You're my best," she goes on, turning on the charm, "and I already told Mr. Devonshire that I was going to send him my best"—she points at me with a ring-covered index finger—"that being you. So what do you say? Can you take this weekend off instead, or perhaps the weekend after next? I really need you on this one."

I sigh and slowly stand up from my desk, shaking my head.

"I really can't," I explain politely, and with disappointment for having to tell her no. "My mom and I have been planning this trip to see my aunt for a few months. They're expecting us next weekend. I made sure to put in for the time off far enough in advance." *And you signed off on it and agreed to it,* I want to remind her, but I don't.

Her red-painted smile fades more noticeably now and she crosses her thin, tanned arms underneath her uplifted breasts.

"It's a huge commission," she stresses. "Not to mention, one of the jobs that will help further your career here at Harrington Planners. Sometimes you just have to set aside your family plans for the sake of what's important."

I say nothing, but instead sit back down and look at the contents of my desk, seeing none of it really. Cassandra isn't going to relent on this one. I know her well enough to realize that.

I sigh and slowly look up at her tall height standing in front of my desk, and I nod. "OK," I say. "I'll change my plans with my mother—I won't let you down." I swallow a lump down my throat, one made up of disappointment and regret and even a little anger.

"Perfect," she says with delight and a bright white smile. She turns on her six-inch black heels and goes toward the door. Then she stops before stepping out into the hall and says to me with long red nails curled around the doorframe, "You're going to go places in this business, Sienna. You're everything an exceptional employee should be, and I'm glad to have you—oh, and you'll be pleased to know that you'll have a new assistant starting tomorrow."

"Great, thanks," I tell her with a forced smile, and she saunters away, the sound of her expensive heels tapping against the floor as she makes her way down the hall.

I let out another sigh, longer and filled with more emotion than before, slumping against my chair. My mom is smiling back at me from a pretty silver frame next to my flat-screen monitor. She's going to be so disappointed.

Looking away from her photo, I prop my elbows on the desk and rest my head in my hands dejectedly. And I think of Luke—I always think of Luke, even though I try so hard to forget him. I've never forgotten the things I learned just being around him, just by knowing him. I thought that maybe once I came back home, the dream I lived when I was there with him in Hawaii would fade as time passed. I thought I'd simply go back to living my life the way I've always lived it, that I was too comfortable in my ways to risk changing any part of the life I've grown to trust. But nothing has faded. Nothing has been forgotten. And in my heart I know it never will.

I look at the five-by-seven of my mom again, the woman who gave up everything for me.

"For the sake of what's important," I say aloud to myself.

Smiling at my mother once more, I get up from my desk and leave my office, heading for Cassandra's at the other end of the hall.

"Congrats on the Bahamas job," I hear someone say, but I don't pay attention enough to know which of Cassandra's many employees it came from.

Weaving my way past offices and then the break room, I make

it to the tall frosted-glass double doors to Cassandra's office. They're wide open and Cassandra is inside talking to a man in a suit.

When he notices me standing at the entrance, he wraps up their conversation and tells her he'll see her tomorrow.

"Come on in, Sienna," Cassandra says with the wave of her hand just as the man is walking past me.

I step inside with a nervous ball in the pit of my stomach.

She sits down behind her engulfing desk. Then she picks up a folder and holds it out to me.

"Here are some of the details of the job," she says. "The rest I'm emailing over to you now."

I don't take the folder.

"Miss Harrington," I say calmly, "I . . . well, I just wanted to say that I will do the job in the Bahamas if you have no one else to fill in for me, but after that I will be resigning. I'm here to give you my two weeks' notice."

The smile drops from her face and she sets the folder back on the desk.

"What do you mean?" she asks, confused. "You're quitting? Why?"

I fold my hands down in front of me.

"I'm sorry. I just don't think this is the job for me," I say. "But I do very much appreciate your confidence in me and your willingness to give me a chance when you first hired me."

Her lavish chest rises and falls heavily. She presses her back against the tall leather desk chair, crosses one leg over the other, and interlocks her hands on her lap.

"I think you're making a mistake, Miss Murphy," she says. She only ever uses formalities when she feels someone is above or beneath her. "You should reconsider."

"I have," I admit. "But ultimately, I've decided to go in another direction."

She laughs lightly under her breath, easily maintaining her air of superiority without appearing childish. "Oh, Miss Murphy," she says, "do you have any idea what you're doing?" She smirks.

OK, now she's beginning to show her true colors.

"Yes, ma'am," I answer with respect. "I'm doing what's important to me."

I didn't need to elaborate on that comment for her to know exactly what it meant and where it came from.

Cassandra raises her chin; it takes her a long moment to say, "Well, if that's what you want, then I suppose this is good-bye." She uncrosses her legs, raises her back from the chair, and begins sifting through paperwork on her desk, no longer looking at me.

"Thank you for understanding," I say. "Please just send the other information over and I'll get to work on the event right away." I go to take the folder, but she puts her hand on top of it and slides it to the side.

"That won't be necessary," she says with a faint sneer, barely looking at me. "I'll find you something…smaller to work on for your remaining time here. Now, if you don't mind, I have work to do."

I nod and make my way out, shocked by how Jekyll and Hyde she had become, but I guess deep down I always knew she was that way. As I step through the double glass doors, at first I feel a great sense of regret, but as I get farther away, a funny thing happens— my lips turn up at the corners. And by the time I make it back to my office, I feel like a huge burden has just been lifted from my life and that now maybe I can truly get *on* with my life.

Or at least try. There's something missing, but I'm strong enough; I know I can do this on my own. Luke would've wanted that for me. He would've wanted me to be able to push myself to greater heights whether he was in my life or not. Luke...

———

I count the following days as if waiting for the world to end. Every day I dread more than the one before it. Every minute that passes brings me closer to the day Luke will be in Norway, the day that might be his last. I come in to work barely smiling back at those who will soon be former coworkers, and I hide away inside my office with the door closed, listening to the sound of fancy shoes tapping against the tile floor outside in the hall. To and from. Happy voices.

The clock ticks on the wall high above my desk. *Tick. Tick. Tick.* There's not much for me to do during the remainder of my employment at Harrington Planners other than sit here, alone with my thoughts that only torture me more every day, the closer that inevitable day looms.

Cassandra decided against sending me on any more planning jobs and opted for putting me in charge of random paperwork—no commissions to be made on paperwork.

Another day comes and goes. Another eight hours with my dark thoughts, my fears that rival anything I've ever been afraid of in my life.

Wednesday.

Thursday.

Friday.

Finally, as that day comes while I'm in Oregon with my mom, I'm thankful to be surrounded by family to help keep my mind off Luke. Futilely, I admit.

And the moment I arrive back at home, I spend all day looking at the photos I took of us. The first one I took with my phone and sent to Paige; the one of Luke crouching in front of his painting at the community center; the goofy one of him next to me on the bus; one of us lying in bed together—I can't bear it. I can't! I shut my laptop harder than I normally would and rush into the kitchen, trying to catch my breath. I stare out the kitchen window, looking into the clear blue sky peeking through the trees that surround my apartment complex, and I imagine Luke being out there, right now, standing on the edge of that cliff.

Then I picture his face, that beautiful smile of his that hides so much pain. And I picture his eyes, looking back at me with so much devotion and passion, and the tears stream down my face.

I picture him looking at me one last time. *I'll be all right,* his smiling eyes say to me.

And then he jumps.

My head snaps away from the window and I sob into the palms of my hands.

For the next week, I try to forget about him. I go to work every single day, forcing a smile and engaging my coworkers in conversation as much as I can. I seek out Cassandra, practically begging—without actually begging—for something more to do. I'll do anything, even if it's cleaning her office and everybody else's, just so I'll have something to do to keep my mind busy.

I try to forget.

I try.

By the end of the week, the day before my last day at Harrington Planners, I'm gathering my things when Jackson, Cassandra's secretary, knocks lightly on my open office door.

"I'm gonna miss yah," he says as he steps the rest of the way inside.

Jackson is tall and lanky with light brown hair spiked up in the front, and he wears stylish black-rimmed glasses.

"I'll miss you too," I say, shouldering my purse.

"So what are you gonna do after leaving the big HP?" He smiles brightly and adjusts his glasses on the bridge of his nose.

"I've got a few things in mind," I say, being vague. As much as I like Jackson, I don't feel like explaining to him or anyone else at Harrington Planners why I left a job making as much as I've been making here for a little more than minimum wage at a nearby arts and crafts store—I was hired three days ago; went in one afternoon after work and filled out an application. They were in desperate need of someone, and I was hired on the spot.

Jackson smiles and nods.

Then he steps up and places a small stack of mail on my desk, like he does about every other day.

"Well, don't be a stranger," he says. "I don't expect yah to come around this place anymore, but don't forget about me next time you go out to Silver's Bar with Paige; we had a lot of fun that one night."

I smile back at him. "It's a date," I tell him. Of course, he knows it's not really a date—Jackson is gay.

"Well, I'll see yah around," Jackson says just before he leaves my office.

"See yah, Jack."

I reach out and grab my soda from my desk and go to leave when something catches my eye. I stop and set the soda back down next to the stack of mail that Jackson just brought by. I rarely ever look at it. Mostly it's junk mail or ads from businesses I'm signed up for where I purchase a lot of things for planning events and such. But buried beneath all the junk is a white envelope with a hand-written address poking out from the side.

I barely notice when my purse slides off my shoulder and hits the floor as I lean over and shuffle the junk mail away from the letter. My heart is racing, my breath is beginning to pick up, with excitement or anticipation or fear—I don't know which, maybe all of them.

But then…my heart just stops cold. I suck in a sharp breath and every bone in my body locks up.

The letter isn't from Luke as I had thought, as I had hoped.

It's from Kendra.

———

One week later…

Paige clutches my black Gucci tote bag against her chest like a mother holding on to her child.

"You're crazy," she says, digging her fingers dramatically into the leather. "You can't give all this stuff away."

I take another blouse dangling from a hanger down from the closet and slide the hanger out.

"I'm not giving it away," I tell her, folding the blouse and putting it in a box on my bed. "I can make some money back on it selling it to consignment."

"That's the same thing as giving it away."

"You can keep the tote bag if you want," I tell her. "Paige, I haven't worn or used more than half of this stuff for six months."

By the time I'm nearly finished with the stuff in the closet, there are three boxes full of clothes and shoes in my room, some of which I'll try to make some money back on; the rest I plan to give to a secondhand store.

"Are you low on cash or something?" she asks, sitting on the end of my bed. "I can loan you some money if you need it. You know that."

"No, it's nothing like that—I'm saving up to buy new camera

equipment," I tell her and close the first box by tucking the flaps in on each other in a crisscross pattern. "I figured I'd get rid of what I don't need to make room for what I do."

We say nothing for several long, quiet moments.

I continue to pack away the last of it—I've been doing a lot of things like this lately when I'm at home, to keep my mind busy.

"Sienna, I'm really worried about you," Paige finally says.

She crosses one leg over the other, pressing the palms of her hands into the mattress, her arms stiff at her sides. "I know you miss him, and I hate it that things didn't work out, but you just don't seem yourself. I'm starting to worry. You're *not* yourself. You're—"

She wanted to say something else, but she refrained. It won't be long though.

I smile at her and close the second box.

"I'm OK, honestly," I tell her. "I've just been making some changes in my life, is all. Things I should've done a long time ago."

"Giving away all of your stuff?" she says, waving her hand about the room. "Refusing to go out partying with me anymore?"

"I told you I'm fine," I say. "No, I take that back—I'm *good*. I miss Luke and I wish things could've turned out differently, but I'm good." I smile hugely and motion my hands out at my sides. "I've spent more time with my camera in a month than I think I have all the time I've had it. I have Luke to thank for that." I point at her briefly to underline that last statement.

Then I add suddenly, "And I have gone out partying with you, Paige, so you can't say that."

She holds up two fingers. "You went twice," she says with a smirk. "And the second time you left early."

"Because the only reason you had me there was so you could fix me up." I grin at her.

She rolls her eyes. "That wasn't the *only* reason," she defends.

Paige gets up from the bed and steps around the boxes on the floor, making her way to my desk by the window. She picks up my cell phone and slides her finger across the screen.

And here it comes…

"Have you called him?" she asks.

I step around the boxes, too, and take the phone from her hand before she can start searching my text messages.

"No." I push the phone into the back pocket of my jean shorts.

"Why not?" I feel her eyes on me, her blond head cocked to one side, but I don't look at her directly.

"Because it's for the best."

Bending down, I grab a box with both hands and stack it and the others against the wall by my bedroom door.

"Now, this is where you can't convince me that you're *good*," Paige says with accusation.

Silence ensues. I stop in the center of the room with my back to her.

"You *need* to know, Sienna." She walks up behind me. Her voice is careful and soft and intent. "Even if you can't be together, it's gonna mess with your head forever unless you pick up the phone and find out if he's OK."

"I can't."

I walk away from her and take the box off the top and decide to carry it into the living room instead. There's no purpose to it other than to *not* talk about this, hoping Paige will drop it. But I know she won't. She never does.

She follows me into the living room.

"Then open the damn letter, Sienna," she says, and I stop cold in my tracks, the box getting heavy in my arms. "If you won't open it, I will."

The box falls against the floor in front of me with a *thud*. I turn around briskly to face her.

"No you won't. And neither will I."

"Sienna, this is stupid—"

"I don't care!" I shout, but then compose myself and say more calmly, "There's only one reason why I would just randomly get a letter from Kendra one day. Out of the blue. Just one week after the day Luke was going to jump in Norway." I step up closer to her and point my index finger upward. "*One* reason. And you know it."

I start to head back to my room for another box, but Paige stops me again.

"Then why keep it?" she asks. "You refuse to open it to find out the truth. You say you don't *want* to know, but you won't get rid of the letter. You're holding on to it for something, Sienna, and it ain't for sentimental value."

I sigh.

"I'm holding on to it because I'm not ready."

She steps up beside me and lays her head on my shoulder. She smells like fruity perfume and chlorine.

"You can never be ready to face something like that," she says, "but by not opening it, you'll never find closure—it'll destroy you either way."

I say nothing and hold my tears deep inside.

Paige hugs me and then picks her purse up from the chair nearby.

"I have to go to work," she says. "Think about Friday night, OK? I miss my best friend."

I look at her without eye contact and nod.

Once Paige leaves, I go back into my room and open my desk drawer. Kendra's letter stares back at me next to some pens and cute stationery. The date stamp reads July. "It's addressed simply to "c/o Sienna" because she probably never knew or remembered my last name. And the address reads "Harrington Planners." It probably wasn't too difficult to get the address of where I worked.

I stand here for ten minutes, unmoving, staring down at the letter, my tear-filled eyes following the pretty cursive flow of Kendra's handwriting, the curvy tail of the "K" in her name, the fancy swirl of the "S" in mine, and I think about opening it again. For a while it takes everything in me not to. I have to know, I say to myself, the same thing I've said to myself since the day I got it. The day the world stopped spinning on its axis.

My heart died that day. It just died. I wondered how I was still able to breathe as I left the office.

But the more I stare at it, the more I realize that I already know. Why would Kendra write to me at all? Why would she write instead of Luke? Why would she go out of her way to track down my address just to send me a letter? And why would she send a handwritten letter anyway? She could have just as easily sent an email through the company website.

Because handwritten letters are more personal.

You don't break up with someone in an email or a text message. And you sure as hell don't tell someone in an email or a text message that someone they cared deeply for died.

I already know what's inside that envelope, but I'm not ready for the finality. Maybe a part of me wants to hold on to the lie for as long as I can. Sometimes lies are more comforting than the truth.

THIRTY-THREE

Sienna

I spend the next few days trying to put Luke out of my mind. But that letter from Kendra haunts me. I can't sleep at night, especially with it being in my room. I think about him every second of every day, and it's only getting worse—the feelings I carry, the fear of him being gone forever, weighing me down.

Every day I come home from work and find myself sitting on the sofa for hours with the television off, listening to the sound of the neighbors walking across the floor in the upstairs apartment.

I expect tonight to be no different, but the second I close my apartment door and slide the chain over, I burst into sobs. Sitting against the front door with my back pressed against it and my legs drawn up, bent at the knees, I drag my hands through the top of my hair and sniffle back my tears. Minutes pass—it feels like an hour—and I'm still sitting on the floor in the same spot, torturing myself with memories of Hawaii, of Luke. I let my head fall back against the door and I gaze up at the ceiling, watching the blades on the ceiling fan move around and around, hypnotizing me, but still all I see is his face.

Finally I get up and storm my way into my bedroom, nearly

tripping over a laundry basket, tears streaming down my cheeks, tears of anger and guilt and fear. I yank open the desk drawer and take Kendra's letter into my fingers. And I stare at it. My eyes burn and I feel sick to my stomach and my head throbs.

Biting down hard, I slip my finger behind the tiny opening at one corner of the envelope and drag it harshly across, ripping it open. My tears get heavier, burning my nostrils and sinuses, blurring my vision. The envelope falls to the floor beside my shoes. The folded paper in my hand feels like the weight of the world. It's so heavy, *so* painfully heavy.

I start to open it, but stop just as my fingers disappear behind the top fold. Choking on my tears, I crush the single sheet of paper in my hand and hold it against my chest, screaming to myself under my breath, close-lipped, teeth gritted, until I can't see straight and my eyes slam shut.

I rip the paper to shreds without reading it and let each piece fall to the floor.

I need air. I can't breathe.

I run out of my room, down the hall, through the living room, and out the front door into the cool night air.

I stop cold in my tracks, and what breath I have left is knocked right out of me when I see Luke staring back at me from the end of the sidewalk, his hands buried in the pockets of his jeans.

THIRTY-FOUR

Sienna

For a time that feels like forever, I can't speak. I don't blink. I feel like I'm hallucinating. Are my feet moving? I never realized I had been slowly walking toward him. Maybe *he* was walking toward *me*. I don't know.

Luke smiles.

I shake my head over and over again, racked by overwhelming disbelief and relief and a hundred other emotions I can't name.

"Sienna—"

Dashing across the sidewalk, I sprint toward him and fall into his arms.

"You're OK!" I cry into his chest, his arms wrapped tightly around me, squeezing me nearly to death. "You're not dead!"

"No, baby, no. I'm fine." He kisses the top of my head.

"But...oh my God, I can't believe you're *here*." I can't think straight. My head feels swollen with emotion and questions and stuffy from the tears.

I pull away from his chest, but I don't let him go and keep my arms wrapped around his waist.

"But I thought—" I look down, the black lettering on his brown T-shirt blurring in my vision.

"Luke," I say, looking back up into his eyes, "how are you here?"

He smiles softly. "I know I said I'd wait for you," he begins, "and I did for a while, but I couldn't wait any longer. I had to see you."

I'm confused. I'm not sure he is answering my question. I was asking how he's alive. Because of Kendra's letter. But the feeling of being wrapped in his arms again takes over and I don't care about that right now.

"Sienna," he says, and our eyes meet, "you're all I've thought about since you left. I *need* you in my life."

My gaze strays again.

I want to be with him too, more than anything, but…

He cups my face within his hands, stealing my gaze back. A tear slips down my cheek. He leans in and kisses it away. I'm so overwhelmed with emotion, just knowing that he's alive, that I can't truly grasp everything right now: that he's here, the things he's saying to me, why I feel like I'll collapse on the sidewalk and die if he leaves.

Finally it hits me.

"But, Luke…the thought of you…I can't stand the thought of you—" Sobs rack my body and my hands begin to push against his chest. "I can't take it! I thought you were dead! I missed you so much! And I thought you were *dead*!" I scream that word into the night air.

Luke's arms collapse around me again and he holds me tight. "It's OK, baby. It's OK. You never have to worry about that again. Do you hear me? Sienna. Look at me." He shakes me, his hands around my biceps, the intensity in his eyes so palpable. "You *never* have to worry about that again," he repeats, as if to drill it into my head.

"What do you mean?"

He looks into my eyes again.

"I went to Norway," he says, "but I didn't jump."

I just look at him for a moment. Confused. Elated, but confused.

"But...but why didn't you jump?"

A smile appears in his beautiful hazel eyes. His fingers tighten gently about my upper arms, and then the smile finds its way to his lips. "Because...I found something more worth dying for."

I can't speak, but my tears say everything that words can't.

"I'm madly in love with you," he goes on, "and I couldn't go another minute without seeing you."

Involuntarily I suck in a shuddering breath, tears streaming down my cheeks in rivulets. He draws his lips toward mine and kisses me deeply. I cry against his mouth, his tongue warm against mine, his hands cradling my head. The kiss is long and hard and passionate, both of us afraid to let go.

Luke holds me in his arms for a long time, just the two of us standing on the sidewalk outside my apartment building. I close my eyes and picture being back on the island with him. I picture the constant rain, us tangled in the hammock, me walking across his back, shaving his face, throwing mud at him. I picture surfing and hiking and the helicopter ride. I think of everything from the very second I saw him to the last moment we shared.

I never want to be without him again.

But a small detail still haunts me.

I pull away and look up at him with wet eyes.

"If you're saying what I think you're saying..." I begin. "Luke, you know you can't change who you are for me. We talked about this, remember? I couldn't live with myself knowing that you gave up an important part of your life for me."

The smile around his eyes becomes warmer.

"But I didn't give it up *for* you," he says. "I gave it up *because* of you. Because you made me understand that as much as I loved BASE jumping, I realized I loved it because it was something I shared with my brother. After he died it became more a responsibility than an experience." He takes my hand and we sit down together on the edge of the sidewalk, side by side with our knees bent and our feet flat on the blacktop of the parking lot. He reaches over and hooks his arm around my leg, our shoulders pressed together. "A part of me—the guilty part, I guess—made me feel like I needed to continue doing what Landon loved most. Because he couldn't do it himself anymore." He sighs and his arm tightens around my leg. His fingers begin brushing the skin around my ankle. "I actually decided not to jump before I left. I went on to Norway with everybody else, but only to make peace with my brother. After everybody jumped and I sat on that rock alone, eleven hundred feet above the ground, looking out at the clouds, I talked to him. On his birthday. Out loud." He laughs lightly. "If I hadn't been out there alone, somebody might've thought I was crazy."

I smile inwardly, and he goes on.

"But I told him all of the things I never got to tell him before he died…

The air was brisk so high up where thin clouds hung in the blue-gray sky all around me. Everybody had already jumped. And they lived. A part of me, more noticeable than usual, was afraid they might not make it, that this would be the jump that killed one of my best friends the same way my brother was killed. But they lived and I was left alone on that rock, just me and the sky and my brother, who I knew was there, sitting next to me.

"I'm sorry," I said as the wind blew through my hair. "I never got to tell you that I'm sorry for abandoning you. But you were right, Landon. You were always right."

I looked out ahead of me, past the few trees on the back of the ledge and into the sky; my legs were drawn up on the rock, my ankles crisscrossed, my arms wrapped loosely about my knees, my back arched into a slouch.

"You were the most important thing in my life, little brother"—I swallowed hard—"I'm just sorry that I realized it too late and I hope you can forgive me."

I choked back the tears, but then I just let them fall.

And then I smiled. I smiled because I knew that Landon forgave me. And then I laughed because I knew he was giving me shit.

"I met this girl," I said. "I've never met anyone else like her, so full of life and passion and so sweet. I'm pretty sure I'm in love with her." I looked over on my right as if looking right at Landon, as if he'd never died. "I'm pretty sure because I feel like I need her to breathe. Every day when I wake up in the morning, hers is the first face I see. And I feel like she took a part of me with her when she left, a part of me that I can't function without." I paused and looked into the sky. "And I need her back."

Then I smiled and said, "You'll always be my brother. But I have to let you go."

I lean over and kiss Luke on the edge of his mouth and then reach up and wipe the tear away from his cheek. And then the one from my own.

"I'm glad you couldn't wait any longer," I say in a quiet voice, and then kiss the edge of his mouth again.

Luke pulls me into his lap and wraps his arms around me, holding me protectively against him; I can feel his heart beating rapidly against my chest—mine is beating so fast I feel slightly dizzy.

His lips caress mine with so much passion that I forget everything else. Through his kiss I relive every moment I've ever spent with him. My fingers wind in his brown hair, and tears of happiness nearly choke me.

The kiss breaks and we sit quietly for a moment, me in his arms.

Then I stand up and grab his hands, elation running through my body, making my arms and legs and chest tingle—I can't believe he's here!

"Let's go inside," I tell him and pull him to his feet, but when he gets up, he grabs me and kisses me again, clutching my butt cheeks in his big hands and hoisting me up, my thighs latched around his waist.

I kiss his face all over: his cheeks, his nose, his forehead, his temples, his very willing lips.

"Which apartment is it?" he asks with a big smile as he carries me down the sidewalk toward the building.

I kiss his lips again, my arms draped over his shoulders.

"One fourteen," I tell him. "How'd you know where I lived?"

"You told me, remember?"

Ah, that's right. I did tell him the name of the complex once.

"But how'd you know where to look?" I ask. "I didn't tell you what building I live in."

He kisses me again. And again.

"No, but you told me what kind of car you drive, so I figured it out."

We come upon my door and my legs fall away from his waist.

"Why didn't you just call?" I ask as I open the door and let him inside, my eyes scanning the floor, hoping I didn't leave anything gross lying around.

"I told you I'd wait for you, remember?" he says. "And I almost called you several times, but then I decided I had to see you. So I took a chance. And here I am." He opens his arms wide out at his sides, a big smile on his face.

"And besides," he goes on, dropping his arms, "I figured if I was standing in front of you, it'd be harder for you to say no."

"You want to know the truth?"

"The truth is good," he says.

"I couldn't have said no to you either way."

He smiles.

I take his hand and lead him to the sofa. We sit down together, me on his lap.

"Why didn't *you* call *me*?" he asks.

"Because I was terrified. Luke, I really thought you were dead. I got a letter from Kendra, and it was like the nail in the coffin, y'know? I couldn't open it. I didn't want to know the truth." There's a strong catch in my voice.

Luke's eyebrows wrinkle and his head rears back.

"You got a letter from *Kendra*?"

"Yeah. About a week after Norway. She sent it to my job."

"You're kidding me, right?"

"No. I'm dead serious."

I jump up from his lap. "Come here and I'll show you."

Luke follows me into my bedroom.

I give him the torn envelope first with Kendra's name and address beautifully written across the front. He looks down at it strangely while I'm picking the pieces of the letter up from the floor. I take them over to my desk and open them all, laying them out so I can put them back together like a puzzle. When I have all the pieces in place, I pat the paper down with the palm of my hand to smooth it out so that it's readable.

And then I read it out loud.

Hey Sienna,

I know you probably never expected to hear from me. And it was a bitch tracking you down, just so you know. I sent an email through the website where you work, but it bounced back. I tried calling once, but I got the voice mail and, shit, I can't stand voice mail. Talkin' to myself and all. And no telling who's listening to it. I hate that. Anyway. Look, Luke is a pretty ~~acwsome~~ awesome guy, and as you know, I'm kind of protective of him. OK, I'm a little batshit-crazy protective of him, but I am of <u>all</u> of my good friends because we're like a family. And I know this might be weird because we didn't know each other real well, but I think of you as family too and I think you and Luke belong together. Like, no joke. You're kinda perfect for him (even if you're afraid of heights) and I guess this is me trying to do right by you both and tell you that he's so fucking in love with you it makes me nauseous. Seriously. He talks about you all the time. It might be sweet and all, but it's weird. I think he needs to get laid. Maybe that'll help. But with you, of course. I don't want any bitches breakin' his heart, y'know?

So anyway, just give it some thought. He quit BASE jumping. Kinda sucks, but we all totally understand. Give him a call or ~~somethnng~~, something (I think I'm dyslexic!). And really, I kinda miss you too. I've never really got along with bitches before, but you're all right.

Yeah, so umm, if anyone other than Sienna (dark reddish-brown hair, short bangs, and with like a million freckles) is reading this letter, do me a favor and get the hell out of my business. Thanks.

Sincerely,

Kendra Morganton

Luke laughs out loud and his hand goes up toward his face, where he rubs his fingers against his jaw—it needs another shave, which I'd be happy to give him.

"Wow," he says with disbelief. "I, uh, well, I had no idea she did that. And I'm really kind of shocked that she'd do it at all. That's not like her."

I look back down at that letter sitting atop my desk in uneven pieces under the lamplight, and I think about how stupid it was that I never opened it before. I could've put my mind at ease weeks ago.

"To tell you the truth, she's talked about you almost as much as I have." He laughs. "She'll never admit it, but she has. She really likes you. So do Seth and Alicia—everybody does, honestly. Even Melinda; she asks me about you all the time."

Luke steps up to me and his fingertips touch the sides of my face as he peers into my eyes.

"Move to Hawaii, Sienna," he says. My heart skips several beats. "I mean it. I want you to come live with me. I mean, if you want me to move to California, then I'll do it because I can't spend another day without you. But if you come to Hawaii, we don't have to worry about buying a new house or anything like that. Mine's not much, but it's paid for. I-I mean, I can have some repairs done, get the ceiling fixed so you don't have to look up at the water stains every time we go to bed; I can put some new cabinets and counters in the kitchen—you probably like that granite stuff. I don't care. I'll do it—"

I kiss his lips to shut him up.

"Yes," I tell him. "I'll move to Hawaii with you."

His close-lipped smile brightens slowly, the look in his eyes overwhelmed with happiness.

"And I don't care about the ceiling or the cabinets," I say. "I don't care if we have to sleep outside in the rain—everything will work out. I just know it. Luke, I want to be with you. Because I'm madly in love with you too." I kiss him again—I can't believe I'm saying these things, so willing to move forward without any real plan, but it feels *so* right. "*Yes*, I'll move to Hawaii with you. Because I love you."

He wraps me in his arms, lifting my feet from the floor.

"Just so you know," he says, "I would've given it up for you too."

"Don't say that," I whisper onto his lips.

He kisses me.

"It's true," he says, carrying me over to the bed and laying me down. "I didn't, but if things had been different and BASE jumping were my thing and not Landon's, I would've given it up for you."

My fingers touch his prickly, gorgeous face as he lies on top of me, looking down into my eyes. "I missed you," I say, tracing my thumbs on the bone underneath his eyes. "I was sick without you. Promise me I'll never be without you."

His lips fall on my eyelids slowly, one and then the other, and then my forehead, and then my chin.

"I promise you'll never be without me," he says. "I'm yours for as long as you want me."

I smile timidly. "That could be a really long time."

He smiles in return, gazing into my eyes, and then his lips cover mine.

EPILOGUE

Sienna

Oahu, Hawaii

The community center has been revamped from top to bottom, it seems. It's stunning! And without my help, Luke, Alicia, Braedon, and Melinda made the charity art event even more beautiful than I could have. Yards and yards of white tulle stream from the ceiling in soft waves, pulled apart in a triangular fashion, with strings of white lights flowing downward amid the fabric. Dozens of white paper globe lanterns are affixed at the top of each fabric display just like I suggested, hanging in clusters above each artist's area as a highlight of the room.

The ceiling is filled with gold, clear, and silver helium-filled balloons, some in clusters, too, their ties strung together with fishing line. The glossy concrete flooring sparkles with the reflections of all the lights above it, and scattered against it around each display are faux white rose petals and glittery silver confetti—Alicia's idea that turned out quite nice.

There are so many people here; I never imagined there would

be *this* many, and it excites me as much as it makes me nervous—because I did donate several of my photographs, after all.

But it's not just the community center—just to be here, in my new life with Luke in Hawaii…it's like a dream. I wake up every morning feeling a whirlwind of emotions all vying for my attention: excitement, happiness, eagerness, even nervousness, as I'm still adjusting to the shock of such a large move, not just in my address, but my whole life. A tiny part of me sometimes panics a little, being so far away from everything I've ever known, but the moment I look around me at the beauty of the scenery—mostly at the beauty of Luke Everett—that panic vanishes in a breath.

I'm definitely living a dream.

With Luke's arm hooked through mine, we walk farther into the room, both of us dressed formally—me in a cute white dress that stops just below my knees and a pair of white heels with silver glitter around the toes; Luke is clean-shaven and dressed in a suit, and oh my God…I think I died when he first stepped out of our bedroom in the dress pants and white button-up shirt, asking me to help him with his tie.

I look up at him now to see him smiling back at me, proud to have me on his arm. I push up on my toes and kiss him lightly on the lips.

"You're the most beautiful girl in the room," he whispers onto my mouth.

I blush inwardly and peck him on the lips once more.

Melinda greets us, taking me into a gentle embrace.

"Oh, it has turned out so wonderfully!" she says with excitement, squeezing me with her thin, frail arms hidden in a pretty black and lavender blouse.

She pulls away, holding my hands in hers, smiling in at me

with such kindness and adoration that I can't help but smile back at her in the same way.

"I couldn't be happier that you could make it," she goes on. "And your photographs"—her eyes get wider and she shakes her head with admiration, tugging on my hands—"they are absolutely stunning, Sienna."

"Thank you." My face is too hot for me to manage more words than that.

I feel so nervous to have my photography on display, as if I'm revealing a private part of myself to the world. Having them on the Internet is one thing, but here, out in the open like this where people can walk by and I can physically see the expressions on their faces, puts a knot in my stomach.

Luke hooks my hip with his hand and pulls me next to him when Melinda drops her hands from mine.

He presses his lips against the top of my hair.

"I have no doubt," he says, squeezing my hip gently, "that every one of her pieces will be sold."

"Oh, I don't either," Melinda agrees eagerly.

"Yours will too," I say, looking over at Luke, trying to take the spotlight off me some because it just makes me that much more nervous. "That's a definite."

He smiles and squeezes my hip again.

Alicia practically runs up, with Braedon close behind—her leg is out of the cast, but she's still got a small limp. "You're here," she says and hugs me tight, even tighter than Melinda had. "So what do you think of the place?" She waves her hand about the room. "Do you like it?"

"I love it," I say. "I mean...*wow*!" I gaze up at the brightly lit decorations. "I couldn't have pulled *this* off. It's awesome."

Alicia purses her lips as if to say, *Yeah, you probably could,* and then says, "Of course, we couldn't have done it without your help, though."

"Oh, no," I say, shaking my head. "I just steered you in a direction." I gesture about the room again. "This was all you guys, and you did a fantastic job." I look at Luke once more, gently bumping my hip against his.

He smiles and bumps me back.

Melinda gestures for us to come the rest of the way into the building. We walk alongside her to see a few of the nearby displays—the photographer who took those black-and-white shots of the old woman is standing in his display area, also dressed in a suit and tie. I meet him and talk with him for a while about his pieces and about our individual techniques and styles. And then Luke walks with me down every row laid out in the room in an intricate pattern to create a labyrinth of extravagant art, all of it situated precisely as if even the layout had been handled with as much care and thought as the art itself.

We drink nonalcoholic champagne in tulip-shaped champagne glasses and meet with the guests—some came by invitation and are dressed up like the rest of us to fit the theme; others are people who came in off the street on a whim: tourists and locals alike, dressed more casually. The night couldn't be more perfect.

Well...I guess it can—Seth and Kendra walk through the entrance and come toward me and Luke, all decked out in formal clothes—my eyes get increasingly wide seeing them like this. Luke I could actually imagine in a suit and tie, but Seth—never in a million years. And Kendra in a little black dress and tall sparkly black heels, with her blond hair all done up in a perfect wavy bun; I do a double take, having to make sure it's actually tomboy, BASE-jumping, crazy Kendra and not just another one of Seth's one-night stands who just looks like Kendra.

"Wow," I say, looking her up and down, "you are rockin' that dress."

"Ain't I, though?" She strikes a dramatic pose and wrinkles her nose on one side to give me a little of that Kendra flare.

I look over at Seth, tall and dark and one gorgeous walking surprise.

"And you!" I take a step back next to Luke and look him over with a dramatic sweep of my eyes. "Did you have to talk him into a suit?" I ask Luke, glancing over at him.

Luke laughs lightly and shakes his head.

"No," he says. "I had nothing to do with this monstrosity."

"Hey, I look damn good, bro, and you fuckin' know it," Seth says with laughter in his voice.

I wince and gesture my hand at him. "Keep it down, Seth," I tell him quietly, trying not to laugh and looking over my shoulder for anyone who might've heard his foul mouth. Thankfully, no one was close enough.

Seth winces, too. "Sorry," he says, realizing.

He really is a sweetheart.

Then I look between Seth and Kendra, the gears in my head churning. They didn't come in holding hands, or even touching each other for that matter, and from what Luke has told me, they're still just friends. But I'm not buying it—or rather, I don't *want* to buy that.

"So," I say suspiciously after taking a sip of my sparkling drink, "you came *together*." I take another calculated sip; my eyes narrow with speculation.

A tiny burst of air moves through Kendra's pooched lips and she rolls her eyes.

"Wash that junk outta your head, Ginger," she says playfully.

Luke laughs next to me, and I gently elbow him in his side.

"Hey, she said it, not me," he defends with laughter, and then kisses me on the head again.

"Pffft!" I take another sip. Ginger? I hate it!

Seth grabs Kendra by her waist and goes to pull her into his big arms mischievously, but she play-fights him off—with a little less Kendra flare here in public than she would normally show when it's just the four of us.

"Keep your Sasquatch hands off me, Seth," she snaps, pulling the thin black strap of her dress back onto her shoulder.

Seth just laughs it off.

Luke and I spend the rest of the evening with our friends and mingling with the guests. At one point, I finally talk Luke into standing with his art and answering questions about it. It took some convincing, because Luke is really shy when it comes to his art. But finally he broke away from me and went to stand by his masterpieces—without a doubt, the most beautiful paintings in the entire room. And he drew small crowds of people in intervals. I watched him from my display just across the room, and he became more comfortable by the minute, it seemed, talking to the guests with that charming, gorgeous smile of his. I catch his eyes a few times, smiling at him across the short distance. He blushes hard and looks away.

After nearly an hour, Luke comes over to stand with me at my display.

"I told you," he whispers against my ear just before another guest comes walking in my direction.

I whisper back, "What did you tell me?"

Before he can answer, the woman steps up, gazing down

fondly at one of the last few photographs I have laid out on the table between us.

"Sorry. My display looks kind of bare now," I say nervously, retaining my bright expression, my hands folded together down in front of me.

The woman looks up from the photograph and smiles.

"Oh, it's fine," she says. "I actually bought three of your largest ones about an hour ago."

"Oh…" I say, surprised. "Well, thank you so much."

"Your work is very beautiful," she says. "I like your style."

Luke squeezes my waist again, since it's mostly all he can do, but I sense a hundred proud words in the gesture, including the words he had been about to say before she walked up: *I told you that all of your photographs would be sold.*

The woman ends up buying the three remaining photos I have on display.

Despite all of my photographs getting sold, that nervous knot in my stomach is still there—I'm not sure how I feel that I sold anything, much less everything! Does that mean I'm really good? Or were they pity purchases? *Geez, Sienna! Just accept that you're talented!* I tell myself and smile so brightly I feel the air hit my teeth.

And like mine, all of Luke's paintings were sold.

A few minutes before the center is to close and the event to shut down, Melinda comes to thank us again, telling us that it was, in fact, their most successful charity event ever. Between my photographs—I did donate them one hundred percent to the center—Luke's paintings, and the many other pieces that sold by other artists, Melinda will be splitting a rather large donation among several different charities in the community. The community that I'm now an official part of—just thinking about it fills my heart with pride and happiness.

As the last of the guests file out of the building, Luke and I go outside to get some fresh air.

It's almost nine o'clock, and the night air is perfectly warm, the breeze light. I can hear the deep pounding of drums off in the distance somewhere, knowing it's the fire dancers that often perform for the tourists.

Luke and I walk slowly down the sidewalk hand in hand, the breeze pushing the thin fabric of my dress against me.

"It wouldn't have been the same without you here," Luke says.

I lay my head against his arm and he squeezes my hand, the delicious smell of his light cologne wrapping around me.

"I can't think of any other place I'd rather be than with you," I say.

We continue on down the sidewalk, making our way slowly toward a cab. People walk to and from in every direction, the night alive with movement and voices.

"Do you miss home yet?" Luke asks.

I shake my head. "I *am* home."

When we finally make it back to the house on Kauai, Seth's Jeep is already in the driveway. When we make our way inside, we expect him to be in the living room watching television or something, but there's no sign of him.

Luke lays his keys on the kitchen table and strips off his suit jacket, laying it over the back of a kitchen chair.

I step out of my sparkly white heels.

I feel Luke's hands slip around me from behind, and then the warmth of his mouth on the side of my neck. I close my eyes softly and lean against him.

Then, just when I feel he's about to kiss the other side of my neck, we both stop when we hear the bed in Seth's room lightly hitting the wall. I turn my head at an angle to catch Luke's eyes.

"Is he—" I start to say, but don't finish.

Luke takes me by the hand, and we move into the living room. Kendra's little black purse is sitting on the coffee table, and her black heels have been kicked off on the floor next to the recliner.

Luke and I look right at each other.

"Seth won't admit it," Luke whispers, "but from a guy's perspective, I think he loves the hell out of that girl."

I whisper back, "Well, from a girl's perspective, I think she loves the hell out of him, too."

Luke picks me up in his arms and carries me down the hallway to our bedroom.

———

Five months later—Kauai, Hawaii

I've never been happier, or so sure of my future, in my entire life. Granted, my future isn't as laid out as it was before; it isn't dictated by a ladder or the money on that ladder, and I may not know what I'm doing tomorrow, but somehow the not knowing is what makes it so exciting. It took a drastic change, and to be blindsided by love, to make me see how much better, how much more peaceful and fulfilling life can be when it's not drowned in stress and expectations and fear. It took giving up what I thought made me the person I am—my job, my stability, my meticulous life—to see that the person I am is so much more than I ever imagined I could be. I'm doing things now that I never would've given a second thought to.

Luke and I do everything together: surfing, hiking, camping for days on end. I've never had so much fun in my life, or felt so free. I'm enjoying my job at a salon on Oahu, doing nails and washing hair and sweeping the floors, while also drawing a small income on the side from my photography. I'm doing what I love and spending more time with those I love, and I wouldn't give up this life for anything.

Luke still works at the surf school as well as co-owning the surf shop, and his paintings have begun to draw the attention of more than just tourists and local business owners looking for a nice piece to put in their offices. He paints on commission now—the last piece he sold was to a businessman in New York who saw his work at an Art Walk while on vacation. That guy told another guy, who told a woman, who told another guy over in Italy, who told another woman in Spain. He's doing what he loves, too, and slowly making a decent living doing it.

Paige and I are still best friends, but we don't see each other much anymore. She moved to L.A. recently and is pursuing a modeling career, even got signed on with a top modeling agency. And she's been dating a guy who, in her words, "surpasses her list of requirements." I'm really happy for her and I wish her nothing but the best in life. But we're such different people living in entirely different worlds now. Despite all that, and the geographic distance between us, it's hard to think about us ever drifting apart. We keep in touch. And she'll be coming here to visit soon.

But I have other friends who are like my family, and I feel at home here with them. Kendra is like a sister to me now, and even though I'm not into BASE, we get along awesomely. I doubt she'll ever be fully over losing Landon, but she's doing better every day, coping in her own private way—being in love with Seth, and finally admitting it, has a lot to do with her healing. And Seth, well, Seth is still Seth and he'll never change. I love him to death like a brother, and he looks after me when Luke isn't around. But he doesn't live with us anymore. Shortly after I moved in, Seth took it upon himself to move out. He wanted to give us our privacy, but also I think maybe it would've happened eventually, him and Kendra moving in together and all. They are a weird and crazy couple; they fight and they make up and then do it all over again—I think they like it. But they're perfect for each other. That's pretty obvious to all of us.

Mom and Dad are going to Cozumel, Mexico, next summer. And they sold the boat.

And as far as me, I'm happy to say that my passion for photography may finally be taking off as a career, too. Aside from my website, I also started selling some of my work on a few stock photography sites. Then I began sharing on Flickr, and to my shock, I had my Flickr Moment and was featured on *The Weekly Flickr* and had an awesome video about my work made.

That has helped change things a lot.

And today is a big day for me—I can hardly sit still.

I hear Luke walking up the front steps, coming back from checking the mail. He's taking his time on purpose because he knows it's killing me. When he opens the screen door, I just freeze, staring at him from the living room.

"Did it come?" I ask eagerly.

He shrugs, acting all nonchalant, a stack of mail in one hand hidden behind what looks exactly like a magazine. I know that's it. And he knows that I know, but I promised him I'd wait.

He walks casually past me and into the kitchen.

"Come on. Is that it?" I ask him from behind, my voice whinier than usual.

"Maybe," he says and slips around the corner.

I know he's grinning.

"How long do I have to stand here?" I call out from the living room.

"Just a minute," he says.

I hear him shuffling paper around, the pages of the magazine maybe. Then I hear the sound of Scotch tape being pulled from its plastic contraption.

Soon he's coming around the corner with the *National Geographic* magazine in his hand.

I press my hands together in front of me against my chest and squeal a little, bouncing up and down on the pads of my feet.

He smiles as he walks toward me and places the magazine in my hand.

I can't get the pages flipped fast enough. First I check the table of contents and navigate my way to the section on the winners of the Old World–New World Photography Contest. Turning the pages quickly, I do that bouncing thing again when I see my winning shot of an old man of Polynesian descent sitting on a rock on the beach displayed near the top of the page. I didn't win first place, but I'm just happy to be in the magazine at all.

I point to it. "Look. My name is underneath it"—I've been talking about this for weeks, about seeing my name in the magazine—"Sienna Murphy. Fourth Place." And then I read the title of my photo: *"Remembering the Old Ways."*

I look up at Luke, going back and forth excitedly between him and my photograph.

"You deserve it," he says, smiling. "You deserve first place, but I'll let this one slide."

I giggle and look back at the magazine.

"I hope to freelance for them someday," I tell him, my eyes scanning over the other winning entries.

"Oh, I know you will," he says with confidence.

I lift my head from the pages long enough for him to kiss me.

He starts to walk away.

I turn another page and my heart stops beating for a moment when I see a photo of Luke taped to the center. He's holding up a white sheet of printer paper with the words: *I want to see your future photos credited to Sienna Everett.*

My right hand involuntarily comes up toward my face, my fingers nervously touching my lips, tears welling up in my eyes.

When I look up from the page, Luke is standing there looking back at me with a ring between his fingers.

My hands are shaking. My heart is pounding crazily. One tear rolls down my cheek. Then another.

I walk toward him, the magazine down at my side wedged within my fingers, tears streaming from my eyes.

"Yes..." I run into his arms, wrapping mine about his neck, the magazine lying against his back.

Luke lifts me, and I lock my legs around him.

I feel breathless. "Yes," I say again and again, looking into his bright face. "Yes, yes, yes," and I smother him with kisses.

"I really do love you, Sienna," he says as he slips the ring on my finger with his free hand.

I stare longingly into his eyes.

"I really do love you, too," I tell him and kiss him passionately.

And this is just the beginning of a beautiful life made by letting go.

Camryn Bennett shocks everyone when she leaves the only life she's ever known. Grabbing her purse and her cell phone, Camryn boards a Greyhound bus ready to find herself. Instead, she finds Andrew Parrish...

Please see the next page for an excerpt from

The Edge of Never

ONE

*N*atalie has been twirling that same lock of hair for the past ten minutes and it's starting to drive me nuts. I shake my head and pull my iced latte toward me, placing my lips on the straw. Natalie sits across from me with her elbows propped on the little round table, chin in one hand.

"He's gorgeous," she says, staring off toward the guy who just got in line. "Seriously, Cam, would you *look* at him?"

I roll my eyes and take another sip. "Nat," I say, placing my drink back on the table, "you have a boyfriend—do I need to constantly remind you?"

Natalie sneers playfully at me. "What are you, my mother?" But she can't keep her eyes on me for long, not while that walking wall of sexy is standing at the register ordering coffee and scones. "Besides, Damon doesn't care if I look—as long as I'm bending over for *him* every night, he's good with it."

I let out a spat of air, blushing.

"See! *Uh-huh*," she says, smiling hugely. "I got a laugh out of you." She reaches over and thrusts her hand into her little purple purse. "I have to make note of that," and she pulls out her phone and opens her digital notebook. "Saturday. June 15th." She moves her finger across the screen. "1:54 p.m. — Camryn Bennett laughed at one of my sexual jokes." Then she shoves the phone back inside her purse and looks at me with that thoughtful sort of look she always has when she's about to go into therapy-mode. "Just look once," she says, all joking aside.

Just to appease her, I turn my chin carefully at an angle so that I can get a quick glimpse of the guy. He moves away from the register and toward the end of the counter, where he slides his drink off the edge. Tall. Perfectly sculpted cheekbones. Mesmerizing model green eyes and spiked-up brown hair.

"Yes," I admit, looking back at Natalie, "he's hot, but so what?"

Natalie has to watch him leave out the double glass doors and glide past the windows before she can look back at me to respond.

"Oh. My. God," she says, eyes wide and full of disbelief.

"He's just a guy, Nat." I place my lips on the straw again. "You might as well put a sign that says 'obsessed' on your forehead. You're everything obsessed short of drooling."

"Are you *kidding* me?" Her expression has twisted into pure shock. "Camryn, you have a serious problem. You know that, right?" She presses her back against her chair. "You need to up your medication. Seriously."

"I stopped taking it in April."

"What? *Why?*"

"Because it's ridiculous," I say matter-of-factly. "I'm not suicidal, so there's no reason for me to be taking it."

She shakes her head at me and crosses her arms over her chest. "You think they prescribe that stuff just for suicidal people? No. They don't." She points a finger at me briefly and hides it back in the fold of her arm. "It's a chemical imbalance thing, or some shit like that."

I smirk at her. "Oh, really? Since when did you become so educated in mental health issues and the medications they use to treat the hundreds of diagnoses?" My brow rises a little, just enough to let her see how much I know she has no idea what she's talking about.

When she wrinkles her nose at me instead of answering, I say, "I'll heal on my own time and I don't need a pill to fix it for me." My explanation had started out kind, but unexpectedly turned bitter before I could get the last sentence out. That happens a lot.

Natalie sighs and the smile completely drops from her face.

"I'm sorry," I say, feeling bad for snapping at her. "Look, I know you're right. I can't deny that I have some messed-up emotional issues and that I can be a bitch sometimes—"

"Sometimes?" she mumbles under her breath, but she is grinning again and has already forgiven me.

That happens a lot, too.

I half smile back at her. "I just want to find answers on my own, y'know?"

"Find *what* answers?" She's annoyed with me. "Cam," she says, cocking her head to one side to appear thoughtful. "I hate to say it, but shit really does happen. You just have to get over it. Beat the hell out of it by doing things that make you happy."

OK, so maybe she isn't so horrible at the therapy thing after all.

"I know you're right," I say, "but..."

Natalie raises a brow, waiting. "What? Come on. Out with it!"

I gaze toward the wall briefly, thinking about it. So often I sit around and think about life and wonder about every possible aspect of it. I wonder what the hell I'm doing here. Even right now. In this coffee shop with this girl I've known practically all my life. Yesterday I thought about why I felt the need to get up at exactly the same time as the day before and do everything like I did the day before. Why? What compels any of us to do the things we do when deep down a part of us just wants to break free from it all?

I look away from the wall and right at my best friend, who I know won't understand what I'm about to say, but because of the need to get it out, I say it anyway.

"Have you ever wondered what it would be like to backpack across the world?"

Natalie's face goes slack. "Uh, not really," she says. "That might...suck."

"Well, think about it for a second," I say, leaning against the table and focusing all of my attention on her. "Just you and a backpack with a few necessities. No bills. No getting up at the same time every morning to go to a job you hate. Just you and the world out ahead of you. You never know what the next day is going to bring, who you'll meet, what you'll have for lunch, or where you might sleep." I realize I've become so lost in the imagery that I might've seemed a little obsessed for a second, myself.

"You're starting to freak me out," Natalie says, eyeing me across the small table with a look of uncertainty. Her arched brow settles back, even with the other one, and then she says, "And there's also all the walking, the risk of getting raped, murdered, and tossed on the side of a freeway somewhere. Oh, and then there's all the walking..."

Clearly, she thinks I'm borderline crazy.

"What brought this on, anyway?" she asks, taking a quick sip of her drink. "That sounds like some kind of midlife-crisis stuff—you're only twenty." She points again as if to underline, "And you've hardly paid a bill in your life."

She takes another sip; an obnoxious slurping noise follows.

"Maybe not," I say, thinking quietly to myself, "but I *will* once I move in with you."

"So true," she says, tapping her fingertips on her cup. "Everything split down the middle—wait, you're not backing out on me, are you?" She sort of freezes, looking warily across at me.

"No, I'm still on. Next week I'll be out of my mom's house and living with a slut."

"You bitch!" She laughs.

I half smile and go back to my brooding, the stuff before that she wasn't relating to, but I expected as much. Even before Ian died, I always kind of thought out-of-the-box. Instead of sitting around dreaming up new sex positions, as Natalie often does about Damon, her boyfriend of five years, I dream about things that really matter. At least in my world they matter. What the air in other countries feels like on my skin, how the ocean smells, why the sound of rain makes me gasp. *"You're one deep chick."* That's what Damon said to me on more than one occasion.

"Geez!" Natalie says. "You're a freakin' downer—you know that, right?" She shakes her head with the straw between her lips.

"Come on," she says suddenly and stands up from the table. "I can't take this philosophical stuff anymore, and quaint little places like this seem to make you worse—we're going to The Underground tonight."

"What? No, I'm not going to that place."

"Yes. You. Are." She chucks her empty drink into the trash can a few feet away and grabs my wrist. "You're going with me this time because you're supposed to be my best friend and I won't take no *again* for an answer." Her close-lipped smile is spread across the entirety of her slightly tanned face.

I know she means business. She always means business when she has that look in her eyes: the one brimmed with excitement and determination. It'll probably be easiest just to go this once and get it over with, or else she'll never leave me alone about it. Such is a necessary evil when it comes to having a pushy best friend.

I get up and slip my purse strap over my shoulder.

"It's only two o'clock," I say.

I drink down the last of my latte and toss the empty cup away in the same trash can.

"Yeah, but first we've got to get you a new outfit."

"Uh, no," I say resolutely as she's walking me out the glass doors and into the breezy summer air. "Going to The Underground with you is more than good deed enough. I refuse to go shopping. I've got plenty of clothes."

Natalie slips her arm around mine as we walk down the sidewalk and past a long line of parking meters. She grins and glances over at me. "Fine. Then you'll at least let me dress you from something out of *my* closet."

"What's wrong with my own wardrobe?"

She purses her lips at me and draws her chin in as if to quietly argue why I even asked a question so ridiculous. "It's *The Underground*," she says, as if there is no answer more obvious than that.

OK, she has a point. Natalie and I may be best friends, but with us it's an opposites attract sort of thing. She's a rocker chick who's had a crush on Jared Leto since *Fight Club*. I'm more of a laid-back kind of girl who rarely wears dark-colored clothes unless I'm attending a funeral. Not that Natalie wears all black and has some kind of emo hair thing going on, but she would never be caught dead in anything from *my* closet because she says it's all just too plain. I beg to differ. I know how to dress, and guys—when I used to pay attention to the way they eyed my ass in my favorite jeans—have never had a problem with the clothes I choose to wear.

But The Underground was made for people like Natalie and so I guess I'll have to endure dressing like her for one night just to fit in. I'm not a follower. I never have been. But I'll definitely become someone I'm not for a few hours if it'll make me blend in rather than make me a blatant eyesore and draw attention.

ABOUT THE AUTHOR

J. A. REDMERSKI, *New York Times*, *USA Today*, and *Wall Street Journal* bestselling author, lives in North Little Rock, Arkansas. She is a sucker for long, sweeping epic love stories; a lover of film, television, and books that push boundaries; and she binge-watches TV series. She hopes to someday conquer her long list of ridiculous fears, find a shirt that she actually likes, and travel the world with a backpack and a partner in crime.

You can learn more at:
JessicaRedmerski.com
Twitter @JRedmerski
Facebook.com/J.A.Redmerski